FOLOVOI

ISOVOI

DRAGOVOI

THE
WASTE

THE VINE

THE MAROVAR

Fallow Vale

LUMILAR

Iron Mine

TRIKOVOI

THE HASSURA PLAINS

◆ Livabai

THE FAN

Quarry

GERBANYAR

Zirevasi

Sea of Beasts

THE ASP

◆ Chalbora

WITHDRAWN

Spindle
Bay

◆ Zareshoma

THE EMERALD COAST

Sabor

THE FAITHLESS HAWK

THE FAITHLESS HAWK

Margaret Owen

Henry Holt and Company
New York

Henry Holt and Company, *Publishers since 1866*
Henry Holt® is a registered trademark of Macmillan Publishing Group, LLC
120 Broadway, New York, NY 10271 • fiercereads.com

Library of Congress Control Number: 2019949488
ISBN 978-1-250-19194-6

Our books may be purchased in bulk for promotional, educational, or business use. Please
contact your local bookseller or the Macmillan Corporate and Premium Sales Department
at (800) 221-7945 ext. 5442 or by email at MacmillanSpecialMarkets@macmillan.com.

First edition, 2020 / Designed by Rich Deas and Sophie Erb
Printed in the United States of America

1   3   5   7   9   10   8   6   4   2

To everyone who is asked to burn, and instead decides to rise.
And to my friends: You're not in this one, either.
They only let me do the cats now.

The sun will rise, even from our ashes.

—creed of the Black Swans

Waste no weapons, least of all your foe's.

—Hawk proverb

PART ONE

KINGS
— AND —
OUTCASTS

— THE THOUSAND CONQUESTS —

FIE WAS TAKING TOO LONG TO CUT THE GIRL'S THROAT.

It wasn't the act itself; in the three weeks since taking charge of her band of Crows, Fie had dealt mercy more than a handful of times. Tavin had told her last moon that killing never ought to get easier, but that it did anyway. Too many lives had ended on the edge of her steel since then to pretend that didn't hold a speck of truth.

No, the sticking point now was the sinner girl.

The girl had been sitting up on her pallet when Fie walked into the quarantine hut, dark eyes imperious, mouth set in a stiff bar like the one sealing the door from the outside. Her short-sleeved linen shift was well made but plain for the Peacock governor's only daughter, her black hair in a clean, glossy braid that hadn't yet frayed and dulled with fever sweat. A scroll had sat half unfurled across her lap. Just enough near-noon sunlight soaked the canvas-screened windows for her to read by.

Fie reckoned the Peacock girl was near her own age, somewhere closer to seventeen years than to sixteen. But delicate rings of dark-veined rash had begun blooming at her temples, slight enough to be only hours old, damning enough to say the girl had only hours left.

Minutes, now that Fie had come for her.

Most of the time Fie found her sinners delirious, dazed, even dead; the Sinner's Plague never let any soul slip through its grasp, and it wrung even the simplest dignities from its victims along the way. Never before had a sinner watched Fie so, like she was a wolf strolling too near a pasture.

Fie ought to have left her mask on. Instead she took it off.

She ought to have drawn the broken sword. Instead it stayed at her side.

She ought to have told the Peacock girl to close her eyes. Instead, she jerked her chin at the scroll and asked, "What're you reading?"

The Peacock girl leaned back, gaze narrowing. Her lip curled. "It doesn't matter. You can't read anyway." She tossed a small, clicking bag at Fie. "There. Do it fast and clean."

The bag was full of milk teeth, and when Fie fished one out, its spark sang loud and harsh in her bones. *Niemi Navali szo Sakar*, it declared, *daughter of*—

Fie yanked her hand out. The tooth had been Niem—*the sinner girl's*, and it'd stay noisy until she died. Others in the bag kept quiet, but Fie picked out the song of Peacock witches among them. The governor's dying daughter meant it as a bribe.

"Not how it works," Fie said, tying it to her belt, "but we'll call it a tip."

"Just do what you're here for already."

Fie shrugged, brushing her cloak aside in the same movement, and drew the swords buckled at each hip. One was from Tavin, the Hawk boy she'd left behind: a beautiful short sword wrought of finest steel, gleaming demurely in the diluted sunlight. The other sword could barely be called such: an old, battered blade, broken half through, its end no more than uneven jags. A Crow chief's sword, good for mercy alone. That sword had come from Pa, who she soon would have to leave behind as well.

Fie didn't care to dwell on that. Instead she held out both blades and asked, "Which do you want?" As the Peacock girl's face turned gray, Fie shuffled closer to give her a better view . . . and to give herself one as well. The letters on the scroll ordered themselves into words for her, faster now thanks to regular reading practice. "Oh. *The Thousand Conquests.* That's a load of trash."

The Peacock girl snapped the scroll up, scowling. "Of course you'd think that. I don't expect a Crow to have taste."

"I'm around conquest . . . two hundred?" Fie drawled. "Out of a thousand? So far the only Crows have been dirty, thieving half-wits. Or monsters. Scholar Sharivi seems to think the Peacocks piss ambrosia, though, so I see the appeal for you."

"It's the truth," the sinner girl hissed. "Peacocks are born to rule. The Covenant made *you* as a punishment."

Fie had heard it before; she supposed that to most of Sabor, it seemed clear-cut. Every other caste was born with a Birthright, an innate gift passed down from the dead gods, like a Crane's way of spotting lies or a Sparrow's way of slipping from unwanted attention. Some were even believed to be dead gods reborn into the castes they'd founded, like the Crane witches, who could pull the truth out of a liar, or a Sparrow witch, who could utterly vanish from sight.

The dead gods, though, had denied the Crows a Birthright of their own. Their witches could only steal the Birthrights from bones of the other castes, and only as long as a lingering trace of its former life lasted in that bone. And as the only caste immune to the Sinner's Plague, their trade was cutting throats and collecting bodies.

With all that, Fie didn't doubt the life of a Crow sounded like a punishment to a highborn Peacock. Most of Sabor believed dead sinners were reborn into the Crow caste so as to atone for whatever crimes had brought the plague down on them to begin with.

And yet . . .

She crouched on the dirt floor, setting her swords between her and the Peacock. "Funny thing is, were I to think on which of us two the Covenant favors right now——" Fie tapped her cheek. "Reckon that's where the scholar Sharivi and I would disagree."

Fie expected the Peacock girl to sneer at her, to lash back.

Instead, Niemi closed her eyes and raised a hand to the Sinner's Brand rash on her face. Her voice cracked. "I . . . I suppose you're right."

A tiny, cold scrap of guilt knotted in Fie's gut. Aye, she despised this soft, clean girl, and not merely because the girl despised her. Yet only one of them would leave this room alive.

Pa would tell her to stop dragging it out.

Wretch would tell her not to play with her food.

Instead, Fie asked, "Do you know why the Covenant picked you?"

The Peacock's lips pressed together. Her finger shook as she pointed to the Hawk sword. "I want that one."

"Rich ones always go for the fancy sword," Fie mused. "You didn't answer me."

"Just get it over with," the girl spat.

Fie lifted *The Thousand Conquests* and began rolling it up. "Been about five years since Crows passed through the lands of Governor

Sakar, aye?" The parchment let out a particularly belligerent crackle. "Heard the last band didn't make it out of here. Most of them, anyway."

The Peacock girl said naught.

"A boy got away. Another chief found him, brought him to my pa. His name was Hangdog."

Was. Two moons since he'd tried to run from being a Crow. Two moons since he'd died on the steps of a Peacock mansion.

When Fie had been old enough, Pa had told her what had happened to Hangdog's first band. Hangdog himself had spoken of it to her only once.

"He told me there was a rich girl who came to their camp. They let her look at the pyre, they let her wear a mask, they let her see the chief's sword, because you don't say nay to a Peacock, even a little one . . . and then that night, the girl led the Oleander Gentry straight to their camp."

The Peacock girl's hands fisted in her pristine linen shift. Another bloom of Sinner's Brand had begun to tattoo her forearm.

Most of Sabor liked to think the Covenant meant for Crows to be punished. By Fie's ken, the Covenant had naught to do with it; they'd just appointed themselves its hangmen.

Niemi Navali szo Sakar turned a furious, glittering gaze on Fie. "I'd do it again."

Fie gave her a humorless, toothy smile and tucked *The Thousand Conquests* into her belt. "Suppose that's why the Covenant calls for you, then. Lie back." The girl didn't move. Fie pointedly hefted the Hawk sword. "Can't steady both you *and* the blade."

The Peacock girl lay back.

Sweat beaded her face. "Will it hurt?"

Fie had seen thousands of lives by now, ghosts darting like minnows through her head as she pulled Birthrights from their long-dry bones.

She'd seen the lives of kings and outcasts, lovers and foes, conquerors and thieves. Some ended in blood, others in quiet. Some had even died at Pa's hand, a cut throat granting them mercy from the agony of the Sinner's Plague. She saw those lives, and those deaths, more than any other.

"No," Fie lied, and rested the blade against the sinner girl's throat.

The clean steel shivered with every heartbeat pounding along the girl's neck, harder with fury, faster with fear.

The Peacock girl drew a shaky breath and caught Fie's eye. "The Oleander Gentry will come for you tonight, you know."

She meant it as a promise. As a threat. As a reminder, even now, of which castes the Covenant favored.

And that was where she'd fouled up.

Fie bestowed her one more smile, cold and benevolent as the steel on the girl's throat. "Let them."

The truth was, it had never gotten easier to deal mercy to sinners.

But sometimes, they made it easier.

———◆———

In the last three weeks, Fie had learned a handy new trick to negotiating the viatik.

When Pa had been the one cutting throats, he'd done his best to at least rinse off his hands after. The blood spooked the next of kin, he'd explained, and sometimes that made them pay the Crows more to speed them along, but more often than not it just made the mourners clutch their purses tighter.

Fie didn't bother. If anything, she made a show of slowly peeling away the bloody rags knotted up to her elbow while the family's representative presented their viatik. No one wanted to count coin into a palm still red and slick with mercy.

And that was the idea.

The Sakars had dispatched a Sparrow to deal with Fie, one who wore the simple fine robe of household servants, one whose red-rimmed eyes said she'd been close to the dead girl. A nursemaid, then. In one hand sat a fat bag of naka for viatik; the other hand skimmed the clinking coins, bitterly weighing out a meager few.

The thing about viatik, Fie had learned over years and years of experience, was that someone was always trying to short them.

Sometimes it was because they thought the Crows couldn't count and wouldn't know they'd been cheated. Sometimes it was because they wanted the Crows to *know* they'd been cheated, to remind them they still couldn't demand fair pay without pushing their luck. This Sparrow woman, Fie reckoned, had the same instructions as too many servants she'd dealt with. Each and every time, they were handed a fat purse, but told to give the Crows as little as possible.

So in the last few weeks, Fie had learned not to let them.

The Sparrow nursemaid flinched back at the gore on Fie's arms, eyes brimming with tears. Fie shook her head, flicking sweat from her hair. They'd kept to the north for most of Crow Moon, but midsummer humidity had invaded even this territory. "Naught to fear. You can hand the viatik to my lad Khoda."

Fie could see the sums scratching through the nursemaid's skull; by the time she'd tallied up that Khoda wasn't a Crow name, it was too late. A rangy, iron-faced Hawk lad stood before her, hand outstretched, a spear leaning rakishly against his shoulder.

The trick, Fie had learned, was to make them hand the viatik to someone they couldn't risk cheating.

A flutter of silk on the nearby veranda caught Fie's eye. Two Peacocks stood there, still in their sleeping robes and clinging to each other, faces hard. The Sparrow servant looked up to the governor and her husband, questioning, as the quarantine hut's door creaked behind Fie.

Last night they'd had a daughter.

Now, Madcap and Wretch were loading aught that was left of her into the Crow's wagon, bundled in bloody linen.

Governor Sakar gave a stiff jerk of her chin, then buried her face in her trailing silk sleeves.

The nursemaid swallowed. Her bag of naka jingled like a bell as it landed, whole and hearty, in Khoda's hand.

Fie caught a muffled snort from Madcap, one that turned into a cough. Not three moons ago, such a bounty would have been unthinkable, even a burden—just one more thing the Oleander Gentry would hunt them for. But now . . .

Khoda was one of five Hawks who had volunteered to escort Fie's band as they answered plague beacons. And since acquiring their escort, a peculiar miracle had occurred. Not only did people start paying them fair viatik, but for the first time, they'd been able to *keep* it. No Oleanders had raided their camps; no Hawk posts had shaken them down for bribes. Fie's band had left generous donations in every haven shrine they'd visited, and still they had more than enough to last until the next viatik.

And now they had a bag of coin near the size of Fie's head. She hadn't even needed to call a Money Dance.

"That'll do," Fie said, and wet her lips to whistle the marching order.

"Wait!" The Sparrow pointed to the scroll cinched in Fie's belt. "That's . . . that was her favorite."

The Thousand Conquests. Where the Splendid Castes were beautiful and wise, the Hunting Castes were brave and true, and the Phoenixes were near good as gods.

Where Crows were thieves and fools and monsters and naught more.

"It'll burn with her," Fie said. The nursemaid's shoulders slumped in relief. Fie added under her breath, "We all win."

The Sparrow woman blinked at that. "Wh—"

Fie whistled the marching order and strode down the road before the woman could sum up aught else.

A familiar jingle said Corporal Lakima had fallen into her self-appointed place a step behind Fie, each thud of the Hawk's boots measured as if rationed out to the greedy road. At first Fie had found it eerie, the creak of leather, the shadow doubling hers. She'd found it near as unsettling when Corporal Lakima asked her for orders.

By now, Fie supposed she was used to both. They made for an odd funeral procession rattling down the dusty gravel: a wiry twist of a girl chief in her beaked mask, a shadow of a Hawk looming at her back, nine more Crows towing their dead sinner in the cart, three Hawks bringing up the rear. They'd left Pa and the remaining two Hawks with their *other* cart, back at the flatway.

Even a second cart seemed an unfathomable luxury. They'd never before had enough to merit a second cart, never enough hands or beasts to pull one. But with Hawks to feed and plentiful viatik, things were a-shift. Now they towed one cart for their supplies and one just for sinners.

"Was there a problem with the girl?" Corporal Lakima's voice ground near as low as the gravel.

Fie shook her head. "Only her mouth. *That* won't trouble anyone again." She picked at the sweaty straps on her mask, more jitters than aught else. They'd keep the masks on until the Peacock manor fell out of sight. "She said the Oleanders will come tonight."

Corporal Lakima was perhaps the stoniest Hawk Fie had yet met; at a decade older and a head and a half taller than Fie, she did not so much stand on decorum as plant both feet into it and wordlessly dare anyone to push her off. She was not prone to a mummer's theatrics. And so when Fie caught an exasperated wheeze before the corporal answered, "Understood, chief," Fie thought at first it had come from the cart. She'd expect a dead Peacock to grumble sooner than Corporal Lakima.

"Did you just sigh?" Fie asked, incredulous.

Lakima coughed. "Did she say when they'll arrive?"

"Just tonight. Suppose I ought to have asked for specifics before I cut her throat. You *sighed*."

"These lowlanders seem to have a surplus of time on their hands."

Fie snuck a look back. Lakima kept her face blank, her eyes locked solely on the road ahead, but a divot between her brows said the corporal was vexed. Oleanders meant a late night for her and her Hawks.

Three moons ago, before they'd smuggled Prince Jasimir across Sabor, Oleanders would have meant rolling gambling shells with disaster. If Pa had been promised a visit from the masked riders, he would have hurried them along through the night, not even stopping to burn the sinner until dawn peeled the cover of dark from the roads.

But Fie was chief now. Fie had Hawks now. And Pa . . .

He'd asked her to bear northwest to the Jawbone Gulf a week ago, and that was when she knew his time had come.

That was a trouble Fie's Hawks couldn't remedy.

Instead, she said to Lakima, "Maybe they'll show up early and get it over with before dinner."

Corporal Lakima lifted her spear in salute. It took Fie a moment to realize it wasn't to her but to the Hawks on duty at the manor's signal post above. Helmeted heads jerked back over the small tower's platform when Fie turned to look their way. A thin wisp of black smoke still lingered from the plague beacon they'd lit to call Crows here.

Likely the Hawk soldiers couldn't fathom why some of their own would accompany Crows. Fie failed to stuff down a smirk at that. She'd won her Hawks fair and square from Master-General Draga, and more importantly, she'd won Hawks to guard the whole Crow caste once Prince Jasimir took the throne. Those soldiers just might be escorting their own band of Crows soon enough.

Rumors had already floated past Fie, rumors of Crown Prince Jasimir, who'd survived the Sinner's Plague like his legendary ancestor Ambra, and tales of Master-General Draga's showy procession to return Jasimir to the capital city of Dumosa. Nobody spoke of Queen Rhusana, but Jasimir had always sworn the queen's first move in a takeover would be to remove King Surimir from power, and so far it seemed the king breathed yet.

Considering the leader of Surimir's armies was personally ushering the crown prince—the one Rhusana had repeatedly tried to assassinate—back to his home, Fie reckoned the queen might be keeping a low profile.

"Why did you take the scroll?" Corporal Lakima asked.

Fie had a score of answers to that: Because it made her feel better about cutting the throat of a girl her own age. Because that scroll told the nobility they were always good, and told Fie she would always be a monster. Because no one in the fine Peacock manor behind them knew that in Crow story and song, the monsters usually wore silk.

"They would have burned it anyway," Fie said instead. "This way I get to watch."

Lakima coughed again. "Ah. Must be *The Thousand Conquests*."

———◆———

Fie shed her mask once the roughway led into the trees, but she kept her eyes nailed to the road, only glancing back every so often to be sure no spiteful mourner tailed them. Five years might be enough for the woods to reclaim the campsite where Hangdog's kin had died, but Crows were raised with an eye to spot potential sleeping grounds, and Fie didn't feel like laying hers on that sad clearing.

She didn't feel like thinking much on Hangdog at all.

Fear had spurred him to turn traitor, that she knew. Fear of what lay down his road as a Crow chief, fear that it would end as the rest of his kin's had. She couldn't fault him for that.

But she could fault him for thinking treachery was his only way out.

Fie felt the flatway before she saw it. The air savored hotter and dustier, the roughway began to even out, and full sunlight stabbed more frequently through the green canopy overhead. Finally they emerged onto the broad, smooth dirt road. Pa and their two other Hawks were sheltering with the supply wagon on the other side of the flatway, in the shade of an ivy-choked hemlock.

Fie's heart gave a familiar sort of pang when she saw Pa, as it had done many a time since he'd asked her to lead them to the Jawbone. Then she kenned the look on his face, and that pang wormed into a deeper worry.

It was a rare look. Fie remembered the last time she'd seen it, all too close, all too clear: when Pa had handed her the sword, the teeth, and the prince, and sent her and the lordlings over the bridge in Cheparok.

It said something had fouled up, and in a way they might not be able to outrun now.

"What is it?" Fie called, striding across the dirt road—but the moment she broke into the sun, she saw.

To her left, a black string of smoke frayed the horizon, half a league away. To her right, another black thread unspooled. Beyond them, even more black trails rose until they'd striped the noon sky like teeth in a giant's comb.

Fie had seen such a sight only twice before, but she knew square what black beacons for leagues and leagues meant.

Even with Prince Jasimir's armies nigh at her door, Rhusana had made her move.

The king was dead.

CHAPTER TWO

——— STOLEN ———

"WELCOME TO OUR ROADS, COUSIN."

Fie cast a palmful of salt onto the pyre, then took a step back from the flames licking up the dead Peacock's shroud and thought a quick prayer to the dead Crow goddess who claimed the plague-dead, the Eater of Bones. Most of Sabor believed the sinner girl would be born as a Crow in the next life, to atone for whatever she did that made the Covenant snatch her so swift from this one.

Fie didn't know if that were true, but if it were, she sore hoped the girl would learn to be less of a hateful hag.

"Didn't sound like you meant that welcome," Pa said by her side.

The Thousand Conquests twisted in Fie's other hand. She'd washed up with soap-shells and salt, yet firelight still painted her fingers red against the pale, crumpled parchment. "I don't."

"She'll be a babe when she comes to us as a Crow," Pa said.

"Better come to someone else's band."

"Fie." Pa set a hand on her shoulder. "It changes naught."

He didn't mean the girl on the pyre.

"It's the last day of Crow Moon and the king dies? They'll put us at fault for it, Pa."

Pa ran a hand over his beard. "And it's been two moons since we were there. Anyone who faults us for it is just looking for something new to blame on Crows. Likely they're already riding with the Oleanders."

"But it doesn't add up, either." Fie shook her head. "We've still two weeks until the solstice, when a proper Phoenix would be crowned. Jas is sure to make it to the royal palace before then to stake out the throne, and he's the one bringing the armies. And now half the nation thinks he's Ambra reborn, sent here to lead us into a new bright age . . . so since when does Rhusana's kind pick a fight they know they'll lose?"

The firelight caught on the knob of scar tissue where Pa's little finger had once been. He'd lost it in just such a fight. "Aye," he said. "It doesn't add up for the queen. But what are you to do about it?"

"What?"

"You're a Crow chief, leagues and leagues away from Dumosa. What are *you* to do?"

Fie wrung the parchment in her hands. She knew the words all too well, yet they felt like shackles tonight. "Look after my own."

Pa squeezed her shoulder and let go. "Let the royals roll their fortune-bones. We've no part in their games now, and however their bones land, we're still chiefs. You've your own to look after. And I've a shrine to keep."

Fie flinched. Most of her wanted to hare dead south to Dumosa, to burn as many of her teeth as it took to send Rhusana to the next life, to settle Jas on his throne and set off on her roads with Tavin at her side. And doing just that would mean keeping Pa with her that much longer.

But Pa was right. Crows needed every haven shrine they could get, and no band needed two chiefs. In the Jawbone Gulf waited the watchtower of the dead god Little Witness. The keeper there kept track of every shrine to a dead Crow god, and would know which ones sat empty and unused.

When old Crows could no longer travel the roads, they lived out their days in a haven shrine built on the grave of one of their dead gods. That close to a dead god, any Crow could keep the shrine's stores of teeth alight, hiding it from other castes. A witch like Pa, though, could make a shrine nigh invincible. No doubt he'd be assigned to one they sore needed.

Fie would deliver him there herself, and then leave him behind her for good.

And from the sound of it, she'd do it while Rhusana seemed certain of her victory. Rhusana, who'd promised the Oleander Gentry they could hunt Crows as they pleased once she reigned. Rhusana, whose mere promise of permission had brought more Oleanders down on Fie's head in the last three moons than Fie had seen in years. Even *after* she'd delivered the prince to safety.

"What if it gets worse?" she whispered. "What if I'm not enough to look after them?"

"You've six Hawks, Fie," Pa said pointedly. "Two swords. Thousands of Phoenix teeth to burn your way clear. If aught can get through all that, it won't be a fight meant for a mortal to win."

That was the heart of her vexation, Fie reckoned. No Crow band in memory had ever had such protection, and still she didn't feel her Crows were safe. A storm squatted on their horizon. All she could do was try to keep them out of it.

Two moons ago, she'd stood in front of two empty pyres, Hangdog at her side, fresh off cutting an oath with the crown prince. Jasimir had tried to tell her then that the Crows' only hope of survival was saving him, and Hangdog had sworn it was all a wash.

Now here she was in front of a pyre yet again, but here Hangdog wasn't after all. The beacons were telling her the last man between the throne and the Oleanders' queen had died. But there was naught she could do about it now.

The smell of burning flesh began to drift from the pyre. Fie stepped back again, mouth twisting. A warning yowl made her jump. She turned and found Barf, the gray tabby she'd plucked from the royal palace, sprawled on the ground behind her.

If the cat kenned the dire tidings of dead kings and grim roads, she didn't show it. Instead she chirped and rolled onto her back, paws tucked neat beneath her chin.

Fie knew that trick too well. Pa, however, crouched to rub Barf's white belly. The tabby promptly latched onto his arm like a snare. He yanked his hand back as Wretch cackled behind them.

"Ought to know better, Cur," Wretch called. Pa's name sounded yet strange to Fie's ear, now that her band called only Fie "chief." "That beast doesn't show her belly unless it's a trap."

"I do know better," Pa grumbled. "Just hoped it'd be different this time."

There was a crinkle as Fie's fist tightened on *The Thousand Conquests*. The parchment had turned gummy with sweat. She tossed it onto the pyre, just as she'd promised.

It smoked and caught almost immediately. Fie knew the value of scrolls, the time and effort that Owl scribes put into copying out a work like *The Thousand Conquests*, how each one was to be prized and protected. Scholar Sharivi had claimed, in a wholly unnecessary foreword, that the tales he'd scrawled within were the unblemished truth. That they captured the history of Sabor, the might of rulers, the wickedness of traitors, the foundations of the nation itself.

Fie doubted with all her heart that Sharivi had captured the foundations of aught but a cowpat, from what she'd read. But in the end, she found he'd given her one scrap of joy: the way *The Thousand Conquests* was there one moment and naught but smoke in the next.

———◆———

The Oleanders came that night after all.

It went as it had the last few weeks: first, Barf sounded the alarm. The cat had no love of Oleander Gentry, not after they'd nearly burned her alive, and since then, she'd yowl and bush her tail out when she caught the rumblings of a dozen or more riders galloping down the road. Even better, she picked up those rumbles at least a full minute ahead of when Fie could.

First the cat howled, then came hoofbeats pounding down the road in the dark, the Crows gathering a bit tighter about the campfire but making no move to flee. The three Hawks on watch would plant themselves between the camp and the road and wait, while the three at rest would sit up, spears within reach.

After that was where Fie had seen the most variation. Once, the baffled gang of Oleanders had offered to assist the Hawks in arresting the Crows. Another time, they had tried to argue with Lakima, then to threaten her, until one rider took a swing at the corporal. Fie had collected the teeth Lakima knocked out of him with particular glee.

Tonight, the Oleanders slowed as they neared the camp, clearly flummoxed by the sight of spears at the ready. Their leader took in the scene from behind a rough rag mask and evidently decided to find some other amusement.

Near two dozen riders trotted past in an awkward, uneasy parade, muttering among themselves and gawking at the guards.

Once, their undyed robes and white powders had frightened Fie. Now she had fire. Now she had steel. Now she had Hawks. The Oleander Gentry looked like children playing dress-up to her, down-right silly as they rode away.

She'd always known their kind only picked fights they'd win. She just hadn't known how it felt when they turned tail and ran.

"Do you think they're lost?" Khoda jested, leaning on his spear. "Should I offer them directions?"

"Off a cliff, maybe," Fie muttered, and went back to sleep.

It took them another day and a half to reach the Jawbone Gulf.

On a clear day, word was you could see all the way out to the tiny island at the most northwestern corner of Sabor, just past Rhunadei. But clear days were rare, even in the summer, and as they crested the hill overlooking the city of Domarem, the noon sun made scarce more than a coin-shaped dent in the overcast sky. Heavy fog blanketed the coast as far as the eye could see—which was barely past the water's edge before the mist swallowed the gulf whole. All that could be seen were the shadows of crumbling spires jabbing from the waves.

Legend said that some long-dead regional governor had gotten ambitious and tried to pry the gulf open for proper trade before the waters were known as the Jawbone. Gulls, with their Birthright of reading the winds, could navigate the fog and shoals in nimble sail-boats; and smugglers, with their time-honored knowledge of the maze of rocks, could slip by like minnows through a shark's teeth.

However, only a Gull witch could command the winds to steer a heavy merchant barge safely through. With less than a hundred of those Gull witches alive in Sabor, that safe passage came at a steep price, one merchants balked at paying simply to deliver to a backwater fishing town, where half the locals were like to strip the ship apart overnight.

Domarem, the governor believed, ought to have been a jewel of Sabor, as great a trading hub in the north as Cheparok was to the south. He also believed he could manage it without paying the Gulls. Instead he'd ordered dozens of watchtowers be built atop those shoals and fitted with beacons so captains knew where to steer clear.

He'd made one fatal error, though. The beacons worked fairly well at night, glowing through the heavy fog to mark safe passage.

They weren't worth a damn during the day.

And since the governor had vexed the Gulls, their witches took his coin no more. So the governor never got his trading hub, and so the towers eroded into ruined fangs, and so the governor's dream starved away, leaving only the mocking name of the Jawbone Gulf behind. Or so the legend said.

Fie reckoned Domarem involved far too many cliffs to make a practical trading port anyhow, though she knew that'd never stop a Peacock convinced of his own genius. Half the city seemed carved straight into the bluffs, and the other half looked as if it had just slid off the rock and piled up closer to the shore. The docks teemed with dinghies, coracles, and sails dyed the vivid, cheery blue that Gulls favored. The sails of southern Gulls tended to fade with sun and seawater, but the mussels they used for pigment grew so abundant here that the silver sands rippled with indigo streaks of crushed shell.

As they drew near the gates, Corporal Lakima asked delicately, "Will we be walking you in?"

It was a dance they'd near-perfected in the last few weeks, though it had taken time. The entire point of haven shrines was to have secret places where Crows, and *only* Crows, could seek refuge. It was one thing to sneak a prince and his bodyguard through two or three as Fie had done. It was an entirely different matter to lead six Hawk soldiers straight into every Crow shrine they encountered.

Yet Lakima's charge was to keep the band safe, and when asked to turn her back while the Crows vanished, unguarded, down secret alleyways and hidden ravines, Lakima had proved . . . reluctant. She'd been more than willing to pick up where Tavin had left off with tutoring Fie in sword combat, but she hadn't believed that a sword and a half would be enough to protect the band.

Then one night they'd encountered more of Rhusana's skin-ghasts, hideous empty puppets made from the skins of the dead. The Hawks' steel left only holes in their still-wriggling hides, but all Fie had to do was call the Birthright of fire from one Phoenix-caste tooth on her string and the ghasts were done for in a trice.

Since then, Lakima had been willing to let Fie protect the band when they went where Hawks couldn't follow.

Fie hadn't been to Little Witness's watchtower, though; only Pa and Wretch had. She looked to them.

Pa shook his head and pointed to a fork in the road ahead. A thinner dirt road branched up toward the cliffs. "We'll be taking a stroll."

"It'll be easier without the cart," Fie said. "Pa, Varlet, and Bawd, we'll go to the shrine. Everyone else, stay here and watch the goods. Wretch, you're in charge."

"Pelen, Khoda, and I can restock the supply wagon from the command post in town." Corporal Lakima gave Fie a significant look. "I'll let you know what they're reporting."

She meant what news they had of the king's death. No rumors of the official cause had reached the roads, which both Fie and Lakima had found troubling.

"Aye. We'll meet back at the fork no later than sundown." Fie fished two packs out of the supply wagon. She'd made them up this morning, stuffed near to bursting with spare pots, dried salt pork, and any other goods they weren't likely to use soon. It would be rude to show up at Little Witness's grave empty-handed. One pack went to Pa, and the other Fie shouldered herself. She swept an arm to the dirt road. "Pa, lead on."

"Lovely day for a walk," Bawd said merrily, hooking her arm through Varlet's. Varlet's grin spread wide as his twin sister's. The two of them had spent near all of their twenty-some-odd years laboring to make it so precious few could tell them apart—cutting their hair the same, mimicking each other's turns of phrase, even dressing as close to identical as they could manage. So far they'd managed to fool Lakima thrice and the rest of the Hawks no fewer than seven times.

Varlet twirled a curl round a finger. "Must say, chief, I'm flattered you picked us to come along. Downright optimistic of you, even."

"You two have survived this long, despite your best efforts," Fie said. There was no mystery to why she wanted extra hands on a shrine visit: Little Witness's watchtower was one of the three great shrines to dead Crow gods, and as such, they didn't dare lose sight of the way in. Someone in every band always needed to know how to find it. "Figured if anyone's safe to keep the way known for a while yet, it's you."

"No doubt Varlet will put that to the test," Bawd drawled. "Cur, where do you reckon the keeper will send you?"

Pa scratched at his bald crown. He was more nervous about this than Fie'd realized. "They send witches to their own shrines, or so my old chief told me. We'll see."

A chill ran down Fie's spine at that. Pa believed, as many did, that when the thousand gods died, they were born again as witches to lead the castes they'd founded. Fie had spent too much time tripping over her own feet to really believe she'd once been a god, though.

And the uneasy truth was that thinking on it felt like standing at the shores of an ocean on a moonless night—something terrible, vast, and unseen roaring before her, waiting to swallow her whole the moment she stepped beyond solid ground.

They soon left the dirt road for a worn footpath that wound through narrow black pines and hassocks of sharp-bladed grass, forking again and again. "Downhill," Pa told the other three. "Always take the downhill branch." Eventually it spilled them out into a cove walled round by basalt cliffs.

Fie knew the moment her sandal touched beach that they had reached Little Witness's grave. Charcoal fragments still freckled the paler bands of sand, remnants of bonfires from the first night of Crow Moon, and even without that giveaway, the rumble of bone magic beneath her feet was all too familiar to miss. Pa strode toward a great mound of boulders crusted over with glistening black mussels, near buried in the white froth of crashing waves. As Fie followed him up onto the rock, the answering hum in her own bones swelled to a muffled roar.

Pa reached the edge of the boulders, then stepped off. By all rights, he ought to have dropped straight into the churning surf below, to be hammered to a pulp between the waves and the basalt.

Instead, he vanished.

"So *that's* how you hide a watchtower," Varlet said.

Fie made herself walk off the rocks as well. As expected, her foot met solid stone, and in a breath she'd broken through the walls of magic shrouding the shrine. Where water had rushed below, now more basalt rose to form the base of Little Witness's tower.

Unlike the shabby towers bristling along the waters of the Jawbone, this one boasted of eight sides instead of four, standing taller, sturdier, and *older* than any of the governor's ruins. The sea had gnawed away

much of the watchtower's ancient embellishments, but the most unsettling survivors were the bricks jutting out from each corner. They'd been
stacked so that every other brick protruded, but saltwater and storm
had worn them down to rounded shells, and they now looked like eight
unfathomably long spines stretching to the tower's rooftop. Windows
cut into eight-pointed stars pocked the surface, letting light in but
betraying naught.

Fie reckoned she could see straight to Dumosa from that roof.
As a god, Little Witness had taken the form of a beggar girl who saw
everyone's misdeeds and recounted them for the Covenant's judgment.
Likely she'd also need a watchtower like this to do it from. If Little
Witness really had started recounting the misdeeds of Dumosa, it was
no wonder she'd died before she could ever leave.

A groan made Fie jump. The iron door at the base of the tower had
split diagonally, the two halves sliding away, behind the walls. In the
entryway stood a little girl, no more than seven, barefoot and clad only
in an overlarge shift of black crowsilk. Her hair had been tied back with
a careless hand, dark strands falling about her round brown face, and
two black eyes burned straight into Fie.

Pa cleared his throat. "Cousin, we're here to see the keep—"

The girl pointed dead at Fie. "What do you call yourself?"

Fie wobbled and nearly fell on a bed of mussels. "What?"

"In this life," the girl said, crossing her arms. "What do you call
yourself?"

Fie shot a look to Pa, who shrugged, mystified as she. "Fie," she
answered.

"Fie. You're first." The girl turned on a heel and walked away from
the doorway.

"I'm not—" Fie sputtered as a wave crashed into the boulders she
stood on, spraying her with foam and brine. "We're here for *Pa*, not me."

The girl poked her head around the doorframe. She blinked at Pa, then vanished again. "Gen-Mara, the Messenger. We can speak in a moment."

"He's to keep Gen-Mara's shrine?" Bawd asked, clapping Pa on the back. Gen-Mara's groves were another of the great shrines. "Now *that's* a place to settle."

"The Messenger's to keep his own shrine," the little girl's voice called from the tower's depths. "You all wait inside—all but you, Fie or Sebiri or whatever it is you're calling yourself now. You come with me."

"*That's* the keeper?" whispered Varlet.

Pa slowly shook his head. His eyes had gone wider than Fie could ever recall seeing. "Lad . . . that's Little Witness."

Bawd and Varlet both swore with equal parts reverence and imagination. Fie stayed stock-still, frozen to the rock, mind reeling. They hadn't come here for Fie. Whatever this was—she wasn't supposed to face it, not yet.

Pa nudged her. "Go on, girl."

The ocean roared round her. "But, Pa—"

"Best not to keep a dead god waiting," he said, and strode into the tower. Fie had no choice but to follow.

Inside was nothing like Fie had expected. Light streamed in from the open windows, catching on wheels, pulleys, and levers lining the walls, and on shelves cluttered with scrolls and stacks of parchment. Most shrines kept a statue of the dead god whose grave they stood on, and while Little Witness's tower was no exception, apparently her recent incarnations had felt the statue could serve a more practical use. The crude stone carving of the little beggar girl now bore planks of wood across her outstretched arms, which hosted dusty jars, roughly folded blankets, and bolts of crowsilk. Clotheslines had been strung between the statue's fingers, splaying out laundry that looked as if it had dried a week ago and simply remained there.

Once all four Crows were inside, Fie heard another creak and snap, and then the iron door's crooked halves slammed shut behind them. A tiny figure darted over to a wooden platform on the ground as wide and as long as the wagon. Thick ropes were fastened at each corner, stretching into the shadows overhead.

Little Witness pointed at the platform and ordered, "Get on."

Fie swallowed and stepped onto the planks.

Little Witness hopped on as well and flipped a lever. Fie heard a rush of water below, and then, to her astonishment, the platform began to rise. "Don't touch anything," Little Witness shouted to the others. "If you need to sit, sit on the floor."

The steps, which seemed reasonably easy to climb, coiled in a slow spiral round the tower walls. As they passed level after level, Fie saw one floor covered end to end with sleeping pallets, no doubt to shelter visiting bands; another held what looked like a viatik stash, the largest Fie had ever seen. A whole level was dedicated solely to jars upon dusty jars of teeth—mostly Sparrow to hide the watchtower and Peacock to weave an illusion in its place. That floor made Fie's own teeth ache and sing in answer, and she was grateful when it sank below them.

"Who put a water-lift in your tower?" Fie asked, anchoring herself on a rope and trying not to look down.

"I did," the dead god answered shortly.

Fie looked pointedly up at the ropes, which seemed to run all the way to the top of the tower. "Wouldn't think you were tall enough for that."

"I used to be. Ten-and-eight lives ago, I fell down the tower steps and died. I prioritized transportation in the next one. And I have time on my hands." She frowned out a passing star-shaped window as Domarem slipped through its frame. "I was the god of remembering. From the moment I am born, I remember everything, in every life and from all the lives before, Huwim or Hellion or Fie."

"Except my name," Fie muttered.

"You've worn a lot of names," Little Witness fired back. "You've worn a lot of lives. Ten-and-seven lives ago, you pushed me down those stairs." She peered up at Fie with a grandmother's eyes in a child's face. "See? Now if you push me off, I will take you with me."

All Fie saw was that, by now, it was a very long way to fall. She tightened her grip on the rope. "I don't feel like killing a dead god today."

"You haven't, the last three times we've spoken." Little Witness smiled in a way that was tired and sweet and bloodcurdling all at once. "You've been a Crow those times."

"Those times?"

The platform drew even with the top of the staircase, and Little Witness hopped off without answering. Fie followed.

"*Those* times?" she repeated. "I'm a witch. If—if we're all dead gods reborn, then wasn't I a Crow god?"

"Aren't you, indeed?" Little Witness led her up five more steps and into a room that could hardly be called one. It spanned the entire width of the tower, but its walls were stone cut with so many of those eight-point stars that they might as well have been screens. Wind whistled through the gaps, and weak light poured in from the overcast sky, giving the room an unearthly pewter glow.

"What you were doesn't particularly matter," Little Witness said, heading for a heap of worn cushions, where she promptly sat. "What matters is what you carry. So first: What will you leave in my viatik stash?"

Fie swung the pack down and settled beside it. "Food, cooking gear—Pa's got the rest of it in his pack—"

"I'll have the teeth." Little Witness pointed to the bag fastened at Fie's belt.

Her heart skipped a beat. She had a sudden horrid hunch where this was going, but she undid the bag's straps anyway, fingers shaking. It was a beautiful work of stamped leather, with pockets and compartments inside to help her order her teeth instead of having to fish around pouch within pouch. Tavin had gifted it to her before she left Trikovoi, with a particular charm stitched into one hidden corner: a milk tooth of his own. His mother had kept them.

In Fie's darkest moments, when she doubted she'd ever see him again, she'd reach for that tooth and the spark still burning within, and know she could yet find her Hawk.

"Not that one," Little Witness said as Fie's fingertips strayed to that tooth now. She pointed to the largest compartment, where the Phoenix teeth were stored. "Those."

Fie couldn't hide a flinch.

"What's the matter?" Little Witness asked. "You're not using them."

A thousand refusals howled in Fie's ears. *They keep us safe. They make us feared. I earned them.*

I need them.

Little Witness's cockeyed smile said she knew square what she asked for. And that only vexed Fie more.

"H-how many?" she gritted, unfastening the compartment.

"How many can you spare?" Little Witness returned. "You've two swords, six Hawks, thousands of fire teeth. How much is enough for you?"

Fie went still.

The dead god leaned forward, her eyes too knowing for her child face. "Truth is, you always like your fire too much. You claimed every Phoenix tooth in the land. Did that fix your problems? You took a Hawk's steel. Was that enough? You cut an oath from a prince, one to change all Sabor. Do you feel safe?"

Wind whistled through the tower. Fie clutched her bag tighter and met Little Witness's gaze with her own. "No Crow is safe with Rhusana climbing the throne."

"But it's not just Rhusana, is it?" Little Witness asked.

Something in Fie's gut rankled at that, and in the back of her skull, a dead Peacock girl whispered, *The Covenant made* you *as a punishment.*

"When the prince is on his throne, will you let your fire teeth go then?" Little Witness pressed. "Will that be enough?"

"You know it won't," Fie snapped before she could rein herself back in. "Aye, it's not just Rhusana, it's the people who ride for her. The ones who know she'll let them. It's everyone who thinks Crows are naught but sinners to abuse as they please. And why shouldn't they? You're the one who can remember clear back to the dawn of days, so *you* tell *me* now: Why did the gods make us like this? Why don't Crows have a Birthright?"

Little Witness leaned back, eyes narrowing, as smug as Barf with a mouse in her claws.

"And who said you didn't?" she asked.

For a terrible moment, Fie knew sore how that mouse felt.

"Wh-what?" she stammered.

"It eats at you every time," Little Witness said, almost sad. "You think wanting more makes you less, when you just want what was stolen. You're right! Rhusana isn't the whole of your problem. She's just the newest thief on the throne."

Fie stared at her. "Stop. Forget Rhusana. We had a Birthright?"

Little Witness wagged a finger at her. "Forget Rhusana and you'll just die again, and you'll never make it here in time in your next life."

"*Enough.*" Fie didn't know if her heart pounded with fury or wonder, but she knew which ruled her now. "The rest of Sabor thinks we have naught to offer but cutting sinners' throats. And you're telling me you knew we had a Birthright this whole damn time?"

"You can't——"

"Crows have *died* while you sat in your tower!" Fie lurched to her feet, Phoenix teeth rattling across the basalt floor. Her very breath came bitter with memories of every pyre she'd lit for her kin, starting with her own mother. "And you couldn't be bothered to, oh, *tell anyone* we had a Birthright until now?"

"It wouldn't have changed anything."

"*YOU TELL MY MA IT WOULDN'T!*" Fie screamed.

"I do hope you don't kill me this time," Little Witness said. "I *just* grew tall enough to work the lift without a stepstool."

Fie's fists balled at her side. "If you don't start speaking plain——"

"I was, at least about the stepstool." Little Witness sighed. "Here's as plain as I can get with you: Aye, we Crows had a Birthright. It was stolen. And if you want to take it back, you'll need to keep your oath."

Fie froze at that. "My——my *oath*? My Covenant oath?"

"Aye."

"Prince Jasimir's safe with his aunt," Fie said, head spinning. "I delivered him to his allies. Twice, if we're being picky. Our end of the deal is kept."

If it wasn't——somehow——

Pa had struck the oath with the prince. And a Covenant oath followed you from life to life, until it was fulfilled.

"Why wasn't that enough?" Fie demanded.

"You tell me. Six Hawks, two swords, every Phoenix tooth in the land, and *that* isn't enough for you." Little Witness undid her hair-tail and set about sorting her long black locks into a plait. "Keep your oath and you'll find our Birthright. You'll not find it sooner. I can speak no clearer."

"What *is* our Birthright, then?"

"Ah." Little Witness smiled one of her dreadful smiles again. "It would be cheating to tell you."

"You told Pa he was Gen-Mara not a half hour ago."

The god in the girl shook her head. "Gen-Mara hasn't failed his duty for hundreds of years. I can't say the same for you."

"I see why I keep killing you," Fie muttered, stuffing teeth back into her bag. When she looked up, Little Witness was holding out her hand.

"I asked for teeth," she said.

"And I asked you what Birthright I'm supposed to find for us. Seems we'll both leave empty-handed."

Little Witness's laugh was even worse than her smile. "Oh, I do miss this, you and me. It was a cruel thing, putting such a spark in you but telling you not to love the fire." She gave a twitch of her hand. "I want twelve, for the chiefs that will come to me in the next moon. We all know the storm's coming; only a fool waits for the lightning to tell them to find shelter."

That was hard to argue with. Fie counted out a dozen Phoenix teeth, feeling the weight of each like lead in her belly.

A dozen teeth she'd never use to defend her own.

A dozen teeth another chief will use instead, her Chief voice reminded her.

It chafed, how she'd never held a Phoenix tooth three moons ago, and now she could scarce bear to part with them.

Fie dropped her teeth into the dead god's waiting palm anyway. Little Witness's fingers closed.

She looked Fie dead in the eye, suddenly sharp. "I can't tell you your own story, little god. Life after life, you've failed, and none worse than when I tell you outright what to seek. But *this* is why the Covenant needs a Crow to play your part, do you see? Your Birthright, your oath, they are truths no one can give to you. You must find them yourself."

"And Rhusana?" Fie snapped. "Can you tell me aught about her? Or am I to go on some journey of self-discovery while she chases all of us into early graves?"

Little Witness began stacking the teeth into a tidy pile. "Only this: she feeds a monster, and each day it grows, and each day she lies to herself that she commands its teeth. She will be Sabor's ruin, if you are not hers. Though I will say, if you want your grave, you'll certainly find it in the palace."

Fie scowled. She'd no patience for more riddles. "I was hoping for something more like 'Here's exactly how she plans to murder the Crows.'"

"You already know how." Little Witness tilted her head. "There's a young man waiting for you downstairs. He isn't a Crow."

The most terrible question yet arose before Fie could stuff it down: "Am *I*?"

Little Witness blinked. "What else could you be?"

"I spent a moon and a half sneaking a prince and a half across Sabor while they mummed at being Crows," Fie said. "They wore our clothes and ate our food and walked our roads, but that didn't make them Crows. Am I any different?"

"Aye." Little Witness stood and dusted herself off. "We're dead gods. And you, you go where you're called. Come on, that young man needs to speak with you."

She led Fie to the platform but didn't get on herself, instead hauling at another lever set into the wall. "Send Gen-Mara up when you get down there. The lever's by the urn of Pigeon teeth." The planks shuddered. Fie wondered for a brief moment if Little Witness had decided to kill her off before Fie could strike first. Then the platform began to sink, steady and even.

"Fie."

Fie looked up. Little Witness stood at the edge of the stairs, watching her go.

"This is a gift," the dead god said. "Something to remember. You are not what you were."

Little Witness vanished back the way she'd come before Fie could ask what that was.

When the platform touched down, Wretch and Khoda were waiting, faces drawn. Pa, Varlet, and Bawd all shared their unease, and so did Fie: whatever called for leading a Hawk into Little Witness's watchtower had to be dire.

"I-I'm sorry," Khoda stammered, "but we need to get on the road as soon as possible. The queen's blaming you for the king's death."

The worst part wasn't her surprise, nor was it her fury, though both rushed ice-cold down Fie's bones. The worst part was that deep down, she'd known it would come to this. Of course Rhusana had found a way to fault a Crow for it.

Still, she asked, "How? There were hundreds of witnesses the night we went to the palace. He never showed his face, not even to watch Jasimir get carted out."

"It doesn't matter," Wretch said with a grim shake of her graying curls. "On Her Majesty's word . . . the king died of the Sinner's Plague."

CHAPTER THREE

TEETH AND MAGNOLIAS

"**W**E WERE THERE WHEN THE MESSAGE-HAWK ARRIVED FROM Dumosa.**" Corporal Lakima dragged the back of her hand across her sweat-beaded cheek. Even in the flatway's blistering midafternoon sunlight, she refused to discard her helm. "Her Majesty says you brought the plague into the palace."

Fie scowled at the dusty road. The moment Pa had finished with Little Witness, they'd swept up the rest of the Crows and all but bolted for the flatway. He'd been right: with Rhusana trying to blame the Crows, they'd need as many active haven shrines as possible, and Gen-Mara's was the largest by far.

"What a load of dog shit," Khoda mumbled, then seemed to recall he was in the presence of his commanding officer. "I mean—beg pardon, corporal. That sounds like . . . like . . ."

"Dog shit," Fie finished helpfully. "You had it the first time. What'd they do with the king's body?"

"Her Majesty claims his most faithful servants burned him this dawn, then threw themselves on the pyre. She says they needed no Crows."

Fie gave a harsh laugh, then coughed at a sudden mouthful of road dust. "Solid dung. If he died of the plague the day before yesterday, and they waited to burn him until today, half that palace would be wearing the Sinner's Brand right now." The Covenant had made a curious punishment of the Sinner's Plague: the disease spread fast and far only *after* its victim died.

"Maybe the Oleander Gentry's leaders are pushing her," added Pa. "They must be worried, with the prince so close to the throne."

Fie tripped, then caught herself. "R-right," she said hastily, brushing it off. In the rush to clear out of the watchtower, she hadn't had time to tell Pa of the oath they'd *both* thought kept, and now she didn't reckon she had the nerve. "Rhusana just gave towns an excuse to turn us away."

Lakima glanced over her shoulder, then lowered her voice. "Whatever the reason, she's also targeting *you*. The report says to look out for a Crow carrying Phoenix teeth."

"She's trying to distract Jas, make him spend time tracking us down," Fie said, scratching her chin. "Where do you reckon he's at by now?"

"The last report had the prince's procession moving down the flatway by the Vine, clearing Lumilar two days ago. If we make haste, we should be able to head due south and intercept them before week's end."

Fie mulled it over. Little Witness had said she wouldn't find the Birthright until her oath was kept. But what would it take to keep it, if not handing the prince to his own aunt? She'd lost her own kin once to keep the oath; what more would it take from her?

What would be enough?

"We get Pa to his shrine," Fie said. "Then we make for the procession, and if I ask nice, maybe Draga saves me some of the queen's teeth."

———◆———

They reached Gen-Mara's temple two mornings later, though Fie didn't know it.

When Pa was chief, he'd never had a call to take the band to a dormant shrine, and in her short time as chief, neither had Fie. Every shrine she'd been to had buzzed and sang in her bones the moment she drew near, but all of them had had a keeper living on the grounds, keeping the teeth awake.

It wasn't halfway to noon when Pa slowed, caught at Fie's shoulder, and squinted up at a hill. From the flatway, all Fie could see were the crests of trees all but sagging with heavy deep-green leaves.

"There ought to be a roughway around here," he said. Something had shifted in his weathered face, as if he weren't wholly in this world. It reminded her too much of Little Witness.

Fie whistled a halt order. She didn't *see* the entrance to a roughway, but that didn't mean one wasn't there. Like the watchtower, Gen-Mara's shrine was too dear to risk just any old scummer stumbling in. "Bawd, Madcap, help us look."

She could have saved them the trouble of poking about; Pa was the one to find it a few minutes later. He'd paused at a dense thicket of parasol ferns, brow furrowed, then set a hand on a gnarled magnolia tree. A moment later Fie felt the sparks of Peacock teeth shift and shiver. Enough of the parasol ferns vanished to expose a smooth, worn dirt road. Another magnolia tree marked the other side of the path, and now Fie saw a clay jar clinging to each, held tight against the trunk by knots of vines. Both hummed with the song of Peacock glamours.

Corporal Lakima motioned for her soldiers and said, "If anyone asks, we're taking a . . . How long will you be?"

Pa shrugged. "I've been here once, years ago. I'd say an hour, two to be generous."

". . . A late breakfast, then." Lakima started toward the road. She stopped to look back at Pa. "This is the last I'll see you, isn't it?"

"Most likely," he said, and tapped his right fist to his mouth and held it out. It was a gesture for greeting colleagues, but also for the parting of friends.

When Lakima's Hawks had first fallen in with Fie's band, it took a full week for them to share the same supply wagon with the Crows. She'd kenned why; on its face, it was fear of the plague only Crows survived, but deeper still, it was fear of something else. She'd seen this dance before, in all the ways Tavin and Jasimir had blundered two moons ago, but still, it had stung.

Now, on the fourth day of Phoenix moon, Corporal Lakima kissed her knuckles and clasped Pa's hand without hesitation.

"Fortune's favor to you, Cur," Lakima said. "Enjoy your rest."

"I'll try." Pa let go. "Keep my girl safe, aye?"

Lakima gave him a nod weighted with meaning. "Yes, chief."

Pa led them down the roughway for, as Fie tried not to dwell on, the final time. The road wound deeper into the forest, sloping just so slightly upward. Fie felt no hum other than the jars of teeth they'd left behind, but the farther they went, the thicker the tree trunks grew and the broader the leaves, until nearly all she saw was green. A faint, clean, lemony perfume began threading the air—and soon she felt a peculiar sort of shudder with every one of Pa's footfalls, like a note struck on a distant bell. She knew the simmer of a haven shrine, but this—this was different.

Then, finally, they reached the groves.

Towering magnolias spread as far as Fie could see, near tall as the watchtower, waxy white blossoms strung like pearls in their branches. Darts of pale sunlight broke through only with significant effort, and even then a faint mist seemed to weigh them down. Thick vines ran over the ground and tangled about the trunks like a drunkard's plait, weaving about strange, almost wartlike knots clustered against the bark. No, not knots—clay urns the same dusty dun as the vines. Some were big as barrels, some no bigger than fists, like the jars of teeth at the head of the road; great masses of Peacock teeth, Pigeon, Sparrow, even a few stashes of gem-precious teeth from Sparrow and Pigeon witches. All sat silent. Waiting.

Pa took one step into the grove, then another. The answering echo didn't sound like a bell to Fie now so much as a song, a chorus, a sigh of pure joy, one that reverberated in the jars, catching like sparks on tinder. Every step forward sent another pulse through the trees, through the vines, through the roots, through the teeth, until Fie's very bones felt as if they'd shake loose.

Pa came to a halt, and the roar swelled and burst like a dam, like a drowning man breaking the surface. Whispers seemed to well up from the vines, then settle, seeping back into the moss below. And then, finally, Fie felt it: the familiar, welcome hum of a haven shrine beneath her feet. The one that said so long as she stayed on this ground, she and hers were safe.

Pa was staring up at the rustling magnolias. Twin lines of tears cut clean tracks down his face. He looked at Fie, wide-eyed.

"I—" His voice broke, bewildered. "I'm . . . home."

Her own eyes burned and spilled over. She stumbled to him, all her fear and fury crashing down as she threw her arms around him, holding on for dear life, for as long as she could.

The groves knew Pa, even in this life. They welcomed him.

He was home, and terribly, he was home without her.

———◆◆◆———

They found the remains of the last keeper curled on a sleeping pallet in the temple proper.

The old Crow had died in his sleep, and it seemed no chiefs had sought out the shrine for a week or so. Or perhaps they'd simply not been able to find the shrine without a keeper to make the dead god's grave buzz in their bones.

There was more than enough firewood in the temple's viatik stash, and Fie set the rest of the band about stacking the pyre while she and Pa surveyed the temple itself. Like most Crow shrines, it was simple; unlike most Crow shrines, it was big. It seemed to be a relic of the days before Crows were run off the roads, its stone walls simple and many, its statue of Gen-Mara near as tall as the great magnolias. The temple roofs themselves had been formed by vines woven with more deliberation than those around the trees, forming broad, tight-knit mats that would funnel rain into wash barrels. More investigation turned up a meticulously tended vegetable patch, a spring of clean water, and even a penned-up goat that seemed to resent Pa's presence on principle.

The groves seemed to have teeth aplenty, even if most were hidden away in knots of vines. Pa made Fie pull a few handfuls from the temple's supply anyway, and in return she left handfuls of Phoenix teeth. Pa had carried them before; she trusted him to ration them out properly. The viatik stash itself was far from overflowing, but it would last Pa alone a fortnight or so, and other bands were now sure to pass through and give more. Nonetheless, Fie hadn't gone to the trouble of dragging their supply wagon this far just to leave Pa scraping by.

Pa helped her unload water skins, sacks of millet and dried beans, strips of dried bison. Then he stood by, brows raised, as she went back for extra cloaks, sandal nails, and spare sleeping mats.

And when Fie spent five minutes digging through the cart for another bundle of dried fruit, he walked over and leaned against its side, giving her a rueful smile. "Fie."

"They're here somewhere." She shoved aside a roll of oilcloth, then frowned and held it out. "Do you need oilcloth?"

"*Fie.*" Pa gently pushed the roll back to her. "I don't need oilcloth."

"You sure? The rainy season—"

"It's no use putting it off," Pa said, not unkind. "The roads wait for no one."

Fie suddenly became very fixated on restoring the oilcloth to its proper place in the cart.

"You've been spooked since Little Witness called you up." Pa climbed into the cart to sit beside Fie. "What's amiss, girl? What did she have to say?"

Scores of answers came to mind once more: That Fie was something she wasn't. That she had failed, again and again and again. That she hadn't kept their oath after all.

That if she couldn't, he would pay the price.

Fie couldn't say any of that to Pa, though, not moments before she left him alone in this empty home. A fragment of the truth would have to do. "She asked for Phoenix teeth."

"Did you give them?"

"Aye." Fie's mouth twisted. "Didn't like it, though."

Pa leaned back on a sack of rice. "Doesn't matter if you like it. The *doing's* what counts."

"Is it enough?"

Pa shot her the look she'd seen a thousand times. He kenned the question beneath her question. "Never doubt it, Fie. Look at all you've done for us in the last two moons. It's enough. You're enough."

She found her damned eyes welling up once more. Pa slung an arm round her shoulders and pulled her close.

"I'd never leave while you needed me," he told her, "but you've gone and grown into a proper chief. And if you find you need me yet, I'll be here."

Fie wanted to say she'd always need him. Between the sniffles and the boiling lump in her throat, it came out as a squeaky croak, and she reckoned he knew anyway.

Pa let her cry her eyes dry, then scooted out of the cart and held out his hand. "Come, you've a prince waiting on you. And didn't you tell that Hawk lad you'd walk his way?"

"Told him Crows go where we're called," Fie mumbled, blowing her nose on a bit of rag. "It's different. Keeps Tavin on his toes."

"Aye. Mind you, sometimes the call doesn't always sound like one." Pa helped her down. "And if I've one thing to pass on before I see you next, it's this, Fie: we can't always wait for a call."

———◆———

It felt wrong being on the road with Wretch, Madcap, Bawd, Varlet, but no Pa. The band had lost Crows before, but those were losses to Oleanders, to sickness, to hunger.

She'd never lost a Crow to time. And none of them were Pa.

Wretch in particular kept close to Fie once they set south on the flatway, and Madcap tactfully eschewed their standard vulgar walking songs to hum something sweet and forlorn under their breath. Lakima too asked no questions, only answering the marching order with a quiet "Yes, chief."

About an hour past noon, a thread of yellow smoke from a league-marker beacon caught Fie's eye. A town was calling for mercy and offering her one as well, a distraction from thoughts of Birthrights, Covenant oaths, and other things she'd left behind. She cleared her throat. "Look alive, all. We've a job on our hands."

A chorus of ayes echoed behind her. Yet not half an hour later, a twinge of frustration wound through her gut as the beacon went out. "Never mind," she called. "Someone must have beat us to it."

Fie couldn't help mulling over the Crow Birthright as they kept walking on. It was a puzzle she couldn't quite fit together: a power they were all born with, yet even now was somehow beyond reach. Moreover, every witch had a stronger, more potent form of their caste's Birthright, like how Owls all had near-perfect memories, but their witches could steal memories right out of one's head.

So if Crow witches could draw Birthrights from bone . . . what power did ordinary Crows have?

And why would it need a kept oath to be found again?

An hour closer to sundown, Fie was dislodged from her puzzling when she saw a blue beacon light farther south, then a green beacon behind them to the north. Her lips pursed. When a town needed mercy, they lit a beacon that burned black smoke. Then the nearest league-marker posts lit beacons in purple, and then the ones that saw purple lit blue, and so on through green, yellow, orange, and red, calling for any band of Crows within seven leagues. The beacons were supposed to go out only when Crows passed the marker on the way to answer a call.

Yet Fie could have sworn this trail of beacons had gone out earlier, only to light back up again.

And sure enough, as she watched, the smoke went out, leaving a short, baffling blue curl in the sky. She whistled the halt order, watching the treetops. Not five minutes later, it lit back up again.

"Why is it doing that?" Khoda asked, spear twirling slow in his hands.

Fie chewed at the inside of her cheek. Tavin had once suggested the Crows could be lured into a trap using plague beacons; Fie had disputed it, saying any town that did so would roll shells with the Crows forsaking that town's next beacon. They'd both been right.

She didn't want to be right this time.

"Something's fouled up for sure," Fie said slowly. "I don't fancy walking us into danger . . . but I don't fancy shirking beacons, either."

Silence crusted over the flatway until Bawd broke it. "Better us than another band, aye? We've Hawks, fire teeth, and the most fearsome chief on the roads."

That got a round of chuckles and ayes. "We'll go where you lead us, chief," Varlet added. "You've the steadiest head of us all. Besides, can't be worse than marching with Vultures."

Half of her steadied at their faith in her.

Half of her wondered if they'd keep that faith, knowing she'd still an oath unkept.

Fie shoved that miscrable half down and set her hands on her hips. "Then we keep a sharp eye and be ready to clear out fast if we need to."

"Or clear out *ghasts* if we need to," Varlet said under his breath. His sister punched him in the arm.

Yet they didn't make it to the blue smoke beacon before trouble found them. Fie heard the shouts first, menacing and gleeful and all too familiar. She picked up the pace. As they rounded the road bend, she found the source: three Crane lads were riding circles about another band of Crows. A small crowd of Sparrow and Pigeon laborers made a loose human fence just clear of the horses' way.

"They turned us away," yelled a Crow man not much older than Varlet. As Fie got nearer, she could make out the string of teeth about his neck that marked him a chief, like her. "We tried to answer!"

"Smells like a lie to me," one of the Crane riders laughed. The Crane caste's Birthright was the truth, but that didn't mean they always told it. "You were running away from your job."

The hair on Fie's arms raised as wrath pricked up her spine. No Crow abandoned a beacon lightly. And all the teeth, swords, and Hawks in the world might not be enough to make her feel safe, but they could at least put an end to this.

"Crows go where we're called!" she shouted. Eyes turned to her. "Leave them be."

"I can handle this if you'd like, chief," Corporal Lakima said quietly. Fie shook her head.

Another Crane rider spat in the dirt. "Keep your own business, bone thief. This doesn't concern you."

"Since we're answering that beacon, I reckon it does," she returned, even as alarms sounded in her skull. This was *square* why she had asked for Hawks. They outranked Cranes. They could run this gang off in a trice.

But she'd left her pa behind today. She'd had the weight of a dead god's words on her head most this week. She didn't feel like letting Hawks fight for her right now.

She felt like looking after her own.

"Last chance," she warned, reaching for a tooth in the string round her own neck. "Ride along."

She didn't really want them to. She wanted to teach someone fear.

If they'd grown so bold as to harangue Crows in broad daylight, there was no saying what they'd do by cover of night—unless they had reason to be afraid.

So it was all for the best, Fie supposed, when a Crane lout drew his horse to a halt between her and the other chief and sneered, "Make me."

She smiled and pushed a Phoenix tooth from her string.

CHAPTER FOUR

ENOUGH

IT DIDN'T TAKE MUCH. THEY NEVER EXPECTED A CROW TO FIGHT back, nor did they expect their threats to quite literally blow up in their faces. The budding mob scattered before the golden blaze. Even the other Crows looked ready to flee until Fie let the tooth's spark go, satisfied the others wouldn't return.

You always like your fire too much, the memory of Little Witness chided. Fie ignored it.

The other chief gaped at her, and Fie stood a little straighter, trying not to preen. If all went as she'd hoped, soon she'd have a Birthright to offer the rest of the castes, and she reckoned that meant hearing "thank you" more often.

Yet gratitude hadn't quite infected the other chief yet, a man two decades younger than Pa, but just as weathered by the roads, and thrice as mistrustful. "That was a Phoenix tooth, aye?" He bit off each word tough and salty as jerky. "*You're* the one the queen's after."

"She's the one who's made a fool of that queen thrice over," Wretch said coldly.

"And aren't we *all* better for it." The other chief pointed at the faltering beacon. "You see that? Karostei called us, then their arbiter turned us away. He said that if even the king could die of plague we brought in, then they couldn't chance it. Whatever feud you've started with the queen just cost us viatik."

"The queen's cozied up with the Oleander Gentry," shot back Madcap. "You've no notion what Chief went through to keep her off the throne and keep *them* from running us all down."

"Would've been faster than starving. They'll just come for us tonight anyway."

"Aye, noted," Wretch drawled. "You'd rather we let you die by mob. We'll remember that next time."

"Enough." Fie swallowed. Her itch to fight had fled with the Crane oafs, and the other chief wasn't wrong. Even if vexing Rhusana was better than the alternative, the rest of their caste would catch trouble for a choice they'd no say in.

Besides, Crows had one rule, and she didn't get to be picky about it. "That queen won't be much longer for her throne, and I wager Karostei won't much longer have an arbiter if he keeps turning Crows away while the town rots. You're welcome to make camp with us tonight, and we'll be safe from Oleanders. At the dawn, we'll head to Karostei. You can come with, or you can head north to shelter in the groves of Gen-Mara until this all settles. Either way, you'll see viatik again soon. Does that suit you?"

The other chief considered a moment as Fie took in the sight of his band. Thin faces, light packs, clothes worn near to threadbare, and more tellingly, none worn so thin as their chief. No wagon at all, let alone one for supplies alone, and precious little time to waste answering plague beacons that didn't end in viatik.

"We've enough to share dinner," Fie added.

The other band traded looks at that, and their chief folded his arms. "Aye, suppose that suits us. You'll deal with Karostei yourselves, though. I'll have no part of that again."

"Fair." Fie tapped her fist to her mouth and held it out. "Fie."

"Drudge," answered the other chief. "When do we eat?"

————◆————

Prince Jasimir had once told Fie the Markahn clan of Hawks thought cats were good luck. When Barf the tabby caught mice in their supplies, or sniffed out wild mint, or sat up and stared down the road a full minute before anyone rode their way, that was true enough.

There was another way the cat was lucky, though: her kills made perfect studies for Fie.

The tabby had learned that laying a dead squirrel at Fie's toes bought her a bite of salt fish and a lap to curl up in later, when Fie went about mastering the Hawk Birthright. The tricky thing about the Birthright of blood was that it could destroy just as well as heal, if not easier, and as one of the Hawk witches, Corporal Lakima had recommended Fie practice as their novices did—on something beyond suffering.

Now, as late twilight hung over the camp, Lakima examined the remains of Barf's latest victim: a tree mouse that had been dispatched with one swift bite. The tooth marks had stoppered up with dried blood, thanks to Fie's work with a Hawk witch-tooth. The corporal held her own hand over the carcass, then nodded her approval. "You've got clotting down, and that alone will buy you time to get to a trained healer."

Fie's Crows were no stranger to her lessons, whether in swords, letters, or healing. Drudge and his Crows, however, took in the proceedings with an array of bewilderment and suspicion. They'd given the Hawks a wide berth, and now they watched Madcap and Varlet toss shells with Khoda as if they were gambling with an asp.

But Lakima seemed to be ignoring it entirely. "If you want to make sure your patient lives, the next thing you'll need to master is clearing out any—" She stopped as Barf jerked awake from where she'd been lounging by Fie's side and stared down the road, yellow eyes wide as saucers. Her striped tail fluffed out, and a warning yowl gurgled up from her throat.

". . . disease," Lakima finished with a sigh. She handed Fie a vinegar-soaked rag to clean her hands after handling the vermin, and wiped her own hands with another before standing and helping Fie to her feet.

"Oleanders coming," Fie called. Drudge's band burst into motion, snatching up aught they could carry, and Fie immediately realized her mistake. "Wait—just—everyone get closer together—you don't need to go to the trees—"

"Mind your own band, cousin," Drudge snapped. "Up, you lot, fast as you can."

Some of his Crows hung back a moment, looking at Fie and the Hawks, but they followed their chief and vanished into the trees. Fie's band just did their best to gather a little closer to the fire, rounding up all the goods about the camp so a spiteful Oleander couldn't trample aught. Madcap made a show of peeling an apple, casual as could be.

Vexed, Fie sat too. She'd *told* Drudge she'd keep them safe.

Two moons ago, you'd be in those trees with them, her Chief voice reminded her. She did her best to ignore it as the Hawks assumed their usual post between the camp and the road.

This time something seemed different about the Oleander Gentry as they rounded the corner. When Fie spied it, a peculiar twist wrenched through her gut. It wasn't the number; nigh twenty riders was high, but naught she and Lakima couldn't handle. It wasn't the weapons; she'd faced down steel before.

It was their faces, plain and furious. Not a single one of them had bothered to don a mask. Gloves, aye, and crude smocks of rough undyed cloth, but no masks.

They'd dressed for bloody business, but not one among them believed they'd be punished for it.

Much as they found strength in a pack, the Oleanders still seemed to have unofficially declared a leader in the man at the front, who slowed to a halt in front of Lakima. Fie heard Khoda suck in a breath and saw why at once: the Oleander carried a Hawk spear.

"Stand down," he ordered Lakima. "We have business with the bone thieves."

"We decline." Lakima planted her own spear in the ground before her, point-up in her own kind of threat: an iron fist wrapped in formality.

"They abandoned a beacon," another Oleander shouted.

"That little bitch burned my arm!"

"They turned their backs when called," the Hawk rider thundered. "Karostei is dying by the dozen. And *she*"—he pointed to Fie—"assaulted citizens we're sworn to guard. We need to make an example."

"Ah yes," Khoda said dryly, "that will certainly convince Crows to answer your beacons in the future."

The stranger Hawk did not look pleased. "As a sergeant in Her Majesty's army, I *order you to stand down*."

Fie's Hawks traded looks at "Her Majesty's."

"Again," Lakima said, icy calm, "we decline."

The Oleander's Hawk drew himself up, nostrils flaring. "On what grounds do you decline a direct order, officer?"

"We have orders to protect every citizen, including Crows," Lakima answered stonily. "And those orders . . ." Her brief pause was the most dramatic flair Fie had ever seen the corporal display. ". . . *outrank* you."

"I doubt it," the rider sneered. "The only one who outranked the queen is dead."

"The queen can't give orders to the military until after her official coronation as the ruler of Sabor." Lakima glanced up at the waxing moon. "Until then, our highest authority is Master-General Draga. Besides, the first line of the Hawk code is *I will serve my nation and the throne above all.* The nation comes first. *Surely* a man who's risen to sergeant in the master-general's army knows the code."

Silence stretched tight as a sunburn over the road.

Madcap chose that moment to take a hearty bite out of their apple. The juicy crunch echoed across the road like a thunderclap, their messy chewing the monsoon in its wake. They stared direct at the Oleander's Hawk the whole time.

He just pointed to Fie. "*She* needs to answer for wounding good people."

"Those 'good people' were attacking unarmed citizens," Lakima said.

"It doesn't matter—"

"Not to your like, aye." That old anger was climbing back up Fie's spine. She got to her feet. "Pray, where were you when your louts were going after Crows?"

"You attacked those men *unprovoked*—"

"Unprovoked?" Fie squeezed between Khoda and Lakima to stand before them, not so far that the Oleander Hawk could snatch her up without risking their spears but close enough to look him dead in the eye. "I asked them to stop hounding the other Crows. Then one of them decided to get in my face, and wouldn't you know it, he was a big, scary lad . . ." She pretended to rub the back of her neck in her best daft yokel impression. "On a big, scary horse . . ." Her fingers caught at two teeth on her string, waking the spark and calling the Birthrights from where they slumbered. ". . . and I felt, oh, *threatened*."

The song of the Phoenix Birthright rang down her bones, almost too swift. Golden fire sparked and spread in a flash to wall off the camp and the Crows whole. The Oleanders' horses danced and shied away, and the Hawk rider swore as his horse gave a fearful buck before shimmying sideways.

It wasn't easy to balance two Phoenix teeth, as Fie found the sparks of their dead owners usually too opinionated to get along, but she kept them in ruthless harmony now as she stared down the Hawk.

She took a step forward, and the flames surged with her.

"Look at all these horses, all these big, scary people," she sighed as flames of brassy Phoenix gold coiled about her hands. "Reckon I still feel *awful* threatened. And you know, the funny thing is, I asked those lads to ride along and leave us be and they didn't, and now here we are." The blaze bowed up and out, closer still to the Oleanders, who shrank down the road another few paces. "So you want my answer? I'll say it once more before anyone else has to burn: *Ride. Along.*"

The Hawk sergeant did his best to stare her down, twitching his spear. She near laughed. *That* was a game Pa had warned her of long before she'd grown to his elbow: scummers like the sergeant would try to startle a jumpy Crow into aught that could be called an attack, then take the excuse to cut them down.

Hawks won the game when it came to steel, mostly. But when it came to fire . . .

"By moon's end, you'll be only a stain on our history," the Hawk swore, wheeling his horse round. "The White Phoenix will wash her hands of you!"

"The *White Phoenix* could stand to be more creative with her nick-names," Fie grumbled as the Oleanders beat a sullen retreat. "She's had what, five years? And that's the best she comes up with?"

"We should try to move out before dawn," Lakima said behind her. "They know you by your Phoenix teeth. If word hasn't already gotten back to the queen about your location from this afternoon, it certainly will after tonight."

Fie called off the fire once the Oleanders faded from sight, vexed more than ever. "Aye, and what would you have done? They weren't going to leave us be without a push."

Lakima didn't take the jab. "I agree, but we still have to account for the risk of them reporting to the queen."

A rush of ire sloshed about Fie's skull before she tamped it down. She couldn't help but notice Drudge's Crows remained in the trees.

She didn't know why she so badly craved the faith of a band of stranger Crows. Or why that faith from her kin felt more like a stone about her neck.

She did know, at least, that Lakima had no business taking the brunt of her vexation. "Sorry," Fie mumbled, pocketing the two Phoenix teeth. Not enough spark was left to go back on her string, but there was enough to store for lighting stubborn campfires and the like. "You're right."

"Will wonders never cease," Varlet breathed in jest. "We must be in sore terrible peril."

Fie shook her fist at him with an exaggerated scowl. "And that's enough out of you, or I'll have you fed to Barf."

The rest of the band chuckled at that, and one of the myriad knots in Fie's gut loosened. It was a little thing she'd noted, as they'd crossed paths more and more with Oleanders and skin-ghasts in the last moon and her band had still looked to Pa to lead out of habit. Once the danger had passed, he'd crack a joke or fool about and snap the uneasy frost that gripped the band. So long as they could laugh, the fear stayed beyond the reach of their campfire.

"I think we'd better keep a standing watch tonight," Lakima said. "We can continue your healing lessons tomorrow, if that suits you."

"Aye." Fie returned to her circle of Crows as Drudge's band slowly began to trickle out of the trees. Most gave her the same wide berth they'd given the Hawks. Fie found that bothered her even more than their flight to the trees had, but scolding them would do naught to calm their nerves. Instead she found a patch of ground to sit, worked her chief's string free, and drew out her tooth bag. It was time for a restock.

Drudge himself didn't share his band's misgivings, or if he did, he'd overcome them. He dropped into the empty dust across from Fie. "Those fire teeth . . . how many do you have?"

Fie glanced up from stowing the teeth she'd just half burned. "Enough," she said cautiously.

"Enough to spare?"

Fie's hands went still.

"The roads won't get better," Drudge continued. "You and I both know it, girl. Whatever you've started with the queen won't dry up for moons. I need to look after my own."

She'd known it was only a matter of time, and yet . . .

The teeth kept her safe. They kept her band safe. She'd *won* them from Rhusana herself. All Drudge had done was eat her band's food and cast doubt at her at every turn, and now he asked for teeth he'd done naught to earn—

When is it enough?

She was back in the tower, a dead god smiling at her and saying that, in life after life after life, she'd failed.

Fie forced her fingers to unbutton the compartment for her Phoenix teeth. "I left a few score at Gen-Mara's groves. This ought to hold you until you reach them." She counted six and held them out. "Try to burn just one at a time. If you do two, they fight."

His eyes lingered on her palm, then flicked up to her. "Reckon that's enough?"

"Aye. The groves are less than a day's walk north."

Drudge looked long and hard at the Hawks, and then at Tavin's gleaming short sword strapped at Fie's side. Then he looked back at the six teeth in Fie's hand.

"There's more at the groves," she repeated.

Drudge took the teeth. "Aye."

Something in his voice told Fie she'd be better waiting to tie new Phoenix teeth on her string until *after* Drudge's band departed. She buttoned up the tooth compartment, closed her bag, and feigned a hearty yawn. "I'd best get some shut-eye, especially if any of those scummers were from Karostei."

"Aye," Drudge said again, toneless.

Fie fetched a sleeping mat from their supply wagon and rolled it out so she could sleep facing the road. She didn't reckon the Oleander Gentry would return after such a scare, but they hadn't the luxury of rolling shells on those odds.

And when she tucked her tooth bag under her head, she told herself it was only to be ready for Oleanders as well.

◆

She dreamed of Tavin, as she usually did.

A poet would say she missed poetic things about him, nonsense like how sunlight caught on his eyelashes or how his smile was bright as a constellation, but the heart of it was that she missed more than eyelashes. She missed falling asleep feeling safer for him at her back. She missed how he'd first sorted out how to tell she was upset, then when to say naught about it, then finally when to say square what she needed to hear. She missed *not* missing him.

And in the dream, it seemed he missed her, too, calling her name from the other side of a courtyard she did and didn't know: *Fie. Fie. Where are you?*

The sun-warmed tiles stuck to her bare soles as she padded across the courtyard. *Here*, she tried to say, but no sound came out.

Fie.

She caught at his elbow and he shook her off, gaze skipping over her like a stone on water. *It's me*, she shouted noiselessly. *I'm right here.*

Fie! He walked away, scanning the arching corridors about the yard, the latticed gallery above.

She followed—and caught her own reflection in a pane of Peacock-green glass.

Red stained her plain linen shift, pouring from a gash across her throat.

Her face belonged to the Peacock girl she'd killed not five days ago.

Fie!

It's me, she tried to say, choking on blood. *It's me—*

"*FIE!*"

She jolted awake with a sucking gasp.

Wretch's and Lakima's faces swam above her. Lakima sat back and let out a long breath, eyes closing. "Thank the Mender."

"You were out cold." Wretch helped Fie sit up. The camp tilted and blurred, all much brighter than it ought to be. "Thought you slept through pack-up on account of burning all those teeth last night, then none of us could wake you."

"It's a healer's sleep," Lakima said. "We put patients in them for serious wounds, but . . . I'm the only other witch here."

"Could Rhusana have obtained one of your hairs?" Khoda asked, rubbing his chin. All a Swan-caste witch needed was a strand of someone's hair in order to twist their desires to terrible ends.

Fie shook her head. "I'd already be dead." She peered about the camp, which seemed curiously empty.

And that was when the answer, horrid and gutting, came to her.

Lakima wasn't the only witch who could use the Birthright of blood.

She twisted about, staring at the sleeping mat, and saw naught. Her throat closed. Her voice came out as a squeak. "Was I moved at all?"

"No," Wretch answered.

"When did Drudge and his band leave?"

"Before dawn."

Fie pushed herself to her feet, heart beginning to pound. "Which way did they go?"

"What's wrong, Fie?" Wretch asked.

Fie's breath came faster and faster. She scanned the grass about her sleeping mat—naught. The ground where Lakima and Wretch knelt—naught.

"What's wrong?"

The head of her sleeping mat—naught.

"He took my teeth," Fie answered, hollow. "The bag. They're all gone."

Quiet gasps swept through the camp.

"I need a moment," Fie croaked. Then she put a good dozen wobbling paces between herself and everyone else, turned to the forest, and screamed every foul word she knew.

Wretch gave her a minute or so before crunching over the dry grass to lay a gnarled hand on her shoulder.

"It's all my fault!" Fie raged, running her hands through her hair. "I brought this on us! I should have just given him the damned teeth!"

Wretch smoothed Fie's hair back down, businesslike. "He wanted teeth?"

"Phoenix teeth. I gave him half a dozen and told him he could get more from Pa."

"And that wasn't enough for him." Wretch sighed. "Aye. One way or another . . ."

We feed the Crows. Fie knew that proverb all too well. "I should have given him more."

"Aye, probably."

Fie winced. She'd half hoped Wretch would tell her she'd done right after all.

Instead Wretch said, "You owe your teeth to no one, and your pa raised no thief. But fear? Fear'll make a monster of anyone that lets it. And that man was afraid for his own."

"Pa never would have let them stay with us."

"Oh, he would have," Wretch said with a shrug. "Cur's soft for anyone who puts their hand out for help, and that's no shame. That's how we got the prince's oath, aye? And doubtless that'll save many a Crow to come. But that's also how Cur lost his finger and how Swain lost his life. There's always a cost to helping folk. Cur knew there's a cost to *not* helping, too. All you can do is decide which you want to pay."

Gen-Mara hasn't failed his duty for hundreds of years. I can't say the same for you.

Fie's eyes burned and watered. "I'm not ready for this, Wretch. Pa hasn't been gone a day and I've already lost our teeth. How do I protect you all now?"

"With the Hawks you won us already. And with those." Wretch pointed to the string still knotted round Fie's neck. "We'll make them last until the next shrine, and we'll carry on just as we did before we had Phoenix teeth."

Before Fie could run off Oleander Gentry with naught but a fist-ful of fire. Her throat tightened once again. Now getting her Crows to Jasimir's procession wasn't just about the oath. She had to get them to safety before they crossed another band of Oleanders who wouldn't back down from Hawks.

"We'll carry on, Fie." Wretch gripped her shoulder again. "They've been at us for hundreds of years, and still the roads are ours."

Shame and fury yet pounded down Fie's bones, but the band didn't have time for her misery. She scuffed a fist over her eyes, took a deep breath, and tried to stand straighter. "Aye. We need to go."

She walked back to the camp with Wretch, where most of the Crows and all of the Hawks pretended they hadn't been eavesdropping.

"Drudge's band went south," Khoda offered. "Just—if that helps at all."

Fie's mouth twisted. If they'd gone north, there was a chance they'd have sheltered in Pa's shrine, and no chance Pa would let them leave with her tooth bag. But south . . . "They've, what, an hour's head start? Two? We could try to catch them, but we'd have to abandon Karostei." She shook her head. "If Karostei's had an unanswered beacon since yesterday, they don't have much longer before it spreads to the whole town. I've enough teeth on my string to get us through that call, then we'll get to Jas's procession fast as we can. Aye?"

"Aye," her Crows echoed.

"Yes, chief," added Lakima.

A curl of purple smoke rose and drifted away—another beacon from Karostei choked out. Fie frowned deeper. "Then let's get to the road."

CHAPTER FIVE

THE ASH HARVEST

THERE WERE A GREAT MANY THINGS FIE NOTICED WHEN THEY emerged from the roughway and took in the sight of Karostei, yet there was only one conclusion to draw.

It would not be saved.

The main town had been carved from the stubble of thinner forests along the northwest edge of the Hassura Plains, and beyond the rooftops, Fie could see rolling fields of ripening maize, buckwheat, even green beads of gourds. The nearest fields' crops, however, were much less traditional: their dirt was covered in scores of rows of tents, sleeping mats, and wagons full of furniture and goods, as if most of Karostei had just moved a quarter league east. Iron kettles smoked over cooking fires, and chickens pecked at the dirt in makeshift pens. Goats and cattle lowed from a pasture Fie couldn't see but absolutely could, and did, smell. Children

☙ 62 ❧

chased one another up and down the dusty lanes, shrieking, as adults watched from tense knots and muttered among themselves.

The town itself sat too still behind a timber wall, one that looked as if they'd been halfway through replacing its older gray wood with newer, still-pale planks. And that was where Fie saw the ugly omen of Karostei's fate: a deep, sickly gray rot spread across the clean lumber in the same stark, veiny rings as the Sinner's Brand.

That was when she knew Karostei could not be saved.

Another puff of black smoke went up from the town's signal post, and Fie spied clusters of black cloaks gathered a dozen paces from the barred gates. Half a dozen Hawk guards stood in an uneasy line between the Crows and the only way in, as two cloaked figures argued with a man in Crane yellow.

Lakima cleared her throat. "Chief . . . how close can we get to those walls?"

"Treat it the same as a corpse," Fie said. "Keep a few paces off. Looks like we'll need you to clear the way, but you'll be safest outside. I doubt there's aught in there but dying sinners now."

"Understood. Shall we take the lead?"

"Aye." Fie let the Hawks form up ahead of her. Better to let Karostei's arbiter negotiate with them first. Besides, she had a single Phoenix tooth left on her string now. She couldn't afford to waste it on cowing an arbiter.

That proved to be the right choice. The Crows on the road ahead parted to let them pass, trading baffled looks when they saw Fie's band in the Hawks' wake. Lakima marched them right up to the arbiter and the two Crows he was arguing with. This close, Fie could see the strings of teeth about their necks that marked them for chiefs like her.

"Corporal Lakima Geli szo Jasko of the Trikovoi fortress," Lakima barked. "Who's the ranking officer here?"

"I am," the arbiter said.

Fie couldn't see the look Lakima gave him, but she had a wonderful view of how he seemed to almost wilt beneath it.

"That's . . . doubtful," the corporal said. She wasn't wrong; though an arbiter was meant to serve as a town's leader, it didn't mean a Crane could give orders to Hawk soldiers.

"The sergeant died two days ago." The voice came from the signal post above, where a fresh string of black smoke had begun coiling into the sky. "We're all guard rank, so until a new officer arrives—"

"*I'm* in command," finished the Crane arbiter. Their arrival had drawn the notice of some idling citizens, who were edging nearer, and that seemed to make the arbiter even more nervy. "Put that out at once. We don't need their help."

Fie ignored him, staring up at the guard by the beacon. "Tell me your sergeant didn't die of the *plague* two days ago."

"Oh, it's much worse than that," one of the other chiefs answered. Lakima stepped aside, and the woman spoke direct to Fie, anger and weariness in her lined face. "The first sinner died *four* days ago. This scummer"—she flicked her hand at the arbiter—"decided he could deal with the body like the dead king and just had a couple Sparrows burn it. *They* were dead of the plague by the next morning, then the sergeant's house came down with it, and next thing you know most the town's run to the fields with what they could carry."

"I'm telling you, it'll blow over," the arbiter insisted. "We burned the quarantine hut, same as they did with the king. Wouldn't we have heard if the palace were rotting from the inside out?"

"Imagine that, it's almost as if the king didn't actually die of the plague at all and the queen is just exploiting an opportunity to further vilify the Crows and consolidate power," Khoda muttered under his breath.

The arbiter blinked at him. "What was that?"

"Nothing," Khoda said. "Though perhaps I'm wrong, but . . . a corporal qualifies as a ranking officer, correct?"

"Correct," Corporal Lakima said, and yet again, the arbiter shrank. Lakima's voice rose. "Guards, stand down and let the Crows in."

The six Hawks on the road didn't need further prompting. Fie couldn't help noting that they took the opportunity to distance themselves from both the arbiter and the decaying wall.

"You can't—these bone thieves just want money! It'll pass!" The arbiter threw himself in front of Lakima. "All they'll do is burn the town to the ground!"

The other chief, a man near Wretch's age, spat into the road with disgust. "Don't blame us because you called too late," he said. "You know damn well how it runs with the plague. If we don't stop it here, it'll take your fields next, and your livestock, and your people, and then the only mercy you'll get is death before the famine."

"We won't pay for you to destroy our homes," the arbiter insisted. "Go cheat someone else."

"Viatik fits the means," the first chief said. She pointed to the ragtag camp. "Your means aren't much right now. Nor are our expectations."

"Let them in!" a woman shouted from the gathering crowd. "If the plague takes the fields, we'll all starve!"

"My father's suffering in there right now! Give him mercy!"

"*I SAID IT WILL PASS!*" roared the arbiter, nigh purple in the face.

Something about that caught Fie's notice. She took a step closer to the arbiter, eyes narrowed. "How many did you leave in town?"

"It doesn't matter—"

"Five score," the first chief said.

The other chief added, "Nigh a quarter of the town."

"It's on his head!" someone shouted from the crowd. "All hundred on his head!"

"He told us we were safe!"

"He said he'd take care of it!"

"And you *believed* him?" Khoda asked, incredulous. No one in the crowd had an answer for that. Or at least not one they'd shout to a Hawk standing with Crows.

"It'll pass," the Crane arbiter repeated, sweat glistening on his brow.

Now it was clear enough for all on the road to see: a dark curl of the Sinner's Brand had begun blooming just below his eye.

"Oh, cousin." Fie tapped her cheek in the same spot. This was the Peacock girl all over again. "Not for you."

He lifted a hand to his face, only to find the rash stippling his fingers. Some believed the Covenant sent the plague to hustle sinners into the next life. Fie suspected that, if they were right, the Covenant certainly wasn't dragging its feet with a man who'd doomed nigh a hundred of his townsfolk with his own spite. Not with how swift the Sinner's Brand was now etching purple-gray vines up his wrists.

"This is a mistake, it can't—"

"You've not long," the first chief said, not unkindly. "We need to get you inside the walls."

"But—*why*?"

The second chief motioned for his Crows. He had considerably less patience with the arbiter. "Because you'll spread it if you die out here. Shrew, Gall, make sure he gets to the gates." Two of his Crows steered the arbiter down the road as their chief turned to Fie and tapped his knuckles to his teeth. "I'm Ruffian. Don't know how you wound up with Hawks for friends, but you have my thanks for them."

"Aye, and mine, too. I'm Jade." The first chief nodded to Fie. "New band, or new chief?"

"Took over for my pa," Fie answered. "I'm Fie. Either of you cross roads with Cur?"

Ruffian bowed his head. "He was a good one. Sorry to hear he's gone."

"No, just lost a finger and couldn't deal mercy. Little Witness sent him to Gen-Mara's shrine."

"That's a blessing, then. We'll be better for having the groves under a chief's watch." Jade tipped her brow at the Hawks. "Looks like he taught you well, if you've already made high friends. Is this your first ash harvest?"

Fie did her best not to fidget. An ash harvest was the Crow name for a hard day like this, dealing with a town beyond saving. "Aye. Saw one from a distance when I was a whelp, but that's it."

"Not much to it, so fear not. With three bands, this ought to be sorted before noon. We'll need firewood, flashburn, and chalk." At Jade's signal, her own Crows began carrying loads of firewood to the gate, and Fie signaled for her Crows to follow suit. "We'll split all our Crows into pairs to check every house," Jade continued. "They mark a cross on the door for any still living, a ring if everyone's dead or the house is empty. We'll be following them to deal mercy, then leave the door open to show we've passed. Once we're sure there're none alive, the town burns, but we start with mercy. How's your stock of teeth?"

Fie's face ran hotter under the climbing sun. She tried not to let her shame show as she pinched at her string. "This is all. My bag was stolen this morning."

Ruffian let out a laugh of disbelief. "Dena's wrath, and you still answered the beacon? Aye, you're Cur's kin to be sure."

"No doubt," Jade said. "Do you know who took them?"

Fie gave an awkward shrug. "We found a band catching trouble last night for leaving Karostei. Their chief saw me run off Oleanders with Phoenix teeth and asked for some. I gave him six and told him I left more at Gen-Mara's groves, but . . ."

I wasn't enough.

Jade and Ruffian traded looks, and Jade's lip curled. "Drudge."

Ruffian shook his head. "He'd cut our throats to look after his band. Can't fault him for it, but two-second clever doesn't last. Here." He started digging in his own bag. "We can spare enough to get you to a shrine."

Jade slung a leather knapsack round to her front to rummage through as well, but she peered up at Fie through a curtain of gray-shot hair. "I have to ask. You've Hawks, and you had enough Phoenix teeth to be loose with them. Are you the one who's got the queen so riled up?"

Fie's mouth twisted. She stared at the dirt. "Aye—but—the queen's got the Oleanders at her back. If she reaches the throne, they ride as they please. My band got the prince away from her, and I got him to his aunt, in trade for his Covenant oath that when *he* takes the throne . . . we all get Hawks."

Ruffian sucked in a breath. "Truly?"

"Aye." Fie braced for a scolding like the ones Little Witness and Drudge had handed her.

Instead Jade's hand thrust into her line of sight, filled with teeth. "Now that's a grand thing. Can't say I hate having a prince owe us a favor."

"No wonder the queen's proper crossed," Ruffian chuckled, passing another fistful of teeth to Fie. "Good for you, giving her throne a rattle. Wager it won't be the last time you do."

"Thanks." Fie reached for her own bag to stow the teeth—and remembered where it had gone. There was a small pouch for her flint at her belt. She stuffed the teeth into that, feeling all the more humbled for how readily Ruffian and Jade had handed them off.

Jade wound her hair into a knot with a twist of rag and nodded to Ruffian and Fie. "Ready?" At their ayes, she twisted about to cry to her band, "Masks on!"

"Masks on," Fie echoed, as did Ruffian. Leather and wooden struts creaked about them in a grim ballad.

"Chief." Lakima caught her as she fetched their chalk from the wagon. Her voice lowered. "The civilians are bound to ask—can any of it be saved?"

Fie looked to the fields and found townspeople staring, bleak, at their homes about to go up in smoke. She'd seen loss before, loss and guilt and rage in a sinner's family, but this was different.

This was familiar.

She'd left Pa behind. She'd lost the only teeth to ever make her feel truly dangerous. Even before then, she'd split from her kin, from her roads, from her ways, all for the sake of the oath.

This time, she knew what it was to lose nigh everything that made you safe.

Yet all Fie could do was shake her head. "It's reached the walls. Everything has to burn."

"Maybe they'll remember this when they pick the next arbiter," Khoda said, bitter.

"More likely one's assigned." Wretch's voice turned muffled as she strapped on her mask. "Town's under a thousand, aye? The governor of the region picks the arbiters for them when they're that small."

So the townspeople had had no say in the arbiter with a hundred deaths on his head.

And so Fie said to the corporal, "If it helps the townsfolk, tell them when they see the smoke, it's the pyres for their kin. That's when they ought to pray. And if that doesn't help . . . tell them the arbiter burns, too."

She pulled her own mask on, the world dimming to a welcome relief of darkness and a beak full of wild mint. For the briefest of moments, she shut her eyes.

The weight of teeth round her neck and at her belt, the weight of her swords, the faith of her Crows, the respect of two stranger chiefs—they all meant something, if she let them. They all could steady her, if she let them.

No matter what Little Witness said, no matter how Drudge had treated her, she was one of them.

She was a chief, with a harvest of ash beckoning.

Fie let the mint flood her lungs, then strode toward the gates.

They'd been barred from the outside, but at first, even with the bar lifted, the gates refused to budge no matter how Varlet and Bawd pushed. Then Jade shook her head with rue and said, "Eater of Bones, this's bound to be a rough day. Try giving it a pull."

Jade was right. The gates swung open with only a little fight when the twins dragged on them, and Fie saw straight away what the older chief meant.

Three bodies lay beneath a shroud of dead bloodflies on the threshold, where they'd collapsed trying to get out. The gates had jammed on them.

"Steady," Jade whispered, and patted Fie's shoulder. "Hand out your chalk." Her voice rose. "My band, start with the western houses."

"My band, we go north," Ruffian called, and shoved the arbiter none too gently over the dead at Karostei's doorstep. Half the bloodflies rose from the corpses with an irate, sluggish buzz. The others rained off in stiff curls, legs folded up in surrender to the plague. "I'll follow once I've dealt with . . . this."

"We'll take east, then." Fie passed out the chalk to her band. "Suppose you all did this with Pa before?"

"Pair up, leave a ring for dead or empty, a cross mark for mercy," Wretch said. The others nodded.

"Then I'll follow. Once every house is marked, gather by . . ."

Fie took a look around the town commons, trying not to grimace at the sight. Dead goats and dogs lay in misshapen heaps, rats huddled like graying warts on the hide of dusty ground already speckled with more fallen bloodflies. Sickly rot wept from nigh every foundation she saw. The market stalls looked about two days gone, canopy stands tilting or buckled in twain where gray ate through the wood and canvas.

The broad stone ring of a communal well in the middle of the open grounds seemed to be the only thing untouched by plague, though Fie wouldn't put odds on its water in the next decade. At least it served as a landmark. ". . . There. That well. Let's be on with it, then."

Surprisingly, Varlet and Bawd split up, Bawd hanging back while Varlet linked his arm through Madcap's and strolled toward a house. "You need company, chief," Bawd informed her. "Can't have you getting jumped in one of these houses. The whole thing'd be like to come down. Besides, I'll not listen to my brother make an ass of himself flirting with Madcap."

"So it's mercy of a different kind," Fie allowed. Normally she dealt mercy alone, as Pa had done, but today . . . today she reckoned she'd be better for company. "No use waiting until someone marks a door for me. Let's clear houses until I'm called."

Bawd followed her down the nearest street, stepping over slicks of gray mire and the remains of barrels that had bloated and burst, spilling apples, salt pork, pickle brine, and aught else into the street. The first house Fie went into reeked even worse of the plague, the humid air seeping through her cloak and gumming the crowsilk against her skin.

A Hawk crest had been carved into the wall, and beneath it several spears listed in a crumbling rack. Cold ashes sat in a small central fire pit, and a long table had sagged and collapsed, shards of broken porcelain strewn among molding beans. A set of steep stairs led up to what looked to be a loft; below them huddled two forms beneath a gray-stained blanket, unmoving.

"Check upstairs, will you?" Fie asked. Bawd loped the steps two at a time, while Fie gingerly pulled back the blanket. If she had to guess, this had been the home of the sergeant, who accounted for one of the bodies before her. She couldn't tell who had been who, arms twined about each other to the last, only that they looked to be long past breathing. A quick press of her finger to each of their teeth confirmed it. Sparks from a living person's teeth would nigh roar in her bones, but these teeth barely sighed at her touch.

Something about the dead Hawk coiled with a dead lover made her furious.

Something about it made her think of Tavin.

Fie stood, breath coming quicker in a warm, sickly rush of mint. For a long moment she wished she'd stuck around to watch Ruffian cut the arbiter's throat.

"Chief."

Fie looked up to see Bawd floating down the stairs with a fine-woven red robe laid over her crowsilk cloak, twirling an ornate parasol.

"I'm the prettiest girl at the dance," Bawd cooed as she draped her dainty self against the wall. It didn't hold, crumbling round her elbow in a small shower of rotting wood. "Oops."

Fie couldn't help but snort. "I don't know that red's your color."

"Right you are." Bawd hung the robe off a tilting spear. "Always did fancy that Gull blue, though."

Fie marked a ring on the door with her chalk. "Rather think you fancied just the trousers. No one else in the loft?"

"Not a soul."

"Then let's be off." Fie glanced back, then shook her head, glad the mask hid her reluctant grin. "The parasol *stays*, Bawd."

"You're no fun," Bawd grumbled. She stuck it in the spear rack, which promptly fell apart.

They left the next house with less cheer, fresh blood on Fie's hands this time. By then, near every house in sight had been marked with rings or cross marks of chalk.

Fie didn't have to tally many of the cross marks to know she had more mercy to deal today than ever before. She'd known, really, since they'd said five-score people had been left to rot in Karostei. She'd just not let herself think on it too long.

Steady. She was a chief. She was a Crow. This was part of her road.

Fie shook blood off her blade and headed to the next door.

At the third house, Bawd's jokes dried up when a thin, gurgling voice inside cried, *"Mama?"*

At the fifth house, Fie handed her mask off to Bawd, too belly-sick for even the mint to help.

By the seventh, she'd stopped cleaning the Hawk sword afterward.

By the thirteenth, she'd no use for a mask anyway; the smell of blood had overrun the stench of the plague.

The rest of her band were waiting for her, passing water skins about, when she finally trudged back to the well. Their masks hung loose, a grudging concession to the cruel noon sun, which had conquered even the dreadful reek of dead and sick. It was an odd comfort to see the three bodies at the gate had been laid out on a proper pyre in the middle of the commons. It was a colder comfort to see the Crane arbiter lying beside them.

Wretch took one look at Fie's hands, near black with blood now, and hauled up water with one of the few pails still intact. No one spoke to her, only patted her back or squeezed her shoulder, a mercy Fie was all the more grateful to let someone else deal.

Ruffian returned as Fie was scrubbing up. "Smart, that. If the blood dries, your rags turn stiff enough to chafe. Now your mercy's done, half your band will go through the houses again for aught that'll serve for kindling, and the other half will pile that and firewood between each house. One or two ought to take flashburn and splash the walls and the heaps, help the fire spread fast when it catches."

Wretch stood. "Aye, we can manage that, chief. Spell yourself a bit."

Fie nodded, wordless. She felt like she might be sick.

Ruffian studied her a moment. "Mind if I rinse off, too?"

"Go ahead," Fie said dully as her band split off. She pulled her arms out of the pail and let them drip pink water on the dirt. This hot out, they'd dry fast enough.

Ruffian sat on the edge of the well, letting his mask fall to the dirt, and splashed his rag-wrapped hands. "Always hard when the Eater of Bones takes her due, but most ash harvests aren't this big," he told her. He didn't have Pa's way of talking to her, as if she should be at study; instead he sounded like a merchant passing a fellow trader a warning of stormy seas. "Only once have I cut more throats in one go, and that was because most of the village caught the plague in the same day. You don't want to know why." Fie did, morbidly enough, but maybe not now. Ruffian continued, "This's the most mercy you've dealt at once, aye?"

"Aye," Fie said, trying not to think of the ones younger than she. The last thing they should've seen was a friendly face. By every damned dead god, she'd done her best to give them one, even with tears in her eyes.

"Most of us get night terrors after our first ash harvest," Ruffian said. "They pass with time. Let others take your watch shift, try to keep yourself busy. You might get short with your band for no reason, or want to run off by yourself, but that's . . ." His brow furrowed as he searched for words. "It's like an asp bite, this. You don't let the poison sit until you lose an arm. You bleed it out. If you can't talk to anyone in your band, find a shrine and talk to the keeper, aye? We have them for a reason."

Fie's throat closed. She told herself her eyes were stinging from looking up against the sun.

"From here it's easy, aye?" Ruffian shook his hands into the bloody water. For better or worse, his tone had tilted closer to Pa's. "Just like any other pyre. Most of the fuel's been built into these houses, these walls. All you have to do is make sure the sparks catch."

A shadow fell over him, shorter for the noon sun—but something about it struck Fie as amiss. She and Ruffian twisted about for a better look.

The first thing Fie saw was red, from blood still bright and slick.

The second was that the daylight filtered *through* the figure. Mere holes where the eyes, the nose, the teeth belonged, as if it were no more than cut from canvas—

Not canvas. Skin.

And the third thing Fie realized, wholly too late, was that the warped face gaping at them had belonged to the Crane arbiter.

The arbiter's boneless hands had already slid onto Ruffian, one on his scalp, one at his chin.

"*NO—!*" Fie reached for him, too late.

The hands wrenched sideways with a crack.

Ruffian didn't move for a moment, still balanced on the well's edge. Then he collapsed, toppling into the pail and hitting the commons ground with a thud. Red water spilled into the dirt about him.

The skin-ghast wobbled over Ruffian's body.

Then its empty face turned toward Fie.

CHAPTER SIX

THE COVENANT SEES

SCREAMS SPLIT THE AIR, AND NOT JUST FIE'S OWN. SHE SCRAMBLED to her feet, snatching up Tavin's sword, and immediately forgot every single one of the combat lessons Lakima had given her over the last four weeks.

The ghost reached for her, its hollow arms drooping deceptively like limp ropes. Fie knew that lie firsthand: though they were naught but walking skin, the monsters had all the strength they'd had in life.

She slashed hastily through its elbows. The forearms fell to the dirt like a wealthy woman's gloves. They wriggled yet toward Fie, dragging themselves on their fingers.

She scrambled back. More screams echoed through the streets. Bloodflies took to the air as one of the bodies on the nearby pyre convulsed, then a second, then a third. It looked as if the skin itself was bubbling and contorting until it split with a squelch. That was Fie's final straw: she keeled over, vomiting.

"*TO THE COMMONS!*" she heard Jade shout. "*ALL CROWS TO THE COMMONS!*" The cry echoed back from Crow to Crow on the western side of Karostei.

Fie wiped her mouth. "All——" Her voice came out a harsh squeak.

The arbiter skin-ghast lurched toward her, the remains of its arms twisting into something like vines. Fie yelped and staggered back, only for the severed forearms to tangle about her ankles and send her crashing to the earth. When she twisted onto her back, she saw the ghast slithering toward her on its belly like an adder. She reached for her Phoenix teeth—and remembered she had but one left.

Gone.

She'd lost the one way to protect them from skin-ghasts.

Bawd's shriek pierced through the air.

The ghast raised itself up at the boneless waist, lunging for Fie. With a furious scream, she lashed out, swinging the sword in a clumsy arc. It sheared through the ghast at the belly. Both halves flopped in the dust like a cast-off shirt and trousers. She drew the chief's sword in her other hand, slashing wildly on her knees, until aught that was left of the ghast were bloody rags yet writhing about her. Fie seized the scraps by the sickening handful and hurled them into the well.

She stumbled to her feet, sucking in the dusty air, and bellowed, "*ALL CROWS TO THE COMMONS!*"

The order caught and spread, echoing back to her from her own Crows on the east side of town. So, too, did a terrible and familiar airy howl, one Fie knew all too well.

There were a great many things she hated about the skin-ghasts, but chief among them was how, when they moved swift enough, the wind whistled through their empty husks. As a chorus of those whistles swept across the commons, Fie finally kenned the enormity of what had come for them.

Karostei had at least a hundred dead on its hands. And if Fie was right, that meant a hundred skin-ghasts were stripping free of their bones at this very moment.

Crows poured from the streets, the slinking forms of ghasts on their heels. The three new ghasts from the arbiter's pyre swayed drunkenly toward Fie, but she had an easier time dispatching these, hacking them to pieces small enough to kick into the well.

Madcap reached her first, the jug of flashburn still swinging from their hand. "Out," Fie wheezed, pointing the chief's sword toward the closed gates, only to find that was a fool's hope: ghasts were already massing before it in numbers Fie couldn't cut through.

"New plan?" Madcap asked.

The lone Phoenix tooth on her string waited, patient, inevitable.

No. Fie wasn't going to burn it here, not with the safety of Jasimir's procession still days away. But they'd laid fuel and flashburn all about Karostei by now. Perhaps fire could still staunch the ghasts' numbers.

"New plan." Fie handed Madcap her Hawk sword, much to their surprise and delight, and fumbled for her flint instead as Varlet arrived with another three of her Crows. That left three yet beyond Fie's sight.

"Where's the closest tinder heap?" Fie asked the new arrivals.

Varlet shook his head. "No good, chief. They're charging right through the firewood and scattering it. And . . ." He grimaced and pointed at the nearby pyre. "They're leaving it too damp to light."

Fie looked, saw what he meant, and wished she hadn't. For most of the dead, their skin had been the only thing holding the decaying flesh and innards together. It would take more than a flint to light the wet mess of a pyre now.

She didn't realize she'd reached for the Phoenix tooth until it was rolling between her fingers.

Then she saw Wretch stumble from an alleyway, Bawd's arm slung over her shoulders. The younger woman was limping swift as she could on a foot bent at a gut-churning angle.

The gray, mottled arm of a skin-ghast coiled about Wretch's ankles and yanked. She fell.

Fie screamed. Her last Phoenix tooth was singing through her bones before she even knew she'd called it.

The skin-ghast shriveled with a rancid crackle as golden fire ate it whole. Fie pushed the tooth harder, the fire farther, and it swelled beyond Wretch and Bawd, driving back some ghasts and devouring others.

"Flashburn," Fie ordered, and Madcap set the half-empty jug by her feet. "Get them clear—"

Varlet and Madcap darted to Wretch and Bawd and half dragged them to the relative safety of the well. Fie tore a strip of her cloak off and stuffed it down the jug's neck. Golden fire snagged on the rag's end, crawling up the crowsilk.

Fie ran a few awkward paces toward the ghasts swelling to the east, then hurled the jug as hard as she could. She didn't see it land, but she certainly heard the shatter and the crack like thunder that followed. A billow of fire tore a hole through the skin-ghasts before her, burning white as it raced along the spill lines and chewed through empty skin.

Even better, droplets had splashed onto the walls of the nearest home, sending fingers of flame prying at the eaves. Fie doubted it would be enough to set the whole town ablaze, but at least some of those sparks would find tinder there.

She pushed the ghasts back with another flare of Phoenix-gold fire and retreated to the well, where she found Jade kneeling over Ruffian's body. Most of the other two bands seemed to have made it back as well, and from the grim looks on their faces, they didn't expect the missing to return anytime soon.

Jade's eyes glistened as she looked up from Ruffian, but she pushed herself to her feet, drawing her own broken blade. "How long will the fire tooth last?"

"Maybe a minute like this." Fie whipped about to take stock of the ghasts closing in. "It'll burn out faster the more fire I call."

"Then here." Jade passed her an open jug of flashburn and pointed at the ghasts piling up between them and the gate. "Last we have. Use that trick again and clear the way out."

Fie tore another strip from her cloak and shoved it into the spout. From its weight, the jug was nigh full, more than enough to blow a hole through the skin-ghasts. "Fall back!" she called to the Crows, then hauled the jug back and took one swift step, a second, swung her arm—

—and crashed to the dust as something caught her by the feet. The flashburn jug landed, unlit and unbroken, in a soft cushion of shifting, gray-mottled skin. It rolled to a rest at the base of the gate.

Whatever had caught Fie dragged her backward. She wrenched about and found the strips of skin-ghast she'd dumped into the well had plaited themselves into something crawling and dreadful that lashed like a serpent round her ankles. Now it towed her through the dust, toward the well, and Fie kenned exactly what awaited her there.

Jade kenned it, too, for the other chief hacked through the plait of skin in one swift blow. It recoiled, then lashed around Jade's wrist instead, her broken sword clattering to the dirt.

Fie called on the Phoenix tooth again, trying not to panic as its spark burned lower. Fire seared through the twists of skin-ghast at her ankles and Jade's arm. The older woman yelped as the rags around her hand caught ablaze, but she shook them off with the charred bits of skin-ghost.

Fie rolled to her feet, fighting to catch her breath in air filthy with smoke and dust and plague-stink. Sparks had traveled in the east, a scattering of little fires licking the sky from thatch roofs, but the west and north remained unlit. Worse, the ghosts were crowding in on all sides. Her last tooth couldn't hold them back much longer.

The gate itself lurched but caught on skin-ghosts weaving them-selves through the bars to hold it fast. No doubt Lakima had heard the screams, but so long as the ghosts blocked the way, no help would come from that quarter.

Fie took a deep breath and scraped together the last bit of Phoenix spark left, fire-song echoing in her own bones, too familiar now. Bits and bobs of the dead Phoenix's life slipped by: a grand duke, the spare to the heir. He had always believed the throne belonged to him; he had seethed when his aunt's daughter was sent to the throne, and then he had found himself sent, repeatedly and pointedly, on diplomatic mis-sions to their neighbors across the pirate-infested Sea of Beasts . . . until he promised to stop trying to poison the new queen.

His was the fire of self-righteous ambition, and as Fie summoned every last ounce of its ghost, she could swear she heard the grand duke whisper, *Hello, cousin.*

The song hitched in her bones a beat, but she forced it back into tune. They were running out of time, and she had none to spare for the follies of some useless ghost.

Golden fire bloomed from the tooth in her fist, and Fie sent it roar-ing toward the gate. All she had to do was catch that fallen flashburn jug, catch that rag.

But ghost after ghost piled themselves over the jug, forming a wall of skin between the flame and the shuddering gate.

Fie pushed harder, her own bones humming, singing, screaming as she poured herself into the song of fire, the dying spark, the last scrap of Phoenix gold carving through slick, hollow hide. *More*, she demanded, *farther*, she *had* to break through, had to get them out—

Goodbye, cousin, the dead Phoenix whispered.

And the fire of her final royal tooth sputtered out.

It was a curious thing: she stood in a black cloak under a blazing sun, sweat rolling down her spine, and yet all Fie felt was the sudden, deadly cold.

A hush fell over the commons as the three bands looked to her and found her empty-handed. The gate rattled fruitlessly against the knot of ghosts.

Every soul left in Karostei knew that even if the Hawks made it through the gate, it would be too late.

Fie turned to Jade. The older chief swallowed, then hefted her half sword, jaw set.

Then her brow furrowed, staring at something beyond Fie.

Fie looked back to the gate and saw a miracle: smoke.

For a moment, she thought she'd managed it, that the rag had caught after all, and she backed toward the well. But the smoke was rising from the other side of the gate.

Lines of gold lit up along the cracks between the gate's boards. Then something flickered near the base—the flashburn rag snared a spark—

"*Get down!*" Fie shouted, and threw herself to the ground.

They came so fast, she could scarce tell one from the other: a whistle. A booming crash. An eruption of white and gold.

When she stumbled to her feet, chips of burning ceramic were bouncing off the commons, raining down through wisps of charred skin floating on the breeze. The rest of the Crows seemed to be stunned but unhurt, dust cascading off their black robes as they picked themselves up. Naught was left of the gate and its ghast blockade but burning wood and grease stains in the dirt.

"*FIE!*"

Through the smoking wreckage strode the last person Fie expected to see, his face full of fury and fear as he took in the commons. Golden fire still rolled off his fingertips.

Fie had thought quite a bit about what she would say the next time she saw Taverin sza Markahn. She liked to think it would be something pithy and full of swagger, to hint that she'd missed him but not *too* much. A teensy, wretched part of her thought she might like something poetic and fanciful, with grand declarations involving souls and hearts and destinies intertwined. Fie usually told herself she wouldn't like that at all. At least . . . not unless he said it first.

But instead of something sly or honey-tongued, Fie found herself just looking to Tavin's still-burning hands and croaking, "I forgot you could do that."

His harrowed gaze landed on her, and that secretly starry-eyed part of her was content, because the look on his face was better than any love song.

Wretch cleared her throat. "You've an audience, chief. And I don't mean us."

Little was left of the ghasts at the gate, but scores stood yet. They'd stopped their uneven swaying and gone stock-still, every empty eye-hole locked on Tavin.

He raised a burning hand, and his voice carried across the commons. "Enough, Rhusana. You can drag it out as long as you want, but we all know it's over."

The skin-ghasts gaped at him a long moment, and Fie was sore sure she wasn't the only one holding her breath. Then, in one swift ripple, every last ghost collapsed, leaving heaps of empty, rotting skin all about the commons.

It still took a heartbeat or two for any of the Crows to budge, eyeing those heaps with a skepticism Fie shared. "We should clear out before they change their minds," Jade called across the square, and tilted her brow at Tavin. "Can your friend there light the town for us?"

"It all has to burn, else plague'll spread to the fields and farther," Fie added at Tavin's quizzical blink. "But the firewood's all scattered, and we used our flashburn on the ghasts, so we need more than flint now."

Wretch muttered something to Jade. The older chief coughed. "You could walk him about town so he stays clear of the plague-dead. I'll see to the wounded."

Tavin nodded, eyes never leaving Fie, and said, "Yes, chief."

The rest of the Crows hurried through the gates, Madcap spitefully kicking a skin-pile on their way out. Ruffian's body had been claimed by his own Crows, along with the handful of Crows who had fallen; they wouldn't leave any of their own to burn with the sinners.

"It's . . . good to see you," Tavin said, with a strain Fie would have found uncharacteristic were they not standing in a sea of corpses. Bawd made a lewd gesture as she limped past, leaning on Varlet.

"Good to see you, too," Fie returned, as stiff as a rusted hinge, a door closed a little too long and sticking on the jamb.

He reached for her. She flinched back. "No—wait—"

Tavin stepped away hastily, tensing. "Sorry—I just—I thought—"

"Plague," Fie blurted out. "It's the plague, it's not—you. I need to wash up before we . . . *do* . . . anything."

He tilted his head, then unfurled a slow grin. "*Anything?*" he echoed.

Fie briefly contemplated revising her stance on spreading the plague. "Anything," she repeated, stern, and waved at the remains atop the unlit pyre nearby. "I have standards. It'll take more than a moon apart for me to roll a lad in a pile of guts. Besides, you'd be dead in a week."

Tavin gave an exaggerated sigh. "Worth it. It's been a long moon."

And just like that, the rust was flaking away. Fie let her own smile creep out, let the door creak open the slightest bit. "It'll only get longer if we don't finish this town off. Come on." She started down a lane to the east, where fire had already begun spreading. "How'd you even find me?"

Tavin jogged to catch up. "When we heard the king supposedly died of the plague, we knew Rhusana was targeting you. Mother agreed to let me bring you and your band to the procession for safety."

"And you and Draga knew I'd be in Karostei how?"

Tavin pursed his lips and swiped a hand at the sky. An arc of flame leapt from one roof to the next, then swept down the rest of the lane. "I'd like to take this opportunity to apologize in advance."

"I don't fancy where this is going."

"You know how skinwitches use belongings to track down the owners? Turns out they can also use people to find belongings." Tavin passed Fie something leathery and scorched. "Like my baby tooth."

"My tooth bag!" Fie tore it open. Her belly sank when she found only charred leather inside. "A damned rat of a chief stole it just this morning. Did you take it off him?"

A shade darted through Tavin's face, and he strode to the next street. "We found it at the roadside. Then Viimo used the trail from the bag itself to lead to you—"

"*Viimo?*" Fie hissed. The last she'd seen the skinwitch was in the dungeons of Trikovoi, and Fie had been more than happy to let her rot there. "You brought *her?*"

"You can't be mad, I apologized in advance," Tavin said.

Fie scowled and crossed her arms. "That's not how it works and you know it."

"In my defense, I was in a hurry." He made a face as a puddle of empty skin caught fire with a crackle. "And with good reason. Though I didn't think Rhusana would throw this much effort into killing you just to spite Jas."

Fie reckoned the queen would put square that much effort, if not more, into it, if she knew all Little Witness had told her. But the thought of telling Tavin that, even after all they'd given up for it, the oath still wasn't kept, made Fie want to find a whole new town to burn to the ground.

Oh aye, and what's your plan? a stern part of her chided. *Don't you think he'd want to know what you're bound to now?*

That was sore true, but the funny thing was, Fie reckoned she wanted him *not* to know, and that took priority.

Instead, she asked, "How is Jas holding up?"

Tavin's shoulders fell. "He's been better. It was worse when Aunt Jasindra died, but I think . . . he wanted to give his father a way out."

"Aye." Fie remembered it too keen, crouching by the fire, saying to the prince, *You wanted to save him.*

I still do, Jasimir had said, *if he's someone I can save.*

She was not sorry the king was dead, and she supposed they'd all known there was no saving him any more than she could have saved Karostei. Still, as she watched Tavin send fire rushing along the walls of one more house, she was sorry for Jasimir, and for the death of the hope that there was aught left of the king to save.

They left the walls of Karostei once every house was ablaze, and not a moment too soon, as she'd grown a bit too appreciative of the way the heat made Tavin's shirt cling to his back.

Lakima and Khoda had posted themselves as close to the gates as was wise, and Fie caught the corporal letting out a relieved breath once she and Tavin emerged.

Fie threw Lakima an exhausted grin. "Don't fool with me. We both know if I'd met my end in there, you lot would be sent to sunnier posts."

Usually, Corporal Lakima either ignored Fie's jests or answered them with a bland "Yes, chief." This time her jaw tightened, as did her grip on her spear.

"I promised your father I would keep you safe" was all she said.

Jade waited for them only a few dozen paces down the road, working through injured Crows with a Hawk's tooth. Their ranks had thinned, but considering the trap the queen had somehow laid, it could have been much worse. Still, she counted five shrouded bodies laid out in the dust. Five too many.

Jade finished straightening out a sprain and stood with a wince as Fie walked over. "So that—those—those skins, the queen's behind them, aye?"

"Aye," Fie rasped.

"You ever see one come off anything still breathing?"

Tavin and Fie traded looks. "No, chief," Tavin said.

Jade stared at the fields, grim. "Then we just found out why she's telling towns to handle their own plague-dead, didn't we? Make her a whole proper army of puppets."

Fie hadn't had the time to do that grotesque math, but the weight of its sum hit home. The ghasts could be sliced to ribbons, crushed under stone, even sunk to the bottom of a well, and they'd still never stop. Only fire could hold them off—and without Fie's Phoenix teeth, there was only one witch in the whole of Sabor who could command fire outside the royal palace.

The boy standing at her side.

"Normally, when a chief passes, we let their band choose who they'll join up with." Jade planted her hands on her hips. "But it seems the queen's got a shine for you. And it's no fault of your own, but it doesn't seem like she'll spare us while she's shaking the country down for you. So I'll take Ruffian's band to Gen-Mara's shrine, and we'll see who starves first: us or this storm."

Fie nodded, guilt drowning even the glow of crossing paths with her Hawk again. "My band's not two days off from safe harbor. You can take our spare cart, and we'll split our rations. If this keeps up, that shrine could get crowded."

"Excuse me," someone said from the roadside.

The Crows parted and found a woman there in a stained Sparrow patchwork apron, holding an old iron kettle. It was filled to the brim with teeth.

"I'm the headwoman now," she said. "Long as the lord lets me keep the name. So I'm here to pay viatik. This is all the teeth we have."

Fie swallowed. She'd never seen so many teeth at once outside a shrine's stores. Even when teeth were all a family could pay, they rarely gave up the entire store, keeping some back for another stroke of ill fortune.

It didn't feel like payment. It felt like tribute.

"Khoda, help the lady," she said slowly.

Khoda took the kettle from her, brows rising at the weight. The new headwoman clenched her empty fists in her apron. "What do we do now?"

"Let it burn to ash," Jade said. "All of it. With this many survivors, you've decent odds someone smuggled out something plague-touched, so keep a sharp eye for the Sinner's Brand. If you see it, carry the sinner into the ashes and light your beacon. We come when we're called."

"Isn't there *anything* we can save?" The headwoman's voice shook. Fie noticed the red rims of her eyes and couldn't help but wonder who of her family had burned.

Fie's voice came out kinder than it had when dealing with the Crane arbiter. "It's not like spotty apples, cousin. The plague rots it whole. Can't just cut parts away when the whole thing's gone bad." The headwoman nodded, eyes glistening. "I'd start rebuilding on the other side of your fields, if not farther. It won't be safe here until it grows green, and that won't come for years."

The headwoman bowed her head. Then she did the unexpected: she raised the first two fingers of her right hand and touched them to her brow.

The fields went still as, citizen by citizen, the people of Karostei followed suit: heads bent, two fingertips pressed to the middle of their foreheads.

The hair on Fie's arms stood straight up, prickling against her stiffening rags.

She'd seen this in old tooth ghosts, in fleeting memories of war heroes riding by, of healers who wrought the impossible to heal scores of wounded in a breath, of Pigeon witches tilting fortune to avert floods or save harvests. It was an old gesture, living now mostly in corners of Sabor that kept those old ways, and it was meant as a blessing. An acknowledgment of great deeds. A sign of gratitude.

One she'd never seen made for Crows.

Two fingers, pressed dead center above two eyes. It meant "*The Covenant sees,*" that it would remember what they had done today, when it weighed their deeds at the end of their lives. It would remember the choices Fie had made. Every last one.

It was supposed to be an honor.

The Covenant sees.

Fie didn't realize her fists were clenched until she felt her nails biting into her palm. She shook out her hands and turned from the headwoman, muttering, "We should go."

CHAPTER SEVEN

SAFE AND SOUND

THEY PUSHED SOUTH FOR A FEW HOURS AFTER LEAVING KAROSTEI, and though Fie saw the sense in it, she felt all too keenly every fleck of dried blood under her short-gnawed fingernails, every bruise, every smudge of what was optimistically mud, but more likely to be some skin-ghast slime.

But there was no use stopping until they found a proper place for all of them to wash up, as every ghast had been pulled off a dead sinner, and every Crow who had tangled with them needed to scrub that sin off. By the time the road wandered close enough to a broad riverbed, the sun was rolling lazily near the horizon.

"The Vine?" one of Tavin's guards asked, tipping his spear at the waters. Master-General Draga hadn't let her only son go haring off with only a turncoat Vulture for protection, which was probably wise considering Tavin was also the dead king's bastard son. Instead, he'd been flanked by three soldiers so stone-faced, they made Lakima look like she had a flair for the dramatic.

"The Sprout," Madcap answered. "It's an offshoot of the Vine, trickles out a score league from here or so."

The soldier's stone face faltered for a moment. Fie reckoned he'd only ever barked orders at Crows and had yet to sort out how he felt when one answered him without bowing, scraping, and tossing in a "m'lord" or five.

"We'll make camp here," Fie announced, catching Lakima's eye. "Best to get everyone cleaned up soon as we can."

"Yes, chief," the corporal said smoothly, and pulled the oxen's harnesses to lead the supply cart to the side of the road. They'd divvied up rations with Jade's band just out of Karostei and sent them off with the cart the Crows usually hauled bodies on, but there was still enough in their supplies to tide Fie's band until they reached the procession.

The newer Hawks traded looks Fie didn't miss but dismounted after a moment.

"Little assistance, if you please," drawled a voice Fie wished she *could* miss. Viimo the skinwitch had been granted a horse, where she sat with her hands bound in front of her, reins wrapped round her wrists, knees lashed to the saddle, and a broad grin on her pale-pink face. "Seein' as all these *precautions*"—she flapped the reins—"was *your* lot's idea." She nudged her horse closer to Fie. "Help a lass out, aye?"

"No," Fie said flatly, and walked away. Wretch laughed and went to untie the Vulture.

"Not even a 'thank you kindly' for all my troubles," she heard Viimo call after her. "I could've let your half-prince lout here wander all about the countryside while the queen made a dress outta your hide!"

Fie ignored her. The skinwitch had been one of the hunters who had hounded her, Tavin, and Jasimir across Sabor; Viimo had helped their leader, Tatterhelm, take Fie's kin hostage; and worst of all, at the last possible moment she'd turned on Tatterhelm, buying Fie time to save her Crows. Fie didn't know if they would have made it out without Viimo's help, and that, to her, was an unforgivable debt she'd never asked to owe.

"Can someone get the salt and soap-shells?" Fie asked Lakima's Hawks, then pointed to the river. "Crows, we all need to wash up, even if you don't think you touched a sinner today."

Khoda rummaged through the cart. "Should we do the same?"

She shook her head, then paused. "You all stayed outside the walls, you're fine. But Tavin . . ."

"You could take him upstream," Varlet said, "to be safe. Can't pick up aught from sharing our water that way."

Bawd fired off a wink with all the subtlety of a rock to the head. "Aye. *Much* safer."

Fie shot her a dirty look, but there was no denying that the last few hours had ground by so slow partially because she'd spent most of it trying not to leer at her Hawk. The easy chatter they'd fallen into had stiffened back into unease on the road, where she had to be a chief and he had to be a king's bastard and neither quite knew how to manage those with an electric storm brewing between them.

Even now Tavin looked taken aback, swinging a pack down. Then he caught Bawd's renewed furious winking. "Oh. Uh. Yes. That would be . . . safer."

"We'll get to work setting up camp." Corporal Lakima tossed Tavin the sturdy satchel Fie made up after every beacon, with a change of clothes, rags for drying off, and its own pouches of salt and soap-shells.

Khoda paused, to Fie's surprise, looking from her to Tavin. "If it's just the two of you, is that . . . er . . . safe?"

Fie buried her burning face in her hands.

"I think we've established everyone's going to be safe," Tavin said, short. "Repeatedly."

Khoda looked annoyed. "I meant—with the skin-ghasts—"

"I can assure you of my personal commitment to Fie's safety, and I suspect she'll be ensuring mine as well, and really I'd like to leave it at that before we ruin the word *safe* any more than we already have." Tavin started toward the riverbank, then stopped, mouth twisting. "Where are we going again?"

"Somewhere safe," Fie mumbled into her palms, then straightened up and set off across the crunching, dry riverbed pebbles. "Come on. The rest of you stay close to camp."

Summer had withered the Sprout enough to leave wide borders of sunbaked mud and long-dead river grass, but the water still ran deep and swift enough in the middle. Fie couldn't make herself look back at Tavin, only trusting his footsteps and the hair prickling on the back of her neck to say he was following her.

Fie didn't stop until they'd rounded a crook in the river far enough from the camp to give them some quiet. "This'll do."

She set her satchel down on the bank and fished out her salt and soap-shells. Tavin's shadow fell over the open bag, and she glanced up on instinct. He was staring down at her, and she could have sworn something troubled flickered out behind his eyes like a snuffed lamp.

He gestured awkwardly at his shirt. "Should I be, er, not wearing clothes for this?"

"I'd rather you weren't," Fie blurted out, then wondered if she could knock Tavin out with a handy rock and insist he'd imagined everything when he woke up.

He just laughed and crouched in place. "That makes two of us," he admitted.

"Wash them or burn them, you choose. Hold out your hands." Fie shook a few soap-shells into his palms. "These first, then the salt."

Despite her candor, she found herself averting her eyes as he pulled off his shirt and waded into the Sprout. It was nonsense; they'd seen each other without so much as a stitch on plenty of times a moon ago, albeit not out in the open like this. Yet whether it was the time apart or something more, something felt unsettled between them.

Fie made herself splash into the water downstream of him, still in her own shirt and leggings, stopping when it reached her belly. "I didn't ask before," she called back as she cracked the soap-shell hulls, "but . . . how do *you* feel about . . . the king?"

She heard Tavin go still, and when he answered, it was with a stiff, surprising sort of anger. "The only bad thing about my father's death was that Jas wasn't ready for it. And that it gave Rhusana an opening. Apart from that . . ." He let out a breath. "We've lost nothing worth mourning."

"You don't think Jas could have gotten through to him?" Fie asked, cautious. The king had left more scars on Tavin than just the burn on his wrist; only Tavin could say how well they'd healed.

"No, I don't." Tavin's voice tightened. "Surimir spent his entire life doing only what served him. He knew people were suffering, dying from problems he could fix, and he just didn't care. People are *still* dying because of him."

Fie sank into the river up to her nose, chewing over her next question and finding no good way to ask it. She ducked her head under, then popped back up in a fizzing cloud of suds and made herself look Tavin's way. "You were born before Jasimir."

He shook his head, back still to her. "I was, but—I was never trained to rule. I have no business sitting on that throne. You might as well put a horse up there." He coughed a laugh. "Twelve hells, *you'd* do better leading the country than me."

"No, I wouldn't." Fie splashed back toward the bank to fetch her salt. *Life after life, you've failed.* "You'd do better with the horse. Come get your salt."

She'd already dusted herself down by the time he reached the water's edge, so she just carried the rest of the bag to him. "Arms out," she said, and rained sparkling flakes over his outstretched wrists.

Then she caught one of his hands and tried not to think too hard about the way his breath caught, too. She rolled her thumb in a steady, even circle over the back of his hand, over tendon and scar, feeling his pulse jump beneath her fingertips with only river water and melting salt between them.

"Scrub with the salt, at least that hard," she said, and let go. "*Everywhere.* I'm not taking any chances." She handed him the bag, then stepped back into deeper water and cracked a grin at him. "And if you miss a spot, I'll know."

Then she ducked her head underwater again before it could burst into flame. Even just touching his hand had sent a jolt through her, one that reminded her in no uncertain terms that it had been a sore long moon without her Hawk.

She stayed under about as long as she could manage, trying to cool her head. Sadly, it was beyond even the river's help.

When she surfaced, Tavin was rinsing salt from his hair. He straightened up, uncertain. "I think I got everything," he said. "Are we . . . Can I—"

"Aye," Fie said. "If you want to be *really* safe, you can pray to the Eater of Bones not to take you, but—"

He crossed the space between them before she could finish, pulling her into his arms.

Then, to her surprise, they stayed that way: up to their waists in the river, her forehead resting against his rattling heart, his arms wound almost too tight around her. Tavin didn't speak, didn't stir, didn't do aught but hold her as close as he could.

First she realized he was shaking; then she felt his chest shudder beneath her cheek and knew something was wrong.

"Tavin?" She tilted her head up to look him in the eye.

Fie thought she'd seen more than enough terrible things for one week, but clearly she was wrong. The boy she loved was crying.

"What is it?"

"I—" He cut himself off, looking like he was about to be sick. He shook his head. "I can't—"

Fie laid her hand against the side of his face, and he closed his eyes, leaning into her palm. "Show me," she said, and moved her fingers to brush his mouth. He sucked in a breath, then nodded, lips parting just enough for her fingertip to catch on a tooth.

The teeth of the living always sang brighter than the dead, even more so when they were still part of the person. There was no need to call Tavin's ghost from a spark in a bone, for there was no spark—only a rush like wildfire that swallowed her whole.

She felt his stab of fear when he'd realized Rhusana had painted targets on the Crows. Unending needle-pricks of anxiety, of impatience, of growing anger as he bartered with his mother for permission to find his chief. The brief reprieve as Viimo traced a steady, clear trail to lead them to the tooth bag.

Then—horror, when he reached it.

Tavin had told Fie he'd found the bag at the roadside, and that much was true. But Drudge hadn't emptied it out and cast it aside like she'd assumed.

Instead, she felt the moment Tavin rounded the bend in the road, found a still-smoking ruin of corpses and ash strewn across the flatway, and drew a catastrophic conclusion.

She felt something irreparable break in Tavin as he all but threw himself from his horse, stumbling through the embers toward a figure burned beyond recognition, lying beside a charred leather bag.

He'd always known she wasn't immortal, that she could bleed and weep and fall like anyone else. But deep down, he'd never really believed it. He'd never believed she'd do anything but simply refuse to die.

And even after Viimo shook him from his screaming, after she told him that wasn't Fie lying dead in the burning grass, that his chief was still alive—it didn't mend what had been broken.

It didn't matter that he'd found her again just hours later, furious and filthy and beautiful in the wreckage of Karostei. For those few, terrible moments, he'd known what it was to see the girl he loved dead. And that could not be unbroken.

Fie jerked her hand back and found tears streaking down her own face. "Oh—*hells*, Tavin."

Tavin bowed his head until his brow met hers. "I thought you were gone," he said, voice cracking. "I thought if I was faster, or if I'd left with you, or . . . I thought I *lost* you, Fie."

"You didn't." She wanted to kiss him. She wanted to fight. She wanted to find Drudge and give his band a proper funeral. She wanted to kick Drudge's fool skull off a cliff. She'd *told* him not to call two Phoenix teeth at once, that he'd lose control. He'd done it anyway, and from what Fie had seen in those fleeting, awful glimpses, it had cost all his Crows their lives. "I'm fine. I'm still alive."

"I know," Tavin said, but his hands still shook as he brushed her hair back from her face. "I just—can't stop seeing it, and then—you're gone again."

She drew him nearer the shore, nearer to her, until their lips met, and whispered against his mouth, "I'm here." Then she kissed him like she'd wanted to since the moment she'd left Trikovoi: like a jealous god hungry for tribute.

She dug her fingers along his spine, grazed her teeth along the pulse in his jaw, seized tangled handfuls of his damp hair tighter and tighter until he gasped her name like a prayer. She answered by dragging them both to their knees. If the fear of losing her had overthrown him, she would be the fire and flood that drove it out.

She took his hand again, no salt between them now, and slammed it over her heart. "Feel that," she ordered, fingers locked in the curls at the nape of his neck, her stare boring into his as her heart thundered against his palm. "Is that gone to you?" He shook his head, wordless. "Am *I* gone to you?" she demanded.

He stared at her, wide-eyed and breathing hard. Then he pulled her closer, his voice low and fierce and desperate in a way she hadn't heard before. "*Never.*"

He said it against her lips, against her throat, against her hipbone after they'd managed to drag themselves mostly ashore and free themselves of their sodden clothes. He spelled it on her with his mouth, with his hands, until it was her turn to make a prayer of his name, and even after that as they fell into the same dance they'd taught each other a moon earlier. Between moments when all he could say was her name and moments when neither of them could speak at all, still he swore *never.*

The sky ripened to sunset well before the ghosts between them were laid to rest. For a while they lay together in the quiet, watching sparrows flit across gold-soaked clouds as cicada-song drifted from the trees.

Eventually, the last of Fie's ghosts shook its chains too loud for her to ignore.

"I—" she started, and her voice broke. She coughed and tried again. "I . . . had to give mercy to—to children today."

Tavin had been tracing an idle pattern across her collarbone; he stopped and shifted to look at her. "Oh, Fie," he said softly. "I'm so sorry."

It was one thing to know her own wounds, but hearing someone else say she'd been hurt always made her bleed anew. Her face crumpled as she curled into his arms. "I've never . . . They were so little, and they didn't have to . . . they didn't *have* to die. It's not right. That damned arbiter killed them all. I had to cut their throats, and he didn't even have to look them in the eye." She buried her face in the hollow of his neck. "It's not *right*."

He rubbed her back until she steadied, chin resting on the top of her head. "I knew . . . this was going to be bad," he said. "But I didn't know it would happen this fast."

"There's thousands of people like that arbiter, all across Sabor. They talk and look like anyone else, but they'll take any excuse to get rid of Crows for good." Fie swallowed. "And all they were waiting for was permission."

"Do you think that's what happened to the man who stole your teeth?"

"Aye. We met because some scummers were harrying his band, and I chased them off with fire. Likely Drudge crossed someone like that after he stole my teeth, and he figured he'd do the same."

"But Phoenix teeth never burned you."

"Reckon he lost control," she said unevenly. "I warned him they'd fight. Did—did you see any teeth in the grass?"

Tavin shook his head. "I didn't see any, but I also had . . . other things on my mind." He grimaced. "Whoever attacked them probably wanted to make sure Crows wouldn't get teeth that dangerous again."

"Covenant forbid," Fie drawled. "Then they might actually have to stop killing us."

"Imagine that." Tavin still drew circles on her back, but the bewildered note in his voice said it was just as much to distract himself as her. "Every time I think we've hit the bottom of how bad it is, we just peel off another layer, don't we? And they'll let their own children die if it means hurting the Crows. What do you even do against something like that?"

The cicada-song shrilled through the quiet but couldn't drown out the memory: *Only a fool waits for the lightning to tell them to find shelter.*

She had an oath to keep, somehow. A Birthright to find. Somehow it would be one and the same; somehow it would change Sabor for good. And she wouldn't manage any of it from the shelter she longed for.

"Save as much as you can," she said instead. "And find better kings."

———◆———

It was a funny thing; Fie thought she'd known how much she missed Tavin while he'd been gone, yet she kept discovering new ways she'd missed him over the two days it took to reach Jasimir's procession.

She'd missed the way Tavin laughed with Varlet and Madcap as they taught him an especially scandalous walking song, the twist to his mouth when he dangled a string for Barf, how he looked at her when he said "Yes, chief," . . . all that and more.

It wasn't all sunshine and flower petals—Khoda had taken a sudden turn for the taciturn, and Tavin's guards curled their lips whenever he slipped his hand into hers, and the two of them couldn't steal a moment to themselves without snickers about *safety*. But they'd both dreamed of a day when he could take to the roads at her side, and with every step, that day seemed closer.

When they arrived at the procession, however, matters grew even more complicated.

Master-General Draga had made camp on the banks of the Vine, in what had once been a rolling, groomed pasture that spread like a blanket of green velvet over the lap of a stately Peacock mansion over-looking the river. Now plain canvas tents studded most of that fine lawn; the only comparatively clear patch was a broad stretch along the Vine, which had been staked out for mammoth pens. The great beasts were making the most of their proximity to the river, spraying themselves down in the late afternoon heat and wading up to their bellies in water that seemed to grow considerably muddier for their presence.

"Now, I know it's been a long moon," Fie said, tallying up the scores of tents, "but last time I saw the prince, all it took to get him across the country was about a dozen Crows."

"Mother figured that once Jas resurfaced, Rhusana would make a power grab," Tavin explained. "So she brought along some, er, light reinforcements. Though, if it were up to me, I'd put my naka on you over an army any day."

"Looks like we get to test that." Khoda nodded at the line of Hawks across the flatway.

Tavin glanced a little too long at the other Hawk. Fie had a notion why: Khoda was only a few years older than Tavin, with a fine-cut face, a promising tilt to his smile, and a too-avid concern for Fie's well-being.

"It should be fine," Tavin said firmly, pushing forward. "They're expecting us."

It was not, in fact, fine.

"You're allowed in," the lieutenant said, motioning to Tavin and his guards. "The Crows go elsewhere."

Tavin frowned. "They're with me. And their chief has business with the master-general."

The Hawk lieutenant didn't seem to find that credible. "The

master-general's orders for the flatway guard are to allow travelers to pass the camp in groups no larger than three. And no one is allowed into the area if they aren't part of the procession, period."

Tavin's face darkened. "I'm sure you were told I'd be returning with a band of Crows."

"My commander told me you left with guards and the renegade skin-witch." The lieutenant glanced over his shoulder as riders approached from camp. "No one gave me orders about Crows. They need to move along and stop blocking the road."

"Fine, I'll order you: let the Crows in," Tavin snapped.

The lieutenant drew himself up. "You'll have to remind me, where does 'bastard' fall in the chain of command?"

Fie bristled on Tavin's behalf. "Think it's well above 'dung-sucking dog-lover,' so I wager he outranks you."

Corporal Lakima abruptly coughed into her elbow. So did a few of the Hawks on the line. The lieutenant, however, was not amused.

"You're addressing your betters, bone thief," he snarled. "I could have you flogged—"

Tavin stepped in front of Fie, eyes burning. "Touch a hair on her head and you'll lose your hand."

Behind them, Viimo cackled. "Love this. Keep it up, lads. This's the most fun I've had in weeks."

"Shove it, turncoat," Fie called back.

"We're entering the camp." Tavin took another step closer to the lieutenant. "With or without your permission."

"Can we all *please* stop posturing for one minute," Fie heard Khoda mutter under his breath.

"Is there a problem here?" a familiar voice called from behind the lieutenant.

The lieutenant made a face that dissolved like candy floss in water as Prince Jasimir rode up behind him, staring impassively down from the back of a horse.

"No, Your Highness," the lieutenant said quick. "These Crows were looking for a place to set up camp."

Jasimir let the silence hang a moment.

When Fie had first met him three moons before, he'd been fussy, naïve, and principled to a fault; if she'd been a thief, she could have emptied his pockets five ways in four heartbeats and convinced him it was for the greater good.

Perhaps it had been the time spent with his aunt, or with Fie, or the loss of his father, but the prince Fie saw now was no longer one painlessly crossed.

"They will be quartered next to me," Jasimir said, icy calm, "and in the future, I expect my guests to be given significantly less trouble."

"If Your Highness commands it," the lieutenant said, looking like his teeth hurt.

Jasimir didn't break his gaze. "I do."

The lieutenant signaled the soldiers across the road, who parted to let them pass. Fie felt looks lingering on the back of her neck but said naught, only marched her Crows through.

Prince Jasimir dismounted and passed his reins to one of his own guards, striding over to Fie, a weary smile breaking free. He clasped her briefly on the shoulder, something Fie supposed would further annoy the lieutenant and appreciated accordingly.

"It's good to——" His face fell as he looked about her band. "Oh no. What happened to your father?"

"He's fine," Fie said. "He's a shrine-keeper now, safe and sound and bored brainless to the end of his days." Then she connected why he'd noticed. "I'm sorry about the king."

He shook his head, rueful. "You don't have to pretend for my sake."

A steward hurried over before the prince could elaborate. "Your Highness, am I to understand that these . . . *guests* will be situated in proximity to your tent?"

"Beside it." Jasimir waved a hand from the man to Fie. "Fie, this is Burzo, my aunt's steward. He'll be assisting us in situating you and your band. Though we can arrange for you to, ah, share quarters with Tav."

"We can?" Steward Burzo blinked, eyes darting between her and Tavin.

"I'd prefer it, if that's fine by you, Fie," Tavin said, still storm-faced. "Apparently there are Hawks who have time to waste hassling Crows. I don't want any chances taken with their safety here."

Fie hesitated. The prospect of a little privacy had almost more appeal than it ought to. That didn't mean she could just leave her band on their own, though.

Lakima caught her eye. "We'll continue to keep watch." The rest of Fie's Hawks nodded, looking nigh as vexed as Tavin.

The steward worried his bottom lip. "Surely the guards on duty will be sufficient."

"You heard Tavin," Jasimir said, steely. "No chances."

"Understood, Your Highness. Ah—if I may." He brushed a dusty patch off Jasimir's sleeve. "I'll see to—"

Something very peculiar happened then, and it happened very fast:

Fie heard the clatter of a spear dropping, saw a blur of leather armor and dark hair, stumbled as it passed between her and Tavin. Then the next thing she knew, Khoda was trying to wrench the steward's arms behind his back.

Burzo twisted swift as an adder, slashing out with a dagger Fie hadn't seen on him before. Khoda whipped away with ease, then swept the steward's feet out from beneath him. In a trice he had a knee on Burzo's back, holding the man facedown in the flatway dust.

"Look." Khoda forced Burzo's hand open. Fie crouched beside them, peering down.

On his palm lay a single strand of dark hair—Fie's, plucked from Jasimir's sleeve.

Fie sucked in a breath. If delivered to Rhusana, that hair was all it would take for the Swan Queen to bend Fie to her will.

"This man isn't working for the Hawks," Khoda said, flicking the hair out of Burzo's reach.

There was a ring, and the second peculiar thing happened then and there: Tavin had drawn one of his short swords, the point leveled at Khoda's throat.

"No, he isn't," Tavin said, "and neither are you."

CHAPTER EIGHT

THE CROWN

"THEY'RE CALLED THE BLACK SWANS." MASTER-GENERAL DRAGA'S voice was calm enough, but she paced about the tent like a tiger pestered by a persistent bloodfly. "Always thought the name was a touch melodramatic. They're spies."

Fie would not put good odds on that bloodfly; nor did she put good odds on Khoda or Steward Burzo, both bound hand and foot. They knelt on plain, sturdy woven mats in the master-general's tent before Tavin, Fie, Jasimir, and Draga herself. They'd offered surprisingly little resistance to being hustled straight to Draga; Khoda had just seemed resigned, and the steward utterly baffled.

Khoda straightened up now, looking almost indignant as he jerked his chin at the steward. "He's not one of ours. And we prefer to be called *specialists*."

"Specialists in infiltrating other castes, gathering key intelligence, and reporting back to their spymaster, the monarch, and myself." Draga folded her arms, coming to a halt beside a rack of spears. "*Spies.* I understand you're trained in identifying potential threats. What do you call a Swan agent embedded with one of Rhusana's prime targets?"

"An asset," Khoda said shortly. "I can assure you, the Black Swans have absolutely no desire to see Rhusana on the throne. If I were on her side, she'd already have Fie's hair."

"That's a fair point," Jasimir allowed.

Fie wasn't sure any of it was a fair point. A whole moon, a *whole moon* Khoda had been spying on her and her band. The notion made her skin crawl. Aye, he'd run off Oleanders, he'd kept watch, he'd played the part of a Hawk all too well. None of it meant a damn if he'd done it to buy his way into her graces.

Tavin shook his head as he moved about the tent, lighting lamps with a fingertip against the waning daylight. "We can't trust anything he says until it's verified by a Crane witch."

"No need to wait." Fie pushed a witch-tooth free from her string with perhaps more enthusiasm than was appropriate. Any Crane tooth could spot lies from him; a witch-tooth could force him to speak plain truth.

Fie rolled the molar between her palms and looked to the master-general. "Who first?"

As Khoda opened his mouth to protest, Draga tapped the crown of his head. He slumped over in a healer's sleep. "Steward Burzo."

The tooth-spark snapped to attention at Fie's call, a stringent old magistrate with little patience for criminals and even less for liars. "How long have you been working for the queen?"

Burzo blinked up at her, and the truth slipped out of him far more easily than she expected: "I don't know."

"You don't know how long or you didn't know you were working for her?" Jasimir asked.

"I didn't know I was working for her," Burzo answered.

Tavin seized his shirt and yanked him close. "You tried to take Fie's hair. You tried to kill her guard. Who do you *think* you were working for?"

"I don't know," Burzo sputtered.

Fie set a hand on Tavin's arm and shook her head. "He's telling the truth."

The master-general waited until her son let the steward go. "Burzo. *Why* did you do all that?"

"I . . ." The tooth-spark gave a hitch, like a net tugging on a bewildered fish. Burzo's open face said as much, his mouth pursing as he searched for words. "I . . . wanted to."

Fie and Draga traded glances, and the master-general tapped Burzo on the back of the skull. He wilted into a healer's sleep as well.

"First the skin monsters, now this." Draga rubbed a thumb between her brows, scowling at the ground. "The Swans have always been cagey about the extent of their witches' powers, but . . . Rhusana knew when to push Burzo into taking Fie's hair. There's a chance that she can see what he sees or hear what he hears. We'll keep him under watch until Rhusana's dealt with."

Fie rolled the tooth a little too hard against her thumb. Spies in her band, spies in Jas's camp, and no knowing what secrets they'd stolen. If one more spy popped out of the woodwork, she was going to skip the questions and go straight to cutting throats.

When Khoda was dragged out of his sleep, he took in the unconscious huddle of Steward Burzo, then smirked at the rest of the tent. "I bet *that* was frustrating."

Tavin looked ready to haul him about by the collar, too, but Draga held up a hand, face impassive as she stared down at Khoda. "What makes you say that?"

Khoda's smile didn't waver as he cocked his head. "I'm going to make a few guesses here, and you'll tell me if I'm off the mark. Burzo didn't know how long he was under Rhusana's control. He didn't know he was under her control, *period*. He *also* didn't know what he wanted Fie's hair for, only that he wanted to take it." His gaze swept across all their faces. "Save your breath. I can tell I'm three for three."

"This is why I hate spies," Draga muttered into her hands. She turned to the rest of the tent, eyes lingering on Fie. "Before we go any further, you all need to understand that whatever you hear does not leave this tent. The Black Swans don't deal in gossip; they deal in the kind of secrets that hold nations together. If you can't keep those secrets, leave."

"Unless you're her." Khoda nodded at Fie. "You definitely need her."

Draga looked sore tempted to knock him out again. "Let's get on with it. What do you know about Rhusana?"

"Not as much as I'd like," Khoda answered, eyes on Fie and her Crane witch-tooth. For some, the truth was a knot to unwind; for others, a thorn to ease out. Fie hadn't drawn truth from someone like Khoda before: what ought to have been stone-solid was instead slippery as an eel and thrice as hard to pin down. That made it all the harder to believe she was getting the whole truth.

"What does that mean?" Fie prodded.

"We haven't been able to get anyone embedded close enough to her to provide hard information. If we could, the king would still be alive."

Fie heard Jasimir suck in a breath behind her.

"The Black Swans believe in keeping the nation stable and whole," Khoda continued, "and in preserving the rightful order. Only Phoenixes are trained to rule the kingdom, and the kingdom will only accept Ambra's blood for a ruler. By birth and by competence, Rhusana is unfit for the throne, and we will do everything we can to keep her off it."

Draga resumed pacing, arms folded. "At least we agree there."

"Why were you following Fie?" Tavin asked, stony.

Khoda shrugged. His truth shifted and slid about, impossible for Fie to force to direct words. "I was already at Trikovoi, and we thought Rhusana might strike at her to distract the prince. Clearly we were right."

"What do you know of the queen's powers?" Jasimir asked, rubbing his chin.

"We *know* nothing," Khoda answered. "We *think* she's a witch. According to Swan records, her father was a Vulture, but the Swan rituals should have guaranteed she'd be born a Swan. A similar ritual should have guaranteed she'd lose her Birthright when she married into the Phoenix caste. We suspect she learned how to thwart those rituals from her mother. And if she was born a witch, with a dual Birthright like Prince Tavin"—it was Tavin's turn to make a noise, albeit one of disgust at the word *prince*—"then she'd have a Swan's ability to manipulate people and a Vulture's command over skin."

"So you get the skin-ghasts," Fie concluded. They'd known for nigh two moons that the ghasts were Rhusana's work, yet there was something dreadful in knowing *how*. "And no one notices her because you already have all three Swan witches. Not the most outlandish theory."

Khoda nodded. "By our count, there should be seventy-eight Vulture witches at all times, one for each of their dead gods. According to our sources, only seventy-seven are accounted for."

"Is it even possible?" Jasimir asked. "The dead gods founded their own castes. Can they be reborn into a different one?"

The Black Swan's glance flicked for the briefest moment to Fie before darting away again. He said evenly, "It wouldn't be the first time."

Fie caught her breath. It didn't have to mean aught; maybe he'd just looked her way to gauge her focus on the tooth.

Still, Little Witness's words echoed back to her: *You are not what you were.*

Whatever Khoda knew about that, she could pry out of him later, without Draga and the lordlings for an audience.

"Doesn't matter how she got her powers, just that she'll keep using them," Fie said. "So where does she foul up? What are her weaknesses?"

Khoda gave an impatient sigh. "Again, we don't have anyone close to her, so it's hard to say. From what we've observed . . . she jumps to easy answers, and she's prone to underestimating people she thinks beneath her. King Surimir never would have handed you Phoenix teeth."

"Do you think she murdered my father?" Jasimir's voice frayed at the very edges.

This time, the truth cut straight from Khoda, unflinching. "I absolutely do. But as with your mother, there's no proof."

Draga straightened at the mention of her sister. "You believe she assassinated Jasindra?"

Khoda hesitated. For the first time, he seemed uncertain how to answer. "Not . . . directly. Only one of our agents saw the queen close-up before the king sealed her chambers and ordered her body burned. They found finger-shaped bruises on her throat. Rhusana wouldn't have been able to overpower a former Hawk like Queen Jasindra. But . . ."

"Surimir could." Tavin's voice rang hollow.

Khoda nodded, grim. "We have no proof. However, it was no secret the king had been visiting Rhusana's pavilion for moons—"

Khoda cut himself off as Prince Jasimir turned on a heel and walked out of the tent.

"I'll go after him." Fie let the Crane tooth fizzle out and tossed it aside, then caught Tavin's hand a moment. "Can you make sure the band's squared away?"

He brushed a quick kiss against her cheek. "Yes, chief."

She sent a warning glare to Khoda and strode out.

Lakima was waiting outside with her three remaining Hawks, looking uneasy as they held a human barrier between the Crows and the rest of the camp, which looked even uneasier for the Crows' presence. Wretch saw Fie and waved a thumb at the river. "His Highness went that way."

"Thanks," Fie called. "Tavin's going to help you get settled. I'll be there in a bit."

A moment later she realized skipping through the Hawk camp by herself was not the greatest notion she'd had all moon. When she turned to Lakima, the corporal was already falling into step behind her as the other guards split off with the band. Fie raised her brows at her.

"You're being targeted by the queen," Lakima said blandly, even as she sized up the nearby Hawks. "Anyone could be a threat."

"Aye," Fie said, and knew she and Lakima both understood it didn't take a queen's influence for that.

They found Jasimir standing by the makeshift mammoth pen, snapping carrots in half and dumping them into a pail as one of the beasts lumbered over. Barf the tabby sat by his side, tail flicking in the grass. She'd had a shine for Jasimir since he'd saved her from a burning cart. Two Hawk guards maintained a respectful distance and a watchful eye; one held up a hand as they approached.

"It's fine," Jasimir said wearily. "Give us some room, please."

Fie had found mimicking the Hawk salute only annoyed them, and so she did just that, and pretended not to relish the guards' sour looks as she passed.

"Do you want to talk about it?" she asked once she was close enough to keep her voice low. The Hawks had stepped a few more paces away, but she wouldn't risk one of them running their mouth.

"What's there to talk about?" Jasimir threw a fistful of carrottops to the mammoth. Sunset had dyed the clouds above lily orange, turning his gold circlet to a band of clean fire cutting through his dark hair. "Everyone else knew he was a monster. I'm the only fool in the kingdom who ever thought otherwise."

Fie watched the mammoth gleefully cram carrots into its mouth. "You thought Rhusana killed your mother. You're probably right. What's it matter if she made your pa do it instead of soiling her own hands?"

"Because it means some part of him wanted Mother dead," Jasimir said, bleak. That much was true; a Swan witch could only twist desires, not create them. "And that's—that's my *father*. He's half of me. He's the only king I've ever known. How am I supposed to believe I'll be any better on the throne?"

"You can't," Fie said immediately. "'Better' isn't what you think you are. Better is what you *do*." The mammoth huffed their way, and she threw it another carrottop. "Your father was a monster, aye. But I'd rather either of his sons sit on the throne than anyone else. And Tavin's spoken for, so that leaves you to take the crown."

They didn't speak for a moment, though true silence was thwarted by the rush of the Vine and the clamor of soldiers sparring, mending armor, and throwing gambling shells in the camp at their backs. The mammoth finished its supply of carrottops and pressed closer to the fence, snuffling about the grass for any it might have missed.

"I really thought—" Jas cut himself off as his voice cracked, then cleared his throat and tried again. "I told you I wanted to save him."

"Aye," Fie said cautiously.

Jas's knuckles paled as he gripped the fence. "I thought I could change him. I thought—I thought I could save him—"

Fury and despair shattered over his face. His foot crashed into the pail. It sailed into the mammoth pen, scattering carrot bits into the grass. The mammoth jerked its head back with a *whuff*, steel charms tinkling on its tusks as the Hawk guards glanced briefly over their shoulders to make sure the only victims were the vegetables. Barf, for her part, simply stopped washing a paw and leapt up on the fence to rub her face on Jasimir's arm.

"I couldn't even save my own *mother* from him!" Jasimir hissed. "I knew I'd been living with a murderer for the last six years. I didn't know I'd been living with *two*."

Fie had the terrible suspicion that the hazy rules of friendship dictated she ought to hug the prince. She also had the absolute certainty that doing so would only further upset them both.

Instead she stiffly patted him on the back. "Rhusana's got a baby, aye?"

Jasimir nodded, eyes glittering. "Rhusomir. She barely lets anyone see him."

"Do you blame him at all for any of this?"

The prince blinked. "He's *two*. I was eleven."

"But you were still a child, aye?" Fie pushed. "And your ma was a warrior and a queen. What were *you* supposed to do?"

"*Anything*." Jasimir looked like he wanted to kick something else. Instead he absently scratched Barf's ears. "I can't even say I didn't see it."

Fie pursed her lips. "Sometimes . . . when I call a Peacock tooth or a Hawk tooth, or even sometimes another Phoenix tooth, I get this *feeling* from it. Depends on the person. Tells me to be quiet, to not make trouble, to look away and move along. It's always these . . . these scummers who knew how bad it could be with a bad person under the crown, but they didn't care as long as the bad royal wasn't hurting *them*." She shrugged. "Sometimes the bad royal would give them aught like a bauble or a sweet talk, keep them addicted to it like poppy-sniffers, and so long as they kept their fine ways and got a chance for another whiff, they'd pretend all was right."

She flicked a bit of carrot into the mammoth pen. "You were eleven, and all the adults around you were telling you naught was wrong. That's no fault of yours."

He nodded, face painfully taut. "There's . . . there's so much to undo."

"Aye" was all Fie had to say.

He pushed off from the fence. "We should get you back to your band."

The Hawks peeled from their posts to trail them as they headed back toward Draga's tent, Barf trotting behind them. "We're only a day and a half's march from Dumosa," he told her. "But of course you and yours are welcome to stay with us as long as you need."

Fie caught looks from the camp's soldiers as they passed: curious, befuddled, a few souring as they lingered on her. "Likely we'll stick with you until you're seated proper on the throne, but unless you hurry, you'll want us back on the roads soon as possible. People are trying to burn their own plague-dead."

He winced. "How bad is it?"

"We had to burn Karostei to ash. Nigh a quarter of the people burned with it." She shuddered. "And Rhusana made ghasts of the dead, so she won't be setting the record straight anytime soon."

Jasimir turned uphill as they passed the master-general's tent. Not far ahead, she saw Tavin laughing with her Crows as they maneuvered the supply wagon around the tents. Lakima's Hawks maintained their wall between them and the rest of the camp, and Fie doubted their grim faces were due solely to Khoda's absence.

Jasimir didn't miss it, either. "I'll tell Aunt Draga about Karostei, but she may want to hear it from you. And I'll tell her your guards could use some reinforcements."

The prince did them one better: once Fie's Crows were settled to her satisfaction, he personally escorted them to the nearest mess tent and joined them for supper. Fie couldn't help but remember moons earlier, when he and Tavin had scrambled to wash up before her band could foul the water; she suspected they both were glad those days were behind them.

Tavin excused himself halfway through their meal, and she didn't see him again until after the sun had gone down. Jasimir had awkwardly pointed out his brother's tent on their way back to where the Crows had made camp. The warm orange glow of an oil lamp soaked through the canvas walls, Tavin's shadow a soft, distinct blur against the light. Fie made a mental note to douse the lamp before doing anything she didn't want to hear crudely recounted by Madcap the next morning.

She glanced back for one more look at her band, who were unrolling their sleeping mats beside the fire. Corporal Lakima stood guard, no more relaxed in a camp full of soldiers than she'd been on the open road. She caught Fie's eye and gave her a slight nod: all would be well under her watch.

Fie returned the nod and slipped into Tavin's tent.

It wasn't much more than canvas pitched high enough to stand in, not even bothering to lay a dropcloth over the grass, but Fie saw bits of him in every corner: his sword belts looped through a support to keep them off the ground, a wooden crate with leather armor stacked neat inside, a modest collection of scrolls.

Tavin himself had stretched out on his belly on a tight-woven woolen blanket in the far corner, and by Fie's guess, it looked cushy enough to be hiding a straw pallet underneath. The oil lamp nearby caught on a scroll unfurled in his hands, one he was frowning at until Fie walked in.

"It's worse than I remember," he grumbled, tossing the parchment aside.

She glanced at it and found square what she expected: *The Thousand Conquests*. "Told you it was awful."

"It's all awful." Tavin propped himself up on his elbows as Fie sat nearby and began to unwind her sandal straps.

Halfway through one foot, a slice of gold caught her eye. She blinked and spotted a circlet like Jasimir's, only this one was buried—spitefully, she suspected—under a heap of dirty laundry. She let out a cackle and swiped it free. "What is *this*?"

"Auugh." He hid his face in the blanket. "Mother said I wasn't allowed to throw it away." He emerged again. "I'm probably supposed to wear it again tomorrow . . . Speaking of awful, the lord of the manor's coming to have dinner with Mother and Jas tomorrow, and we have to go."

Fie twisted about to look at him, still holding the circlet. "'We'?"

"I told her I wouldn't go if you couldn't."

"And that was supposed to get you out of it." She dropped the circlet on his head. It landed askew, slipping over one ear.

Tavin gave a rueful grin and pulled the circlet off. "Guilty. Mother called my bluff. I shouldn't have said we *have* to go; I don't know if you need to stay with your band. Would you *like* to join me for dinner with the lord of the manor tomorrow?" He dropped the circlet on Fie's head, where it sat even worse, sliding to rest just over her brows. Still, he pulled a polished-brass mirror from a nearby crate and handed it to her. "There. Much better."

Fie tried not to stare at her reflection, at the bar of bright gold striping her forehead.

She tried not to admit how some ancient ache in her bones stirred at the sight. How somewhere deep down, eons away, lives and lives and lives past . . . some part of her felt whole for wearing a crown.

She tossed her head swift and hard, and the circlet popped off with a mellow ring, rolling to lay in the grass like a snake eating its own tail.

"Too big for me," Fie said, and she didn't know that for a truth or a lie. "But likely I can manage dinner."

Tavin reached up to twist a lock of her hair in his fingers. Then his smile splintered a bit. He ducked his head, patting down the blankets of his bed as he searched for something, and a moment later he surfaced with a pair of sewing shears. "I . . . have another favor to ask."

Fie continued unwinding her sandal straps. "If it's to cut the lawn, you'll need bigger shears."

He shook his head. "Will you cut my hair?"

She stopped, letting the leather sandal strap fall to the grass, and cocked her head. "I like your hair." That was the truth: it had grown out a bit since she'd left Trikovoi, curling about his ears long enough to bury her hands in when she felt like it.

Tavin gave a half shrug, staring at the shears. "Fie . . . Burzo has been in my mother's service before I was born. If all it took was a hair for Rhusana to turn him, I don't want to—I *can't* take any chances."

He'd held up a steady front all evening, teasing Lakima and jesting with Varlet, but the scratch in his voice said this wasn't just about Burzo.

Fie reached out, turned his chin until he met her eyes. "You're not the king."

He swallowed. "That's not enough."

And in her bones, Fie knew he was right. She took up the shears. "I'll need rags and water."

Once Tavin's hair lay in damp waves against his skull, she got to work. She'd watched Wretch trim hair short often enough, and usually with no more than the chief's blade or a shard of broken pottery. Shears made for much quicker work, and it wasn't long before the rags covering Tavin's shoulders had darkened with shorn hair.

Something about the silence felt too grim for Fie to abide. "How did you know Khoda for a Swan?"

"When he pushed me aside, I . . . felt it," Tavin explained. "The Hawk witch-finders trained me to read caste in the blood, in case any assassins tried disguising themselves." He blew out a breath. "Not that it was good for much. He's been spying on you since before I arrived, and I didn't notice a thing until today."

Fie raised an eyebrow he couldn't see. There was something both tiresome and delicious about what sounded like jealousy from Tavin. "Reckon that's all that bothered you?" she prodded, tugging another lock between her fingers.

To her surprise, he answered swift and blunt: "The guard on the road. I don't care that he was a . . . How did you put it?"

"Dung-sucking dog-lover?"

He gave an exaggerated dreamy sigh. "You have such a way with words. I'm used to people like him. But I can't stop wondering, how many of them are Hawks?"

"Plenty. But you saw it yourself—he backed down when Jas showed up. They care about the lad at the top, and if he fancies Crows, they'll learn to do it, too."

Whatever Tavin had to say to that, he kept to himself, and Fie was more than willing to distract herself with running her fingers through his hair. She'd cut near all of it down no higher than a knuckle-width when he asked, "Do you feel safe here?"

Fie fumbled the shears.

She had the protection of a prince and a master-general, two swords, a bag of teeth. Yet not a dozen paces away, even in the middle of scores of the kingdom's finest warriors, Corporal Lakima still kept watch over Fie's band.

"Safe enough," she lied.

The last curl fell to Tavin's shoulder with a decisive snip. She bundled the rags off his shoulders, taking care not to let any hair fall loose. "There. Done. We'll throw this in the river tomorrow."

Tavin twisted about on his knees, and when she looked up, she wasn't quite sure who she saw. It wasn't just that his hair no longer softened the harsher lines of his jaw; it was his face. Even when things had been at their most dire on the road, even when she'd nigh killed herself burning too many teeth or he'd good as killed himself letting the Vultures take him, he'd kept the faintest embers of a grin or a jest, like letting them go cold meant some kind of surrender.

She couldn't see any ghost of laughter in him now.

"Fie." He cradled her face in his hands. "I—I will *never* let anything happen to you. No matter what. You know that, don't you?"

Fie didn't know why the notion made her eyes burn, why it stole the words from her burning throat. Then she thought of Pa, tears streaming down his face as he said in wonder, *I'm . . . home.*

She reached to douse the lamp, voice cracking. "I know."

As he drew her to him, she whispered the most terrible truth she knew against the pulse of his neck: "I feel safe with you."

It wasn't that he watched her back, put her at ease, or made her soft in ways she both reveled in and despised. Fuss as she might, she loved him for those and more.

The terrible part was one they both knew and neither could say into the dark: he made her feel safe, and that was not enough.

A quarter hour into the dinner with Lord Geramir, Fie had learned three facts about the man.

First, he was wholly, predictably insufferable, shoveling praise onto the prince and the master-general like dung into flower beds, yet curling his lips at Fie and Tavin as if they were the ones who reeked.

Second, he was deeply insecure, boasting of his expensive Dovecraft robes, his unmatched vineyards, how often the regional governor invited him to dine in his grand fortress in Zarodei.

And third: judging from the way he couldn't stop staring at Fie, he was *terrified* of her.

Not that she was doing much to soothe his nerves, staring right back at him, jaw clenched, as he dithered, "We'll all just be *so* relieved when this . . . unpleasantness blows over."

Fie was weighing how much longer she could abide the company of the Peacock lord. Draga had promised she wouldn't even need to say aught, just enjoy a fine dinner with Tavin, and like a fool, Fie had believed her. Instead she'd had to leave her swords and teeth in Tavin's tent, don a laughably large tunic of Draga's, and pretend she didn't want to drown Geramir in the soup course.

"I'm sure His Highness will remember your hospitality," Draga said crisply, not even blinking as a serving boy set a plate of fine greens and plum-drenched beef before her. The master-general had apparently insisted Lord Geramir come to them if he wanted the prince's ear, and he had not arrived empty-handed, bringing a host of his own Sparrow servants and platter after gleaming platter of Hassuran delicacies.

Now those same servants swarmed thick as bees about the tent, which had been set up just for this dinner as far as Fie could tell. It wasn't near big enough for all the attendants darting about with trays, bowls, platters, pitchers, and more; it was made all the worse as they tried to give Fie a wide berth, turning her corner of the table into an oasis in a storm. Fie had been sure to scrub herself even cleaner than the prince, but the servants had apparently caught word that a Crow would be in attendance.

"Lord Geramir," Jas said, "are you aware some towns are attempting to burn their own plague-dead?"

The Peacock lord coughed into his wine goblet. A plate landed before Fie with a thud. The server scuttled away near as abrupt as they'd appeared.

Lord Geramir dabbed at his mouth with a fine silk hand towel, then flicked it away for a server to pluck from the ground. "I'm sure they're just following the queen's example."

Fie snuck a look at Draga to see how she'd gone about managing the slab of beef. It seemed to involve the delicate forked tongs beside her plate. She didn't miss Geramir's uneasy glance when she picked up a silver knife.

"I would appreciate it if you made it clear to your arbiters that the Crows must handle any outbreaks." Jasimir's own knife scraped against the plate as he sliced through the beef. "It's not safe for anyone else to dispose of the bodies."

Lord Geramir bobbed his head. "This will all pass soon enough."

"Geramir." Draga set her forked tongs down. "The words you're looking for are 'Yes, Your Highness.'"

He squirmed, tugging at his collar. "It would be unseemly to directly contradict Her Majesty . . . There are those who would think I am showing favoritism to, er, to the . . ." Geramir's gaze skimmed over Fie and Tavin a moment before darting back to his plate. "You know what I *mean*."

"Do I?" Tavin asked, artificially pleasant. The lamplight gleamed off the circlet sitting in his short-cropped hair as he tilted his head.

Draga cleared her throat, but Prince Jasimir blinked at the

governor, slow and deliberate. "I'm afraid we *don't* know what you mean, Lord Geramir." He let the Peacock fidget a moment. "If you're saying your only two options are to let the Crows continue to keep the Sinner's Plague in check as they've done for centuries, or to let your land rot because this week's queen told you to, the choice seems fairly obvious to me."

"No, of course . . ." Geramir looked about for another hand towel, then settled for dabbing his brow with a sleeve. "I'm just saying, you can issue your own orders after you're crowned a week from now, and it makes no sense for me to burn bridges when we could just wait it out—"

"'Wait it out'?"

The tent fell silent as everyone looked at Fie. She was staring at the Peacock lord, cheeks burning.

"I'm not particularly concerned," Geramir said, waving a hand. "The arbiters know what's best for their towns, and—"

"The arbiter of Karostei was the one turning away Crows," Fie snapped, anger spiking up her gut. "He died wearing the Sinner's Brand, along with a quarter of Karostei. We left that town in ashes. Can a quarter of your population *wait it out*?"

Lord Geramir's face darkened. "This is absurd," he said. "Did you ever consider you might be *biased* because it's your job to take the dead? You're wading around in it all day, but—"

"You aren't concerned that the plague will reach your home." This time, it was Jasimir who cut him off. Lord Geramir shrank a bit but gave a noncommittal shrug. "Do you think my father died of the plague?"

"Her . . . Her Majesty says so," Geramir stammered.

Fie made herself put her knife down. "But you don't think *you* could catch it. You think the gentry are above the plague."

"It's called the Sinner's Plague for a reason," he returned. He picked up his goblet, found it empty, and set it back down with a scowl.

"Forgive my indelicacy, Your Highness, but your father was not . . . known for his temperance. Besides, surely the Covenant would not have sent someone *unfit* to the Peacock caste—"

"Last week I cut the throat of the Sakar girl," Fie said. "You know the family? Nice estate up north. Beautiful cedars. No more children. Their only heir showed the Brand at sunrise, and I burned her corpse by sundown. Not four days ago I watched the plague take the Karostei arbiter where he stood for damning a hundred souls rather than call for Crows. You can tell yourself what you please about the Covenant, and you can tell yourself the plague's no concern of yours. One way or another, you'll still feed me and mine."

For the first time, fear flashed through the Peacock lord's eyes. But something about it struck her as wrong—and then she placed it.

Peacocks got a certain look when the plague took one of their own: rattled, as they could no longer deny that, for all their fine ways and sturdy walls, their house was vulnerable as any other.

But Geramir didn't look like a man invaded by doubt. His fear was that of the gambler who'd wagered the whole of his fortune only to realize that the bones had landed bad.

The hush over the table stretched unnaturally long.

It took Fie a moment to ken why: the only people in the tent were seated at the table.

"Where are the servants?" she asked, and the weight of the quiet seemed to push back. The camp ought to have been ringing with noise as they prepared to march at dawn. Her stool tipped as she bolted to her feet, heart pounding.

No—not just her heart. A rumble shook the earth, then another and another, turning the table into a clattering mess. Strange, low cries echoed through the walls of the tent.

For all its soldiers, the camp was no safer than any other house.

And from the flicker in Master-General Draga's eyes, that realization was dawning.

Fie started for the tent flap. Tavin caught her shoulder. "Wait, we don't know what's—"

"No—" She twisted free and stumbled out of his reach. "My band—I need to—"

Fie yanked the tent flap aside and found—nothing.

Twilight had drenched the camp in dark, dusty shades of blue, but not so much as a breeze stirred the canvas, stillness lying like a fog over the rows and rows of tents. Then Fie picked out darker, stunted shapes along the lanes: Hawk soldiers staring into the oncoming night, faces blank.

Every single one was on their knees.

Something monstrous and impossible swelled near the banks of the river, then a second, then a score. Fie heard Tavin's sharp breath at her back but couldn't tear her eyes away; her head couldn't quite process what she saw until it was too clear to deny.

Not a hundred paces off, bleeding, empty mammoth skins swayed in an unyielding march toward them, trampling an unswerving path through tent and frozen Hawk alike.

And above the muffled screams and the crunch of tentpoles, clear, musical chimes pierced the air, needle-sharp.

More empty-faced Hawks stamped up the path in inhumanly even time, bearing a glittering covered sedan on their shoulders. Gauzy white silk curtains fluttered demurely with each step, dusk catching on the silver and pearl wrought into its supports.

"Fie," Tavin said, "please, get behind me."

Jasimir's voice rose behind them before she could argue. "Tav—"

Fie's belly dropped further. She knew that tone. She finally tore her eyes away to look back.

Lord Geramir had drawn a dagger on Jasimir. That wasn't what had stopped the prince in his tracks, though, one hand frozen halfway to a knife up a sleeve.

What had stopped Jasimir was the blade Draga now held at his throat.

There was no way out.

There was no way out for any of them.

The footsteps of the sedan-bearers stopped with a flourish of chimes; the thunder of mammoth footfalls persisted like a dwindling pulse.

In a whisper of satin and a cascade of silvery-white hair, Queen Rhusana glided out from the curtains of the sedan, drawing herself up to her full height. The shadows of mammoths rose behind her like a tide.

A shallow smile sliced across her face like the birth of a waxing moon.

"I'm here to make a deal," she said.

CHAPTER NINE

—— NEVER ——

The last time Fie had been in Draga's tent, Khoda and Steward Burzo had knelt before them.

Now she was the one on her knees, a knifepoint pressed between her shoulder blades to keep her there. Jasimir stood at her side between her and Tavin. Both lordlings had been allowed to stay on their feet, but their hands were bound behind their backs like hers, with a half dozen Hawks just waiting for either of them to make a move. Lanterns pressed muted light against the canvas walls, the daylight long fled.

"I have to admit, I'm proud of this one," Rhusana allowed as she slipped through the tent flap. The master-general herself stood at guard outside, face rigid and blank. "Your aunt wants so much, Jasimir, and yet hurting you . . . not an option." She shook her head, drifting to a halt before the three of them. Chimes in her headdress tinkled, swaying with thick snow-white braids that hung in intricate loops along the sides of her skull, crowning a long, sleek fall of unadorned hair. "She doesn't even want her own son on the throne. It took some *real* creativity to find a way in."

Sweat was beading along the queen's upper lip. Rhusana might be a witch like her, but they were both still human. A display like this had to be pushing her limits.

"You can't hold the whole camp like this much longer," Fie spat.

Rhusana locked eyes with someone behind Fie and inclined her head. The tip of the knife sank, just a hair, into her back. Fie yelped and jerked forward.

"When I want a parasite's opinion, I'll ask the Peacocks," the queen said, smooth as silk, and nodded again. The tip of the knife dug into Fie's back once, twice, less than a knuckle deep but far enough to draw blood.

"*STOP*—" Tavin jolted forward only for a Hawk to lodge their spear between his knees. He stumbled to the ground. The Hawk pressed the spearhead to his throat.

"She's right," Tavin snarled into the grass. "You can't keep Mother in check forever. She's fighting you, isn't she?"

Rhusana glowered down at him. "You always did underestimate me. She may not want to hurt Jasimir, but killing him would hurt the king's legacy. Believe me, her desire for *that* runs deeper than a god's grave. And once I feel like letting her go . . ." She flicked a hand and the spear lifted from Tavin's neck. "I have hostages. So if we're done with the pleasantries, we have business to discuss. Believe it or not, I'm not just here to show off."

"Which of you killed my mother?" Jasimir rasped, the first time he'd spoken since they'd been captured. "You? Or Father?"

Rhusana rolled her shoulders. "I didn't ask him to do anything he didn't want. But that's in the past. It's time to think of Sabor's future."

"What do you care about Sabor?" Tavin pushed himself back up onto his knees, eyes burning.

"It's my home," Rhusana answered, "whether it wants me or not. Something I think *you* of all people would be familiar with, as the king's toy bastard. Regardless, this"—she waved a glittering, gem-armored hand at the walls of the tent—"isn't good for the country. Asking them to pick sides, asking them to choose a new queen over a worn-out dynasty. No one wants a civil war; they just want to go about their lives like always. They want stability."

"And how does fouling up plague outbreaks help *stability*?" Fie spat.

She heard the knife shift in the grip of the Hawk behind her and braced for Rhusana's wrath. Then Tavin barked, "Touch her again and I will die stopping you. Try keeping your hold on Mother then."

The Hawk behind her went still as the queen's silver-clawed fingers curled into a fist.

"The outbreaks," Rhusana said slowly, "are a reminder that every caste fears the same thing. I want to unite the country as it has never been united before, beyond our outdated divisions, by uniting us against a common threat. We will no longer be twelve castes but one nation."

A chill ran down Fie's spine.

"I'm not following. You'll unite Sabor against the plague?" Tavin asked.

"Against the Crows." Fie wanted to laugh; she wanted to scream.

"Both, really," the queen admitted. "Most of the country can't tell the difference. They're already on my side, whether they know it or not. Everything they lose to the plague, they'll blame it on the Crows, and nothing brings people together like a common foe. In the meantime, they'll adapt to handling plague-dead on their own, and any Crow with an ounce of sense will find some other nation to pollute."

Jasimir stared at the queen a long moment. Then he said, "I don't know what you're going to offer us, and I don't care. I don't want any part of it."

Some part of Fie eased at that, even if she didn't want to own to it. It didn't change that they were prisoners with enemies at every side, but if she'd lost Jas, she'd lose all hope.

She just had to let Rhusana gloat and preen and burn out her strength on the camp. Then Jas and Tavin could do something clever to buy Fie time, and she'd get her teeth, and they'd save her band, and—and—

There was still a way out.

There had to be.

Rhusana was laughing. "We don't have to do things *my* way. I told you I was here to make a deal. I want to arrive in Dumosa tomorrow with Prince Jasimir at my side, and I want us to be coronated together as King and Queen of Sabor, to give the traditionalists the descendant of Ambra they want. Rhusomir will be our heir, and your brother will be kept as a very comfortable hostage, to guarantee the master-general's obedience. You'll be of your own independent mind, free of my influence. We'll rule a united Sabor." She extended a hand to Jasimir, then realized his hands were still bound and brushed a lock of hair from his temple. "You'll be able to come home."

Jasimir spat in her face.

"You may be willing to sell the Crows for your throne," he said, cold and dark and sharp as obsidian. "I won't fail my people. I'd rather die than rule with you."

Something serpentine flickered in Rhusana's pale, silvery eyes. She carefully, gracefully wiped the spittle off her face with a silken sleeve, but Fie saw how her hands shook.

A horribly serene smile flexed across her face. "When I said 'Prince Jasimir,' I didn't mean just you."

She slipped a hand under Tavin's chin and tilted it up.

"Tell me," she murmured, "haven't you wanted to be a king?"

"Tavin, you can't." Jasimir's voice rose. Tavin tried to twist out of her grip, but she tightened her fingers on his jaw.

"You're the eldest. You're the son of a Hawk and a Phoenix, just like your brother. So why does *he* get the crown and you get to pay for it?" She looked pointedly at the burn scar tangled around Tavin's hand, the mark King Surimir had left on him. "Why should *you* suffer for the king's choices?"

Fie ground her teeth, scouring the tent for any scrap of an opportunity she could use while Rhusana's focus was on Tavin. The queen could offer Tavin a hundred thrones, and he'd spurn them all.

Sure enough, Tavin gritted out, "You have nothing to offer me."

"Don't I?" Rhusana tilted her head. "You've already spent so much of your life pretending." Tavin swallowed. "Pretending you had the power to do what you want . . . the power to protect what you care for. Don't you want the real thing?"

The prince's voice shook. "Don't—don't give up on me, Tav."

Rhusana leaned down to whisper in Tavin's ear. The only word Fie caught was *crown*. Then the queen straightened, flicking her hair over her shoulder with a shattered screech of chimes. Tavin looked nauseous.

Beyond that, though—a flicker of hunger.

A thick, sickening hush curdled over the tent.

Tavin's eyes landed on Fie, and for the second time that night, her blood ran cold.

She knew that look. She'd seen it on a bridge over a dust-choked canyon, screams all around them, moons ago.

I will never *let anything happen to you.*

Tavin turned from her.

"No—" His voice broke, and her heart leapt with a terrible, vain hope that he wouldn't, he *wouldn't* do this to her, not for any price, not even for a crown.

That hope crumpled when he continued, "No . . . harm comes to Fie."

It felt like the moment he'd cut the ropes of the bridge, stone cold and irreparable. But this time, only Tavin stood on solid ground. This time, she and Jasimir were falling into the jaws of their foes.

"You *can't!*" she shrieked as Jasimir thundered, "*She will damn Sabor!*"

"That's quite enough of that." Rhusana snapped her fingers. The butt of a spear slammed into the side of Jasimir's jaw. He dropped, eyes shuttering.

"She'll get us all killed," Fie screamed. "Me, Wretch, Madcap, Pa. You can't—*you can't*—"

"I'm saving what I can." Tavin stared at the ground. "And putting a better king on the throne."

"Twelve *hells* you are—"

"I'm doing this for you," he whispered.

"Remove her," Rhusana ordered.

At that Tavin looked up. "No harm comes to Fie. Swear it."

"I swear," Rhusana said. "She'll be kept in Lord Geramir's mansion for her own safety, and you can"—her lip curled—"*visit* her as you please once things settle down."

Arms stiff as iron yanked Fie to her feet, though she thrashed and clawed and howled like a furious cat.

"You come to me again and I'll tear you apart," she hissed, humiliated to feel hot tracks of tears burning down her cheeks. "You've killed us all, you bastard, *you've killed us all.* I'll cut your throat before you lay so much as one of your traitor hands on me."

He wouldn't look at her.

It took two Hawks to drag her to the tent flap, screaming and twisting and looking for any flash of flesh she could dig her teeth into. Rhusana accompanied them, saying loudly, "Take her to Geramir's estate, with my orders to keep her confined and in good health."

Cold blue night slammed down on Fie's sight as she was hauled outside, only a sliver of golden lantern-light cutting through the sudden muffling dark. It vanished behind Rhusana as she let the tent flap fall, stepping in close to the Hawks.

"Drown her," the queen breathed, then slipped back inside. Her voice rose. "We'll be leaving for Dumosa within the hour . . ."

The last Fie saw of the tent, Tavin still knelt, head bowed, with Prince Jasimir fallen at his side.

She screamed her fury, for all the good it did her, as the two Hawks bore her through the wreckage of a camp she only saw in blurred, convulsing glimpses. She wept and fought and cried out for her teeth, for her swords, for her pa, for anything or anyone, as they passed Hawk after motionless Hawk still on their knees.

Naught came but the clammy damp rising from the river as they drew nearer.

Hysterical laughter gasped through Fie's sobs. She didn't know why, for even a second, she believed the Covenant would answer a Crow.

Maybe Little Witness was wrong. She'd never been destined for aught more than drowning like a rat in a barrel.

Or maybe, in yet another life, Fie had failed.

Her feet slipped and slid on the suddenly slick ground, and for a moment, she thought she'd missed the rush of the river under her own screams. Then the air soured with something heavy and metallic and almost sickly sweet. Fie had cut too many throats to *not* know the smell of blood.

The Hawks bore her past great mounds of meat and tripe, baskets of carrot tops spilled amidst the gore. Black spots speckled every one she saw, and the mammoth handler nearby shared the same glazed look as the rest of the camp.

That was when Fie gave in to pure, rotten laughter. They'd never even once had a chance. Seizing control of Draga, manipulating Geramir— it was all just flash, just Rhusana making it worse because she could. She'd won the moment she had a mammoth handler's hair and given him enough poison to slay all the beasts for their skins.

No wonder the Covenant didn't think her oath was kept. Jasimir had never once been safe.

The moon flashed with a red edge off the river as the Hawks towed Fie in. Mammoth blood had turned the waters flat scarlet.

She was laughing yet when they thrust her beneath the surface.

Blood and muddy river water caught in her nose, in her mouth. She tried to cough them out only for more water to rush in, coppery and gritty and foul.

All Fie could think was that if Tavin had refused, at least she would have died swift.

She gagged, wheezed, inhaled more blood and mud and river. Hands like iron weights kept her under, even as she clawed at them, at elbows and shoulders, trying to find purchase, trying to find a tooth she could rip free, anything—

Tavin had done this, Tavin had damned them all—

She had failed in this life, *she had failed them all*—

—the darkness was sucking her under, the river was eating her whole. One tooth, one breath, one granted prayer, anything, anything, *anything*—

One set of hands suddenly let go, then the second.

She broke the surface. Everything was on fire, her eyes, her throat, her belly—she spewed up the bloody water and aught else she'd eaten that night, gasping and wheezing and crying as hands held her until she steadied.

"We don't have much time," Corporal Lakima grunted, and pulled Fie ashore.

Her band waited there, faces taut with fear and relief. Two huddles of armor and limbs marked the Hawks who'd tried to drown her. Fie didn't care to find if they were alive or dead.

Wretch wiped Fie's face down with a rag and laid a spare cloak round her shoulders.

"H-how?" Fie stammered to Lakima.

The corporal produced a bag and a string: Fie's teeth. A stitch dug in the side of her jaw. "She's trying . . . but . . . she can't make me want to hurt you."

"What about the lordlings?" Madcap asked.

Fie couldn't choke back a sob. She shook her head.

"They're not—she didn't—" Bawd faltered.

"She's taking J-Jas captive," Fie forced out. Lakima held out her swords. Fie took them, then dropped the one from Tavin in the mud. "Tavin is . . . siding with the queen."

After a moment, Lakima picked the sword up, wiping mud off the hilt, and handed it back. "We have a saying in the legions: waste no weapons, least of all your foe's. Don't throw this away." Her stern face turned even harder. "Return it."

Fie wanted to throw it into the river. She wanted to bury it in Tavin's heart. She wanted—

Her grief was a wildfire, her fire was a flood, and both would devour her whole the moment she let them. She couldn't. She *couldn't*.

"You need to go," Lakima said. "Don't tell me where—she'll know. You need to get out before she can look through my eyes."

Varlet's voice broke through the hush. "Do we try to take the prince with us?"

Fie swallowed, agony in her every bone. No fire teeth, only one Hawk, and half-drowned—yet she'd overcome greater odds before. She might die trying to get the prince out, or she might save him yet.

She'd given up everything to keep her end of the oath; she'd left her kin, she'd left her roads, she'd left their ways.

And in this life, same as any other, still she had failed.

She could hear Jas still: *Don't give up on me.*

But she'd been raised on words older and harder than that: *Look after your own.*

That was how Crows had survived. For years, decades, centuries, that was how they'd lived for another dawn.

She'd tried, Covenant help her, she'd *tried* to do right by Sabor, but at the end of the day . . . none of it—not her swords, not her teeth, not her oaths, not the scrolls she read, not the boy she loved—*none* of it would save them.

She might be able to save Jas, but Jas couldn't save them.

Fie shook her head. "We need to go."

Lakima led them along the riverbank, past the eerie quiet of the wrecked camp, up to the bridge over the river. No Hawks blocked the flatway anymore.

"They'll send riders after you. I'll hold the road as long as I can." Lakima planted herself in the pale, moonlit dust as Crows spilled onto the road behind her, and Fie realized she would not see the corporal again.

"Just buy us an hour or two," Fie said. "Then get yourself clear."

"Yes, chief."

Fie's vision streaked with tears. "You're a terrible liar, Lakima."

"Yes, chief." The Hawk allowed a stiff shade of a smile, then turned her back. "Please . . . tell your father I kept my promise."

Fie nodded, her throat nigh too tight to force out aught but a ragged "Thank you."

She didn't have to whistle the marching order for the Crows to know it was time to go.

When they reached the flatway bend, Fie looked back and found Lakima and her spear waiting in the thin moonlight, alone in the empty road.

PART TWO

LOVERS

— AND —

FOES

CHAPTER TEN

THE MESSENGER

THEY RAN FIRST, FOR AS LONG AS THEY COULD WITH CLANKING packs and an unhappy tabby clutched in Madcap's arms.

When Fie's band could run no more, they walked as swift as possible, still heaving for breath, still wordless. Fie kept two Sparrow teeth burning, tossing spent teeth into the brush by the side of the road. Each time the orange glow of a campfire blossomed ahead, she lit a third and felt it ring in her bones like a hammer. No camp sentries looked her band's way as they passed.

She'd learned two moons ago that burning three teeth for too long left her a hollowed wreck, but letting her third Sparrow tooth go each time felt like letting safety slip through her fingers.

By every dead god, she wanted to feel safe again.

They marched on through the bitter dawn, quiet and hurried, and stopped only when hooves thundered up the road. Then they took to the trees, and Fie burned three teeth until the patrol of Hawks passed.

Once the hoofbeats faded, Fie said, "Eat, drink, piss if you need to. Then we get back on the road."

"Where are we going, chief?" Madcap asked.

Fie opened her mouth to answer—then thought of Lakima and closed it. A moment later she said, "North, and that's all I'll say. If any of us are taken by Rhusana . . ."

Murmurs rippled through her band. Madcap swore softly, then set Barf on their shoulders for the climb down. "Cunning, our chief."

Long ago, Wretch had told her history would give her a name: *Fie Oath-cutter. Fie the Cunning. Fie, the Crow Who Feared No Crown.*

Mammoth blood still fouled her tongue. She didn't deserve any of that.

She couldn't fail them again.

They stopped once more before the sun set, to let another Hawk patrol pass. This time, Fie knew none of their weary legs could carry them into the trees in time. Instead, she had them shelter in the brush and called a third tooth, trying to ignore the sting as copper burned in her nose.

Her band pushed on through a second night as Fie kept her Sparrow teeth alight. No one spoke to her but to offer a water skin, a blanket round her shoulders, a strip of dried pork. She didn't like to think of giving off hurt like a stink, but she'd spent too much of the day scrubbing tears from her face to convince herself otherwise.

The trees began to run together for her, and the stars, and the moon, and the sky, until she marched through an endless dimming gloom—but this was the chief's way, wasn't it? Forever caught on the road, only drifting from beacon to beacon, never finding peace, never finding home.

She'd been a fool to think any other road could wait for her.

Near midnight, Fie stumbled and fell to the dust, and found her legs would not push her back up.

The next thing she knew, she was being hoisted into a cloak turned makeshift sling. "You keep those teeth alight, chief," she heard Varlet say. "It's our turn to carry you."

"You don't know where we're going," she slurred, trying to climb out.

Wretch pushed her back, gentle but firm. "We do, girl. Tend to your teeth. We're almost there."

Fie didn't have it in her to scrap with Wretch, and when Barf leapt up and curled on her chest, the fight was good as over. Instead she slid into a fog, rolling Sparrow teeth in her fingers, letting them slip into the sling when they burned out, focusing on staying awake even if she couldn't walk.

She reckoned no one in her band knew how Tavin had carried her when she'd burned herself out in the Marovar.

Near dawn, they turned off the road. Fie only barely registered the change, wavering in and out of her haze—then, beyond the tang of blood still in her mouth, she caught the fresh, sweet perfume of magnolias.

Voices rose around her, first in welcome and then in alarm. She caught Pa's voice in the din and finally let the teeth fall from her hands.

There were scores and scores of Crow shrines across Sabor, and she was sure they'd passed at least one. But with all she'd crossed since they'd parted, she only trusted Pa, and the shrine of Gen-Mara, to keep her band safe.

Of course Wretch would know where to go.

"Pa," she croaked, "Lakima kept her word."

And with at least that one oath kept, Fie let exhaustion drag her into the dark.

———◆◆◆———

She dreamed of blood. She dreamed of drowning. She dreamed of Tavin. She dreamed of Jasimir, cursing her for abandoning him. She dreamed of Lakima, cut down on a lonely road.

She dreamed of Tavin again, of the night before he'd turned, drawing her to him and leaving his plain crown in the dirt.

She didn't want to wake from that, and still she did.

It took her a moment to place where she was. Before, she'd just woken in Tavin's tent, curled in his arms on a soft pallet in the honeyed glow of morning light.

Now she woke alone on a thin grass-woven sleeping mat over a dirt floor, mossy stone walls blocking most light. A few weak shafts broke through the mats woven of living vine that made up the roof. Someone had spread a blanket of crowsilk over her.

Pa. She'd fled to Pa.

She'd given up on the prince. On the oath.

Tavin had given up on them all.

There was no more running from it. She curled in on herself like a withering leaf and finally let the weight on her heart cut itself open.

Her whole body shuddered with sobs. Not the quiet ones that she could hide in a sleeve, or the ones that squeezed between angry words, but terrible, guttural things that tore from her chest like furious beasts, sucking the wind from her as they clawed their way out.

That was how Wretch and Bawd found her, racked with grief and wrath and guilt beyond words. The next thing Fie knew, she'd been gathered to lean beneath Wretch's chin like she was five again and wailing for her dead ma. Once again, Fie couldn't scrape together a protest, weeping into the older woman's shirt as Bawd sat beside them, rubbing Fie's back.

Eventually Wretch said, "You can't carry this alone, Fie. What happened with the queen?"

"Rhusana w-wanted one of them to rule with her." Her voice rattled in fits and spurts. "She—she—wants to turn all Sabor on the Crows. Jas said n-no." Fie tried to think of a way to say the next part without saying Tavin's name.

"Why did the Hawk lad say aye?" Bawd prompted after a moment.

Fie couldn't help a shiver, but she had to say it, had to tell them what he'd damned them all for. "He asked for Rhusana's word that no—no harm would come to . . . me." She gasped a broken laugh. "I told him earlier, we need to put better kings on the throne, and he—and he—"

She broke down again.

"He cares for you," Bawd said.

"Then how could he do it?" Fie choked out. "How could he trust her? How could he sell us all for—*me*?"

"Deep breaths." Wretch let out a sigh. "I'll never doubt that boy loves you, Fie. But loving someone doesn't make us choose right, for us or for them."

Fie didn't want to hear aught about how Tavin cared. She wanted to cut his throat for being such a fool to trust the queen's word. For choosing a throne over an oath. For forsaking her kin, her caste, her king-to-be.

"What are we going to do now?" she whispered.

"I don't know about the next moon, or even the next week." Wretch propped Fie up and pushed a clay plate with a stack of panbread her way. Fie saw bits of soft cheese and a drizzle of honey, the way Pa made it specially for her. "But we'll scrape it together as we always do. You need to eat."

Fie shook her head, even as another sob bubbled up her throat. "I'm the chief, *I'm* supposed to be taking care of *you*."

"You think that's how it works?" Bawd scowled and tore off a strip of the panbread. "We look after our own. That didn't stop when you became our chief. You're the cleverest, meanest chief on the road, and we'll follow you straight into the twelve hells if you ask, but if you fall, we carry you. If you're sick, we carry you. If you need us, we carry you, and I swear on Varlet's head that if you don't take care of yourself, we will *make you*."

The strip of panbread was shoved in Fie's face. She grudgingly took a bite, and then another, and something about filling her belly made tears roll down her face anew. The panbread vanished in short order.

The hurt went nowhere, still dragging thorns about her every thought—but her hurt never truly went away. Wounds became scars, pain tempered to bitter wisdom, and from the embers of her grief always, always rose rage.

She let Bawd and Wretch lead her to the temple's makeshift wash-chamber, where rainwater had been diverted to a great stone cistern surrounded by barrels and basins. They left her with soap-shells and a change of clothes, and it wasn't until Fie scrubbed the reek of old blood from her stiff hair that she realized it had clung to her like a curse.

Pa was waiting for her when she left the temple. One look at his troubled face unraveled her again, but he'd come prepared; he handed her a clean crowsilk rag to mop up her face, slung an arm around her shoulders, and led her away. "Come on, girl."

He took her behind the great statue of Gen-Mara, to a sun-dappled grove where a handful of boulders made a ring around a long-cold firepit.

They sat together on the largest stone, and she told him everything. She told him how Little Witness said she was a failure, how the dead god had said their oath went unkept, how she'd charged Fie to find a Birthright but Fie had chosen the oath instead.

She told him how she'd failed Jasimir, how she'd failed the Crows. She told her pa how she'd failed him.

And then, head bowed, she waited for his judgment.

Pa didn't say aught for a while. She heard the scratch as he ran his hand over his beard, and a sluggish hot breeze passed through the grove, heavy with the smell of magnolias.

"Could be worse," he finally said.

She looked up, startled.

Pa shrugged. "Won't lie to you, Fie: it's bad. But if you hadn't sent Jade here with a wagon full of supplies, we'd have days instead of weeks. If you hadn't given your heart to that lad, likely he never would have bargained for your life, and you and your band would be feeding the crows now. If you hadn't cut the oath to start with, the prince would be dead, and likely, so would we all. Could be worse."

"Could be better," she said thickly. "And that's on my head."

"Aye, that's the way of being a chief. Blow your nose." Pa waited until she'd done so. "Every chief fouls up. And when we foul up, we don't do it small, we do it with lives in the balance. Like Skelpie."

Fie swallowed. Pa rarely called her ma by name, and even rarer did he speak of the night the Oleander Gentry had taken her. It was Fie's oldest, fiercest wound. "Ma didn't get up the trees in time because . . . she was passing me to Swain."

"And I was the one who didn't think it out *before* the raid. See? We should have had a sling ready for you, a plan, anything. Skelpie shouldn't have had to figure it out herself. We're supposed to look after our own. But I fouled up."

"That's no fault of yours," Fie argued. "The Oleanders killed her. Not you."

He gave her a long look. "Aye. I could have thought ahead, I could have given myself to save her, but it was the Oleanders who chose to ride our way. My sins were those of a new chief. Now why can you forgive me for those, but can't forgive yourself?"

She wanted to say it was different. She knew it wasn't.

"I'm not the chief I was," he said. "And neither are you."

You are not what you were. She'd all but forgotten Little Witness's last words to her.

If only she could forget the rest. "None of it matters anyhow, Pa. Sabor's going to rot itself to stone, and we're going to starve waiting for it to pass."

"I asked Little Witness what she wanted with you, you know," Pa said. "She wouldn't say much, some spooky blather about a storm and teeth and thieves. But she did point out one thing. You know how many Phoenix gods there are?"

Fie's brow furrowed, trying to recall. "Twenty-four, aye?"

He nodded. "Now, how many Phoenix witches walk this land?"

Tavin had told her King Surimir was the only one, though that was before he'd shown he'd inherited the fire witchery from his father. But the king was dead. That left . . .

"One," Fie said. "Only one. What does it mean?"

He rubbed his beard, grave. "Little Witness told me we're on the edge of an end. She didn't say what's ending, but I know one thing: change comes with a cost, and even Phoenixes need ash to rise."

"So we wait?"

Pa pressed his lips together. "No, Fie. Not you."

She stared at him.

"The Fie I raised couldn't sit about a shrine and trust the nation to sort itself out before she starves," Pa said. "You wanted better for us *before* the queen brought hell to our door. You weren't content with a chief's lot, you weren't content with a Crow's lot, and you were right to ask for more. So I'll not cast you out, girl. But can you tell me true: You'd be content to waste away in a shrine, hoping the prince survives to keep his oath?"

She shook her head, fear trying to strangle a terrible, eager relief. "I can't take the band into that kind of danger."

"They'll stay here until you've done what you need to."

"A Crow alone on the road is good as dead."

A strange look crossed Pa's face. He reached for where his chief's string had been, only it had been whittled down to but a few scarce teeth. He touched one and said to the empty air, "It's Cur. Send the visitors round back, if you please."

At Fie's bewildered look, he gestured to the statue. "Gen-Mara, the Messenger. Little Witness told me the witchery would be different on my own grave. Outside of her tower, she's naught but a tot with a sharp memory. Here I can speak to anyone so long as I have their tooth. I'll knot one of yours into the string before you go."

"I'm not going, Pa." There was something doubly vexing about arguing against something she hungered to do. "You really want to roll shells on the odds of one Crow against the queen of Sabor?"

"I'd take those odds," a familiar voice called, footsteps crunching closer.

A moment later, two figures stepped into the clearing, two she'd figured good as dead.

Khoda gave a half-baked rendition of the Hawk salute as Viimo looked about, sizing up the statue and the firepit.

"Homey, this," the skinwitch concluded.

Pa set a hand on Fie's shoulder. "You're not going alone."

CHAPTER ELEVEN

GOOD LUCK

"FOUND THEM LURKING OUTSIDE A FEW HOURS AFTER SUNUP." PA gestured for them to sit on the boulders. "Apparently Khoda here remembers the way."

"Did Khoda here also tell you he's a Swan spy?" Fie asked.

"*Black* Swan," Pa drawled.

"It turns out your father *also* has a considerable supply of Crane teeth," Khoda said wryly as he lowered himself onto a stone, folding his arms. "And if it's any comfort, I only remembered it was in this stretch of the road. Viimo was the one to find the entrance, and even then . . ."

Viimo tossed a handful of leather scraps to Fie. "I had something of yours to follow. And your trail still went cold a few paces off the flatway."

Fie unfurled the leather, recognized the stamp work, and couldn't speak a moment as a hot lump swelled in her throat. They'd even managed to salvage the part of the bag where Tavin's tooth had been stitched in. If she called its spark now, would it tell her why—

No. The *why* of it didn't matter. What Tavin had done was done.

"How did you get out?" she asked instead.

Khoda flashed a grin. "The real question is why I stuck around to begin with. The nice thing about Hawks is they assume all you have to do is tie someone up and put them under watch, and that's enough to keep them in place."

"That's usually how it works, aye," Viimo said. Fie sneered at her on principle.

"Well, if the master-general didn't want me to escape, she could have been a bit more thorough, that's all I'm saying. Rhusana had to collect hair from every Hawk in the procession; you'd think at least one of them would have spotted it like I did. And then I needed this one"—Khoda jerked a thumb at Viimo—"to make sure we were going the right way."

Four days ago, Fie would have found Khoda's sass more palatable. Now it only reminded her of Tavin. She narrowed her eyes. "And just why were you looking for me?"

He coughed. "Right. To business. I figured you might be interested in finding another way out of this that doesn't involve seeing who dies first, the Crows or the rest of Sabor."

Fie traded looks with Pa. "I'm listening," she said slowly. "But if you're looking for a conqueror, you've come to the wrong witch."

"We have a saying among the Black Swans," Khoda said, looking about the ground until he found a long stick. "The only difference between a conqueror and a thief is an army."

"Just so happens that we're short on armies in these parts, too."

"Then it's a good thing we need thieves." Khoda drew three circles in the ashes of the firepit. "Rhusana's plan is a three-legged stool," he said. "She needs three things to maintain her power: the military, the aristocracy, and the lack of an alternative. Tavin's cooperation gives her the aristocracy, because a descendant of Ambra legitimizes her reign. Tavin and Jasimir are both functionally hostages, so that gives her the military, because the master-general won't endanger her son, and she can't risk Jasimir dying in a coup. And Jasimir's captivity means there is no alternative—Tavin and Rhusana are the only eligible rulers."

"Two of those count on Jasimir." Fie frowned.

Khoda ventured another grin and pointed the stick at her. "Exactly. She's keeping Jasimir imprisoned in the royal palace. If we can break him out, then Rhusana loses her leverage against Draga. A stool with two legs wobbles." He drew a slash through one circle, then another. "We prove Jasimir is . . . well, the *real* Jasimir, and Rhusana's plan falls apart in front of all of Dumosa. All she'll have left is the king's illegitimate son."

Fie stared at the remaining circle. Ambra's descendant. A bastard boy. A Hawk who hadn't, in the end, believed she could win against the queen.

"I can take that from her," she said, icy as a Marovar wind.

Khoda carved a line through the final ring. "And that's why I'm here. Like I told you before, Rhusana's biggest weakness is that she underestimates everyone else. She didn't understand why giving you Phoenix teeth would be a problem until she'd already done it, and she doesn't see you as a threat without them. So she's going to account for Draga's warriors, she's going to account for Jasimir's fire, she may even foresee an asp or two from a disgruntled noble. But she's never going to expect you."

Fie frowned, a thousand questions, fears, and rages running roughshod through her skull. "How long do you reckon this takes?"

"Well, the game is up if the solstice coronation goes through," Khoda said with a shrug. "Then legally she'll have command over the military whether Draga likes it or not."

"Solstice is in four days." Fie shook her head. "We'll never make it."

"Viimo and I brought horses," Khoda said. "It'll be a hard two days' ride to Dumosa. If we can disrupt the ceremony, that will buy us time, but if we can't end Rhusana's reign before Phoenix Moon ends, I'd say we won't end it at all."

"Pa?" Fie turned to him. "How long can you hold out?"

He scratched his beard. "Jade's band, Ruffian's band, and your band . . . We'll make it to the end of the moon, aye. But it'll be tight, and if any more bands seek shelter here, it'll be tighter."

Part of Fie wanted to say no. But she'd be giving up on a future. She'd be giving up on the Crows.

She'd be no better than Tavin, and that she could not abide.

"Aye," she said. "I'm in. Now how exactly do we break a prince out of a palace?"

Viimo let out a cackle. "Well, it starts with something you'll like."

⊱—◆—⊰

"That ought to tide you over for Sparrow teeth."

Pa dropped a dozen into Fie's hand, and she tucked them into a pouch as they made their way through the shrine's teeth storage. Viimo and Khoda had assured her they had most every other supply covered; they'd arrived with a third horse for Fie, one that had been weighed down with enough Hawk rations to perhaps buy the shrine a few more days, even.

That even included a few changes of clothes. She'd traded her crowsilk leggings and shirt for a Pigeon's loose gray linen shift, painted leather vest, and trousers; her ragged black cloak had been replaced with one of striped gray, and a scarf round her throat hid her string of teeth.

It felt odd to wear aught that wasn't crowsilk. It felt worse to wear it in a Crow shrine.

"Vulture, you're set; Swan won't do much good . . ." Pa tapered off, and Fie saw why. The jar he'd come to was painfully small and painted with the Crow mark for "Phoenix."

Part of Fie wanted the whole jar for herself, wanted that weight in her bag, wanted the knowledge that if all else failed, she could burn her way clear.

But that wasn't the part that won.

"You heard Khoda," she said. "Rhusana's accounted for fire. Keep them for if it gets bad and we need to go out and get viatik."

"You sure?" Pa asked.

Fie let a hand stray to her scarf. If all else failed, she had one Phoenix tooth left to burn now—or at least, one last tooth from a half Phoenix.

"Aye," she said. "I'm sure."

He pushed his lips together, then waved a hand. "Come on, girl."

They left the tooth stores, and Fie tried to ignore the looks from the other Crows. If she saw someone in Pigeon garb stomping about a shrine, she supposed she'd be antsy, too, especially after a Vulture and Swan had shown up on their doorstep hours ago.

Pa led her to one of the massive magnolia trunks, running a hand over the bark and vine until it stopped at a dusty clay urn. He knocked off a layer of moss, then rattled the lid back and forth until it squawked free and fished inside until he emerged with six teeth.

"Here." He passed them to her.

They sang so loud when they hit her palm that she thought for a moment their owners lived yet. Then she kenned what she held: six witch-teeth, three from a Sparrow witch and three from a Pigeon witch.

The teeth of a Sparrow witch would let her pass not just unnoticed, but wholly unseen. Those of a Pigeon witch would let her skew fortune her way. Both could mean the difference between life and death when she reached Dumosa. Both were rarer than gold.

"Can you spare it?" she couldn't help blurting out. "The shrine—"

"Has enough," he said. "Especially with those fire teeth. Let the queen watch for fire or steel or asps. She'll never see you coming."

Fie wanted to say something full of salt and smoke, about how she'd throw Rhusana out and keep the oath and bring all twelve hells down upon any who had crossed her.

Instead, her throat knotted around the knowledge that whether or not Rhusana saw Fie coming, the queen would still have Tavin to watch her back.

Pa saw her face drop and shook his head. "It passes," he said. "Well, not truly. It's just another scar, aye? Hurts like hell even when naught's scraping at it, and we don't live a life that gives you time to just let it be. But it'll heal over, and as it does, it'll ache only but once in a while."

What would grow over her wound might be hard and ugly, but it would be a reminder. One she sore needed.

"You've still got one of my teeth, and I've one of yours," Pa said, tapping one of the teeth in his pared-down string. "I don't know if I'll be able to reach you outside the shrine, but you may be able to reach me if you burn my tooth. But if that calls for burning it out . . . make sure you need it."

She wrinkled her nose at him. "I'll not waste it weeping to you about a mean merchant."

He laughed. "You should also take Barf. The cat's good luck."

"I've teeth for that now."

"Teeth burn out," Pa said. "How do you feel about your odds once they're gone?"

Fie took the cat.

She did not linger taking her leave of her band; she told them and herself she'd only be gone a week or two. If she let herself believe anything else, she'd never set foot outside Gen-Mara's groves.

Only Wretch had parting words for her, and those she saved for when she embraced Fie and could whisper them into her hair: "Remember, just because the lad loves you doesn't mean he does right."

They were on the road a few hours before sundown, with Barf tucked into a sling on Fie's chest. Fie had only ridden a horse a handful of times before, and her distaste for it was wholly validated when they had to dismount for the evening and she found her legs reduced to little better than the salt pork in her travel rations.

She'd resumed taking laceroot seed each night when Tavin had fallen in with her band, for she had no intent of getting with child for years, if ever. It ached to take it now, just to keep her bleeding at bay, but she did still. Too much hung on her head now for cramps to lay her low.

It was a strange thing to camp with just the three of them and only have Khoda on watch. It was stranger still to cross travelers on the road the next day and not feel the sting of suspicious looks. Khoda had picked a Sparrow's patchwork apron, but Viimo had donned a Pigeon cloak like Fie, and none of them drew so much as a stray glance.

The ride to Dumosa passed with only as much chatter as Fie could stomach. They talked through the plan each night, exchanged no more than a few words when setting out each morning, and barely spoke on the road. That suited Fie just fine; she still didn't trust Khoda, and she'd rather roll through broken glass than act chummy with Viimo.

More than once they passed plague beacons dragging long fingers into the sky, and she bit her tongue. Each was an accusation: as a chief, she was bound to answer. Each was a reminder: Rhusana had good as lit each beacon herself, waiting for Fie to take the bait.

She told herself another band might answer and pressed on.

By noon of the second day, they could see the crest of the royal palace over the trees, and it didn't take long for the rest of the city's hill to swell above them. They ducked into the brush before they hit the gates proper, and Khoda and Fie went to work pulling the saddle and bridle off Viimo's horse, while Viimo herself shed her Pigeon cloak for one of dusty black crowsilk.

"Remember," Khoda told the Vulture, cinching a pack to her former mount, "nothing until we're at *most* two carts from the gate. We don't speak, you don't know us, and you don't make your move until—"

"The guards see. Aye, I know." Viimo cackled at him. "You're workin' with professionals, can't you tell?"

As if to drive the point home, Barf leapt up onto the packs, stuck a hind leg in the air, and began to groom a very undignified place. Khoda made a little disgusted cough but heckled Viimo no more.

They waited for nigh another quarter hour, peering from the brush while Khoda sized up the passing travelers. Finally he spotted a cart laden with squash and maize and signaled Fie.

She called on two Sparrow teeth, and they slipped onto the flatway behind the maize cart, keeping a good number of paces behind it. The farmer didn't notice them, even after she let one tooth go and focused the other on Viimo.

They followed the farmer all the way up to one of the Lesser Gates into Dumosa, reserved for Common Castes and Crows, and sat in line on the bridge over the Hem. Viimo lingered a pace or two behind them, but with Fie's Sparrow tooth turning notice from her, the farmers and laborers waiting to enter the city paid her no heed.

It wasn't until the maize cart drew within easy eyesight of the Hawk guards that Khoda nudged Fie. She let her remaining Sparrow tooth go cold, then reached up to grab Barf from the horse's back, a signal for Viimo.

Right on cue, the skinwitch ducked around the horses, hovering at the edge of the maize cart. When the farmer scooted off her wagon seat to speak to the Hawks, Viimo made a show of swiping one, two ears of maize, then a squash, practically flapping her crowsilk cloak for attention.

"*HEY!*" The farmer bolted for Viimo. "Damned dirty bone thief! You trying to steal from me?"

Viimo swore, stumbled back like a drunkard, and all but heaved the produce into the air. Somehow, in righting herself, she managed to send another squash flying.

"Subtle," Khoda muttered. "Ready?"

"*Guard!*" the farmer shouted. "Thief! Get her!"

Viimo took off running. There was a flurry of leather stamping on stone, and then four Hawks streaked past in hot pursuit. Fie rekindled both of her Sparrow teeth and readied a spare for if a tooth burned out.

"Ready," Fie said.

She'd borrowed this idea from when Jasimir had saved Barf before. Khoda made sure the horses' reins were clear of their feet, then smacked one on the rump. It reared, startling the other two and only adding to the chaos. Shouts and curses spilled over the bridge as Fie and Khoda backed toward the gate. Every eye was either on Viimo or on the horses now shying down the cobblestones.

Fie and Khoda slipped by the stormy-faced farmer and past the vexed Gull merchants waiting at the now-clear gate. The two Vulture witches on guard were watching the chase with glee. Then Fie saw them narrow their eyes.

"That's not a Crow," one said. "Look—that hair's like one of us."

The other swore under his breath. "Reckon that's the tracker who turned on Tatterhelm? The queen might want a word with her . . ."

The skinwitches didn't so much as blink as Khoda and Fie strolled through the gate, then ducked into a nearby alcove. Barf wriggled until Fie set her down.

Two Hawks shoved Viimo through the gate a few minutes later. She moped and twisted about, the picture of sullen defeat, and Fie couldn't help huffing a laugh. Viimo had been right about that much: starting the plan with her arrest was something Fie enjoyed quite a bit.

Once they were out of sight, Khoda stepped out, trying to get his bearings as he pulled two painted vests from his pack, both marked with the stripes of a Pigeon courier. "My handler will be waiting in Magistrate's Row. Then after that . . ."

"I know." Even from the alcove, Fie could see their next target: the golden spires of the royal palace, carving into the sky like beacons.

CHAPTER TWELVE

— FROM OUR ASHES —

K HODA'S HANDLER DID NOT BOTHER TO GIVE HER NAME. SHE looked as if she could blend in among the Owl scholars, with deep mahogany skin and thick hair braided tight to her scalp. The orange embroidery on her violet robe marked her for a legal scribe—or at least a credible fake. It wasn't quite the same orange hue as the roof tiles of Magistrate's Row, but judging from the number of scribes darting between courthouses, record houses, and the Advocate's Guild, that orange thread would let her go anywhere she pleased.

She also did not seem pleased to see Fie at Khoda's heels, dark eyes flicking between the two of them. "Courier. What are your rates?"

"Ten naka to deliver inside Dumosa," Khoda replied. "Four more inside the palace."

The handler nodded, jaw tight, and said through her teeth, "Who else are you planning to recruit? A stray dog?"

Barf chose that moment to flop into the dust between them all and roll over for a belly rub. The handler closed her eyes.

Khoda nodded and held his hand out. His lips barely moved as he hissed back, "Tell me a Crow witch with a grudge and a bag full of teeth isn't an asset. Besides, this is the one that got Jasimir all the way to Draga in the first place. She can manage herself."

"And there won't be a . . . distraction for you?" his handler asked pointedly.

Khoda coughed. "Women typically aren't."

Fie raised her eyebrows but said naught. She couldn't help thinking Tavin would have been less thorny with Khoda if he'd known.

"Hmph. Four naka more for the palace." The handler counted naka into Khoda's palm with an air of significance that told Fie this wasn't just about the coins. "So far, it's been worth the new investment. We would have lost half our staff to a . . . policy change, if we hadn't had early word. But it's a risk to have someone so—"

"I'm keeping an eye on it," Khoda said swiftly. "Where do you want this delivered?"

The handler blinked at him, gaze darting to Fie once again, then passed over two scrolls, two heavy clay tokens, and two slips of parchment. One read *Ebrim Kamiro, Repairs Master, Maintenance Division*; the other *Yula Haovi, Cleaning Manager, Maintenance Division.*

"Be quick," the handler said. "Two dawns from now, the crown burns white."

Fie had given up trying to parse their double meanings, but that one she got all too clear. Two days until Rhusana took the throne, and with her, the Oleander Gentry.

"The sun will rise," Khoda said shortly.

His handler nodded, grim. "Even from our ashes."

That seemed to be some sort of signal, for Khoda turned on a heel. Fie followed him, feeling the handler's eyes on her as they strode from Magistrate's Row.

"What in the twelve hells does *that* mean?" she hissed to Khoda once they were a respectable distance away.

"It's our creed." He handed her a scroll, a token, and a parchment slip. "It means we do whatever necessary to keep order. The master-general was right, Black Swans deal in the kind of secrets that can tear a nation apart. Our entire purpose is preventing that, no matter what. Even if we ourselves must burn."

"Sounds uplifting," she drawled.

Khoda tucked his scroll into his belt. "My creed is what kept Steward Burzo from sending your hair to the queen with the next message-hawk. I had to make a call about which was better for Sabor: keeping my own cover, or losing it to keep you free of Rhusana's control. You know how I chose."

"I don't think the fate of the nation hangs on one Crow girl," Fie returned.

He pursed his lips. "You're just a Crow girl to people who benefit from you being *just* a Crow. From what I've seen, you're a witch who can use every Birthright with the right tools, and you understand how to exploit what people expect of you. That's how you got the queen to give you Phoenix teeth, how you fooled the master-general of the royal legions into saving your family, and how you convinced her to honor Jasimir's oath. You don't just survive, you turn tables on the most powerful people in the nation." He shot a look at her. "And now I'm betting that's how you're going to get Jasimir on the throne."

There were too many *you*s in there for Fie's liking. She'd done what any chief could do, and only because Pa's soul had been tied up in it all.

And now Khoda was making it sound like if things got dire enough, she could just whip up a miracle on demand.

He meant it as encouragement, that Fie knew. But all she could hear was *Even if we ourselves must burn.*

———◆———

It was dismayingly easy for them to walk into the royal palace.

Khoda had explained on the way up that this was the easiest way to smuggle a witch in; Pigeon witches were so rare and so powerful that Sabor was doubly sure not to let any slip through their grasp. Every single Pigeon witch was strictly accounted for at all times.

Pigeon couriers, on the other hand, were both harmless and commonplace. There was precious little point in screening for witches that were already accounted for. When they approached the gate for servants' use, the Hawks just eyeballed them for weapons, validated their courier tokens, and waved them through with a spare guard for escort and a warning to keep the cat under control.

All Fie had to do was maintain the Peacock glamour that covered her witch-sign. She made a mental note to warn Jasimir about it once they cleared him out of the prison.

Then she remembered she'd all but abandoned him, and wondered if he'd speak to her at all.

The guard led them down corridors tiled and graveled, some walled in lattice, others no more than a fine roof supported by slender columns carved like spouts of golden fire. Whatever wind may have made it into the palace grounds seemed to get tangled between its intricately carved walls, leaving little relief from the smothering afternoon sun.

Khoda named different buildings they passed under his breath: the library, the dining hall for servants, the servants' living quarters. Fie tried not to ogle the splendor, even of the plainest buildings. The first and last time she'd been in the royal palace, it had been dark as pitch. She still resented the gilt and filigree with every bone in her body, but it was easy to see now why Jasimir had missed living in such finery.

The farther into the palace grounds they got, the more the ground hummed below her feet with the steady, hungry song she heard in Phoenix teeth. Pa had told her all the Phoenix gods were buried below the royal palace, making such a well of power that any Phoenix could call fire on royal ground, whether or not they were a witch. She'd missed it before, when she'd not yet called on the fire Birthright, but it was nigh impossible to ignore now.

The Hawk guard walked them to a square, sturdy building, still laden with flourishes of gold flame and curling feathers. He jabbed his spear at the door. "Their offices are on the second floor. Have Kamiro or Haovi show you out, and don't forget to show your tokens."

Khoda bowed. Fie, unaccustomed to bowing to anyone unless she was mocking them, hurried to do the same. The guard didn't seem to notice as he headed back the way they'd come.

Fie and Khoda went inside, Fie blinking to adjust to the dark. A set of stairs led them to the second floor, where they found Ebrim Kamiro's office labeled in a neat, clear hand.

"Courier," Khoda called at the sliding canvas-screen door. "Messages for Ebrim Kamiro and . . ."

"Yula Haovi," Fie finished.

The screen door slid aside, and a woman in her fifties peered out. "From Magistrate's Row?"

"Ay—yes," Fie said.

The woman winced. "Oh, you're going to take work. Come in, hurry."

A man stood at the shelves in the back of the office, digging through a wooden crate of what appeared to be various tools. "The entire point of having *my* office, Yula, is that *I* decide who's allowed in."

Yula rolled her eyes at him and shut the door behind Khoda and Fie, nearly catching Barf's tail. The tabby flicked it out of the way with a disdainful glower. "Well, you can decide who's allowed in, *Ebrim*, if you ever decide to answer your own wretched door."

He vaguely waved a pair of pincers at her, then set them on a shelf, grumbling into his crate. A moment later he surfaced with another, smaller pair of pincers, frowned at those, and started for his desk. "You can speak freely here; at this hour there's no one but us on this floor. Just keep your voices down. You'll change into servant's uniforms, and then we'll stow you in the sick room for the Sparrows, long as there's no need for it." Ebrim shook out a plain roll of hide, and with a start, Fie realized it was a map of the palace grounds. "This can't leave my office. Hawks check for it every day. Here's where we are." He jabbed a finger into a corner. "I have open repair requests for most every part of the palace, so you can go anywhere you need to search. Your first order of business is finding His Highness, right?"

When Ebrim looked up, Fie found a surprising amount of distress in the man's eyes. He was younger than Yula by a good decade or two, his sandy-brown face clean-shaven but his dark hair still graying at the temples; likely he'd been in palace service before Jasimir was born and had watched the prince grow up.

Khoda shifted. "Our top priority is making sure the coro—"

"Crown prince is safe, then getting him out," Fie interrupted. Khoda shot her a look. She ignored it. "I'm one of the Crows who came for him back in Pigeon Moon. No way he pulled that stunt off without help from your ranks, aye?"

Yula ducked her head. "His Highness was known for . . . intervening," she said. "When the king was in one of his rages, or when a courtier wanted to show off how they toyed with us, His Highness would sway them to mercy as best he could. It cost him plenty of friends a royal could use. We owed him."

"Aye. Sparrows were the only ones I saw mourning him for true." Fie folded her arms. "We'll need anything you can tell us about the coronation ceremony, too. If we can't throw it off, the prince won't have a crown to claim."

Yula nodded. "They've had half my crew scrubbing down nigh every inch of the Hall of the Dawn. We'll keep open ears."

"There are some places they can't possibly be holding the prince." Ebrim scoured his desk, then picked up his pincers and dropped them on the Hall of the Dawn and the Hawk barracks. He added a pot of nails over the library, scraps of parchment over the servants' quarters, and a small potted plant over the armory. "The library's too open. Same with the armory, and we'd know if he's in any of our buildings."

Khoda stepped closer to the map, brow furrowing. "We'd be looking for a room that's probably been cleaned out in the last week. It would be isolated, probably the only one on its floor in use, and somewhere one or two people could come and go without drawing much notice."

"Let me look through our requests," Yula said. "I'll have a list for you this evening."

"Our thanks," Fie said, then squinted at the map as well. "Maybe look for aught that's close to the royal quarters, too. Rhusana won't want to inconvenience herself when checking on him."

"Nor will that faithless bastard Hawk." Yula's face darkened. "All those years he's been at His Highness's side, and now he turns."

That caught Fie like a sucker punch. Khoda must have seen, for he piped up. "I don't know what the queen offered him. I can only hope it was worth it."

My life. The knowledge burned at Fie like a coal caught in her throat. The price was not worth it, yet Fie had every intent to show Tavin the worth of what he'd bought.

———— ◆ ————

That night, they narrowed down Yula's list to seven rooms near the royal quarters, debating each by lantern-light in the servants' quarters' sick rooms as Fie reworked her chief's string to add new teeth, more string, and a small clay Vulture charm-bead from Viimo. When she was done, it was long enough to be a belt, one she could hide under her plain linen shirt and royal servants' golden sash if need be. She'd always found it easiest to call a tooth to life as it rolled between her palms, but the tooth just touching her skin would have to be enough. One glimpse of a tooth necklace and she'd give them all away.

They had only a few hours of sleep before Ebrim arrived with the toll of the palace hour-bells in the dim predawn, bearing repair request slips for each area. He also had day-old sweet rolls stuffed with dates and almonds for their breakfast and a fish head for Barf's.

"Remember," he told them, trying to ignore the tabby rolling glee-fully on his sandals, "you say you're there to assess the issue that needs repair. If anyone asks, show them the signed request. If a Hawk or Peacock tells you to clear out . . ."

"Aye, you don't need to tell me," Fie said around a mouthful of stale roll. "We'll clear out."

Ebrim gave her a meaningful look. "*Yes.* And you'll do it with a bow and an apology."

Fie swallowed with a grimace. "*Yes.*"

They tried to leave Barf shut in the room while they slipped down the dark, silent hall; most servants wouldn't be up for another half hour. However, they had not planned for her squeezing through the bars on the window, and they had no more than set foot out the door when she trotted up, chirping. Khoda swore under his breath.

"Pa said she's lucky," Fie said with a shrug. "And I've only three Pigeon witch-teeth, so we'll need what we can get."

They hurried first to the archives, where several large closets had been cleared out in a mostly empty tower. The Hawks on guard let them in with a yawn, and Barf entertained herself terrorizing the local rodent population, but their "assessment" only turned up the tax records for provincial grain farmers of a hundred years ago.

The next room was in a corner of an unused cellar near the icehouse on the other side of the palace grounds . . . or at least, that's where Fie thought it to be. Khoda was the one who knew the palace's layout.

The sun hadn't quite climbed over the horizon, and by the easing gloom, all the buildings looked like coiling limbs of the same terrible creature, with their scaly tiled domes, fans of golden feathered trim, and spines of arched windows. The dreadful hum of dead Phoenix gods simmered beneath her soles like a drawn-out pulse.

Somewhere in this gilded beast was Tavin. Somewhere was Rhusana. Would they come to Fie, or would she have to carve them out herself?

She could only hope to end this all before she had any need to learn her way around the palace's tripes.

They had just strolled past a row of columns, each large as one of Gen-Mara's magnolias, when a shout echoed from the open walkway behind them. "You there! Sparrow!"

Fie caught her breath and turned. Twenty paces away, a Peacock lord was beckoning them, looking peevish.

"Keep looking," Khoda muttered in a rush, shoving the repair request slips at her, "and use Viimo." Then he shouted, "Right away, m'lord!" and jogged off before Fie could so much as squeak a protest. All she could do was watch him walk away with the Peacock lord, bowing intermittently, until they vanished round a corner.

For a moment, Fie couldn't breathe.

She was alone in the home of her enemies. She didn't know where she was going. She didn't know how to get back to Ebrim's office. She didn't dare ask for help.

If she froze much longer, a Hawk patrol was bound to notice, and then it'd all be over.

Pa would know what to do. Fie's hand crept toward his tooth—then dropped. It was too soon to burn it already. She had other teeth. And that had been all she'd needed before.

The rhythmic stomps of a patrol caught at the edge of her hearing. Fie reached for her Sparrow witch-tooth, then paused. The invisibility would only last so long, and unless she knew where to go, she could burn that tooth clean out and never find Jasimir.

Instead, she chose the Pigeon witch-tooth.

Pa had never given her a Pigeon witch's tooth to use before now; he'd only had her practice burning two plain Pigeon teeth at once and tweaking fortune in small ways. The footsteps drew nearer. She ducked into an alcove, fishing under her shirt to pry the tooth free. If she was to call on one now, she'd do it proper.

The tooth keened as Fie rolled it between her palms, the spark popping free like a cork. She blinked. Abruptly, the world shifted, unshifted, and rattled with potential.

Naught looked different; naught looked the same. She could hear, see, *taste* the currents of fortune: a whorl of bad luck on the walkway where Khoda had been called away, a bloom of good fortune unfurling around her. The footsteps of the Hawk patrol stopped.

"Tell you what, soldiers." The voice seeped out from beyond a nearby gate. "If we leave now, we can beat Unit Seventeen for breakfast." A chorus of assent later, the footsteps had retreated in the opposite direction.

Fie let out a breath, then tried to focus. She needed to find Jas. If there was any time for a stroke of fortune in her search, it would be now.

Another servant passed them, looking almost bewildered by the tray in his hands. Barf perked up, shedding ripples of good luck like a winter coat. She chirped and scurried over to follow the Sparrow man, the end of her tail twitching like a flag in a trifling wind.

Fie didn't see any other sources of luck; Pa seemed to have been right about the tabby after all. She followed her cat.

They turned into a peculiar parade, the servant weaving through gates and corridors as Barf mewed at his heels, Fie darting behind statues and columns every time he turned to try to shoo the cat away to no avail. The few Hawks in sight peeled off from their posts as fortune nudged them away, recalling an errand or struck with an urge to use the privy.

The hum of Phoenix god-graves rose the farther they went, until they turned into a grand, arcing hall. Rich gilt and scrollwork crawled up the columns, and six towering golden statues stood sentinel in alcoves along one wall, facing six more across the way. Fire wreathed the bottom of each in a shallow moat, enough to deter anyone from laying hands on the towering statues, but not so much to damage the urns, lesser icons, and other trappings clustered into the alcove with them.

Fie didn't know the Phoenix gods all too well, but their graves sang below her feet loud enough to tell her where she stood. Ebrim's map had showed two great curved chambers flanking the Hall of the Dawn to the north and south, standing over the two burial grounds of the dead gods. They'd been labeled as the Divine Galleries.

The servant slipped behind a statue, fiddled with something, sent one more furtive look around, and tried to take a step back.

Barf had coiled round his ankles. He toppled to the ground with a yelp and a clang as the tray went flying. The smell of fish stew reached Fie even from the tapestry she'd ducked behind, as did the man's flurry of curses. Moments later he stormed out of the hall, mumbling something about finding the cleaning staff.

Fie bolted to the back of the statue. Barf was far too fixed on cleaning up the fallen stew to pay her much mind, looking very satisfied with herself. Fie's Pigeon witch-tooth was starting to burn low, but it didn't take a work of fortune to see that the head on a guardian dog statue had turned at a strange angle, one that didn't match the dog statue beside it. She pushed it all the way around.

A door-size section of the statue's pedestal lowered over the flames, carving a path across them and into the statue's base.

The fading currents of fortune had little to say about this development. Whether that meant going in would be good or bad, Fie couldn't tell.

"Stay here," Fie muttered to the cat, knowing she had absolutely no say in the matter, and headed in.

Firelight cut the darkness, revealing a marble staircase that wound down in a spiral, studded in cut-iron lanterns burning with a pale flame. Fie had made it halfway down when a voice echoed up, distant and familiar.

It was a voice that nailed her in place where she stood.

". . . talk to me." A long pause. "Please, Jas. I-I'll get you out of here, I'll get you somewhere better. Just say *anything*."

Fie had thought quite a bit about what she would do the next time she saw Tavin. Mostly it involved knives, and demanding answers, and leaving him bleeding out in despair; always it made her weep.

She found now that for all her fury, more than anything, she just wanted to run.

There was a low mumble. Tavin didn't answer for a moment. When it came, all he said was "You wouldn't understand."

She had to get out. She had to get away from him before she did something foolish. She had to run.

She took a step back, and her luck finally gave out: her servant uniform slipper had picked up grease from the stew. It skidded out from under her. She slipped and smacked into the marble steps.

A tense silence fell. She scrambled to her feet fast as she could.

"Hello?" Tavin called up the stairs. "Who's there?"

Fie tore her slipper off and bolted up the steps two at a time, clutching it in her hand. She heard Tavin hurrying up the stairs behind her, mercifully still out of sight.

"Stop!" he shouted. "Identify yourself!"

Fie stumbled out of the passageway and back into the grand gallery. Barf was still licking the splatters of fallen stew. If Tavin saw her . . . Fie tossed her slipper at the cat, who sent her an indignant glare and scuttled off to sulk behind an urn.

Tavin's footsteps had nearly reached the top of the stairs. She couldn't hide fast enough without burning one of her precious Sparrow witch-teeth, she couldn't flee the hall fast enough for him to miss, *nothing* was fast enough to get out—

The notion struck swift as lightning. Fie ran to the other side of the statue, calling a Peacock tooth in her belt.

You, it seemed to hiss as its spark snapped free. Fie sucked a breath through her teeth, then called a Peacock witch-tooth to life as well.

The harmony was hard to strike—two different notes, two different songs—but she didn't have time to negotiate. She yanked them into cooperation and wove the image around herself in a blink of an eye: the vivid memory of a long, glossy braid, a rich brocade gown, bracelets and armbands as befit a Peacock family's heir.

The spitting image of Prince Jasimir emerged from behind the statue, even though Fie knew it was Tavin wearing his face.

And Fie turned to him with a look of genteel surprise, wearing the face of Niemi Navali szo Sakar, the Peacock girl whose throat she'd cut just two weeks earlier.

CHAPTER THIRTEEN

— LADY SAKAR —

IT WAS UNNERVING, SEEING JASIMIR'S FACE ON A FIGURE THAT moved like Tavin. She'd woven plenty glamours just like it for him before, when they'd fled across the country, but it was different when she'd painted those features herself. Besides, whatever Peacock witch they'd found to do it was clearly skilled; if she hadn't known Jasimir to be locked away somewhere below, she'd have wondered if he'd broken out on his own. They'd even foregone a topknot like the one Jasimir once sported, spinning instead the same finger-length straight, dark hair he'd had at Draga's camp.

But all it took was the sharp way he scanned the hall, shoulders stiff, for Fie to be certain. Tavin's eyes narrowed on her.

"Excuse me," he said tightly. The voice was still unmistakably his own, yet close enough to Jas to fool all but the few of us who knew them well. "No one is allowed inside the Divine Gallery at this time. How did you get in?"

Fie stared at him, score upon score of curses and questions and threats banging about her skull, none so loudly as *Why?* Panic and rage warred behind her eyes.

None of it would help her now.

Tavin frowned and took a step closer. "Can you understand me?"

Answer, she had to answer—all she wanted to do was push him into the fire herself—what would a Peacock girl say? She'd seen but a brief glimpse of the Sakar girl's life before shaking the memories down to build her glamour; Niemi had been a gossip, a liar, and beloved in the mansions of the north.

Oh, let me, the spark of the tooth sighed impatiently. Fie's head flooded with words, gestures, like a mother teaching her child the steps of a dance.

"I apologize," Fie said with a graceful bow, shocked to hear her voice smooth out to a delicate purr. "Your Highness startled me. I was simply out for a morning walk, and I'm afraid I seem to have gotten lost. You see, my family's only here for your coronation."

He smiled a flat smile, only as polite as custom dictated. She hadn't shaken his suspicions yet. "Where were you trying to go?"

Out of the corner of her eye, Fie saw Barf sidle out from behind the urn to sniff at the remains of the stew. It took everything she had not to throw her other slipper at the cat. *I need a distraction*, she thought frantically.

Then stop trying to be clever, the Peacock girl's spark sneered back.

Fie felt her features relax into something empty and pleasant. "Only around the gardens, Your Highness. I thought I'd walked back to the guest quarters, since I saw a servant leaving in such a hurry." Astonishingly, the spark nudged her back toward the statue, words bubbling to her lips. "Is there an exit over here? I'll just leave this way."

The moment Fie took a step in that direction, a hand wrapped around her arm. "*No*—!" Tavin cut himself off as she turned to face him, eyelashes fluttering like palm fans.

He's hardly going to let you go back there, Niemi's voice whispered between her ears. *Now* he's *the one scrambling for excuses.*

Sure enough, he looked stymied, even rattled.

"Your Highness?" Fie asked, hating the Peacock girl's satin-sleek tone.

A frown tugged at his mouth. "I . . . need you to tell me about the servant you saw."

Another dilemma. If she accidentally described a real Sparrow servant, she'd be bringing a hell down on their heads—

You little fool, the Peacock spark scoffed. *They're* servants.

"I must apologize, Your Highness," Niemi said through Fie. "I do not pay them much attention."

"Nor do I." To Fie's horror, Tavin's dark eyes roved over her rigidly blank face and seemed to like what he saw. He let go, but calloused fingertips grazed her upper arm, brief but shocking. A jolt went through Fie's gut.

Anytime he'd reached for her in the last moon, his hands had lingered just so, as if to delay letting go just a heartbeat longer.

She missed it.

She hated it.

She thought it had been only for *her.*

"Forgive me," Tavin said with a bow of his own, blissfully unaware that she wanted to tear his heart out with her bare hands. How *dare* he lay hands on her again, while she wore a stranger's face. "I've been atrociously rude. I'd introduce myself, but . . ."

Fie didn't need a Peacock's help to say, sweet as poison, "I know who you are."

He smiled as he righted himself. How *dare* he forget her so swift. A dagger hung at his belt. If she was fast enough—no. She'd seen how fast he could move.

Fool! the Peacock girl scolded again. *Pay attention! He asked for your name!*

Already Fie was doubting her choice to call *this* tooth. Yet she had an answer that would serve her purpose, *and* vex the ghost in the bone, a victory on every front.

"I am Niemi Navali szo Sakar," Fie lied.

The spark in the tooth sputtered with rage. Tavin extended a courteous elbow. "It's a poor apology, but I insist on escorting you back to the gardens. Or would you rather return to the guest quarters, Lady Sakar?"

"To the gardens, if you please, Your Highness," she said hastily. They had to be coming up on the hourly bell, when it would be time to send a signal to Viimo. "I was trying to find the amber-pods."

She twined her arm through his and tried not to shiver where they touched, fear and anger not quite stifling the part of her that still leapt at the contact.

"You must have just missed them," Tavin said. "They're on the west side of the guest quarters."

Keep playing the fool, Niemi commanded. *You're adept enough at it.*

Fie rankled, but the dead girl had a point, and Niemi had guided her this far. "I must have," she agreed. Behind them, Barf let out a quiet, grumpy mew as she trotted to catch up. Tavin started to look behind him.

"Are you nervous?" Fie blurted out, capturing his gaze once more. "I mean . . . for your coronation ceremony."

He smiled thinly at her, steering them out the entrance she'd snuck through to begin with. "You could say that. It's been a . . . difficult time."

Fie smiled with empty sympathy as they exited the Divine Gallery, mind racing. Getting lost was only a half lie; she still had no sense of where she was in the palace. This was a chance to map more of the grounds for herself if she could light an Owl tooth for memory . . .

but when she'd called on two teeth or more, they'd always been of the same Birthright. The glamour itself wasn't the problem: once she woke the witch-tooth and told it what to do, they more or less sustained themselves until the tooth burned itself out. The problem was that she needed the dead Sakar girl to *keep* whispering in her skull, and for that, Fie had to keep her spark singing.

Say something! the Peacock girl hissed, even now.

"I can't imagine taking the throne at your age," Fie fumbled. Not her best, but at least it was Tavin's move now.

Each step was an opportunity lost. She couldn't lose her guide to this dreadful, glittering world. But they didn't have time for her to sort out the lay of the palace.

Fie gritted her teeth and called an Owl tooth to life.

This time it clanged against the Peacock song in her bones. She shut her eyes, trying to find a balance; it felt like listening to two different conversations at once and following neither.

Then, suddenly, they settled into harmony. No, not quite harmony . . . alliance. The teeth sang in her bones as two separate songs, uneasy but aligned for now. Glimpses of Niemi's memories flared in her mind bright and sharp: a thousand conversations she had performed like a surgeon, slicing with backhanded compliments, stitching feigned sympathy, winching a tourniquet of rumor.

Tavin was asking her something. She blinked up at him, trying to focus. "S-so sorry, Your Highness, I was distracted by"—Fie waved a hand vaguely at a passing marble sculpture—"that statue. It's quite . . ." It appeared to be a Phoenix queen stepping on a pile of dead invaders. ". . . lifelike."

Tavin ran a hand over his mouth. Even with Jasimir's features, the expression was wholly his own: she'd managed to sell herself to him as a fool, one who was only mildly amusing. "The Phoenix heritage is a glorious one," he said, bland.

It was what he'd given her caste up for. Fie bit her tongue on that, but the curl of wrath went nowhere, searing up her spine.

The voice of Niemi rang in her head, borne louder and stronger now on the strains of Owl memory-song. *You can still make him bleed for it, little fool. You know his every wound.*

That she did. Besides, her head swam with the seasick feeling of burning dissonant teeth. She needed Tavin distracted before her fool act gave way.

And she didn't need steel to make him suffer. "It must be terrible, losing your father like that. He was such a wonderful king."

Tavin's left fist curled, his Peacock glamour hiding the burn scars King Surimir had left.

"We all miss him," Tavin said through his teeth.

She wasn't done with him, not by a league. Not when she had mere weeks to save her kin from the death he'd chosen for them. "And the queen is *also* being crowned? Will you be consorts?"

He looked like he'd stepped in surprise dung, and nearly ran into a line of servants bearing perfumed garlands toward the Hall of the Dawn.

"No," Tavin said quickly, "no. We will both rule, and both be free to find our own consorts. Come on, this is a shortcut." He stepped off the walkway, leading them through hedges trimmed into tigers, phoenixes, gods; they passed grand lapis lazuli–encrusted fountains and beds of sunrise glory blossoms tentatively unfurling in the morning glow. The Owl tooth hummed steady in her bones, charting it all for her.

Part of her despised it, for every time she remembered this garden, she would be drawn back to Tavin once more.

A heady perfume flooded Fie's nose, and a moment later, they strolled through a pristine archway into a grove of amber-pod trees wreathing an empty pavilion. Branches dangled like garlands, thick with waxy leaves and clusters of translucent gold petals. Some were painstakingly woven into the roof of the pavilion to make a ceiling of shimmering blooms.

"Here we are. You'll be at the ceremony tonight?" Tavin unwound his arm from hers.

Fie tried to ignore how her side felt cold for his absence. "Ay—yes."

"I'll keep an eye out for you, Lady Sakar." He caught her hand, bowed again, and brushed his lips to her knuckles.

She froze.

Tavin straightened, smiled, and slipped through the archway without another word.

All her teeth dropped from her command, cold and silent. The glamour vanished, the song died, and she was no longer a makeshift duchess but one more nameless Sparrow servant. A false one at that.

The amber-pods swayed before her, but it took a wave of belly-sickness to ken why. She sat hard on one of the pavilion's stone benches, the chill of the carved granite creeping through her linen trousers. Barf emerged from the shrubbery a moment later and leapt up to curl beside her, grooming a forepaw as Fie rested her head between her knees.

She'd gone light-headed when she'd first learned to call three teeth at once, so of course calling two different Birthrights would turn her belly. It wasn't quite alike; calling three of the same teeth felt like the difference between spotting a ship at sea and viewing it through a spyglass, if she were the spyglass. Balancing two different Birthrights at once, though . . .

They didn't swell or howl or rattle her bones. They made her balance them like cogs in a great machine, finding just the way to turn one so it moved the other. But there was a curious strength in it: none of her teeth had burned out, or even come halfway. They should have been nigh used up by now.

It wasn't just the teeth, though. It was the feel of Tavin's mouth on her skin, even for an instant.

She was too sick to cry, too furious not to. She buried her face in her hands, still curled over, and let the sobs shudder from her. Not ten days ago he'd sworn she would never be gone to him. One chance for a crown and he'd tossed that oath aside. She should have known better to trust anything promised between her legs.

She should have never believed him to be better.

But now for all he knew, she was being kept caged up in the countryside like his pet, to visit for his pleasure when it suited him, and he was free to woo a proper consort from a worthy caste. Her people would starve, Sabor would rot, and that was an acceptable price for a throne.

Even if we ourselves must burn.

Her belly roiled; her knuckles yet seared where his lips had been.

"I'm going to kill him," she breathed into the silence of the perfumed air. The amber-pod blossoms only shivered on their branches in reply. Fie didn't care. She'd sworn as much when she was dragged screaming from Draga's tent. And she had come to the royal palace to keep her oaths.

Something fluttered as she sat up. Fie's head whipped about just in time to see a crow take off from its perch on the shoulder of one more Phoenix statue, and rise into the sky.

CHAPTER FOURTEEN

— A PRISON FIT FOR A KING —

FIE HAD JUST ENOUGH TIME TO DRY HER FACE AND CONTEMPLATE burning the palace down before the hour-bell rang. When it did, she closed her eyes and made herself call on a Vulture witch-tooth, focusing on the clay charm-bead Viimo had given her.

The Vulture Birthright sparked and flared, lighting up Viimo's trail in Fie's senses. The end of it shifted, moving north, south, north, south. Then it stopped in the north for a long moment, only to resume moving north, south, north, south. After a minute or so it stopped in the north once more.

This was the message system they'd set up: Viimo had a tooth from Fie, a trinket from Khoda, and the Birthright to find where they stood at every hour-bell. If either Fie or Khoda sought out a particular place in the gardens at the chime of the hour-bell, it was to send a message. Waiting east, in the amber-pod grove, meant Fie had news.

Viimo could pass that message along to Khoda through his own spies in the prison, but Fie had no such network. Instead, Viimo paced north to south in her jail cell, a signal Fie would sense through a Vulture tooth. That pacing meant Viimo had a message from Khoda. Pausing a while in the north was a signal to meet at the next bell.

Their meeting spot was the statue behind the Hall of the Dawn, and the hall itself sat between the wings of the Divine Galleries. Now that she'd memorized the way from the gallery, Fie knew she could make it there several times over before the hour-bell chimed again. If she hurried, she could look over Jas's prison before she and Khoda met up; if luck was still with her, Tavin wouldn't have gone back.

She blotted her burning cheeks one more time, then took a deep breath and ducked through the pavilion's archway. Thanks to the Owl tooth, she picked out landmark after landmark to guide her way.

No one looked twice at a Sparrow servant hurrying through the palace gardens, especially with more Sparrows up and hurrying about the walkways with armfuls of garlands, silk, perfume oils, fineries, and decorations of every kind. Fie didn't have a repair order for the Divine Galleries, but the vestiges of the Pigeon witch-tooth's luck seemed to have kept the guards at bay. She darted in before that luck could fade, Barf at her heels.

She couldn't quite remember which of the towering statues had concealed the passage, but the cat had no such issue, scuttling behind a golden figure pouring out a pitcher of flame. Fie followed and found her licking a patch of marble where the spilled fish stew must have been hastily mopped up. Even better, Fie's slipper had tumbled behind a column. The calluses on Fie's feet were thick enough that it hadn't made much of a difference to her, but she yanked it back on for symmetry's sake, at least.

She wrenched the dog statue's head around, and the panel in the statue base lowered once more. Fie eased halfway down the steps, holding her breath and waiting for any telltale noise. The walls themselves seemed to rattle and thrum around her, making it all the harder to focus. God-graves always sang in her bones, and it was tolerable enough when she tread on only the one. If the legends were right, the Phoenixes had dumped all twenty-four of their dead gods under the two galleries, and the drone of their song ground into her very teeth.

There was no time to dawdle, not when she'd no notion if guards would pass by the statue or if Tavin would return. Fie rushed to the bottom of the steps. They opened to a short, narrow stone passage lit with more oil lamps. A line of bars walled off the end of the hall, making a small, enclosed chamber furnished with cushions, a bed, and a low table. A stack of dirty dishes sat near a narrow metal flap.

There were no Hawks on guard that she could see. Fie didn't know if that meant Rhusana couldn't spare any, or if the fact that it had taken a Pigeon witch's Birthright to find this prison meant secrecy was its main defense.

Jasimir lay on the bed, reading a scroll, but he sat up at the sound of her footsteps. His eyes widened. "*Fie?* What are you doing here?"

She planted her hands on her hips and cocked her head. "I'll give you two guesses."

Jasimir let out a laugh almost like a sob, hurrying to the bars. "F-fair point. I just didn't think Rhusana would leave you alive, no matter what she promised . . ." His face buckled briefly. Tavin's unspoken name hung over both of them like an executioner's sword.

"As far as she knows, she had me drowned. Lakima saved me. I'm sorry, Jas. I ran—my band, I had to—"

He shook his head. "You've been through enough for me. Of course you needed to get your family to safety. I can't believe you didn't . . . you didn't give up."

She winced and stared at the stone floor. "I did. I figured it was all rutted, all I could do was wait to starve with the rest of my kin. But some miserable wretches reminded me I owe the queen a whipping."

"You have help?" He straightened up, a light sparking in his face. "Is Tav in on the plan?"

She swallowed, voice knotting into a rasp. "No."

They both went quiet a moment, recoiling from the salt in the wound. Fie cleared her throat, then called her Owl tooth back to better cement her memory of this moment. "I haven't long. Tell me about this cell."

"It's made to hold royalty." Jasimir frowned. "*Technically*, only the royal family and their most trusted servants are supposed to know about them, and even then, Owl witches have been called to wipe memories if anyone got too loose-tongued. I'm sure Rhusana's only sending servants under her control." He shook his head. "And you just . . . walked in? Just like that?"

"Pigeon witch's tooth," Fie said by way of explanation, but couldn't help feeling the teensiest big smug. The palace was fine, but clearly it had not been Crow-proofed. "How do we get you out?"

"Ah. That I don't know." Jasimir twitched his fingers. A tiny golden flame ignited over them, then snuffed out. "Any of us can call fire in the palace, since we're so close to the god-graves. But these cells are built so that if I tried it, I'd burn up all the air and suffocate long before the bars got hot enough to bend. There's one under every statue in the Divine Galleries."

Fie closed her eyes, letting the words stamp into her mind with the memory Birthright. Anything that could help break Jas out, she needed to note. "Walls are stone, bars are metal, no fire. How'd they get you in to begin with?"

"I don't know. The last thing I remember is Aunt Draga's tent, and then I woke up here."

"Sounds like a healer's sleep," Fie muttered as she looked around, just to commit the words to memory along with everything else. "So Rhusana has at least one war-witch, along with a glamour-weaver. You're getting meals through that?" She pointed to the metal flap beside the stack of dishes, and Jasimir nodded. "No other locks, levers, anything?"

"None that I've seen."

Fie scowled about the room. She couldn't see any sort of mechanism that would open the cell, and they didn't have time for her to hunt for one. It stung, getting this close, but Jas's rescue would have to wait.

"I'm sorry, I have to get help, but I swear—I'm not giving up again."

The prince bit his lip and nodded, eyes glistening wet in the lamplight. He held out a hand through the bars. "We still have an oath to keep," he said, hoarse. "We'll make them pay."

Fie clasped it hard and fierce. "We'll burn it down."

He let her go, but when she reached the stairs, he called after her. "Fie."

"Aye?" She looked back.

Jasimir was pressed against the bars, hollow and desperate. "Everyone . . . my mother, my father, Aunt Draga, Tavin . . . They're all gone. You're all I have left. If I lose you, too . . ."

She knew that break in his voice; it matched hers, when she'd laid all her failings at Pa's feet days ago. So she gave him a sad grin and said, "Not just me. You've got the cat, too. Now sit tight for a bit, aye? Help's on the way."

Barf had apparently grown bored of the fish stew and moved on by the time Fie emerged. Fie wasn't troubled; she knew the tabby would show up again when it pleased her. The guards were just returning as she scuttled from the Divine Gallery, and they paid her no heed thanks to the Sparrow tooth she burned. The ground still buzzed beneath her slippers, but the overbearing song faded with the more distance she put between herself and the graves.

Khoda was already at the statue when she arrived, kneeling in the grass and studiously scrubbing the snowy marble pedestal. The statue itself loomed taller even than the ones inside the gallery, a golden woman crowned in flames wrought of amber, a sun rising from her outstretched hands, just like the royal crest. This had to be the Mother of the Dawn, patron of the monarchs. All the gods were supposed to have statues in the Divine Gallery, but apparently being their favorite got you an extra one outside, overlooking the gardens.

"You're here to help with the mildew?" Khoda asked gruffly, jerking his chin at a scrub brush nearby. From what Fie could see, there was no trace of scum on the marble, but an excuse was an excuse.

"Aye." She picked up the brush, then caught Khoda's frown. "*Yes.*" She knelt next to him and began to scrub. "I found him," she muttered.

"This side's clean enough," he announced. "Let's start on the back." They scooted until they were behind the pedestal, with the Hall of the Dawn behind them. If Fie had sorted the palace's layout right, then the wall of iridescent glassblack a few dozen paces away was the only thing between them and the thrones inside.

"Where is he?" Khoda hissed.

Fie opened her mouth to answer, then closed it as a notion struck. "Keep scrubbing," she told him, and fished out a new Peacock tooth and her half-burnt Owl one. She'd built glamours from memory just an hour ago; perhaps she could do so again.

The sparks and the songs took a moment to find their balance, but it helped to give them the structure of her own fresh memories as well. She set her Peacock tooth on the ground, and a miniature copy of Jasimir's cell spun itself into place, down to the dog statue that opened the way.

Khoda wasn't scrubbing anymore. She scowled and thrust the brush back in his hand, hissing, "I shouldn't have to tell a spy boy to keep his cover up."

"I've never seen anything like this," he said. "How did you get the image so accurate?"

"Owl tooth. That memory Birthright's coming in handy."

"And you can use Peacock and Owl at the—" He cut himself off. "We can talk about this later. The Divine Galleries weren't on our list. How did you find him?"

Fie grimaced and relayed as much as she could stomach: burning a Pigeon witch-tooth, following the servant, catching Tavin's eye. When she was done, Khoda was back to frowning.

"I don't like it," he admitted. "But if you've snagged his attention—"

Fie was already flicking the water from her scrub brush into his face. "*You* glamour yourself up like a Peacock and charm him then! I'd rather have split his skull in the amber-pods!"

"Well," Khoda said, wiping dirty water off his face with an air of faint disdain, "that makes what I'm about to suggest much more of a poppy dream, I suppose." Fie regarded him with the kind of suspicion she usually reserved for street meat. He shrugged. "I think we can use this. After the prince is free, of course. But the Sakars haven't exactly been bragging that their daughter died of the Sinner's Plague, and they'll be in mourning at their manor until the next moon at the earliest. The odds you'd be recognized as a dead girl are low, and in the meantime, Tavin may let something useful slip. You've already caught his eye. Let's see what else you can catch."

Fie had been scrubbing at the same patch of pedestal so hard, she felt likely to leave a divot. "I'd rather catch his throat and be done with it."

"Yes, I'm aware, and I'll save that honor for you once all this is over," Khoda sighed. "But this isn't like dealing with sinners or Oleanders. You have to think about strategy and spectacle. Hundreds of high-bred witnesses saw you take Jasimir's corpse moons ago, only for him to return in triumph. If you kill Tavin while he's posing as Jasimir, do you think the public will buy that the crown prince *miraculously* came back to life yet again?"

It's a divine mandate when a Phoenix prince survives the plague. It's a cheap hoax when his guard conveniently lives, too.

Tavin had made nigh the same point back at the beginning of Peacock Moon. Fie had to gulp down the hard knot that memory left in her throat.

"The same goes for Rhusana," Khoda continued. "She's the most powerful person who knows Tavin's a fake. Remove her and he'll just be harder to dethrone. We need them to take each other down." He studied the miniature jail, eyes lingering on the tiny Jasimir pacing behind the bars. "The first step is getting the prince out. Our two favorite traitors will blame each other for it, and we can use that. I've seen cells like this on Yimesei. I'm pretty sure I can break him out with a proper distraction."

Fie eyed the angle of the sun in the sky. "Coronation starts at sundown. You'll need to work fast."

At that, Khoda cracked a decidedly sharkish smile. "You've sorted out how to hold a Peacock glamour while using other teeth, right?" She nodded. "While you were off sniffing out the prince, one of my sources got me the program for the entire coronation ceremony. And I think . . . we can kill two birds with one stone."

THE SILK CROWN

Fie had been in the Hall of the Dawn once before, when she'd helped steal a crown prince faking his death. This time, she was here to stop a fake prince from stealing the crown.

It had been only slightly harder to break into the massive hall than it had been to sneak into the palace itself. Every entrance was guarded by Hawk war-witches reading caste in the guests' blood to verify only Splendid Castes and a select few Hawks were allowed within. Any witches were also sent to Vulture skinwitches to have the witch-sign on their wrist marked for tracking during the ceremony.

However, like Pigeon witches, the nation kept their few Sparrow witches all accounted for and on a tight leash, so much so that a stray witch was unthinkable. All the gentry waiting to enter had been lined up to the left of each entrance. The right side was kept clear for those who wanted to exit.

So when Fie called the first of her three Sparrow witch-teeth in the shadow of a hedge and vanished whole from sight, not a soul stirred to stop her from strolling right into the heart of the royal palace.

True to Pa's word, no one saw her coming.

She'd been right about the Mother of the Dawn: she could see the statue's silhouette behind the two thrones, streaky and warped through the wall of rainbow-hued glassblack. A great gold disc and spray of golden rays made a sun cresting behind the dais, but now solstice eve sunlight streamed in through the statue's fingers as well, gilding the hall's lacquered blues, scarlets, and violets in a dazzling peach-gold color that Fie found wholly unnecessary. According to Ebrim, the hall had been built with the thrones in the west so Phoenixes could watch the dawn through the matching glassblack panes at the eastern end, where Fie stood now.

The ground itself was patterned with ornate wheels of marble in green, black, and white, and immense cut-iron columns marched down the main walkway, each carved like a lantern with the image of great Phoenixes of the past: Bright Hamarian, Suro the Conqueror, and of course, Ambra. Fires in every column blazed without mercy, even in the heat of midsummer, and the air hung just as thick with perfume oils and incense as the night Fie had pulled two dead princes from the palace's guts.

The stream of gentry was beginning to congeal into a glittering crowd, mingling to the strains of musicians in the two galleries lining the upper levels of the hall. Sparrow servants wound round the multitudes, offering trays of pale wines and delicate pastries, brandishing palm fans to keep the gentry cool, and swiftly snatching away any empty goblets or plates. As Fie watched, a Peacock noblewoman in an emerald-choked headdress popped a thumbnail-size stuffed crab into her mouth, chewed once, wrinkled her nose, and motioned for a servant. The nearest Sparrow held his hand below her mouth, face stiff, as the Peacock daintily spat wet crab into his palm.

Fie winced, sick to her stomach. Back in Gen-Mara's shrine, Pa was counting out rations and stretching every grain, every drop, every crumb, to last until the end of the moon.

All the more reason to end Rhusana swift. Fie ducked behind a tapestry in a secluded corner to let her Sparrow witch-tooth go before it burned too low. A Peacock witch-tooth wove Niemi's face over her own once more; Fie borrowed the glimmering gown of another aristocrat, the elegantly dressed hair of a nearby countess, the swinging jewelry of a young woman she'd passed in line. When she was done, the teeth she'd strung at her wrist had turned to bangles, the swords at her hips hidden beneath a flowing skirt.

More importantly, everything was fine enough to blend in, but not so fine as to draw attention. She could barely manage speaking like a servant on her own; talking to any of these gentry would mean consulting another of Niemi's teeth for aid, and Fie reckoned she'd rather let someone spit crab on her.

Fie slipped out from the tapestry and drifted onward, careful to look purposeful enough that no one interrupted her. Wherever she ended up, she needed to have a clear view of the ceremony. But the highest of nobility had already packed the front of the hall, and she doubted they'd move for her. She squinted, trying to spy a way to squeeze in—

And the crowd shifted briefly, just long enough for her to catch sight of Tavin in the heart of the throng.

Her heart seized. From a distance, it didn't matter that he wore a glamour of Jasimir's face; it was close enough to his own to hurt. He was laughing. He looked *happy*. He looked—

Straight at her.

She tried not to flinch away as they locked eyes. Niemi wasn't there to tell her to be charming, but Khoda's reminder still was: *Let's see what else you can catch.*

Academically speaking, the expression Fie gave Tavin could have been called a smile. It also could have been called a death threat.

She hurried off before she made good on it, only to run into a Sparrow servant who'd slid into her path.

Fie stiffened. Not even a minute and she'd already been found out. She didn't even have her Phoenix teeth to burn a way out anymore, just the one from Tavin—

The servant gave a deep bow, and Fie tried not to let her relief show. Even after he straightened, his head stayed bent, his eyes cast to the ground. "Lady Sakar, a thousand apologies for the interruption of this unworthy one."

He paused, waiting for her. Fie gulped. It was a good day when a Sparrow didn't spit in her wake, normally. She'd at least find that less disconcerting. "Go on," she said, trying to sound aloof instead of unsteady.

Only then did she spot the crest sewn into his golden sash: two hands cradling a sun. The royal emblem. That meant he was a personal attendant, either of the prince or of the queen. "His Highness wishes to offer Your Ladyship a more favorable place to observe the coronation, should you so desire it."

She'd certainly caught something of Tavin's, then, and it was sore useful and sore repulsive. Fie hated it the way she hated viatik sometimes, when the goods were dear but the givers dreadful. And she knew better than to trust anything given freely.

"Very well," Fie said in her best highborn snob voice. "Where . . . is it?"

A flicker of curiosity darted through his face. "I will escort Your Ladyship there, if it pleases."

This felt like a game, a back-and-forth like Twelve Shells. She'd spent so long playing games like this from the other side of the board—for every viatik, every Hawk bribe, every Money Dance—but it was always just to keep from losing too much.

For the first time, she was meant to have the upper hand. Fie tried not to panic. She'd already told the man she would go, hadn't she?

But a Sparrow servant wouldn't give a Peacock orders. He was waiting on her approval.

It was a very strange feeling.

"It pleases me," Fie echoed. "Lead on."

The Sparrow man bowed once more and guided her through the crowds as seamlessly as a needle through gauze, evading trains of satin that spilled like rivers across the marble, unsteady crystal goblets swung for emphasis in silver-crusted hands, fellow servants darting to and fro on business of the Splendid Castes. Finally he deposited her at the edge of the front row of onlookers with another bow and a sweep of his arm. "Does Your Ladyship desire anything else?"

She could barely hear him over the musicians nearby, who had begun a jig that rang too cheery in this grand sprawling hall. About to ask for a different spot, she changed her mind. Other nobles were sneaking glances at her behind palm fans and elaborate collars. Surely they wondered about her and what it meant that a prince would want her to see him become a king.

But this close to the music, no one would try to make conversation with her, which meant she could leave Niemi's voice out of her head that much longer. She'd also have no need to fear someone bumping against her and finding a sword where there was only supposed to be silk.

She shook her head and then, as an added touch, flicked her hand in dismissal. The servant melted into the crowd almost too swift, and

Fie realized most of the Sparrows had to be calling on their Birthright. Even though they couldn't vanish outright like their witches, anytime Fie tried to look straight at a servant, she found her attention skidding off to land on a sparkling jewel or a pounding drum.

Whether that was the Sparrows' choice she couldn't say, but she remembered Niemi's blithe derision that morning. It was equally likely the gentry only wanted to be offered trays of delicacies without having to think too hard about who held them.

The pounding drum swelled in Fie's ears as the sunlight began to dim. Solstice had kept the sun long in the sky, but finally it touched the edge of the cliffs looming over the royal quarters at the west end of the palace. The drum fell silent. A hush flooded the hall as two lines of gold-cloaked priests filed in, one from either side of the thrones.

Khoda had told Fie of the ceremony details, and she'd committed it to her memory with one more Owl tooth to be safe. All the priests before her now had been born royal Phoenixes, but either they'd been too far from the line of succession to hope for a crown, or they'd assessed—correctly, Fie would say—the average life expectancy of a monarch and decided it not worth the risk. Instead, they'd sworn a Covenant oath forsaking any claim to the throne and bound themselves to the service of a dead Phoenix god instead.

Once they were in place, the Phoenix Priesthood regarded the room with an odd kind of sobriety, Fie thought. There was a peculiar charge to the silence in the Hall of the Dawn, glances flicking between painted nobles like little shocks of static, as if to ask, *Is this really happening?*

Khoda had warned Fie of this, too; Rhusana was not universally beloved, and with so many of the most powerful families in the nation present, there was a chance they might take matters into their own hands.

But no one stirred, save the sun that sank a little lower, and save the priests who, after a long moment of unease, raised their arms and cried in one voice, *"Now begins the night before the dawn!"*

Music burst forth from the galleries, forcefully joyful and triumphant, as the Phoenix Priesthood began to sing. The first hymn praised the rulers of the past, the next Mother of the Dawn, and then the rest of the dead Phoenix gods got their due, and so on, until Fie was certain the only thing keeping her from falling asleep on her feet was the musical accompaniment blaring in her ears. Finally, the last of the sunlight drained away and the priests fell silent. All but two filed away, then returned, bearing two basins of sharp-smelling oil and two long, narrow strips of plain, undyed silk.

The two priests who had stayed positioned themselves before each of the empty thrones. They both picked up silk strips, then submerged them in the golden oil. "Warriors, have you chosen who rules you?" the priests asked as one.

With a pang, Fie saw they were addressing Draga, who stood near the center of the room. The master-general's face glistened with sweat, like she wanted to vomit. Whether that meant she was still straining against Rhusana's will, Fie couldn't say. Draga gritted out, "We have chosen."

A ripple went through the crowd, almost like a sigh. The priests called, "Noble houses, have you chosen who rules you?"

There was a pause. For a moment, Fie thought perhaps no one might answer and she wouldn't have to do aught to foul up the ceremony at all.

Then a man called from behind Fie in a cold, decisive voice, "We have chosen."

Heads turned, and Fie couldn't help it; she turned, too. The man stood only a few paces behind her, and he wore a fine robe in deep Peacock green, but she was close enough to read the elegant pattern of pearl, jade, and gold embroidered in petals and leaves over his shoulders. It formed a mantle of oleanders.

Her breath caught even as her own sense made her whip back around. Oleanders were no threat to a Peacock girl. Even though her hair stood on end, she couldn't let it show.

More mutters of *"we have chosen"* pattered through the hall like reluctant rain, rising to a hum, until the priests were satisfied. "People of Sabor," the priests cried, "have you chosen who rules you?"

This time the answer came like thunder, rolling about the room from soldier and noble alike: *"WE HAVE CHOSEN."*

Fie couldn't help but notice the lines of Sparrow servants banished to wait at the walls until the ceremony was over. Not a one had so much as mouthed the words.

"Let them come forward." The priests nodded to either side of the dais.

Fie caught a shuffle nearby. Tavin was being led from beneath the shadows of the nearby gallery in a simple, well-made tunic and trousers of undyed, unadorned linen. Once again, his eyes found her. The corner of his mouth lifted.

Then, as he passed by, he gave her a slow, deliberate wink.

Some small, miserable worm of hope in her had clung to the notion that earlier had been a fluke; that she didn't understand the ways of princes and palaces; that, at the very least, since Jasimir didn't shine to girls like that, Tavin would have the sense to refrain.

She had been granted one small boon, though: any who saw her cheeks darken now would take it for the blush of a flattered young noblewoman, and not the rising bitter-burnt fury of a girl whose last scrap of faith had shriveled.

Khoda had told her not to kill either Tavin or Rhusana, not yet. But that didn't mean she couldn't get creative.

She'd nearly missed Rhusana's own entrance from the opposite side of the dais. Tavin and the queen passed the great mammoth-tusk horns that bracketed the dais; they would be sounded to announce the new monarchs once the ceremony was complete.

As Tavin and Rhusana knelt on velvet cushions before the thrones, Fie swore to herself that those tusks would stay silent a long, long time.

The two priests lifted the silk from the basin, dripping ribbons of golden oil onto the marble.

"The first crown," the priests announced in unison as the sky behind them cooled to a grim blue-gray through the glassblack panes.

"Wear it," the priest standing over Rhusana said, winding the silk around her brow, "and think on what it means to rule."

"Wear it," echoed Tavin's priest as she cinched the strip on him, "and think on what it means to burn."

"Wear your first crown," they said together, "and think on what it means to rise."

Fie slowly reached for a tooth she'd knotted into the string at her wrist just for this occasion.

Tavin and Rhusana stayed kneeling as the priests began another back-and-forth chant, some nonsense about the glory of the Phoenix gods and signs of their favor. In Fie's experience, talk like that was naught more than a garland to drape around a misdeed or a knife at the throat of someone you wanted to rob.

Instead, she kept an eye on the growing dark, and on those silk crowns.

The rest of the ceremony was meant to be straightforward. The priests would ask for Ambra's blessing upon the new rulers-to-be. Then, Khoda had told her, would come what the priests called "the Miracle of the Burning Crown": the silk would burst into flame as a sign of Ambra's favor.

"And by Ambra's favor," Fie had pointed out as they ran through the plan in Ebrim's office that afternoon, "you mean the fact that even a royal toddler could light those crowns, since they're practically kneeling on dead Phoenix gods."

Khoda had tilted his head with a lazy grin. "I guess the presence of the Phoenixes makes it a miracle?"

"Shitty miracle," Fie had observed.

But now she watched a bead of oil slide down the side of Tavin's face as the priests droned on, and she thought of what it meant to burn.

Doubtless he would light the crowns for himself and Rhusana. Or maybe he would light his own, and a Peacock illusion would serve for hers. The point was to show the crowd they were Phoenixes true and could not be harmed by fire. Then they would meditate until dawn, and when the final ashes of their silk crowns were swept away, they would be given crowns of gold and rise with the sun.

Fie's eyes stayed on that twist of silk.

He'd called her the girl he loved. He'd enjoyed her in his bed. He'd sworn she would never be gone to him. But all it took was a palace and the promise of a golden crown to burn it all to ash.

Fie made sure the tooth at her wrist was still securely wrapped in a bit of rag, for if it touched her skin, it would sing double, no, triple as loud as any other she carried. For one thing, the Phoenix god-graves rumbled beneath her toes, calling to the scrap of bone she held now.

For another, the teeth of the living always sang louder than those of the dead. And Tavin lived yet, though how long she would abide it, Fie no longer knew.

The priests wound down their chant, the sky well and truly black with night now. Torches and lamps had been lit about the hall, but the great lantern-columns cast the brightest light.

"And now, O Ambra of the Sunrise, Queen of Day and Night, Tiger-Rider, Fire-Drinker, God-Sent, Conqueror of the Highest Lands, we beseech your memory and your name," Rhusana's priest proclaimed, holding his arms aloft.

Tavin's priest raised hers as well. "Grant your favor to these new rulers, that they may follow in your ways. Show us that your flame burns on in them."

Fie took a deep breath and called first an Owl tooth. The spark of the scholar within jumped with curiosity, eager to unravel a new mystery, but Fie offered a plea instead: *I need to find a memory*, she told it.

And swiftly, she slipped Tavin's tooth from her wrist into her palm, rolling it to call out the spark.

His thoughts, his memories, surges of blood and fire, they all threatened to drown her as she tried and tried and tried to shut them out. She didn't want to see him, she didn't want to feel—

This, the scholar said, picking a memory out of the maelstrom in her bones. Fie lunged for it and fell into a dark night moons ago, one she knew well—but this skewed different, this was through Tavin's eyes—

He crouched on a branch in the dark, the Crow girl and Jas beside him. Until a moment ago, they'd been utterly invisible; Fie had called the Birthright of a Sparrow witch as easily as slipping on a sandal, and they had only appeared now so she could call on a Phoenix tooth.

She was too good at her work, he thought, and a rebellious part of him wondered what would happen if the Crows ever decided they'd had enough of carting around plague-dead. Perhaps that was why the Oleander Gentry were so hell-bent on keeping them unarmed and starving.

Though since they'd acquired Phoenix teeth, perhaps that would all change. Even now, Fie seemed about to put out a hearty campfire, a trick he hadn't mastered until he'd practiced his firecraft for a few years.

"It's not working," Jas whispered, and Tavin swore silently, knowing that had to have shattered the girl's focus.

Sure enough, the fire roared with glee as Fie hissed. She drew a sharp breath, no doubt trying once more. Tavin debated a moment; she was too clever by far, and if she noticed someone else's hand in putting the fire out—

Hoofbeats said they'd both be distracted soon. He didn't have a choice.

The fire called to an ugly part of him, one that knew what it wanted and wasn't afraid to take it. He breathed it in a moment, that need to ignite and devour, then exhaled, just as a Phoenix priest had secretly taught him, banishing the hunger and the flame.

The campfire went out.

He glanced sidelong at Fie. She didn't seem to have noticed a thing, fumbling for that Sparrow witch-tooth again.

There was something in the way her brow furrowed that called to that hunger in him, hooked in his ribs like the point of a spear—

Fie dropped the memory like a hot coal, yanking her thoughts from the teeth before they could show her anything worse.

She had what she needed.

Just then, the silk crowns began to smoke.

Both the fires were real, little tongues of flame licking up the outside of the silks. Rhusana was sweating. Fie inhaled swift, feeling the fires call to the ugly part of her, the one that wanted to burn this hall down with them all inside, burn Sabor from mountain to coast, just to make them all reckon with a Crow for a conqueror.

And then—she cast it from her, breath and fire and rage.

The silk crowns snuffed out.

A gasp swept the crowd.

From where Fie stood, she had a truly perfect view of Rhusana's face as it shifted through first bewilderment, then anger, then accusation. The faintest of snarls bared her teeth as she shot Tavin a furious glare. He shook his head ever so slightly, as if to say, *This isn't me.*

Rhusana kept staring at him. Tavin swallowed and closed his eyes, and a moment later, the silk crowns ignited again.

There were many, many things Fie could not forgive Tavin for. Something about *that*, though, something about him still trying to light the damn crowns, still trying to make *that* work when he'd been so ready to give up on her and Jasimir—

That was something no chief would abide.

Initially, Fie had thought to just blow out the crowns, again and again, until the ceremony was called off. But Tavin's own tooth had barely been tapped of its power, especially here on the Phoenix graves. It practically begged for her to put it to use.

And she'd made her plan back before Tavin himself had shown her the truth: in the end, she was one more thing to burn for a crown of gold.

Khoda had said the difference between a thief and a conqueror was an army. Tonight, it would be just a tooth.

Fie took another breath, letting memory and bone guide her, and this time she tasted it: every fire in the room, from lamp and torch and blazing column, simmering on her tongue. When she exhaled, it was a decree of exile.

Out, she told the lamps, and all along the walls, they obeyed.

Quiet, she told the crowns, and they fell silent, bleeding smoke.

Go, she commanded to every last towering column, to the fires within that carved dead Phoenix monarchs from the black iron.

One by one they went dark, plunging the Hall of the Dawn into unbroken night.

Fie caught muffled yelps of alarm, the rustle of fabric and clanging of jewelry, and allowed herself a vicious grin. Then she stuffed it below a mask of dismay and called on the Phoenix Birthright once more.

The Hall of the Dawn fell silent as fire bloomed into uneven letters over the dais, each nigh tall as Tavin.

MURDERER

BASTARD

TRAITORS

She let the words hang over their heads a long, terrible moment, then spun that flame into the shape of a bird whose fiery wingtips spanned near as wide as the hall itself, burnishing the iron columns to either side.

Awestruck gasps swept through the hall as it hovered well above the thrones. Rhusana's face had twisted with fury and astonishment; Tavin only stared, wide-eyed. Apparently even this wasn't enough to rattle him.

Then again, Fie thought, what good was conjuring up a phoenix if she wasn't going to *use* it?

The fiery specter beat its massive wings once, twice—then dove for the crowd.

There were real screams then. Fie was sure to keep the phoenix well above them, if for no other reason than that she didn't want fire catching a wayward headdress and spreading to the rest of the Hall of the Dawn while she was still inside. Someone crashed into her and she stumbled, only to get knocked aside as another noble shoved past.

Hawk soldiers shouted orders, trying to calm the pandemonium, but even if they could be heard over the cacophony of shouts, cries, and tearing fabric, Fie doubted any Peacock would listen. Hysterical babble burst from the crowd—"*The gods are angry!*" "*Ambra has turned her face—*" "*—false?*"

Khoda had wanted a distraction. She reckoned this would do it . . . but it never hurt to make sure.

Fie ducked behind a now-cold column that broke the throng like a boulder in a river, trying not to laugh, then swung her phoenix about for one more swoop at the crowd. A fresh tide of screaming nobility fled for the exits as soldiers hustled Tavin and Rhusana off the dais. The monstrous phoenix soared so near to their heads, Rhusana flinched away.

The bird crashed into the wall of glassblack, and with a flash of inspiration, Fie smeared the fire over it like butter on panbread. The great gold disc, the bejeweled rays, they all sagged and wilted, bleeding scorched gemstones. Even the gilded edges of the thrones themselves seemed to dull.

Fie muffled a cold laugh in her sleeve and let the fire go, and darkness swallowed the Hall of the Dawn once again. But not perfect dark this time—a fading glow spread over the chaos, cast from the ruin of molten gold behind the dais.

And through it, Fie saw Hawk guards surrounding Tavin, hurrying him through the tumult of fleeing gentry and toward the nearest door.

She needed to get to Khoda and Jasimir, she needed to go back into hiding, she needed to get out—

Her Sparrow witch-tooth had barely been spent. Tavin's tooth dug into her palm; his sword hung heavy at her side.

Return it, Lakima's memory urged.

The embers of fire-song in Fie's own bones did not argue. All through the dark she heard the shrieks of nobility crashing into one another, not caring who they trampled in their desperation to escape. The finest, stiffest, most high-bred Peacock families in Sabor had turned to little better than beasts trying to claw their way out.

She felt dangerous, she felt raw and undeniable, like vengeance made flesh, like a walking curse. And she was not done with any of them yet.

The Sparrow witch's Birthright stole Fie from sight once more as she wove through the masses like an asp, her eyes fixed on Tavin's charred silk crown.

CHAPTER SIXTEEN

A SHOW OF STRENGTH

SHE CLUNG TO THEIR TRAIL LIKE AN ANCIENT GRUDGE, NEVER too far from reach. Every time Tavin's guards looked back, their gazes passed right through her as they hustled their makeshift prince down a walkway that hummed under Fie's soles with the bones of dead gods. They'd chosen to leave through the other half of the Divine Gallery, where Fie had not yet tread.

The eyes of the statues seemed to burn on her, as if the Phoenix gods took issue with her mummery of fire. Fie refused to be sorry.

Tavin's guards did not slow as they cleared the crowds. If anything, they quickened their pace, striding down the mostly empty lantern-lit colonnades and shoving aside the few servants who didn't duck off the path in time. As Fie passed one fallen woman, she was tempted to begin snuffing out the lanterns ahead of Tavin's guard, row by row, just to see them run.

But she'd learned long ago the hard difference between what she wanted and what must be done. If they ran, she would lose them in the dark long before the blade at her side could be returned.

"What do you think—" She heard one Hawk begin.

Another Hawk cut her off. "It was a threat, that's all we need to know."

At the rear of the squad, two guards traded looks. One cast an uncertain glance behind them, scouring every shadow for signs of an intruder. Fie knew they'd only find an empty walkway.

She gave in and blew out a lantern—just the one. The guards' eyes widened. They hesitated a moment, then whipped back around to keep their eyes on Tavin.

The escort wound into the royal gardens, cutting through tunnels cleverly hidden between hedges and behind falls of vines. Fie kept at their heels with an Owl tooth burning in her bones, committing every step, every shadow, every mutter to memory.

Every drop of sweat or oil running down the back of Tavin's neck.

The farther they went, the further a strange, dreadful feeling welled up in Fie's bones. It wasn't a sickness, no, nor a weakness she knew; it didn't feel *wrong* in the way that skin-ghasts set her on edge.

It felt . . . it felt like she'd felt at Little Witness's tower, standing at the edge of a measureless sea, one that meant to swallow her with barely a ruff of foam to mark her drowning.

She clung tight to her teeth until it passed. Not too long after, they emerged into a wide, open courtyard, its intricate tiles little better than an unruffled lake in the dim moonlight. From its center rose an island of a structure, bedecked with domes, fringes of gold, tiled roofs that flared like skirts, intricate friezes, and balustrade-laced verandas that looked high enough to see most of Dumosa sprawled below.

The royal quarters. Where Rhusana slept. And her son. And Tavin. Fie didn't know if a Crow had ever set foot inside.

She supposed she'd best leave an impression, then.

The guards led them into a grand foyer clearly meant to impress people far more important than Fie. It was like a vision of paradise from *The Thousand Conquests* with its elegant marble fountain, lacy golden lanterns casting constellations onto an ebony ceiling, and floor inlaid with brass and tile of deepest blue.

Fie's band hadn't had to scrape for meals in a while now, but she still couldn't help measuring every ounce of gilt and finery against every night she'd slept with a hot coal of hunger in her belly.

She did not have long to weigh it, as Tavin's guard divided, half taking posts at the foot of one of two matching stairways, the other half continuing up the steps. She followed them up one, two flights of stairs, passing more guards whose heads bowed but whose eyes narrowed in Tavin's wake. Any servants in the halls flattened themselves to the walls, then knelt, staring at the ground.

Fie's skin crawled.

It wasn't just the guards and the servants putting her on edge, but it took three dark hallways sweeping by to ken why: they were the *only* people she saw in this grand jewel box. The royal quarters weren't a home; they were a Money Dance unto themselves, a show of strength, shoving fingers of gold into visitors' eyes and saying *See, this is what Saborian royalty is worth.*

But they were also, in a haunting way, empty. When Fie had called memories from Phoenix teeth, the royal quarters were always filled with chatter, light, life, heated debates and petty triumphs, a minor uproar every time the current monarch walked from one wing to another.

These weren't the same royal quarters. The hushed, still shadows in nigh every corner made Fie feel like a beetle crawling about the guts of a gaudy corpse.

She nearly ran into the back of a guard and caught herself just in time. They'd stopped outside a chamber with two guards already positioned by the doorway.

"Sweep the halls again," the leader of the guard ordered. "We need to be certain nothing and no one followed us."

The guards posted at the door traded looks at "nothing." The rest saluted and turned on their heels. Fie scrambled back, but they were walking down the hall three abreast, leaving no room for her. At their pace, they'd catch up before she could get to the end of the corridor—

Something in her spine gave a *tug*, and when she blinked, she saw it: the threads and currents of fortune as a Pigeon witch saw them. They were drawing her toward a shallow alcove.

Wretch had a saying: *When the Covenant grants you a favor, don't waste it asking why.* Fie scuttled back toward the arch, which was identical to one on the opposite side of the corridor—but when she pushed against the back wall, it gave so suddenly that she near fell on her rear.

The back panel had split down the middle like veranda doors, opening to a still, quiet dark. The tide of luck nudged Fie, and she did not need another prompting. She bolted in and eased the panel halves shut again, holding her breath until the footfalls of the Hawks had faded.

The luck current led on into the unbroken dark. Fie swallowed. Then she registered the faint hum in her own bones and the simmer of a tooth on her string.

The Pigeon witch-tooth she'd burned out this morning had, somehow, sparked back to life.

Fie swallowed. The tooth had been cold, empty bone, she'd swear it on any of the two dozen dead gods' graves she had to choose from here. She'd only left it on the string because she hadn't found a good place to throw burned-out teeth yet.

Her Sparrow witch-tooth, too, seemed to have recovered enough of its spark to buy Fie more time, but she let it go cold. Part of her wanted to get out of the royal quarters as swift as possible, go find Khoda and Jas, and sort out their next move from the safety of the Sparrow quarters.

The rest of her had made it this far, and still burned with the wrath she'd kindled in the Hall of the Dawn. Besides, whatever hidey-hole the currents of fortune had led her into, it seemed the only way out would be to keep following them. She didn't have time to waste asking why.

She made her way along the trail of luck, hands stretched before her. It wasn't too long before they brushed up against startlingly rough canvas. When she pushed it aside, milk-pale moonlight bloomed before her, carving out a strange and lifeless chamber.

The fortune trails coiled inside, smug and gleeful like a hound who had led its master to a kill. Fie stepped into the room, staring about. Only dim moonlight gave her any reprieve from the dark, peering in from a glass dome overhead like a half-lidded eye. Cloth-covered furniture jutted from the flat sea of the cool tile floor like shoals.

In the far corner, Fie saw something that picked at her memory a moment until she placed it: a spear rack identical to the one in Draga's tent.

No wonder it felt so cold and still—still as death. Instead of Tavin's or Rhusana's rooms, fortune had brought her to the chamber of the late Queen Jasindra.

Now she just needed to find out *why*.

Fie paced about, frowning. Khoda had said the king sealed the room years ago, yet she saw no dust on the furniture covers, nor on the windowsill, nor the floor. It all looked clean as the day the old queen died.

She reached for the dustcloth over the bed. Something brushed across the back of her hand like a cobweb. When she went to pluck it off, she saw . . . naught.

Fie went still. Then she looked up again at the glass dome. A half moon stared back.

Solstice always fell on the middle of Phoenix Moon, when the moon had swollen to its fullest.

Someone had cast a glamour over the entire room.

No wonder luck had led her here. Fie closed her eyes, trying to think. She didn't know if a Peacock tooth could undo a glamour the way Tavin's tooth let her snuff out fires. Maybe the truth Birthright— but she'd only used it to draw the truth from people, not clear away an illusion.

Then again, she'd sorted out how to balance Peacock and Owl. Lips pursing, she found one tooth each of Peacock and Crane and kindled them both.

They clashed horribly, like a flute and a lyre in a tavern brawl, but she knew the trick of it now. It took a few tries to get them to settle into cooperation, but then—then she saw it, the glamour over the room, glowing too vivid to be real.

Show me the truth, she told the teeth.

It was as if they had pulled the cords on a curtain, sweeping the glamour aside in uncanny folds of another world. The true room unrolled before her, lit by the glare of a full, unblinking moon.

Fie couldn't help a sharp breath. Her hands curled to her chest, nausea crawling up her throat.

Everywhere she looked, she saw hair.

Long, silvery strands strung about the room like sick garlands, knotted with other, darker hairs. Shelves and shelves of shorter hairs, all fastened to neat squares of parchment with names scrawled out in a neat square hand. More of those parchment squares broken out over the bed and the windowsills, even tacked to the walls like a papery rash. Bundles of hair like skeins of yarn, each bearing a single label: *Livabai. Chalbora. Teisanar.*

One bundle had been left unwound on a desk, its label next to it: *Karostei*. Beside it were strange, gray, papery curls. Fie made herself squint closer, only to stumble back, trying not to vomit.

Skin. They were strips of dried skin.

It took a moment for Fie to conquer her mutinous belly. When she saw a nearby shelf of tidy jars packed with more bits of skin, she had to fight that battle all over again.

But Fie had work to do and an oath to keep and time that was running short. She glanced about to take in the whole of the room.

There were two doorways she could see besides the passage she'd taken. One had been boarded shut for good, but the other stood agape, planks sitting nearby with the nails still protruding. If that was Rhusana's way out, then likely it would work best for Fie, too—or at least it was better than popping out into the hallway with no way to check for patrols first.

A thick mantle of dust had accumulated on the higher shelves of the room, but mostly everything was where it had been in the glamour. One low dresser had been revealed as a tidy stack of crates holding envelopes, inks, parchment; a station had been set up nearby with parchment squares, a glue pot, and a quill.

That was the worst part, Fie reckoned: the *order* of it all. She'd expected a monster. She had not expected one so organized.

More squares sat on the desk. Fie picked out names she recognized: *Draga, Jasimir, Burzo, Kuvimir*. She made herself get close enough to riffle through them all, telling herself it was just to make sure her own name was not among them. Then she checked the shelves and their rows of squares lined up like toy soldiers, ducking the long strands of what she presumed to be Rhusana's hair.

She did not find a square with her name.

Nor did she find what she'd been looking for true. She checked every square, every name. None of them were *Tavin*.

She hadn't expected it, she told herself, but the sinking twist in her chest called her a liar.

Expected, no. Hoped for, yes.

As she passed the shelf of jars, something caught her eye: a second row of jars tucked behind the row full of skin. Their contents looked more solid, weighty—

She drew one out, and her heart leapt into her throat. The jars were full of teeth, and not just any teeth. Fie dug out a handful and let them sift through her hands like grain, near choking down a laugh of pure relief.

Finally, *finally*, a boon.

They were Phoenix teeth. They were *hers*. It must have been Rhusana's own killers who took them from Drudge and bore them here to make sure nothing so precious, so *dangerous*, ever fell into the hands of a Crow again.

"Ha," Fie muttered to herself. "Guess again, you dog-faced hag."

She stole one of the pillows from the bed, cut it open, pulled out the stuffing, and poured the Phoenix teeth in, jar after jar, until she'd emptied them all. Just the weight of it alone made her want to sing. She'd soft-footed her way around this miserable palace for fear of the terrible price of getting caught. Now, if it truly came down to it, she could burn her way free.

Fie hefted her teeth, about to swing the bag over her shoulder, and paused. Her eyes traced the web of gossamer hairs spun about the room.

Fortune had brought her this far. And it wasn't just so she could take what was hers.

In the end, she left one thing: a single tooth, sitting on the bed in the middle of a heap of parchment squares cleared from every shelf. Fie had even made herself empty the skin jars into the pile.

As she padded quickly to the open doorway, gold fire spilled out from the molar. By the time she reached the end of the hall, the moonlight at her back had blushed rosy.

There was no canvas drape over this exit, but the faint orange glow showed a sliding screen. Fie called on her Sparrow witch-tooth again to wipe her from sight. No lantern-light filtered through the screen, but that didn't mean the room was empty.

She eased the screen aside, and moonlight lit her way again, this time from a whorl of skylights that cut the shape of the sun into the domed golden ceiling. The chamber itself was practically a wheel of gold, sprays of carved and gilded plumage coiling from every arch, every bedpost, every column and only interrupted by graceful blades of carved golden fire. It didn't feel like a bedroom. It felt like a shrine. And if it adjoined the dead queen's chambers, Fie had a strong notion who that shrine was for.

But unlike the queen's room, this one was occupied. A figure lay in an achingly familiar sprawl on the gold-draped bed.

The king had slept just fine in this temple to his own divinity, and now it seemed Tavin would too.

There was something awful about his sleeping face, something that froze her feet to the cool, moon-washed tiles. She'd loved it once, waking up first so she could see the heart of him beneath all his flash and charm, perfect peace without guile.

Somewhere in Sabor, Oleander Gentry were riding down Crows this very night. Somewhere, another child was dying of plague as their village argued over beacons. And in Pa's shrine, their rations were dwindling, and they were one more day closer to starvation.

Fie hated the peace in Tavin's face now, near as much as she hated the part of her that didn't. The part of her that still lit up at his touch and his smile and his laugh, the part that yet starved for him—the part of her that had mercy for a bastard boy.

She hated it, hated him, hated herself so much, the dreadful garish room swam with tears. She could remind herself of how he'd betrayed her, the death he'd signed her people to, and still part of her would do anything to lie in that foul golden bed with him.

She wanted to cut that part of her out, let it burn with the dead queen's room, just to end the agony she craved.

And since she couldn't cut herself free, she would cut out the next best thing.

Fie drew the Hawk sword.

Her slippers skimmed the tiles without a sound. She took care not to let her shadow fall over his face as she ghosted closer to the bed, moonlight dripping along the glistening steel.

Return it.

Was Lakima even still alive? Or had he signed her death warrant, too? Tears spilled down her face, hot and furious and horrified with the weight of the blade in her hand.

Stop, that soft, broken part of her wept as she raised the Hawk sword, *don't——you can still love him, you can leave him be——*

And the coldest part of her whispered back: *Not if I want to live.*

Once, she'd thought she could be like the girls she saw in the sparks of teeth. Fie *wanted* to be like them, beaming at the attention of a lover, laughing at their follies, making space in even the hardest of hearts for ballads and sweet poetry and the unspoken oath in the touch of a hand.

Now she knew the bitter truth: that softness came at a price she would not pay. And she would not forgive Tavin for trying to make her pay it.

He'd made her feel safe; he'd made *only* her feel safe. He'd been willing to give up all the Crows for it.

And that was not enough.

He didn't stir as the shadow of the blade fell under his chin.

Fie supposed she ought to say something clever and vicious, but there was nothing clever about cutting a boy's throat in his sleep, and her viciousness had no words. His Peacock glamour had been called off for the night, so it wasn't even Jasimir's face below her but Tavin's own, every scar and bump and mark that she knew by heart, no Owl tooth required.

Pa would tell her not to drag it out.

She couldn't make herself lay the edge to skin. The blade hovered less than a finger over his throat. The sight horrified her.

Fie whipped fury through her veins, but grief answered instead. She'd *wanted* to walk the rest of her roads with him. She'd wanted more. And Little Witness had told her she was right for wanting it, but how could she be, when this was where it led?

End it, her frost-cold self said. *He dies now, or he dies by Rhusana's hand. What you want is already dead.*

It was never going to get easier to deal mercy. She didn't know why she'd hoped it would. All she could do was make it swift.

Fie lifted the sword, braced herself over Tavin, let the point of the blade hang over his throat. All she had to do was fall, by every dead god she could fall—

Too late, she felt a tear roll off her nose. It landed on Tavin's throat.

His eyes flew open.

Fie yanked the sword away as he bolted upright. She slapped a hand over her mouth before she could gasp aloud. The Sparrow witch-tooth kept her out of his sight. It would not keep her out of his earshot.

Tavin touched a hand to his collarbone, where her teardrop had slid to rest. His gaze swept the room, passing right through her.

His breath tangled in her hair. She didn't dare stir, heart thundering in her ears like an alarm.

So close she could taste him.

So close she could feed him his own blade.

Tavin scoured the shadows of the king's room again, wide-eyed, his own chest heaving.

Then he whispered into the night: "Fie?"

Just then, a storm of footfalls boiled up from just beyond a doorway Fie hadn't noticed, the trill of chimes like rainfall in its wake. "*Get out,*" a familiar voice spat behind the closed doors.

"Yes, Your Majesty." The stamp of Hawk boots was impossible to miss. Once it faded, the doors were thrown open with a bang, lanternlight spilling into the bedroom. Tavin flinched back, blinking, and opened his mouth.

Rhusana didn't wait, little better than a knife of a silhouette in the doorway. "Jasimir's gone."

"*What?*" Tavin squinted at her.

"Don't play the fool with me." The queen swiped a lamp from the wall and stalked in, slamming the doors shut behind her. She had changed from the linen shift of the coronation ceremony into a simple, sleeveless silk gown, her pale hair in three heavy braids that swayed like asps. In a swift motion, she'd seized Tavin by the neck, her jeweled claws digging into skin. "What do you know?"

Fie decided she could take a step back now. She did so slowly, keeping her Hawk sword close.

"N-nothing," Tavin ground out. Then he fouled up: he glanced at the wavering flame of her lamp.

Rhusana jammed it closer, the oil sloshing in its reservoir, and Tavin couldn't help a wince. "Surimir made certain you weren't fond of fire, didn't he?"

"I don't have to like it," Tavin said coldly. "It still won't harm me."

"How sure are you?" Rhusana gave the lamp another swirl, and oil splashed up near to the brim. "What if it's not just the flame? What if it's oil boiling on your skin? Will you burn then?"

Without the Peacock glamour to hide behind, the burn scars of Tavin's hand caught the lamplight all too clear.

"I told you I don't know anything," Tavin growled. "What do you mean, Jas is *gone*?"

Rhusana glowered down at him. Slowly, she let him go, leaving five dark divots on his neck. "The servant who was *supposed* to bring him dinner was found unconscious in a storeroom. The Divine Gallery guards swear they saw him enter on time anyway, but don't remember him leaving. The coronation fiasco was just a diversion. The cell is empty."

Tavin glared back up at the queen for a long moment. Then he asked, "Where is Fie?"

That took the queen by surprise. She frowned, setting the lamp on a bedside table, and folded her arms. Chimes on her bangles gave a fidgety tinkle. "Geramir was careless," Rhusana said carefully. "She escaped after we left. Doubtless she's long gone now."

Tavin narrowed his eyes. Fie knew that face. He was summing up figures in his head. This time the numbers were plain enough: How Rhusana had stormed into his room, rabid with paranoia over the *chance* Tavin might have betrayed her. How casually the queen dismissed Fie's absence now, like she was little more than a runaway pet. Like something she wanted him to forget.

"What did you do to her?" he snarled. "My *one* condition was that no harm—"

Rhusana burst into melodious laughter. "And what does it matter? What will you do now, tell everyone you've committed an act of treason? Are you so thirsty for execution?"

Tavin's whole face seemed to fracture before Fie's eyes. *You damned fool*, she thought wretchedly. *You thought she wouldn't drag you down with her.*

"You should work on finding a *suitable* consort," Rhusana told him. "Something a little less embarrassing, perhaps."

He didn't answer.

Fie couldn't stand to watch anymore. She hated them both so much, she didn't know if she could do as Khoda wanted and let them tear each other apart. But it was easy to cut a boy's throat while he slept. She might die trying to take them both on now, alone.

Instead Fie fed her wrath to the tooth still burning in the dead queen's bed. It didn't need to balance against the Sparrow witch-tooth, instead snapping up her fury like meat thrown to a tiger.

The blaze had already crept across the floors and crawled up the walls, but now it roared with new hunger. Fie would leave naught there for Rhusana, not one strand of hair, not one scrap of skin, naught but a message unwritten and still crystal clear:

When she came for them, there would be nothing left but ash.

"Do you smell—" Tavin started.

Rhusana had already straightened up, staring at the ripe golden glow now pushing through the screen. Then she let out a scream and charged for the hall in a swirl of silk, near crashing into Fie. A breath later, two Hawk soldiers burst into the room. "Your Majesty, what—"

Rhusana had torn the screen aside. The fire didn't need Fie's help anymore, slinking down the hall toward the queen's silhouette.

"PUT IT OUT!" she roared.

The Hawks ran out, mumbling something about water, as Tavin got to his feet. He stared at the blaze, at the undeniably Phoenix-gold tongues of flame. What Fie could see of the chamber was burning like the sun. There was no chance that any of Rhusana's collection would survive.

"*I said put it out!*" Rhusana howled, and Fie realized she meant for Tavin to bring the fire to heel.

But he only eyed the inferno, grim, and shook his head. "It's too much," he said. "I can't stop it now."

Fie couldn't say if he glanced around the room behind him once more, or if it was only a trick of the dancing firelight.

Fie backed through the door with her steel and her teeth and a soft part of her heart that refused to die. The queen's screams of rage followed her all the way down the hall, down the stairs, and out into the night.

CHAPTER SEVENTEEN

——— THE BLOODLESS WAR ———

"**W**ELCOME BACK," KHODA SAID STIFFLY, TACKING PARCHMENT TO a wall as Fie let herself into the servants' sick room. "Would you like to tell me why the royal quarters are burning?"

She didn't have to ask how he knew; alarms had sounded all over the palace, summoning servants and priests from their beds to help douse the blaze. The funny thing, she'd realized, was that the palace was meant for an abundance of royalty who could snuff out fire with a whim. No one had ever worried about the royal quarters being little better than a tinderbox.

"Someone must have knocked over a lamp." Fie dropped the bag of teeth on the floor. "And look what fell out."

But the Black Swan was not impressed. "You were supposed to meet us back here. Instead you did what, exactly? Arson with a side of improvisational dentistry?"

"She got her Phoenix teeth back." Jasimir stood from the pallet he'd been tucking into a corner of the room. He offered her a weary smile. "You had me worried, though."

Already there was something about his company that made the whole dreadful endeavor feel less like staring down a hurricane. Barf had immediately claimed the middle of Jasimir's blankets, and the room felt more whole with him there. It was no longer an uneasy alliance between her and Khoda but . . . something closer to a band.

"Nice to see you out of a prison," Fie returned. "And I got more than teeth. Rhusana had . . ." She wavered a moment, the old queen's name sticking in her mouth. "She'd turned Queen Jasindra's room into her, well, workroom, I reckon."

A muscle jumped in Jasimir's jaw. "My *mother's* room?"

Fie grimaced in sympathy. "Aye. She was keeping all her stolen hair there, like a *collection*. There were all these long strands about the room, too, and papers with names and hairs on them, and some were just wads of hair of everyone in a town, and it was one of the foulest things I've ever seen, and I burn plague-dead for a living. So I'll give you two guesses what part of the royal quarters is burning right now."

Jasimir closed his eyes, rubbing a hand over his mouth. "Thank you."

"Don't thank her," Khoda snapped. "Are you serious? You found evidence the queen is a witch, that she's manipulating people, and you just—you set it on *fire*?"

"She had Jas's name on one of those papers!" Fie fired back.

Jasimir planted his hands on his hips. "Fie reclaimed one of her most valuable resources and cut Rhusana off from most, if not all, of hers. Any general will tell you that's how you win a war."

Khoda stared at them both. Then he stalked over to his own pallet and dropped onto his back, hiding his face in his hands. "Brightest Eye preserve me, I'm going to strangle them both."

Jasimir drew himself up, mouth tightening. "I was under the impression that the entire *point* of this endeavor is to overthrow Rhusana as quickly as possible so I can start fixing this mess. Fie just put us a lot closer to that, so what, precisely, is your problem?"

"My problem is that *this isn't a war*." Khoda sat up again, scowling. "Winning a war requires an army that you don't have. You have spies and you have servants, and if you treat them like soldiers, you're just going to get them killed."

"I burned the hair Rhusana took from Draga," Fie objected.

Khoda shook his head. "You burned *one* of them, I'm guessing. We don't know if the queen was carrying more hair on her, if that room was her only stash, anything. And by taking the teeth, you all but wrote your name in the ashes. Until we learn more, the only good thing we can safely assume is that you've dealt her supply a serious blow, and now she'll be preoccupied with restoring it."

Jasimir narrowed his eyes. "If we're not making war with her, then what *are* we doing?"

"Making an argument." Khoda pushed himself back to his feet and turned to one of the empty walls, producing a piece of chalk. "A bloodless war, more or less. We need to prove that Tavin and Rhusana are unfit to lead. That's not going to be hard, because it's the truth." He wrote both names on the wall, with two branches under each: WEAKNESSES and ASSETS. "Rhusana is an unregistered witch, a murderer, and legally has no claim to the throne, even through her son."

"Father officially recognized Rhusomir as his own," Jasimir pointed out.

Khoda wrinkled his nose. "You nobles and your names. Rhusomir? Really?"

"What did you think the 'Jasi' part came from?" Fie returned. "Jasifur, the king's pet dog?"

Jasimir cleared his throat. "The point is, as far as the nobility know, her claim is legitimate."

"Not if we prove that she's still a witch." Khoda wrote *witch* under both Rhusana's WEAKNESSES and ASSETS. "The marriage ceremony takes away even a witch's Birthright, and it should have given her at least the ability to withstand fire in return. Preferably, we could goad her into using her own powers in public, but really"—he added *fire* to WEAKNESSES—"she still burns like anyone else. If *that* happens in front of the right witnesses, it's evidence that she sabotaged the marriage ceremony, which means she was never officially married to Surimir. That nullifies *her* claim to the throne and makes Rhusomir's claim only as good as Tavin's."

"Then maybe it's a good thing we have a bag of Phoenix teeth after all," Jasimir said frostily.

Fie shot him a grin. "I knew springing you from jail was a good call."

Khoda threw dirty looks at each of them before turning to Tavin's name on the wall. "This is trickier. The fact is that, as far as the public knows, he's . . . well. You." He gave a semi-apologetic head tilt to Jasimir as he scribbled *passes for Phoenix* under ASSETS. "And unlike Rhusana, he's fireproof."

"Hawk witches can read caste in the blood," Jasimir said. "Could one of them expose him?"

"Draga could, if she's truly out of Rhusana's control now. She's likely the only one powerful enough to make a difference. But we'd be asking her to send her own son to die as a traitor."

Fie remembered the look on Draga's face the last time she thought she'd condemned Tavin to a terrible end. It had been hard enough for her to leave him to die by someone else's hand. To ask her to do it herself . . . Fie shook her head. "I don't like those odds."

"Neither do I," Khoda said. "We could try to figure out who's doing his glamour work, but you could throw a rock in the Hall of the Dawn and it'd hit a Peacock witch and bounce off four more. And there are only so many terrifying but specific omens Fie can manufacture around Tavin before it looks less like the work of angry gods and more like an angry lov—" He caught himself. "Lady."

"Subtle," Fie said, stony. "They teach you that in the Black Swans?"

"You know what they *did* teach me? How to keep my feelings out of a mission. And it would help if you did the same." Khoda jabbed the chalk at the distinct lack of entries in WEAKNESSES. "Our biggest opening with Tavin right now *should be* that he's currently interested in 'Lady Sakar.' Especially because I've heard Rhusana is pushing him to marry off fast."

Fie's gut twisted. She could still hear the queen's coo: *A suitable consort. Something less embarrassing.*

"Do you know how many nobles he slighted, pulling you up to the front like he did?" Khoda continued. "Almost every single one of my informants was talking about how he was showing off for some backwater Peacock girl. For a prince who's never been interested in women, that's a pretty big giveaway, don't you think? But I can't trust you to stick to the plan, so—"

"That's *enough*." The last time Jasimir had taken that tone, it was when Hangdog had heckled Tavin about his parents. "Tavin signed a death warrant for Fie's people, and you want her to *seduce* him? You have no right asking that of her. We'll find another way."

Khoda pursed his lips. It wasn't hard to read him in that moment: they might find another way, but it wouldn't be as swift or as easy. And her Crows didn't have the luxury of time.

"What . . ." Fie's voice cracked. She coughed. "What was your plan?"

Khoda looked from her to Jasimir and back. "Nothing too sala-cious. Let him chase you around enough to start raising serious ques-tions. He could say Jasimir's tastes have changed, but . . ."

"I, er, had opportunities to be interested in women," Jasimir said awkwardly, cheeks darkening. "I was not."

Fie's eyes widened with wicked glee. "Oh, I need to hear about *that*."

"*Later*," Khoda said. "But between that and you writing *bastard* over his head in fire, the rest of the palace ought to start catching on." He scratched the back of his neck. "Rhusana needs to reschedule the coro-nation. I suspect she'll be throwing parties and revels left and right to keep the nobility busy and happy in the meantime. That's where we'd start, making sure plenty of people see him haring after you. The prince and I can pose as servants to eavesdrop and get a sense of who's having doubts."

There was a knock at the door. "Food for the sick," Yula called from outside, their code for entry.

"Come in," Khoda answered.

The door swung open only wide enough to allow Ebrim and Yula to slide in, both bearing large clay pots and a few rough bowls. Once the door shut, they both bowed deep. "Your Highness."

"Please—I think we're past that now," Jasimir said, slightly strained. "Besides, you're risking so much for me. I owe you a tremendous debt."

The Sparrows straightened, but both Ebrim and Yula looked every-where but at the prince, uneasy. Ebrim set his pot on the floor and revealed a fluffy, steaming heap of rice. "You've raised quite the hell in one day. The queen's saying the Phoenix priests used the wrong oil, that it gave everyone fever visions. All the priests are being interro-gated, and word is she thinks *they* sabotaged the ceremony. She's push-ing the coronation back two weeks, to the first of Swan Moon."

"There was half a riot in the guest quarters," added Yula, unveiling her own pot of a stew heavy with chicken and lentils. Fie's stomach growled. "The nobles are furious they're being asked to stick around that long. Some say it's disrespectful, waiting until after Phoenix Moon." She passed a bowl to Jasimir first, then Khoda, then Fie. "We've placed someone to intercept any messages sent to 'Lady Sakar,' but we can also give you an empty chamber to keep up appearances. His Highness may be more comfortable in the guest quarters as well."

Jasimir ducked his head. "I'll be fine either way. Fie and I have slept on much worse on the road." He frowned. "Not to imply that this is bad, of course. Just—you don't need to go to any trouble for me."

"What His Highness means is '*Yes, thank you,*'" Khoda drawled. "Weren't you the one just lecturing me about resources?"

Ebrim and Yula traded looks. "Let us know what you decide," Ebrim said delicately. "And there's something that's come to my attention. No one's come forward themselves, but I'm hearing rumors of other servants having, oh, *encounters* with the queen. Strange ones. She wasn't what I'd call beloved among us, but this is new."

"What kind of new?" Fie asked warily.

Ebrim ran a finger along the bridge of his nose, eyes squeezing shut. "Mind you, it's all hearsay. But the story always starts with three or more servants on a job. One, just the one, gets called off by an attendant of the queen. They don't return for at least an hour, maybe more, and when they do . . . they can't remember a damned thing about where they've been."

"Not a scratch on them," Yula added. "Same clothes, no sickness like they've been drugged, nothing to say what they've done. The last thing they all remember is the queen's attendant leading them away."

Khoda set down his bowl, face sour. Then he got up with a grumble of "Of course she has one" and wrote below Rhusana's ASSETS: *Owl witch.*

"Seems like an awful lot of trouble to keep her secrets," Fie said around a mouthful of stew. "Why not just kill them?"

Yula covered a small gasp with a sleeve.

"What?" Fie blinked at her. "She murdered a whole score of Crows just to take my teeth."

Ebrim eyed her like she was a feral cat. "The queen could pick off a half dozen Sparrows, certainly, but there'd be too many gaps in the schedules, too many worried families looking for them. Someone would notice."

Fie let the unspoken question hang over them all: *And no one noticed twenty Crows dead in the road?*

That was the pinch of it, though. They'd notice. But so long as the plague beacons were answered, they'd look the other way. And since the Crows would starve without viatik, those beacons would keep being answered.

Khoda turned back to the rest of the room. "I take it no one's named names, for fear of the queen." The Sparrows nodded. He started pacing in a circle, scowling. "I'll check with my other informants, but if she's only targeting Sparrows, then you two will be my best sources. And I'll need everything, as soon as possible. If she's going to this much work to keep something quiet, especially at a time like this . . ."

"It's ugly," Fie finished.

Jasimir nodded. "Maybe ugly enough to sink her."

"The night kitchen shift has also been hit with a rush order for more savory finger foods," Yula said. "And the wine-master was given orders to have more casks of dry white wine ready by noon. Lights are on in the calligraphy scribes' offices, too."

"Invitations," Jasimir said. "Light refreshments and white wine? She's throwing an afternoon revel."

Khoda looked at Fie. "Well?"

"You don't have to do this." Jasimir put a cautious hand on her shoulder. "We can find another way."

Fie thought of Pa and Wretch and all her Crows, all the Crows across Sabor, waiting for the queen's knife to fall to their throats. She'd made an oath; she'd bought them a king. She meant to keep it.

"Aye," Fie whispered. "I'll do it."

Khoda only nodded shortly. Then he lifted the chalk to Tavin's name and wrote, under WEAKNESSES, *Lady Sakar.*

———◆———

In her dream, she knelt before a throne, silk knotted too tight round her head. It took but a thought to light it, and in the glassblack panes she saw her own reflection crowned in golden fire.

We have chosen, *a crowd chanted at her back.* We have chosen.

You chose wrong, *she wanted to tell them, oil seeping into her scalp and down her brow, down her cheeks, until her reflection's face was streaked with fire.*

———◆———

You walk like a mammoth, grumbled the undead spark of Niemi Navali szo Sakar.

Better a mammoth than a ghost, Fie thought back. She'd known she'd need the dead Peacock's help to survive mingling with the gentry, but that didn't make it any easier to have her voice rattling around Fie's skull. It was one thing to borrow her face for a moment. It was another to shroud herself in Niemi's face, her thoughts, her memories, for the whole of an afternoon. Fie could only hope she never saw the memory of Niemi leading Oleanders to Hangdog's band; with any luck, batting her lashes at a false prince would be enough to keep the Peacock ghost occupied.

Since she'd called on a brand-new tooth of Niemi's, though, the spark had no notion why Fie had brought her along. There were a great many things that vexed the Peacock girl, but none quite so much as the fact that she'd never had a chance to see the royal palace in person, and now a Crow was using her face to sneak into the queen's own revel.

Not that much sneaking was required; an invitation had arrived just that morning, requesting the company of the Sakar family in the Midday Pavilion. Fie had surrendered that invitation at a gate made of an ornate gilded trellis, where vines thick with gold-orange blossoms were molded into the form of a phoenix perched on the apex of the arch. Trailing vines made up a fantail like a curtain over the entryway.

Perhaps Rhusana meant to say that she had no fear of phoenixes, even after the previous night. Or perhaps she'd just picked the easiest pavilion.

Now Fie strode down the sandstone walkway, taking in the terrain. The pavilion itself was a grand round structure, its roof like a bronze-laced parasol of amber-hued glassblack, the columns painstakingly brushed with gold leaf that faded into rose gold at the base. More of those climbing vines twined about brass lattices connecting the columns, their frilled petals fluttering down like drops of sunlight. The rim of a turquoise-tiled reflecting pool skirted the pavilion's marble base like a moat, and more bands of turquoise tile ringed the pavilion like ripples in a pond.

Thankfully, stands of palms and cypress also offered shelter from the sun, which had passed noon an hour ago but refused to lessen its onslaught. A few Peacock gentry were milling about, but Tavin and Rhusana weren't in sight, and Fie had no doubt the rest of the nobility were waiting to be fashionably late.

At least the plain gown they'd stuffed her into was made of light, gauzy silk. Both Khoda and Yula had insisted on it. Even though Peacock witches frequently glamoured their own outfits, they dressed in a base garment of the same cut so no one would reach for a sleeve and find bare skin instead.

"That's all part of the Peacock game," Khoda had remarked with a roll of his eyes. "It doesn't have to be real. It just has to be real *enough*."

She'd made sure to give Khoda a particularly unfortunate face when she glamoured a Sparrow attendant's disguise for him.

Neither he nor Jasimir looked to be among the Sparrows Fie could see, but it was hard to focus with Niemi berating her with every step. *Glide, you lumbering cow! Sway!*

Fie clenched her fists and tried to glide. Instead she nearly tripped on her own hem.

Hopeless, the dead girl scoffed. *And you thought you could be* me.

I know, Fie spat back, *that I'm* better. *Now show me what to do.*

Niemi's spark stayed spitefully silent. Fie fetched up against a cypress, seemingly to escape the sun.

I'll embarrass you, Fie thought. *I'm wearing* your *face, after all, taking* your *name, so they'll think you're the one——*

Rage flushed from Niemi's sulking spark. Fie felt her back straighten, her chin lift, then she was walking like she was suspended from a wire, graceful and smooth. The skirt of her glamour-gown trailed behind her, smooth as a lily on a pond, a cobalt blue color Khoda claimed the Sakars favored.

It's only until you can sit somewhere seemly, hissed the Peacock girl. She marched Fie over to a wrought-bronze bench within the pavilion and plunked her down, only to stand her up again as a cry rang through the gardens.

"*Her Majesty, Queen Rhusana! His Highness, Prince Jasimir!*"

"Canape, Your Ladyship?" a familiar voice asked, dry. When Fie turned, she found the grizzled, drooping face she'd glamoured on to Khoda. He swung his tray to her, head down, and muttered, "Eat while you can. Try not to stuff your face."

She took a delicate pastry, looked Khoda in the eye, and deliberately shoved it into her mouth while the rest of the garden's attention was on Rhusana and Tavin. Niemi's spark sniffed with disgust. Khoda wrinkled his nose at her, bowed, and swept away to bestow pastries closer to Jasimir. It was a risk bringing the prince here, but Khoda's people had seeded rumors of Jasimir fleeing to the Shattered Bay overnight. Rhusana had already taken the bait, flooding the docks with guards; as far as she knew, he was halfway across the Sea of Beasts at this very moment, never to return.

". . . condolences for Karostei."

Fie's head snapped round to find the speaker. Two Peacock lords stood nearby, and she recognized one: the man who had spoken for Rhusana from under his mantle of embroidered oleanders the night before.

He wore pale green today, but the subtle pattern of oleander blossoms had been wrought about his cuffs. Once could have been coincidence. Twice was a choice.

The other man was shaking his head mournfully, stroking a salt-and-pepper beard in a way that, with a sharp pang, reminded Fie too keenly of Pa. "It's a disaster," he sighed. "The high magistrate ordered an aid effort, so we'll lose half the regional taxes for this moon just to rebuild it. They won't even use the same land."

"Old-fashioned superstition," the Oleander lord murmured. "The king died of the plague, and here we stand. The Crows burned the whole town?"

"Even the walls. Their headman was supposed to weather it out. Supposedly they . . . *overruled* him."

Khoda would tell her not to get involved. *Pa* would tell her not to get involved. Men like that had already decided what the way of it was, and until they paid for shutting out the truth, they wouldn't change their minds. Sometimes even that wasn't enough; even now, Fie could feel hums of assent from Niemi's spark.

But what good was all this, the finery and gliding and mummery to make her into a Peacock lady, if she wasn't going to do aught with it but lure a false prince?

Don't you dare, Niemi warned too late.

"A band of Crows, one sword among them, overpowered a village headman and all the Hawks in his command?" Fie asked them loudly, trying to mimic the stodgy highborn affect. "Nonsense. This folly puts all Sabor in danger."

The Oleander lord was staring at her with a peculiar kind of cool calculation, not because he cared for her thoughts but because he was running the numbers on the cost of vexing her. "Forgive us, young lady, but these matters do not concern you."

Lord Urasa's right, Niemi hissed frantically. *You're making a scene!*

Good. Fie set her jaw. "Am I to wait until the plague spreads from his lands to ours, then?"

"If your family wants to keep letting bone thieves extort them for a service any peasant can provide, that's your business," the other lord huffed. "The queen proved they've been swindling us for, what, centuries now? And doubtless spreading the Sinner's Plague themselves the whole time."

Every throat Fie had ever cut flooded her head until every thought bled with rage. All she could think of were the children of Karostei. "And when the Covenant marks you for—"

"What's all this now?" Tavin's voice cut through the pavilion. Fie found him striding from the walkway, sun bouncing almost too bright off a sash of cloth-of-gold over his ivory silk tunic. The circlet he'd claimed to despise sat in his hair, and more gold flashed in rings cluttering his fingers, bracelets and armbands clasped round his wrists, even hoops through his ears. His features, though, belonged to Jasimir.

He took the steps up two at a time, a small act so familiar it made Fie's teeth hurt. He nodded to the man Niemi had called Lord Urasa, the one wearing oleanders on his sleeves. "Don't stop on my account. What could possibly have Lady Sakar so aggrieved?"

"Your Highness." Lord Urasa bowed, as did the lord beside him. "This is all a misunderstanding. I believe the young lady places more faith in the Crows than either I or Lord Dengor."

"You find their work distasteful?" Tavin asked, frowning.

"Unnecessary," Lord Dengor answered. "We've seen adequate proof that anyone can burn plague-dead. I believe the only reason to persist in humoring the Crows is . . ." He shot a sideways look at Fie, and said with great meaning, ". . . *sentiment.*"

It was a tone she'd heard before, when Geramir had fretted that summoning Crows could be seen as favoritism. That simply treating them like any other caste had become, in their eyes, an act of unmerited generosity.

Be silent, Niemi half ordered, half begged. *Leave it be.*

But when fine lords left it be, it just meant Crows like her would have to deal mercy to children.

"How many deaths are you willing to answer for when the Covenant calls you to the next life?" Fie said instead.

Lord Urasa glanced at something over Fie's shoulder and smiled. "Surely," he said loud enough to ring across the pavilion, "the young lady is not calling the queen a liar."

"Surely not," a sharp voice echoed behind Fie.

Urasa bowed. So did Lord Dengor and everyone else in the area.

Fie's stomach sank as she turned. Queen Rhusana was behind her, ice-pale eyes narrowed on her. Today her chimes were gone, replaced by a fine headdress of white gold shaped like a phoenix, its twin wings forming a diamond-studded fan in her silvery hair.

She was also wearing the same white tiger pelt Fie had first seen her in moons ago, the one Surimir had given her. But that was not enough for the queen: at her side paced a living, breathing white tiger, with pearls in its collar and a chain linked to a cuff on Rhusana's wrist. Even that chain was wrought in the shape of oleanders.

This time, Fie was all too happy to let Niemi pull her into a graceful bow.

"Prince Jasimir." Rhusana twitched a finger, and Tavin stepped forward, a furrow in his brow. "It seems our guest would benefit from expanding her *perspective*. Will you show Lady Sakar around the gardens?"

That sounded too much like an honor to be anything less than deadly. Fie's stomach jolted as Tavin said, "Certainly, Your Majesty."

"I think a visit to the western end may, perhaps, provide some . . . clarity."

Tavin flinched so swift Fie barely saw, but he nodded. "Understood."

Whispers swept around the pavilion, but what rattled Fie most was the glimpse she saw of Jasimir's glamoured face in his Sparrow disguise, standing just on the other side of the pavilion's bronze lattice screens. He looked stricken. Khoda had his elbow in a pale-knuckled grip.

"My lady." Tavin was offering his own elbow, stiff and grim.

"Your Highness." Fie bowed again, took it, and let him lead her from the Midday Pavilion, into the west.

CHAPTER EIGHTEEN

PLAYING THE FOOL

Tavin didn't speak to her for an uncomfortable few minutes, pacing slowly down the sandstone walkway, her arm tucked into his. Fie didn't know what awaited her, but from Jasimir's face, it had to be something grotesque. Maybe it was a prison, or a scandalous exile from the palace grounds. Maybe something worse.

Fie dragged each breath in time with her steps, trying to steady her pounding heart. Rhusana would want her timid and trembling; Fie'd give no such satisfaction to her, nor to Tavin as her surrogate.

The silence swelled between them until a croak burst it like an overfilled water skin. Startled, Fie looked up.

Two crows perched on a nearby arbor shawled in purple wisteria. A third landed and cawed as she and Tavin drew closer.

Tavin's brow furrowed at the sight.

"Are they not common in the south?" Fie asked after a moment. Her voice creaked from disuse. "Crows, that is."

He blinked, almost as if he were startled to find her still there. "Not in the palace."

Fie prodded the spark of Niemi's tooth. *If you ever wanted to flirt with a prince, now's your chance.*

The spark had kept its peace since Rhusana had cast them from the pavilion, no doubt seething that a Crow girl could tarnish her name so badly. The prospect of snaring a prince, though, was one too juicy for Niemi not to bite.

"I imagine there are much finer sights to see in the royal menagerie," Niemi cooed through Fie. "Is it as marvelous as the rest of the grounds?"

"Well, it's down a white tiger now," Tavin muttered under his breath.

Fie felt her head tilt. "Is something amiss? I know I let myself get carried away earlier, but . . . we can still be friends, can't we?"

She didn't catch Tavin's answer. A jolt had clutched her as they turned onto another pathway—the same strange, nameless dread that had clung to her in the hedge tunnels the night before, when she'd trailed him from the Hall of the Dawn. Every step seemed to send a clear, uncanny note through her bones until they hummed back.

Mercifully, if Tavin waited on a reply, he didn't show it, marching stone-faced past another grand pavilion in shades of scarlet, violet, and orange—the Sunset Pavilion, no doubt. If he felt anything like the radiating tone of *wrong*, he didn't show that, either. Instead he steered them closer to the royal quarters, which swelled up above them to provide a better view of the gardens. They passed an arch with a stone phoenix perching on skulls at its crest, marking a set of stairs that descended belowground, and instead climbed a flight of marble steps, emerging to a small plaza under the main veranda of the royal quarters.

That was when Fie saw it, less than a pace away.

It was as if the gods had simply punched out a great, perfect circle in the middle of the paving stones. Fie reckoned she could lie her entire band down in a head-to-foot line and still not touch both sides. Its walls were slick, unbroken glassblack, and the surface of the water could have been one more unmarred pane, still and black and seemingly bottomless. It lay too far below to touch—

Too far below to climb out.

And suddenly Fie knew, without words, that the horrible ring in her bones was coming from below the surface.

"I take it they don't talk about the Well of Grace in the north," Tavin said quietly.

She jumped, and his grip on her arm tightened. The edge was much too near for comfort. "N-no," Fie stammered.

He was staring at the water. "It's against the law, and the Hawk code, to raise a blade against royalty. So that rules out beheading. And Phoenixes can't exactly die by fire. So this"—he waved his free hand at the waters—"is for when a Phoenix needs to be executed. The *grace*, you see, is the ordeal—fighting not to drown for as long as you can. It can take hours, even days. It's supposed to be terrible enough that when the Covenant weighs the sins that got you executed, it's balanced out by the suffering you endured, and then you can be born a Phoenix again."

"How many—?" Fie couldn't finish the question. From what she'd seen in the memories of Phoenix teeth, they were inordinately fond of recreational murder. There could be dozens, perhaps more than a hundred bodies at the bottom of that well. No wonder her bones ached so, from all that wretched, hopeless death.

"No one can say," Tavin admitted. "Sometimes they fish out the bodies once they start floating, if they're still worthy of being buried in the royal catacombs. Not always. And it's not just for Phoenixes, but also for the people who cross them. Not even a Gull witch could summon enough wind to carry themselves out. They've tried."

Fie shot him a sidelong look. Tavin was slipping, calling the Phoenixes *them*.

But suddenly his eyes cut to her. "Lady Sakar," he said, terse. "Do you understand why the queen asked me to bring you here?"

The people who cross them.

Fie froze.

It had been a long, long time since she'd looked at Tavin as a boy who could kill her.

It would be so easy, a quick shove, and once she wore herself out screaming and trying to stay afloat, she'd be one more body at the bottom. They could call it an accident.

And every way she could fight him off, she would lose—she knew that as sure as the sun rose. He'd win with steel, he could not be touched by fire, and whatever she might wreak with a Hawk war-witch's tooth he could easily undo with his own healing.

She'd just always trusted that Tavin wouldn't hurt her, not when he needed her help, and then not while he held her heart. That wasn't the boy Fie knew.

But this was a traitor with a stolen face.

She should have cut his throat while he slept.

"I know why I'm here," she rasped.

He took a step back from the well's edge, drawing her away with him, then unwound his arm from hers. "I'm going to play the fool," he said tightly. "I'll tell the queen I thought she just wanted you taken away from the party, and if you're asked, we only passed by the well as we walked about the gardens. But if you ever speak openly against her again, she will know, and *she will kill you*."

To Fie's humiliation, her sight blurred with tears. She couldn't help it; the well still droned in her spine, her heartbeat still crackled down her veins, she still hated him, missed him, she hated this awful palace and everyone in it and she wanted to go back to her roads and her crowsilk and her pa.

The words choked themselves free: *"How do you live like this?"*

Tavin's face fractured the way it had the night before. He turned his head away and said, voice cracking, "They're all short lives."

Fie wanted to push him into the well for quoting her own words to a different face. She wanted to cry more because he'd remembered them.

All she did was scrub her face with a sleeve until she could speak again. "W-why are you helping me? Won't the queen be angry?"

Tavin didn't look at her. "I don't want to answer to the Covenant for any more than I already have to," he said heavily. He hesitated a moment, then turned to the stairs, offering his arm once more. She took it. "The palace is full of dark secrets. You don't have to be another one."

Fie gulped. She needed to manage *something* today, or Khoda might send her back to the well himself. "And if I like dark secrets?" she made herself ask.

Tavin's eyebrows shot up, as if to ask, *Even after this?* He gave her a long look, one that ended with a hint of a smile. "Then I have a lot to show you, Lady Sakar."

Niemi's tooth-spark flickered at Fie, prompting. "You saved my life, Your Highness. If I may be so bold, I think you can call me Niemi."

Something hitched in Tavin's face, only to smooth over. He reached over to rest his free hand on hers. "Thank you, Niemi. And you may call me Jasimir."

Jasimir and Khoda were both waiting for her at the meeting statue, and they fell in line behind her, seamlessly shifting from palace servants to personal attendants as Fie strode toward the guest quarters.

Once they reached the empty chamber Yula had set aside for them and the door had shut, Fie found herself wrapped in an abrupt embrace.

"I'm fine, Jas," she wheezed, but she hugged the prince back anyway.

Jasimir didn't let go, but still managed to point a finger at Khoda. "You're not allowed to yell at her," he said, voice muffled in her shoulder. "I—I forbid it, do you understand me?"

"Yes, Your Highness." Khoda sounded less acerbic than Fie had expected, but twice as tired.

"I thought they were—I thought he would—" Jasimir pulled back but kept a tight grip on her shoulders. "How did you get away?"

"He's just going to play like he misunderstood." Fie ducked her head. "He didn't want to kill me. Let others kill the Crows, aye," she added bitterly, "but he's not up for drowning Peacock girls yet."

"His Highness was right." Khoda folded his arms. "We're asking too much of you. I should have warned you about Dengor and Urasa—"

Fie shook her head. "I can do it. Hells, now Tavin and I are on a first-name basis. Isn't that what you wanted?"

"Not if you had to take a trip to the Well of Grace to get there!"

Jasimir let her go, only to turn to Khoda, rubbing his chin. "No, no, we . . . we can work with this. The aristocracy will smell that lie a league away and know he intervened for her. It already looks suspicious that he's courting a woman. If that becomes a point of conflict between him and Rhusana . . ."

"The strength of their alliance would also be questioned," Khoda said.

Jasimir nodded. "Making an argument."

Khoda pinched his eyes shut, rubbing the spot between his brows. "Yes. But no. But yes. Ugh." He blew out a breath and fixed his stare on Fie. "We'll take Tavin's approach. You play the fool from now on, all right? A beautiful, elegant, empty-headed fool. The queen will have an easier time believing you're just a naïve country bumpkin than a Peacock who puts the welfare of Crows over her own status in court."

"And if Rhusana thinks you're a fool, she may let something slip in front of you," added Jas. "That's how I survived five years of her."

Fie shuddered, remembering the look on Tavin's face when she'd asked how anyone lived like this. "Has it always been this way?"

Khoda and Jasimir traded looks. "Not always . . . this bad," Jasimir said slowly.

A knock rattled the door. Fie scrambled to throw herself onto the nearest low sofa in a genteel swoon, as Jasimir stationed himself behind her with a palm fan, straight-faced. "What are you *doing*?" he whispered, bewildered.

"Being a fine lady," Fie muttered back from behind a sleeve.

"You look like you're dying in a tragedy play."

"*Silence*, manservant," she hissed, pinching her mouth at him as Khoda shot them both dirty looks and answered the door. Fie caught a ruffle of murmurs and the clink of silver. A moment later, a tray appeared in Khoda's hands and the door swung shut.

"Refreshments for my lady," he said loudly, then jerked his head at the door.

A shadow still lingered in the gap between the bottom of the door and its frame. They had an audience.

"Well then, bring them here!" Fie called in her most petulant snob voice. "What are you waiting for?"

Jasimir tapped her shoulder. When she looked up, he pointed to his open mouth, then drew a finger across his throat and shook his head.

Khoda set the tray down on a nearby low table. "At your leisure, Your Ladyship."

The shadow at the door slipped away.

Jasimir tossed the palm fan aside, then went to the window, pushed the screen aside, and plucked a fresh frond from a palm outside. Then he approached the tray, tapping an index finger to his chin as he studied a plate of flower-shaped sweet biscuits, a soft white dome of cheese, tiny jars of jewel-colored sauces, and pitchers of chilled tea and water. He dipped the palm frond in the water; naught happened. He tried the tea next.

The tip of the frond withered instantly, and black lines spidered up even the untouched green. Jasimir hastily let the frond go. It sagged over the pitcher's edge.

"Already trying to poison you, that's a good sign," he remarked, and picked up an envelope. "Oh, but she sent an invitation to her party tomorrow in the Midnight Pavilion. That's a smart touch. It's harder to argue that she'd bother inviting someone she thought would be dead." Then he read something and wrinkled his nose. "Or perhaps not. '*The pleasure of your company is specifically requested by His Royal Highness, Prince Jasimir.*'"

Khoda lifted the tea, careful not to splash any on himself, and pulled aside the serving cloth beneath it. A slip of parchment waited there. He unfolded it, scanned a moment, then nodded to himself. "Yula says we can leave the food in the chamber pots and she'll smuggle meals to us when she sends cleaning staff to the room." He glanced at the door again, mouth twisting. "Rhusana's still interrogating the Phoenix priests. She thinks they're behind the failed ceremony and the prince's escape, so that's pressure off us for a bit. Two servants are missing. Both were called away from a team job, one yesterday, one shortly before the coronation, but they both returned. They only went missing after they left the palace and went into Dumosa."

"Sounds like runaways," Fie said. "Took off and didn't look back."

"Running from what, though?" asked Jasimir.

No one had an answer for him. Fie couldn't help watching the rest of the palm frond blacken and die as it absorbed the tea.

Maybe Tavin was trying to protect her—not her, *Niemi*—by giving her status as his guest. Or maybe Rhusana meant to kill her publicly this time.

She couldn't trust either of them. And no matter what Tavin said or what he did, it was all for a dead Peacock girl.

In her dream, she drifted on her back in cold, dark water, staring up at the sky.

"You can't stay in there forever," a woman's voice called nearby. She came into view in between bright scarlet petals floating on the water: a soft, lined brown face, black hair braided in a crown over her head. The hood of her long, black silk robe lay flat over her shoulders.

"Watch me," Fie heard herself answer, and let the water swallow her whole.

The Midnight Pavilion could not have been more different from the Midday Pavilion. Instead of vivid oranges and turquoises, this was a work of black marble, wrought iron, and lapis lazuli of deepest blue, all trimmed in gold. Instead of reflecting pools, alabaster fountains sent a fine mist across the warm night. Jasmine perfume hung in the air, wafting from vines stringing constellations of star-shaped blossoms below the clear crystal panes of the pavilion's roof. Strings of silver and gold lanterns cast a shimmering light around the grounds.

More notable, though, were the hedges enclosing the garden,

dotted with snow-white oleander blossoms. There was no chance that was a coincidence. If anything, Khoda had said, it was so open now that it was near becoming an opening: Rhusana was so busy signaling her support of the Oleander Gentry that she'd become overconfident in their popularity.

Fie had kept her thoughts to herself on that front, but all she could think of was the Hall of the Dawn, when the Peacocks had been asked to speak for the queen.

None of her skeptics had spoken for her then, but none of them had argued when Lord Urasa did, either.

The murmur of polite conversation hitched when Fie entered the garden on Tavin's arm, letting the strains of flute and lyre songs well up in the gap. Her pale teal glamour-gown had been the subject of much debate between Jasimir and Khoda; it was meant to show deference to the queen, but too close to white and she'd make herself a challenger. Too intense a hue and the message would be lost. They'd settled for a muted seafoam silk with beading in blue and green to add the pattern of a fantail to the skirt.

It was all so beautiful, Fie had thought as she'd spun the glamour, recreating the work of days, weeks, months in an instant.

And with every sunrise, it was getting harder to remember that none of it was real.

But with every eye fixed on her now, it was all suddenly, horribly real. The conversation resuscitated itself with gusto after a moment, palm fan after palm fan snapping up to hide lips as the flurry of whispers rose.

The queen regarded them from a modest throng near the entrance of the pavilion, her white tiger seated beside her, tail flicking. If she was vexed that her Hawks had found no trace of Jasimir but the rumors he'd fled across the sea, she gave no sign.

"It'll be fine," Tavin said quietly. "Just follow my lead."

Her grip on his arm tightened without even thinking. Irate, she started to loosen her hold—

Don't, Niemi's spark ordered, unbidden.

Fie near tripped over her own hem again. She'd meant to call the tooth only if she had to make conversation, but it had somehow come back to life on its own.

He thinks himself our savior now, Niemi continued. *Let him.*

She didn't have a chance to argue; they'd drawn close to the queen. "Welcome, Prince Jasimir," Rhusana said with a deep nod, then: "Lady Sakar."

Niemi guided her into a peerless bow.

Stay down until she dismisses you, the Peacock girl whispered. *Don't look her in the eye.*

"I trust you enjoyed your walk in the gardens with the prince."

"Indeed," she said, Niemi feeding her every word, "it was most instructive."

From her bow, she could see the tiger's tail lashing back and forth, like Barf's when she spied a beetle.

"I am glad to hear it," Rhusana said glossily. "I hope you enjoy this evening just as well."

That's your dismissal. Niemi lifted her back up but kept her head bent.

It's also a threat, Fie snapped back. As if it wasn't bad enough that Rhusana had tried to have her killed twice yesterday, she wanted to make sure Niemi Navali szo Sakar knew she might try a third time tonight. At least it would be hard to drown her in a pavilion. "Your Majesty is too gracious."

Tavin steered her away before the queen could say another word, and Fie felt the stares of the rest of the garden on her back. His shoulders were shaking. When Fie looked up at him, startled, his lips were pressed together, cheeks flushing dark.

"What's wrong?" she asked. "Did I say——"

"*'Gracious'*?" he said, sounding a little choked, and Fie realized he was trying to hold back laughter. "Of all the . . ."

Play the fool, Niemi reminded her.

"I've no notion what you mean," she said smoothly.

Fie ventured a glance behind her. The queen was watching them go, her cold, pale stare on Tavin. Whether or not she realized it, though, even more of the Peacocks were watching the queen.

And not all of those stares were kind.

Jasimir caught Fie's eye as he wove past, bearing a tray of appetizers. Somewhere beneath his glamour was a Peacock tooth on a string round his neck. Fie hadn't wanted to risk it wearing off and revealing the true crown prince of Sabor serving stuffed mushroom caps in a servant's uniform.

"Hold on," Tavin said suddenly.

Jasimir stopped dead in his tracks. Then he bowed, face blank, his voice gravelly. "What does His Highness desire of this unworthy one?"

Fie's pulse rose in her throat. Had she fouled up the glamour? But——

"These are really quite good," Tavin said, passing Fie a mushroom cap. "Here, try it. That's all," he added to Jasimir.

The true prince bowed once more, fingers tightening on the tray. Then his face dropped, eyes widening. He didn't remember to change his voice as he shouted, "*Look out——!*"

Fie whirled in time to see Lord Dengor, deep in conversation with a terribly bored woman, walk right into Khoda's back. Khoda stumbled, a pitcher of wine flying from his grasp.

It shattered at Rhusana's feet. Red drenched the bottom of her lily-white satin skirts.

The Midnight Pavilion went silent.

Rhusana looked down at her skirts. Then she looked up at Khoda.

Even if he'd wanted to pin it on anyone else, scarlet wine had splashed all over his own uniform, ruining even the cloth-of-gold sash. He dropped to his knees, staring at the ground.

The queen cocked her head and somehow made it look like brandishing a dagger. "Manservant," she said thinly. "How old are you?"

"This unworthy one is forty-three, Your Majesty," he said, for Fie had given him an older man's face tonight.

"And how much do we pay you per year?"

Khoda's mouth twisted. Fie had to give him his due as he paused: even facing down a queen, he kept his guise up, working out the figures like a Sparrow servant who rarely dealt with great sums of coin. "About a thousand naka, Your Majesty."

Rhusana glided over to him, just the way Niemi had showed Fie, her pet tiger shambling in her wake. She lifted his chin with the tip of one of her silver claws.

"So what you're telling me," she said sweetly, "is that you could work in the palace for the rest of your *wretched*"—she backhanded him across the face, leaving red gashes over a cheekbone—"*useless*"— another slap, another set of scratches to match—"life and still not make up for what you've just done to me."

Fie heard a faint scuff. A mushroom cap rolled off Jasimir's shaking tray. Fie glanced out of the corner of her eye and saw the faintest bit of smoke coming from where he gripped the silver.

Tavin had frozen beside her, eyes locked on Khoda and the queen, but Fie didn't want to count on that holding up. Slowly, she shifted her weight, then tapped Jasimir's foot with her own. Jasimir blinked. The smoke went out.

"Let's think of another way you can pay." Rhusana tapped her lips. "What about an arm? Or an eye? Which would you rather pay?"

Fie heard Tavin's sharp breath.

Khoda's face went gray. He opened his mouth, then closed it. "Please, Your Majesty—"

Rhusana raised her hand again, the rings and claws tipping her fingers now speckled red. Khoda flinched. "Are you not *sorry*, manservant?"

"I—this unworthy one is sorry, Your Majesty, so sorry—"

"Then *show me* how sorry you are," she cooed. The queen yanked her tiger's chain. The great beast lumbered closer, sniffing. "Make your choice, or Ambra here will be happy to make it for you. An arm or an eye?"

The tiger nosed Khoda's bloody face. A heavy pink tongue lolled out and lapped at the scratches.

No one moved. Not even Tavin.

There were Phoenix teeth on her string, Fie knew, and there was steel in the blade beneath her skirt, and Jasimir could call fire down, but there were Hawks all around them, and it was a long way to the palace walls.

She didn't know if she could stop this. Not without giving up everything they'd worked for here—not without giving up her chance of stopping Rhusana.

Here she was, garbed in all the power of a dead aristocrat, on the arm of a prince, and she couldn't even save one servant.

What good was *any* of this?

"*Choose*," Rhusana ordered in a singsong voice, eyes dancing. She curled her fist. The tiger shuddered, its tail lashing faster. Its whiskers flicked back in a snarl.

"Your Majesty, if I may . . ." The woman Dengor had been nattering at stepped forward and spread her hands in apology. "I'm afraid this was all an accident, my brother wasn't looking and—"

Rhusana's nostrils flared. Her tiger lurched forward, swiping a massive paw. It caught the gray-haired older woman across the arm and thigh. Her scream rebounded through the assembled Peacocks, but no one moved. She crumpled to the ground. The beast's jaws closed on her wrist.

The queen dragged at her tiger's chain again, and it let go with a muffled roar, shaking its head. A hand fell out of its jaws, only to be snapped up again. Droplets of blood flecked its fur and Rhusana's skirts alike. The woman below her moaned, sobbing but still alive, clutching the stump where her hand had been. Blood bloomed all across her side. Not even Lord Dengor stirred to help her.

Rhusana smiled serenely at the assembly. "Would anyone else care to contribute their opinion?"

No one said a word.

Fie had seen that lost, unsteady look before, on the faces of Splendid Castes and upper Hunting Castes, when there was a rare case of the Sinner's Plague among their own. She'd seen it on Geramir's face, when she reminded him of the dead girl whose face she now wore.

They had not thought themselves in danger from a queen who'd come from Swans, someone whose lot in life it was to sing sweet songs, dance sweet dances, and perhaps bring sweet pleasures to their beds. They thought they knew the rules: the Peacock aristocrats paid and the Swan courtesans did what they were asked. Even if Niemi had *accidentally* slipped into the Well of Grace . . . Well, that was an accident, and it was to be expected at the hands of a Phoenix prince.

Rhusana was the Swan Queen, and they would tell themselves she was more style than substance, easily manipulated, a puppet monarch. So long as she only savaged servants, and only murdered challengers to her crown, they figured themselves safe. Their money and their rank and the promise of their support—that would protect them above all else.

And not a one of them knew what to do with a queen who cared for none of it.

Not even Tavin, who had not moved once from Fie's side.

"Remove this mess," Rhusana said, waving a hand, and Fie felt a knot in her spine slip loose. Khoda would likely have scars, but compared to Lord Dengor's sister, those were a light price to pay. Hawks emerged from the shadows to hurry both Khoda and the wounded Peacock out.

The glint of red on Rhusana's diamond-tipped claws caught her eye, and she pursed her lips.

"Do . . ." Tavin cleared his throat. "Do you want me to send for a new gown, Your Majesty?"

Rhusana wiped the blood off in a slow, deliberate movement, leaving a trail of rusty stripes across her skirt.

"It already has red on it," she said flatly.

Fie looked around the Midnight Pavilion, almost desperate. She found hesitation in the faces of the gentry. She found calculation. She found cold, quiet triumph.

She also found fear. Anger. Helplessness. Horror. This wasn't the way it was done. This wasn't how highborn were supposed to behave in the open.

But no one moved.

No one moved.

No one moved.

CHAPTER NINETEEN

— REAL ENOUGH —

"I'll admit," Tavin said, "that was not what I had planned for the evening."

His tone was light, but there was a measured clip to his words, and Fie knew it was due to the Hawk guards who had joined him in escorting her back to the guest quarters. She'd held out for a few minutes after Khoda had been hauled away, but once it wouldn't be terribly conspicuous, she'd claimed a "poor constitution" (Niemi's words) and asked to retire.

Even now, for the life of her, she couldn't manage to sort out how she should answer as the guest quarters drew nearer—was she supposed to *flirt* after that? Niemi's spark surged at the opportunity, and for once Fie was grateful for it. "And what *did* you have in mind for the evening?"

Tavin let out a tense, short laugh. "Let's just leave it at . . . not that." They came to a halt outside the entrance to the guest quarters.

Don't let him follow you in, Niemi warned. *It would be unseemly if you were to take him to bed so soon——*

Oh, been there, done that, Fie told the dead girl, tired. *Repeatedly. Reckon it worked out* real *well.*

"Perhaps tomorrow you'll allow me to make it up to you." Tavin slid his arm free of hers but let his fingers run along the inside of her arm, up her palm, lifting her knuckles to his lips. "Just the two of us. Wherever you'd like to go."

Home. The thought was a dagger, sudden and sharp.

She'd learned better, though. There was no home for a girl like her.

"When?" Niemi asked for her, breathless.

"Midmorning. I'll send a messenger." He let go and spun on a heel, then threw a too-familiar grin over his shoulder. "Don't worry, I won't make you wait."

Both their smiles faltered the slightest bit. Niemi kept Fie's face iron-still, but inside, Fie was screaming. The last time he'd said those words, he'd called her the girl he loved, he'd sworn he would find her no matter how long it took. And from his flinch, he remembered.

It just didn't matter anymore.

She waited until Tavin and his escorts were gone, then sank into the shadows, trying to swallow down the tears burning in her throat. Then she called a Vulture tooth, found Viimo's charm-bead, and traced its path.

Viimo was still in her cell, pacing west, east, west, east. She stopped in the west. That meant *Return to home base.*

Fie switched to a Sparrow witch-tooth, the one near burned out from her trip to the royal quarters two nights earlier. Once it had wiped her from sight, she hiked up her skirts and sprinted across the palace grounds.

"I can't believe," Khoda was saying as Fie burst into the sick rooms, "that she named the damn—*ah*—tiger Ambra."

"Sorry." Jasimir paused from dabbing a sharp-smelling green paste onto the gashes on Khoda's face. He looked up at Fie with a strained smile. "We have a code word for the door, you know."

Yula closed the door behind Fie. "We've put out word that the people in here have a very contagious fungus. You won't get many folks barging in."

"I'm sorry I didn't stop her," Fie blurted out. "I didn't—I couldn't—"

"You *shouldn't*," Khoda said so sharply that Barf sat up from where she was curled in his lap, ears flattening until he gave her a pat. "You both did exactly what you needed to, which was to keep your cover. *You*"—he pointed at Fie—"have the ability to assume disguises at will and to memorize and reproduce so much information, it's not even funny. If you ever get tired of working for the Crows you should talk to me about a career in espionage. And you—" He turned to Jasimir just as the prince was reaching to dab more paste on a scratch. Instead, it smudged over the tip of Khoda's nose. "Er."

"Sorry," Jasimir mumbled, and handed him a rag.

Khoda waved it off, then wiped his nose. "As I was saying, *you* are literally the only person who has the training, the temperament, and the lineage to take the throne. You, Tavin, and Rhusomir are the only living descendants of Ambra now who aren't sworn to the Phoenix Priesthood." He scowled and muttered, "I *still* can't believe the tiger. Of all the gall."

"And you thought I was joking about Jas being named for his pa's dog," Fie said.

"That would have been preferable," Khoda scoffed. "The point is, you're the best candidate for the throne. It's my job to keep you alive at any cost."

"*Not* any cost," Jasimir said, suddenly irate. "I asked that of Tavin once, and I have never been so ashamed as when I got it."

Khoda shrugged. "Get used to shame. You're going to be a king. Anyway, neither of us needs to be spying in the parties anymore. Fie, you may have to keep going as Lady Sakar if we can't get you an excuse, but they'll be useless for scouting for defectors now. No one in their right mind will do anything but blow smoke up Rhusana's"—he coughed—"face. Yula, is there any particular role that will give us free run of the palace?"

She frowned at the ceiling, then snapped her fingers. "Oh!" Her face fell. "But it . . . it's beneath His Highness."

"I'm willing to test that," Jasimir said, grim. "Chamber pot duty?"

Yula shook her gray-streaked head. "Pest control. There isn't a corner of this palace that mice won't get into, and the tabby there seems to have a shine for you. We'll round up a few more mousers, and then you can be our new cat-masters. Well, one of you is cat-master. The others are deputy cat-masters."

Khoda gave a resigned sigh. "Brightest Eye help me, if these scar over"—he gingerly tapped a cheekbone between the scores and winced—"I'll have the whiskers for it. Cat-masters it is."

"*Deputy* cat-masters," Fie corrected. "Jas is obviously the ranking cat-master."

Khoda scowled at her but was interrupted by a knock at the door.

"Food for the sick," Ebrim grunted outside.

"See? Password," Khoda hissed at Fie, then called, "Come in."

Ebrim slid in, then caught the door before Yula could close it. "Hold on. We have a visitor for the patients."

A man slid in behind him. He was a lanky fellow, looked to be in his late thirties, wearing Pigeon grays with surprisingly long sleeves.

He was sweating, and from the way he fidgeted with those sleeves, Fie reckoned it wasn't just from the heat.

Ebrim closed the door, then motioned for them all to huddle in the middle of the room, as far from the window and the hall as possible. Barf mewed in protest as Khoda moved her from his lap, then curled up on his pillow instead.

"This is one of our missing Sparrows," Ebrim said in a low whisper. "What do you want us to call you?"

The man's mouth wobbled. "Just . . . just Sparrow will do."

Ebrim patted the man on the back. "Sparrow here sought me out. He still remembers what happened when the qu—" Sparrow flinched, and Ebrim stopped. "When *she* called for him. Will you tell them, or should I?"

Sparrow took a deep breath. "I'll do it. It was just yesterday, after the solstice, around noon. I was working on the retiling project in the west wing of the archives, on the fourth floor, you know the one." Ebrim nodded. "Her Maj—*Her* footman said she needed assistance at once. I . . . My sister, she, she was called more than a week ago, just like that. Doesn't remember a thing. I thought I could find out what happened to her."

"Brave man," Khoda said. "What happened next?"

"I was taken to the royal catacombs, near the well. The footman gave me a torch and told me to go to the Tomb of Monarchs and wait until I was called back. The hour-bell was ringing when they sent me down, and I-I think it rang again right around when they called for me. The—*she* was waiting at the bottom of the stairs, with a man in an Owl robe. They asked if I heard anything, and I said no. Then she said if I told anyone, she'd—" He covered his mouth and shook his head. "The man also said he could make me forget everything, everyone I ever loved, all of it. I swore I wouldn't tell. They let me go."

"She had you there for an hour," Jasimir said. "For . . . nothing?"

Sparrow gnawed at his bottom lip, then shook his head again. "I lied," he whispered. "I heard . . . something. It came and went, and I couldn't tell where from, and I knew if my sister heard it too, she would have told them, so I lied."

"What did you hear?" Khoda asked.

Sparrow shuddered. "It sounded like someone weeping. Like . . . like a soul in torment."

A cold hush fell over the room, prickles dancing over Fie's arms. It only broke when she said, soft and slow, "What the *fuck*?"

Jasimir reached over and gripped the man's shoulder. "I know what it's like to feel powerless against her," he said. "Like everything you hold dear can just be taken from you, if she feels like it. It was incredibly brave to come back. I won't forget it."

Sparrow nodded, eyes on the ground.

"Look at me," Jasimir said, and waited for Sparrow to meet his gaze. "Thank you." He let go.

"I'll get you back into Dumosa." Ebrim took a step toward the door as Sparrow fussed with his sleeves once more. "If you'd like, we can try to get you farther."

"I just want it all put right," Sparrow said hoarsely. "The way it was."

I don't, Fie thought but didn't say. *I want better.*

Once Ebrim and Sparrow were gone, Khoda started pacing. "So. Now we need to figure out how to break into the royal catacombs." He looked up to Yula. "I don't suppose you get a lot of cleaning requests down there."

She shook her head. "They also need to be unlocked by a member of the royal family. They're the only ones with the keys."

"*Damn.* I was hoping we could send Fie in."

Fie squinted out the window, thinking. She hadn't yet told Khoda of her plans for tomorrow. "Maybe we still can."

———◆◆◆———

"I'll admit, again," Tavin said, "this was not what I had in mind."

Fie propped an unlit torch against her shoulder as they passed under the stone arch, its carved phoenix sneering at them from atop its skulls. "I told you, I like dark secrets."

A fern could flirt better than that, Niemi scolded.

Fie swallowed. She'd dressed practically, with a minimal glamour to turn her linen tunic and leggings into finer weaves with thicker embroidery. There was no chance of dazzling Tavin with a spectacle of a gown today.

He'd gone first, headed down the steps to a set of heavy-looking bronze doors, a ring of keys swinging from his fingers. She leaned closer to the back of his neck and breathed, "And you said you had a lot to show me."

Tavin dropped the keys with a clatter. "Er," he croaked. "That's . . . fair."

There, Niemi said. *Better. You might land us a prince after all.*

Fie didn't know if the swell of nausea came from that notion, or from the fact that the Well of Grace had to be only a few dozen paces above her. Either way, she ignored the dead girl and tried to fix her head on what the queen might be hiding.

The bronze doors swung open. Tavin tapped the iron torch in his hand. It kindled with a flurry of gold sparks. He reached for Fie's torch. "May I?"

It had taken Fie nigh a week to teach him to ask before reaching for her. He'd figured it out in under three days for a Peacock girl.

She gave him a tight-lipped smile and held her torch out.

Once it was lit, he led on. The passage continued down in a shallow, broad slope; Fie knew a hall designed for pallbearers when she saw one. It was simple, well-cut masonry, the ceiling fitting in a smooth arch over their heads. If the well above leaked into the ground, she saw no sign; the stone looked mostly dry and free of mold streaks.

She felt it all the same, dragging at her belly. Naming the fear made it easier to face, but easier was not the same as easy. When her torch wobbled, Tavin looked back. Whatever he saw in her face spurred him to hold out a hand.

Fie loathed herself for taking it. She loathed herself more for the way it felt right.

Halfway down, they passed two figures standing in armor bolted to the walls, one on each side of the hall. Torchlight caught on bone, on empty eyes peering through helmets wrought of gold-trimmed bronze.

"There are going to be more of those," Tavin warned. "They're former master-generals. They guard the catacombs even after death."

Fie sucked in a breath as they passed. The thought of Draga standing on duty down here until she crumbled away didn't sit well.

Then a strange pressure began to push on her ears, like a note too low to hear anywhere but in her gut. The deeper they went, the cooler and stiller the air became, until she winced at every crunch of her footsteps.

They passed three more sets of dead Hawks before they found the bottom, and Fie could only hope they were wholly below the bottom of the Well of Grace now. Her torchlight caught the edges of columns a few paces out; everything beyond it was a sea of dark.

Tavin found a small brass wheel in the wall and gave it a full turn. There was a soft gurgle. Then he touched his torch to a brazier mounted beside the wheel.

Fire caught on oil and spilled down channels cut along the walls, unfurling into a spiderweb of flame over the whole of a great, round room near as wide across as the Well of Grace. Doors lined the chamber in dark arches, gaping like toothless mouths. More dead generals were stationed beside every one, and great curving beams held up an eight-sectioned dome above.

More bones lined the room, set into morbid mosaics around each door, curving ribs outlining flames, fingerbones forming the rays of a backbone sun. Over each door sat a skull.

It all felt . . . *different* from the royal palace. Familiar. Fie couldn't place why until she realized every column was studded with the same eight-pointed star she'd seen in Little Witness's tower. *All* the stonework reminded her of the watchtower the longer she looked at it, if it had been buried underground instead of thrust into the sea.

So the catacombs were at least as old as Little Witness's grave. The notion felt peculiar to her.

Tavin waved his torch at the doorways. "There are different crypts for different, well, kinds of Phoenix. The priests have their crypt there, and then there's one for spouses of the monarch if they want it, and one for the immediate members of the family who never hold the throne, like siblings. Cousins get their own crypt, too. Or they did. Phoenixes are . . . fewer, these days."

Fie squinted at the skulls over the doorways. Something was off about their jaws. She blinked. "Where are their teeth?"

"They're pulled out in the burial ceremony," Tavin said.

"For the Crows?" she asked, like she didn't have near a half dozen Phoenix teeth stashed on her at that very moment. Tavin nodded. She frowned. *Play the fool.* "But . . . why would you need to pay the Crows? You survived the Sinner's Plague."

It was his turn to give her a tight, thin smile. "My father didn't. But it's been part of our traditions for so long, I don't know what would happen if we changed it. Maybe the priests would all quit." He barked an uncomfortable laugh. "Let me guess. You want to see the Tomb of Monarchs."

"Do you *want* to show me the Tomb of Monarchs?" she asked, sly, and realized with a curl of revulsion that she hadn't even needed Niemi's help to flirt back.

He laughed again, more genuine this time, and pulled her forward.

It was like the first time she'd approached the Well of Grace all over again. Each step seemed to ring and rebound and hum in her ears, that pressure building and building in her skull. Tavin's hand became less a comfort and more an anchor. She heard whispers—voices—chanting—

Bones, she realized. The Well of Grace had to be directly overhead, and that was bad enough, but everywhere she looked, she saw bones. The most dead she'd seen at once had been Karostei, one hundred scattered across the village. There had to be hundreds, maybe thousands of dead here, packed tight and dry, their bones singing to her in their sleep.

Tavin led her to a set of double doors across from the hallway and pushed them open. Inside was another round room, but it climbed like a massive chimney; the fire-lines had lit in here as well, carving bars of light all the way to the ceiling high above Fie's head. Great stacks of what looked like spokeless wheels rose above them, studded in toothless skulls. At the eye-level wheel, Fie saw a stone casket for every skull; the ring of skulls was not complete, though, with four empty caskets lying in wait.

"Once it's full up, there's some kind of mechanism to raise all the rings," Tavin said, letting go of her to turn in a slow circle. "Then they wheel in a new one and start filling it in. Oh. And, of course, there's Ambra."

Firelight fell across an ornately carved casket in the dead center of the room, raised on a low dais. A skull was set into a tarnished gold wreath atop the casket, a crown of gold wrought like feathers fused to the bone.

Fie couldn't help noticing the Queen of Day and Night had managed to keep her teeth.

"Oh," she said faintly. Wherever she set her eyes, it was as if the room skidded out from under them. She tried to steady herself against a wall, only for her fingers to brush skull.

The spark-song blared in her bones, resonant and demanding. She yelped and yanked her hand back, only to stumble on the shallow dais, dropping her torch. Tavin seized her wrist before she fell.

"Are you all right?" he asked, steadying her.

Fie stared at him, trying to scrape together an answer through the droning of the well, the chanting of the bones, the song of dead monarchs echoing off the walls of her skull—

"Fine," she said dizzily.

He frowned, peering close, too close. "You don't sound fine. We should get you out of here."

Her heart rattled in her ears, a drumbeat to the cacophony. She hadn't been this close to him, not like this, in too long. It still ached, it still burned.

He'll know, some distant part of her warned. *You'll lose control of your teeth and he'll figure it out, he'll see your face, you have to get out, you have to—*

Distract him, Niemi whispered.

Fie leaned forward and pressed her mouth to his.

It doesn't mean anything, she told herself, *none of this is real—*

Tavin's torch fell to the ground with a clatter.

Shaking hands skimmed her face, drew her closer, and she hated how much she missed this, hated how she curved into him like a bow he was stringing, hated her heart for leaping as he traced the line of her spine.

None of it's real, she lied to herself as she curled her fingers in his too-short hair, trying to shut out the brief, flickering gasps of his thoughts whenever his teeth brushed her. *This isn't you, he doesn't want Fie, he wants a dead girl——*

Just don't look at her face—

The thought broke in as his teeth grazed her jaw, the need and sorrow burning bone-deep.

You can do this, just don't look—

Fie didn't know whether to laugh or cry. Of course it was all mummery on his part, of course none of it was real.

Tavin still wanted her, the real her. By every dead god, she hated him for it.

By every dead god, she couldn't let him go.

None of it's real.

That was the way of Peacocks, though, just as Khoda had said. It didn't have to be real. It just had to be real enough.

They half shifted, half fell against Ambra's casket. The marble cover grated in protest but only moved a hair as Fie let herself lean back, shivering first at the chill of the stone, then at Tavin's hands slipping under her tunic, his mouth burning on hers.

She hated him still. She wanted him more.

She thought she might have him right here, on the grave of the Queen of Day and Night.

His fingers were too clever by far. Then he pushed her tunic up and knelt to press a kiss to her ribs. Fie sucked in a breath. Her knees faltered, and she scrabbled for a handhold on the casket.

For the second time, her fingers met bone.

But this time, there was no venom-sharp spark.

Fie blinked, gut lurching, at the sight of her fingers hooked in the empty eye socket of Ambra, Queen of Day and Night.

And then—simply, inescapably—she was pulled under.

———————◆———————

She knelt before a throne, silk knotted around her head. It took but a thought to light it, and in the glassblack panes she saw her own reflection crowned in golden fire.

"*We have chosen,*" a crowd chanted at her back.

You chose wrong, she wanted to tell them. Oil dripped down her face until her reflection was streaked with fire.

———————◆———————

She lay in a sea of sweat-stiff satin, and she was dying. Twelve figures stood around her bed, watching her gravely from beneath black silk hoods.

"You know the price," a voice said, one Fie had heard before. "Will you pay it?"

"M-my word," she coughed.

"A Covenant oath," the voice said, firm.

She lifted her arm. "Cut it," she croaked. A small silver dagger was produced and drawn swiftly across her palm, and a hand clasped hers.

"In flesh and blood do I make this oath," she ground out. ". . . I will give up my crown and join you on your roads, as one of your own."

"In flesh and blood do I make this oath." The speaker stepped forward. It was the woman Fie had seen in a dream before, with her lined face and black silk robe. This time Fie saw a curious, well-made necklace wrought about her neck in silver and steel and bone, like a row of spikes—no—*teeth.*

It was a chief's string.

They were *Crows*.

But their robes were silk, their hands gloved instead of wrapped in rags, the chief had wielded a proper knife—

She missed the chief's side of the oath, drowned in coughing. "To the Covenant I swear it," she gasped. "Now *do it*, damn you."

"To the Covenant I swear it," the chief echoed. "May my oath be kept in this life and, if I fail, the next."

The chief waited, giving her a pointed look.

She relented, choking out the last few words. "May my oath be kept, in this life or the next."

She drifted on her back in the cold, dark water of her favorite pond in the private royal garden, staring up at the sky.

"You can't stay in there forever," the chief called from nearby, black robe wafting on the mild breeze.

She knew what the Crow chief was here to collect. But she was not ready to leave all this. She was not ready to pay.

"Watch me," Fie heard herself answer.

This time, as she sank into the water, she heard the chief's muffled cry: "*You swore to the Covenant, Ambra!*"

Dark water closed over her head, and all was still.

Fie was back in Little Witness's tower, the sea roaring around them, held back only by the stone walls. The dead god was smiling at her.

"Aye, we Crows had a Birthright. It was stolen. And if you want to take it back, you'll need to keep your oath."

Fie was only dimly aware of Tavin shaking her, of the blood running from her nose, of him carrying her from the Tomb of Monarchs. She only barely heard the chanting of the bones around her, singing what almost sounded now like *Welcome, welcome, welcome.*

Her mind was little but fog and dust devils of thought, spinning threads that snapped before she could pull them taut. But one kept winding round her skull, again and again, and that thought was not a dust devil nor a spindle, it was a hurricane, too immense to see it all from the shore.

It had never been Pa's Covenant oath unkept, but one she'd sworn lives and lives ago.

It had been Ambra's to keep.

And now, in this life, it was Fie's.

PART THREE

CONQUERORS

— AND —

THIEVES

CHAPTER TWENTY

— THE HEIR —

SOMETHING COOL AND DAMP BRUSHED OVER FIE'S MOUTH. HER eyes flew open.

She saw mahogany and teak and linen and red; then everything blurred again.

"Easy," Tavin said somewhere above her. "Don't push yourself."

"Where am I?" She blinked until her vision cleared again.

"A spare room. We're in the royal quarters."

The room about her was—strange, she thought. Small for a royal bedroom and worn in a way the palace usually painted over. The walls were soft golden teak, the bedposts lacquered Hawk red, a familiar thick-woven blanket covering the mattress—

The last time she'd seen that blanket, she'd been sharing it with Tavin in Draga's camp. This was his room, his *real* room.

She saw a modest collection of weapons neatly racked on the wall, light streaming in from a screened window facing a mossy cliff. Across from her sat a small shelf of scrolls, along with a washbasin and brass mirror beside a dish of what had once been rings, necklaces, and other jewelry before they'd conspired to knot into a solid ball the size of her fist. On the table beside the bed stood a simple brass lamp, a mammoth carved of ebony, an amulet of mammoth ivory with the master-general's personal seal.

It was like a window into a part of Tavin she couldn't bear to look at.

It was a room Niemi wasn't meant to know.

"Sorry," Tavin said after a moment. He was sitting at the foot of the bed, wringing a rag stained with blood. "Other than the nosebleed, you didn't have any injuries that I . . . saw, and I didn't know where else to take you."

"This is fine." She pushed herself up, and he handed her a mug of water. "Thanks. I . . . don't know what happened."

It was half a truth.

Tavin passed her the bloody rag and tapped his chin. "You've still got some, er. Would you like me to get a doctor?"

Fie mopped at her face to buy herself a moment. When she surfaced, she had the best answer she could scrounge together: "Allergies," she blurted out. "It's just—allergies."

"I see," he said, in a way that meant he did not see at all. Then he rubbed the back of his neck, sheepish. "I apologize, I . . . may have moved . . . things . . . a little too fast, earlier." She gave him a blank look. "In the tomb."

Fie's brow furrowed, still groggy. He hadn't seen the visions of Ambra's life, had he?

"When we kissed," Tavin clarified, cheeks darkening. "I-I got a bit carried away."

"Oh." Fie shook her head distractedly. "No, I liked it."

She'd seen Ambra's life. She hadn't called the spark from that bone. It had swallowed her whole anyway. Animal bones did that, aye, because they knew no better. Human bones knew to wait, not to offer their gifts or their secrets so freely.

But Ambra's skull had just drawn her in, like it was part of her.

Tavin's voice jostled her from her thoughts. "I want you to know," he said, fumbling for words, "that if you feel like you have to go along with whatever *I* want, because of who I am—you don't."

His fingers were tracing unseen patterns on his wrist, where a glamour hid the scars.

Fie couldn't stop herself; she reached over and caught his hand. "I know."

Now, Niemi hissed. *Take him. Finish what you started in the tombs. He'll be ours.*

The notion turned Fie's belly. So did the notion of hearing him say Niemi's name in the close, shuddering way he'd once breathed hers.

She let go. "I should probably go lie down. In my rooms. For a bit."

She didn't want to. She wanted to stay here with him, in a room that felt *real*. Fie wanted to unroll all his scrolls, look in his mirror, pick out the tangle of jewelry, run her hands over every bit of it until she could find a way to forgive him for selling her Crows to the queen.

But Fie had come to the palace to keep her oaths. So she let Tavin walk her back to the guest quarters, let him leave her with a quick, soft kiss on her cheek, made herself ignore the tension in his shoulders as he left.

She'd expected her room in the guest quarters to be empty. Instead, her door swung open to a chorus of mews.

Fie blinked. Jasimir and Khoda were seated on the ground, try- ing to wrestle a black-and-white cat into some sort of vest. More cats were lounging about the room, pouncing on carpet fringe, napping on the bed, or grooming an ear. Barf herself rolled on the carpet beside Jasimir, squirming in another of the vests.

Jasimir looked up and grinned, tapping a new-minted badge on his Sparrow uniform. "Cat-master," he said brightly. Then his grin slipped. "What's wrong?"

"What happened in the catacombs?" Khoda asked.

Fie sat in one of the overstuffed chairs. A small cat with a tortoise-shell coat immediately leapt onto her lap and curled up. She buried her face in its fur. "I didn't hear anything. It all made me sick, there were too many bones, I just—" Fie made herself lift her head and take a breath. "In the Tomb of Monarchs, I touched Ambra's skull." Khoda tensed. "It wasn't supposed to—bones aren't supposed to do aught unless I ask, but it did, it showed me Ambra's life."

"Why would it show you that?" Jasimir asked, bewildered.

She didn't want to say it out loud; it was the same as the feeling from the Well of Grace, from Little Witness's watchtower, the same droning dread. She said it anyway.

"Last moon, I went to the watchtower of Little Witness. The shrine-keeper there *is* Little Witness reborn, and she remembers everything. She told me the Crows have a Birthright, but it was stolen. That if I wanted to get it back, I had to keep my oath. I thought she meant *our* oath, Jas. I thought getting you to Draga wasn't enough, that I had to put you on the throne. But Ambra . . . Her skull *grabbed* me, and I saw her—I saw her swear a Covenant oath with Crows, to save her life."

"But she didn't keep it," Khoda finished, quiet. "And now it's yours."

Jasimir twisted to look between him and Fie, letting the black-and-white cat in his lap go. "What are you saying?"

"Fie is Ambra reborn. Well, the latest one, that is." Khoda leaned back, trying to sound casual. "Congratulations. You're now in on another of those secrets the master-general mentioned. You know, the kind that holds nations together."

Jasimir and Fie both stared at him.

"The Black Swans keep count of witches, right?" Khoda continued. "When they first started, the numbers didn't add up. A witch of one caste would die, but we wouldn't see another witch born to take their place. It took a few decades to figure it out, but every one of them had died of the Sinner's Plague, and a few years later . . . a new Crow witch would be registered. Eventually they get sent back, after a life or two with the Crows. But Ambra has stayed. Most of the nation thinks Ambra's rebirth is supposed to set off an era of peace. It's already happened"—he did a quick tally on his fingers—"thirteen times, I think? That we know of?"

"You knew this whole time?" Fie asked, numb. "You knew who I really was?"

Khoda pursed his lips and didn't answer for a moment. "I wasn't lying when I said we thought Rhusana would target you. But this is part of why. You have every right to be angry with me for keeping it from you, let's just get that out of the way. But what good would it have done if I told you? What would it change?"

"*What would it change?*" Jasimir exploded. "It makes her the heir to the fucking throne! The rightful queen of Sabor!"

"*No.*" Fie pushed herself back into the chair. "I don't want it. You can't make me."

You don't want to be queen? Niemi demanded. *What's wrong with you?*

Khoda was shaking his head. "Even if you did want it, it doesn't matter. You have to keep your oath."

The oath . . . Fie's belly sank. "Ambra swore to give up her crown and join the Crows. How am I supposed to keep *that?*"

"You need a crown to give one up," Jasimir said.

Khoda scowled at him. "It's not happening."

Jasimir ran his hands through his hair. "Khoda, you've told me for the last week that all the gentry care about is that the crown goes to a descendant of Ambra. Tav, Fie, and I almost died, *many times*, in order to convince people I *might* be Ambra reborn. Now we have the real thing, and suddenly it doesn't matter?"

Khoda didn't answer.

Fie did for him. "It doesn't, because I'm a Crow."

She heard Little Witness's final words to her: *You are not what you were.*

She also heard Niemi's: *We could be the queen, you insufferable fool!*

"Because you don't have proof," Khoda corrected. "How are you going to convince the Peacocks? The Hawks? The rest of Sabor?"

Jasimir's face went stony. "She can't be killed by the plague, *like Ambra*. She can control fire and keep from being burned, *like Ambra*. That's all it would take for anyone to believe *I* was Ambra reborn."

"You know it's not that simple," Khoda snapped, getting to his feet. "And I can't believe you're willing to just throw your throne away."

"It's not throwing it away!" Jasimir stood as well. "I've given *everything* to make myself the best king I could be for Sabor. Do you think I'd give that up for anything less? But if the Crows have a Birthright and this returns it, it's not just about Ambra. It's about helping my people—*our* people. You can't tell me that doesn't give Fie the right to the throne."

"It's not just *having* the right to the throne!" Khoda was angrier than Fie had ever seen him. "It's *being* right for the throne!"

"My father abused his power in every way imaginable just to prove he could," Jasimir hissed, "and your all-knowing Black Swans did *nothing* to stop him, because you thought he was good enough for the throne."

Barf climbed onto Fie's lap and plopped down with seemingly no regard for the fact that her belly was planted on the tortoiseshell's face. Fie closed her eyes and let her head fall back.

Niemi wouldn't shut up in Fie's skull. Her tooth should have burned out hours ago, but somehow it was still alight. *Marry the prince*, the dead girl sang, *take the throne, make us queen!*

Fie ripped the tooth from her string and flung it across the room.

"I'm going to scalp the next person who says *throne*," she announced, eyes still shut.

She heard Jasimir stomp toward the door. He paused before opening it.

"If being a Phoenix was all that made my father right to rule Sabor," he said, tired and furious, "and being a Crow makes Fie wrong, then I don't even know what we're doing here."

"If you're leaving to go sulk, *cat-master*, don't slam the door," Khoda sighed.

Jasimir did not slam the door. Somehow it still sounded angry.

"It's not just that you're a Crow," Khoda said after a moment.

Fie cracked an eye open to give him a look of disbelief. "Please. Continue telling me how I'm unfit to rule."

Khoda put his hands on his hips. "Fine. Let's say we have a heat wave, early spring, and the Marovar glaciers dump snowmelt into the Lash. The Hassura Plains flood, and Lumilar loses a fifth of the crops they've sown and a quarter of their cattle herds. How do you keep the city from starving?"

"Tell the lady-governor of the realm to pay them," Fie said with a shrug. "Have you seen her mansion? She can afford it."

"Oh no, she didn't like how you phrased the order!" Khoda threw up his hands. "She's saying she doesn't have the resources, and your appropriations council won't approve the expense of direct aid, either! What do you do?"

"Have them all executed," Fie said darkly.

Khoda scowled. "Joke all you like, but this is exactly what I mean. Surimir wasn't good enough for the throne, but he *was* trained to keep the nation running and the Hawks and Peacocks happy. I don't have to tell you leadership isn't for amateurs. If Jasimir tried to run your band, even now, do you think he'd manage?"

Fie *hmph*ed. Khoda had a point. But . . . "I've always been in this for the Crows, Khoda. Maybe you're all right about us after all. Maybe I'm still with the Crows because the gods really did make us to be a punishment, and Ambra fouled up so grand that I'm still paying for it. But we *had* a Birthright. I hate this palace, I hate these people, and I bet whatever the crown looks like, I'll hate it, too. But if taking it gets us our Birthright back, there is nothing you can say or do to stop me."

He gave her a long look. Both of them knew that if it came time to test it, it would not end well. But Fie didn't care; things rarely ended well for Crows without someone wrenching them the right way.

The door rattled on its hinges, then opened. Yula entered with a cart of cleaning goods, finger pressed to her lips until the door closed behind her. "Apologies," she said under her breath, and hurriedly shoved aside the cleaning supplies. "We had to clean out the sick rooms, they're needed. Here, your things." She unloaded a few sacks of spare servant uniforms, base gowns for Fie to glamour, and Khoda's own stash of varying disguises. Then she paused, worrying her bottom lip between her teeth.

"What's wrong?" asked Khoda.

Yula turned to Fie. "Will . . . will you come look at them? The patients, that is. There's three."

Fie's face dropped. "Is it the plague?"

Yula worried her bottom lip more before answering. "We don't know."

That sat strange. The plague usually made itself known within hours. Fie reached for one of the Sparrow uniforms. "Aye, I'll take a look."

Once she'd changed, she and Yula hurried across the palace grounds, Khoda staying behind in case Jasimir returned.

Caws ruffled the garden as they strode through, black wings rustling in the topiaries. Fie stopped counting the crows once she passed a dozen.

Something was drawing them to the palace. She didn't know if she wanted to find out what.

Three Sparrow servants were waiting for them in the sick rooms, two women and a man sweating in the stifling room—yet they wore the long-sleeved tunics of winter uniforms, and gloves over those. Fie's nose wrinkled. She didn't smell the telltale plague-stink, but they also didn't look like sinners to her, eyes still bright and alert, no pallor, no rash of Sinner's Brand on their faces.

"I brought the Crow," Yula whispered. "You can show her."

They traded looks. The man stripped off a glove and rolled up his sleeve. Fie came closer.

She saw it, faint but clear enough: the Sinner's Brand carved whorls down his arm, all the way to his fingertips. It was the same distinct pattern she'd seen on Niemi before cutting her throat, but nowhere near as dark, and Niemi's had only been a few hours old.

"How long?" Fie asked.

"One day," one woman answered.

"Since the solstice," the other said.

The man swallowed. "Five. Five days."

Her brow furrowed. She looked up at him. "Any fever?" He shook his head. "Spewing? Coughing blood?" He shook his head after each. Fie took a step back and turned to the women. "And you? Only the Sinner's Brand, too?"

"Yes."

Fie stared at the man's arm again, utterly flummoxed. The Covenant did not send the Sinner's Plague with equal speed, to be sure. Pa had suggested once that it seemed to linger on those who had great wrongs to atone for, making them feel every weeping sore, every bit of their lungs giving way. Others it took swift, usually when it had spread from an unburnt corpse and caught those whose crime was simply negligence.

She'd never heard of the Covenant simply marking sinners, then leaving them be.

"Is it the plague, or no?" Yula asked.

"I-I'm not sure," Fie said.

"You *have* to be sure. If it is . . ." Yula's voice shook. "They can't stay in the palace."

Fie didn't get it at first. Neither did the Sparrows behind her.

"Why?" the man asked. "If it's our time, we'll go to the quarantine huts."

That was when Fie understood. Her blood ran cold.

"Take them to the city," she told Yula. "Fast as you can, and *anywhere* that can quarantine them."

"I said we'll go—"

"It's not you, it's the queen," Fie interrupted. She made herself face the Sparrows. "I've never seen plague like this, and maybe—maybe it'll be different. But if the queen finds you, I know one thing: she'll die wearing the Sinner's Brand herself before she calls for Crows."

CHAPTER TWENTY-ONE

── RED LANTERNS ──

A QUIET FELL OVER THE SICK ROOM. THEN ONE OF THE WOMEN spoke up. "It spreads if we die and aren't burned, right?"

"Aye," Fie said. The Sparrows all traded looks.

"If I asked now, would you give me mercy?" The woman stared at the floor.

"Aye." Fie's belly sank. "But your only symptom is the Sinner's Brand."

"I have——" The woman's voice cracked. "My sister and her children live in my house, in Dumosa. If I carry the plague there . . ."

"If you had the plague I know, you'd already be dead," Fie said. "If the Covenant wanted you to suffer, you would be suffering."

"It's not for us to know what the Covenant wants," the man said softly. "But if it spares Dumosa and the palace, it's worth it."

Fie could only think of the Black Swans' words again: *The sun will rise, even from our ashes.*

How much more would have to burn?

The door burst open before she could answer them. Khoda stood in the doorway, wide-eyed and taut.

"Fie, we need to go. The queen's rounding up the Sparrows and having all of them caste-tested. She's looking for us."

"But—"

The stamp of Hawk boots ratcheted down the walkway outside.

"No time, we're going." Khoda seized her by the elbow and hauled her into the corridor.

Fie yanked free, then locked her arm in his in a much more manageable position. "Stay close to me," she said, and called a Sparrow witch-tooth to life. Both she and Khoda disappeared.

"Don't you need to be saving these?" Khoda hissed.

Fie headed toward the stairs. "It's . . . complicated," she hissed back, because it was the truth.

She still had all three Sparrow witch-teeth Pa had given her. All three Pigeon witch-teeth. She even had *Tavin's* tooth still knotted in a bit of rag on her string, because every time she thought she'd burned one out, a day later the spark was back, good as new.

The Sinner's Brand on healthy people. Teeth that wouldn't burn out. And, as Fie and Khoda passed a window screen on the first floor, crows clamoring in the gardens.

The Sparrow man had been right. It wasn't for her to know what the Covenant wanted with them now, because absolutely none of it made a lick of sense.

Fie yanked Khoda to the side as Hawks marched down the hall. They flattened themselves against the wall, the spears passing less than a hand-width from Fie's nose. Door after door crashed open, and the offices' occupants were marched out to line up.

A Hawk with the bronze-and-carnelian badge of a war-witch passed from Sparrow to Sparrow, gripping each bare wrist a moment, then moving on. Once the war-witch had passed them by, Fie gave Khoda's arm a tweak and scuttled sideways for the door.

They eased out into the too-bright sun. Shouts of surprise and dismay echoed from every floor of the servants' quarters; at least a quarter of the staff had to have been sleeping before their night shift.

A sudden dreadful thought struck. "Where's Jas?"

"He came back to the guest quarters," Khoda answered. "We'll be safe there. Rhusana's only testing the palace servants right now, not any of the Peacocks' attendants."

Fie remembered the way the war-witch had tested the Sparrows and stopped in place. Khoda nearly yanked her off her feet by accident, not seeing she'd ground to a halt.

"What—?" he spluttered.

"This just got a lot worse," Fie said. "We need to see if—"

She heard boots behind them and shoved Khoda into a hedge, joining him fast as she could.

"We're *already invisible!*" he whispered, irate.

"They can still run into us," Fie whispered back. "*And* hear us, so shut up already. I'm watching for something."

The footfalls of Hawks pounded down the stairs, but it was the trio of Sparrows from the sick room who emerged through the doorway first.

Fie bit her fist, thinking *no, no, no, no, no.*

A squad of Hawks followed, keeping them at spear's length. Fie caught "*quarantine hut*" and bit down harder. Khoda muttered a curse beside her.

The Sparrows were marched out and away. Once they had passed, Khoda asked, "How long do they have?"

"I don't know," Fie answered. "They only have the Sinner's Brand, no other symptoms. They've all had it for long enough for the plague to kill them. It could be hours, it could be days. Weeks, even."

Khoda swore again. "And the queen won't light a beacon, because she didn't light one for Surimir, and people will start asking why. *Damn it all.* I know your father can hold out to the end of the moon. . . . But I don't know if Dumosa can."

Fie had no answer for that, so she helped him out of the hedge instead. "Let's get to the room."

The jeers of crows followed them all the way back to the guest quarters.

In her dream, she was swimming again, in her favorite of the private gardens. Her tiger was lounging in the other end of the pond, dozing among the lantern-lilies. She supposed he missed the chill of the Marovar nearly as much as she did, but he made it much easier to cow the Peacocks of the south. One look at a queen riding in on a tiger and they gave her everything she wanted.

Something caught her eye. She lifted her arm from the water and squinted.

If she looked close enough, there was a strange whirl of a pattern on her forearm, well above the witch-mark on her wrist. It almost looked like . . .

Something impossible. She'd just wear long sleeves until it passed.

A faint, piercing sound made her jump. It was familiar—too familiar. A whistle, muted but clear.

She knew it. Didn't she?

The whistle came again. It was a Crow signal, an order.

Up. *That was what it meant.* Up.

Fie woke with a start. The room around her was dark, the faint snores of Jasimir and Khoda both holding steady. Jasimir had claimed the couch, and Khoda a heap of cushions, both inundated with sleeping cats. Last time she'd counted, they now had seven in their purview, including Barf, but Barf had staunchly refused to share the bed with anyone or anything except Fie. The intricate window screen had been left ajar just enough to let the mousers come and go as they pleased.

It gave a slight rattle. Fie saw no sign of a cat.

Every nerve afire, she slid from the bed and crept to the window.

The screen rattled again. This time she was close enough to see the culprit: a thrown pebble.

She barely held in a noise of disgust and peered outside. Sure enough, Tavin was standing below, only a few paces away, lit in moonlight that had only diminished slightly since the solstice. His face broke into a grin when he saw her.

Fie made a bewildered gesture. He pointed to the ground, then held out his arms, mouthing, *I'll catch you!*

She debated a moment, then lied to herself that she might gather valuable information, coaxed the screen open, and threw a leg over the jamb. Barf yawned from the foot of the bed but curled into a tighter ball.

It isn't even that far of a drop, Fie thought with the kind of disdain she invoked for things she secretly enjoyed. The window was just high enough to discourage intruders, taller than Tavin by maybe half his height.

He reached up to help Fie scoot off the frame, fingers pressing into her hips in a way that was distracting and not helpful at all, and there was a wretched moment when he looked up and she looked down, bracing herself on his shoulders, only to find their faces much too close again, and all she could think of was how he didn't smell the same in the palace as on the road, but close enough that it was still him—

Tavin set her on the ground, then took her hand in his, jabbing a free thumb toward the royal quarters. She goggled at him. If he'd woken her up just to tumble somewhere private, she might murder him ahead of schedule.

Tavin read the look on her face and frantically shook his head. "I want to show you something," he whispered, then cringed. "That . . . didn't come out right. There's something I want you to see?"

"Is it in your trousers?" she asked doubtfully. "Because I—" Fie caught herself. She'd almost said she'd seen it before, which Niemi certainly had not. "I . . . can guess," she mumbled instead.

His teeth flashed in a sheepish laugh. "No, nothing like that. It's not even in the royal quarters, just the private gardens."

Fie waited for Niemi's spark to feed her an answer. There was only silence. Belatedly, she remembered throwing the tooth across the room. She swallowed.

She was on her own with Tavin now.

"Oh," Fie said. "That's, er, fine."

He didn't tarry in the gardens, instead cutting as straight a line to the royal quarters as possible. There was a magic to it: no Hawks on guard troubled them, only bowing their heads as he passed. They even opened the doors to the royal quarters for him, easy as could be.

Tavin led her right through those too, avoiding the stairs entirely. He didn't even stop to pick up a lamp, letting a golden flame roll off his hand instead to light the way. In less than a minute they were back outside, on a stone path bordered in dense, dark hedges.

"You don't have to, but it's better if you close your eyes," Tavin said.

Fie weighed it a heartbeat, but decided if this was any sort of trick, she was rutted anyway. She shut her eyes and let him steer her down the walkway, one hand between her shoulder blades. The air grew cooler, damper on her skin, a soft rush building in her ears. The scent of some strange flower drifted through the air, honey-sweet and light as a soap bubble.

They came to a stop. "You can look now," Tavin said, close enough to her ear to send goose bumps down her arms.

Fie opened her eyes.

They stood at the edge of a broad, dark pond, facing the stone cliffs that made up the westernmost end of the palace. A waterfall traced a white veil down the stone, splashing into the far end of the pond. To either side, dozens, maybe hundreds, of thin streams fell like threads, some filling the smaller pools bracketing the main one.

A golden glow lit the waters, cast twice: once from patches of rock-moss along the pond bottom, and once from clusters of scarlet lilies bobbing on the pond's surface, the pollen at their hearts shining like candleflames. The lilies were *everywhere*, spilling over the edges of the smaller pools, drifting in sedate rafts on the main pond, even sprouting in the tiny pools carved out of the cliff face by stubborn, tiny waterfalls.

Dimly she saw ornate statues, majestic fountains, an absurd gazebo or two, but she knew this was what he'd brought her here for: the one thing no craftsman could shape, no king could commission.

"They're called lantern-lilies," Tavin said, his hand warm on her back. "They've tried growing them in other parts of Sabor, but this is the only place where they'll shine by night." He ducked his head. "Everything you've seen here has been disasters and death threats and the worst of all this . . . this trash. I wanted you to see something beautiful."

There was a shaking edge to his voice, one she knew he couldn't fake, one that matched the tremble of his hand on her. This wasn't real enough; it was *real*, in the way his room had been real, in the way that said it mattered to him. He might not love Niemi, but he would at least do this much for her, offer as much beauty as he could in a court of monsters.

Fie found herself reconsidering her stance on tumbling him

somewhere private. But it would be selfish, lying with him just to tell herself she was in control, and it would be cruel, making him continue his mummery all the way to bed.

"Why have you been so kind to me?" Fie asked instead.

Tavin looked so sad for a moment, she wanted to cry herself. When he spoke, he sounded tired, but he gave her his best attempt at a smile anyway. "You remind me of someone."

Fie couldn't make herself smile back, didn't know why the next question couldn't stay bottled up. "Is that why you kissed me earlier?"

Tavin winced. "Yes."

Fie raised her hand, let it lie against the side of his face. "Would you like to do it again?"

His breath caught. "Yes."

She drew him to her. It wasn't feverish and feral, like that morning in the tomb. The way their lips met this time was deliberate, slow, gentle in a way that broke her heart, so sweet, too sweet. It was peace in the storm, one more scrap of beauty to hold on to.

And like all beautiful things, it ended too soon. Tavin pulled away, resting his forehead on hers a heartbeat or two. Then he told her, "I should let you get some rest. I'll walk you back."

She wished, for a terrible moment, that she could be the kind of girl who would be happy with him like this. That all his kindnesses here, all his sorrow, all his regret—they would let her forgive him for the choice he had made in Draga's tent.

But the awful truth they both knew, and neither could say, was that it was not enough.

Tavin didn't speak again until they reached the guest quarters, though his fingers stayed laced with hers. "The queen is holding a ball four days from now, on the twenty-first, to mark one week left until the coronation. Honestly, I'm pretty sure she's doing it just to prove she can throw an event without casualties for once. Will you do me the honor?"

Another opportunity to spy, she told herself, not convinced at all. "Yes," she told him. "I'd be . . ."

She trailed off, startled. A familiar sight had snatched up her attention whole.

"What's wrong?" Tavin followed her gaze over the rooftops of the palace buildings. His own eyes widened.

Two unmistakable columns of fire and smoke rose from two of the palace's three gates.

With or without the queen's permission, the plague beacons burned.

CHAPTER TWENTY-TWO

— DEPUTY CAT-MASTER —

"THE BEACONS ARE OUT NOW," YULA ANNOUNCED IN A LOW VOICE as she unloaded breakfast from the cleaning cart.

Fie pushed an overly interested orange tomcat away from the pan-bread and set it on the table. The beacons had given her a handy excuse to sneak back in the night before, claiming she'd seen smoke in the sky and gone out to see what it was. "Did Crows answer?"

Yula shook her head. "The sick are all still here, and then some. They found another five Sparrows with the Sinner's Brand, on top of the first three. Some of them have to sleep outside the quarantine hut. There's no room for them inside."

"That's faster than it usually spreads, right?" Jasimir asked Fie.

She chewed a strip of panbread, thinking. "It doesn't spread like this, period, unless there's a dead sinner somewhere that's been left to rot. Like with Karostei. But Khoda saw it. It didn't just spread fast, it killed fast. No one's gotten worse since yesterday?" Yula shook her head. "None of it stacks up right."

Khoda blew out a slow breath, thinking. "I need to go check in with my sources," he said finally, scratching at the still-healing lines on his face. "I'm sure the Hawks had direct orders not to light the beacons, so I need to find out who's willing to spit in the queen's face. You two stay here. Especially you, cat-master. You can try to get harnesses on your employees."

Jasimir made an annoyed noise but didn't argue, picking at his panbread as Fie wove Khoda a glamour and tossed him the tooth to keep it going.

Once Khoda and Yula had left, the prince waited until they were sure to be well on their way out, then turned to Fie and asked, "What are your thoughts on breaking into the royal quarters?"

She choked on her panbread. He pounded her on the back and shoved water her way, and eventually she coughed out, *"What?"*

"Breaking into the royal quarters," Jasimir repeated, as if he'd merely proposed a walk around the Midday Pavilion. "You and me. We know Rhusana's hiding something. Maybe we can find some clue about what it is. Why are you looking at me like that?"

"What happened to Prince"—Fie fluttered her hands, warbled her voice, and mummed dewy-eyed dismay—"'*Oh no we can't, it's the la-a-a-w!*'"

"First of all, 'we can't, it's the law' is not the wildly unreasonable statement you're pretending it is," Jasimir said peevishly. "Second, you know what happened, you were there for most of it. Do you want to do it or not?"

"I want to know *how*," Fie said.

Jasimir picked up a cat harness and gave it a shake. One of the cats raced over, a handsome silver fellow with darker spots. "Good Patpat," the prince hummed, and picked up the cat.

"*Patpat?*"

Jasimir scowled at Fie. "He pats you when he wants attention. Look, I had to come up with a lot of names at once. Point is"—he started feeding Patpat's forepaws into the harness, a curious little canvas-and-leather vest—"Patpat's a mouser. And he's *quiet*. Rhusana leaves food everywhere in the royal quarters. When I left in Pigeon Moon, the mice problem was so bad, they'd already had to triple the number of summons to the pest control office. The guard will be on high alert and reading castes at every entrance, but you can sneak us in with a Sparrow witch-tooth, and no one will ask questions if we're already inside."

Fie nodded thoughtfully. "We can let the cat run around, go where we please, and if the tooth burns out, we'll just say we're looking for Patpat."

"Exactly."

"Khoda will hate that we didn't run this by him," Fie said.

Jasimir nodded. "Correct."

"But I can wear the deputy cat-master badge."

"Correct."

Fie considered a moment. "So we should definitely break into the royal quarters, is what I'm hearing."

Jasimir grinned at her. "Correct."

———◆———

"We ought to have a talk about your security," Fie whispered to the prince a half hour later, as they crept into King Surimir's personal study and closed the door.

Jasimir looked about the room, hands planted on his hips. "They're doing their best. Besides, if you weren't here, I'd need a sophisticated team of specialists to replace you—a Sparrow witch, a Peacock witch, a Vulture witch . . . A little over their paygrade." He walked over to the desk and pulled a drawer open. "It's all been cleaned out."

Fie squinted at the empty shelves, running a finger along the gaps. Enough dust to account for a few weeks' absence, and no more. The queen's official study had been dustier, with only a few scattered quills and scrolls to ratify the illusion that she used it.

But . . . "She wouldn't win over the Oleander Gentry with empty words. And if they only cared for her powers, they'd have turned once her hair collection went up in smoke. There has to be more, something on paper, that they *only* get once she's crowned. Where haven't we looked?"

Jasimir sighed. "Almost everywhere. There's the library, the bathing chambers, the parlors, the bedrooms—"

Fie perked up. "She made your mother's bedroom into a nightmare den. Why not yours, too?"

"*Eugh.*" Jasimir's lip curled. "You may be right. There's a small study attached. Nobody would think to look there."

Fie called up the Sparrow witch-tooth again, and they edged out the door with their arms linked so as not to lose each other while unseen. Jasimir pulled Fie down the hall, pausing until a patrol of Hawks went past, then guided her up a narrow, unadorned flight of stairs she reckoned the servants used. It took them to a much finer hallway, where the prince slowly pushed open the first door on the right. The room was a midmorning sort of dim, the curtains drawn against the heat to come. Fie was tugged inside. She pulled the door shut behind her.

When Fie let the Sparrow witch-tooth go again, she found Jasimir utterly sucker-punched. One look at the room told her why.

The walls had been painted in soft swirls of silver, white, and gold, the bed much smaller than would fit Jasimir now. Toys were scattered all about the floor, wooden soldiers with the points sanded down, fluffy plush birds, a carved horse on wheels. It was a room for a young child, not an almost-king.

It was Rhusomir's room now. And from the way Jasimir was searching the corners, every last trace of him had been painted over.

"Jas." Fie elbowed him. "There's a better room waiting for you. I've seen it. It's got so much gold it's foul."

"That room is yours by right, not mine," Jasimir said grimly, and headed for the door on the other side of the room. "I was saving a bottle of wine in here. She better not have touched it."

Fie followed him into the study. Sure enough, Rhusana had clearly made camp in here, but from the way Jasimir was trailing fingers over his bursting, dusty shelves, the queen hadn't had the time or care to clear them out. They were crammed with scrolls, with rolled-up maps, even rare bound tomes from across the sea. One shelf was a great collection of seashells and dried starfish; another was cluttered with strange spiral rocks, like snail shells turned to stone. A window seat overlooked the waterfall Fie had stood beside the night before, the lantern-lilies still violently red by day.

But a map of Sabor had been tacked over the far wall. Tiny flags dotted dozens of spots that might have seemed random to a stranger's eye, matching no label or symbol on the map itself. Fie drew closer, throat closing.

Rhusana couldn't have—

She had.

Little Witness's watchtower, marked with a flag.

The shrine of Maykala, marked with a flag.

The groves of Gen-Mara, marked with a flag.

Crow shrines, the only places left for them to seek shelter in Sabor, marked with flags. Not all of them, though; Fie saw blanks where she knew shrines lay, like Dena Wrathful's temple, and Crossroads-Eyes' great tree. But so, so many. Too many.

They should have been unfindable. Peacock teeth to weave an illusion, Sparrow teeth to ward off attention—these were sown in every shrine. Fie had never heard of anyone but Crows finding the way in on their own, not unless the keeper wanted them to.

She found the answer in a dish beside the map: a skein of hair and scraps of skin. Her own memory supplied the rest. The first and last time she'd tried to use a Sparrow tooth on skin-ghasts, there had been no gaze for her to turn away. A Peacock glamour would fail too.

Rhusana was using her ghasts to scour every last bit of Sabor, until she found every last shrine.

"Fie." Jasimir's voice said he'd found something near as bad. She turned and found him thumbing through one of the many stacks of parchment on the desk. He looked ill. "These are official decrees. This one bans Crows from owning property within Sabor. This one bans anyone from representing Crows before a magistrate. This one says anyone who does business with a Crow will be jailed for a year." He flipped through more. "You . . . you get the idea. Rhusana has signed them all. They've even got the royal seal. But they can't go into effect without signatures from 'Prince Jasimir' and Draga."

It felt like a nail pounding into Fie's heart, each order, with the horror of the map on the wall. She pointed a shaking hand at it. "Those are all Crow shrines, Jas. She's—she's going to tell the Oleander Gentry where the shrines are."

Jasimir put a hand to his mouth. A breath later, it curled into a fist.

"All right," he said swiftly. "We're not going to panic."

"We aren't?" Fie asked, trying and failing to keep her tone from hitting a glass-shattering high.

"No. This is bad, but—we can do . . . something." He snatched up a blank parchment and a quill, laying it flat over one of the orders. "I'm going to try to copy her signature and we'll figure out the seal. We'll draft an order to cancel those orders, or postpone them, or *something*. We can't take the map—Rhusana will ransack the entire palace to find it—but you can move the flags around."

Fie pulled a flag out, then stopped. "They leave holes. She'll know where they belong."

"Then put more holes in," Jasimir said with a strained kind of calm. "Really, Fie, since when do I need to tell you to stab things?"

"I'm starting to think helping you fake your death was a good thing," Fie said under her breath. She started with the great shrines, Pa's and Little Witness's, poking the flag in a few times before settling somewhere off the mark, then she carried on to the smaller shrines. But it was slower work than she thought, and she'd only scattered a dozen or so flags before Rhusana's voice carried down the hall.

"Window seat," Fie hissed, shoving a final flag wildly off its marker.

Jasimir grimaced at his copied parchment. Fie could see Rhusana's signature was mostly done, but there was no time. He shoved it under the other parchment sheets, dropped the quill in the inkwell, closed the study door, and rushed to join her on the window seat. Fie called the Sparrow witch-tooth back to life a moment before the door slid open.

"—take long. You just need to sign some decrees." Rhusana breezed in.

Tavin followed in her wake, face stormy. "They won't be legally binding until after the coronation, you know."

"I'd rather avoid any unnecessary delays." Rhusana swept up the parchment slips and handed them over. "Here."

Tavin scanned one after another, a trench deepening between his brows. "You want to send Hawks to raid Crow shrines?" he demanded, tossing the parchments back on the desk. "What is the matter with you? Why can't you just leave the Crows alone? They've done nothing but their job."

Rhusana narrowed her eyes, then, surprisingly, leaned against the desk. Perhaps it was the fact that she needed him to sign the decrees; perhaps it was that, with plague swelling in the palace and spies in every shadow, the queen wanted just one person to speak plain with, and Tavin was the one who couldn't betray her without risking his own neck.

Either way, a forlorn crack wormed through her porcelain façade. "Do you know what my mother told me, when I was old enough to know I was neither a Swan nor a Vulture?"

Tavin stared back, then folded his arms. "Fine. I'll bite. What childhood trauma do *you* think justifies mass murder?"

The queen shook her head. "Hardly. I asked my mother how I could be a witch when witches are supposed to be the old gods born into their own caste, but I was born of two. And she told me what I'll tell you: that just makes us new gods. Do you get it?" She waved a hand glimmering with pearls and white gold. "The old gods are dead, and *we're* supposed to keep the caste system they locked us into? *Forever?* That's nonsense. Only children look at the world and think twelve little boxes is enough. It's no way to live."

"You seriously want to dissolve the caste system?" Tavin asked.

"You can't tell me it's working as the Covenant wants," Rhusana answered. "You can't tell me it's rewarding the virtuous by sending them to the Phoenixes. Surimir was proof enough of that. So yes, I want a world where the best person can rule the nation, not just the one who happened to be born to the right family, the right caste. If that means letting the plague take all the sinners it wants, I'll let it, because what's left will be the strongest of us. It will be *united*. I don't hate the Crows. They're just the price I'm willing to pay to fix this country."

Tavin looked at the parchment slips on the desk, then up at Rhusana. "Horseshit," he said mildly. "It's miserable being caught between two castes, I know. You don't belong anywhere, you don't have the protection from either caste, and the only thing you can do is try to make a place for yourself, make your own safety. But you can tell me this is for some better version of Sabor all you like. I'm guessing your version still has you as queen."

Rhusana gave an elegant shrug. "Like I said. The best person for the job."

"Like I said." Tavin returned her shrug, cold. "Safety. You think you can get rid of the labels but keep the hierarchy and call that *united*. I'm also guessing your Sabor has no room for a king." Rhusana's mouth twisted. Tavin didn't wait for an answer that wouldn't come. "I figured you'd only let me live long enough to win over the Peacocks. I'm not wasting any of my time signing any of your garbage. Besides, you already broke your side of the deal with whatever you've done to Fie."

Jasimir's hand found Fie's and held it tight.

Rhusana straightened up, and, even in the full clutch of midsummer, a frost seemed to roll through the room. "Whatever I've done," she repeated, slow as her white tiger stretching. "Why do you think I can't do *worse* to her?"

"Because if you could, you'd make me watch," Tavin returned, so matter-of-fact it sent ice through Fie's gut.

Rhusana didn't smile, didn't frown; her face was an eerie sort of blank. She picked up the parchment decrees, then held them out to Tavin once more. "And what makes you think I can't do worse to your newest little conquest? What was her name again . . . Niemi?"

It was Fie's turn to clench Jasimir's hand.

"Do you think they teach their daughters about poison in the north?" Rhusana asked gently. "The ones that take a full week to kill you, so you can watch your fingers and toes fall off one by one? The ones you survive, but every breath is torture for the rest of your life? Do you think the Crows would give her mercy——"

Tavin tore the parchment slips out of the queen's hand.

She smiled and handed him a quill. "Remember to sign as Jasimir."

Fie wanted to scream, she wanted to throw herself at Rhusana and claw her eyes out, she wanted to curse Tavin all through the twelve hells for signing the Crows' deaths into law. She wanted to burn this study down, burn the royal quarters down——she would burn the palace down with all of them in it if it meant bringing this sick mummery to an end.

Tavin's hands were shaking as he signed, again and again and again. It brought her no comfort.

He reached the bottom of the stack and paused, blinking at the page. Rhusana wasn't paying attention, frowning at her map of the shrines, but Fie could see it was the blank parchment Jasimir had forged most of Rhusana's signature on.

Tavin nudged it back under the stack so only the signature line was showing. "You forgot the seal on one."

Rhusana pointed to a drawer, then pulled one of her finger-claws off, still studying her map. "The wax is in there."

Tavin removed a stick of golden wax and flicked a flame to its end until it dribbled onto the page. "Done."

The queen had extracted a signet ring from her jewelry apparatus. She pressed it into the wax, swift and firm, then yanked it back as if waiting for Tavin to snatch it from her grasp. Tavin rolled his eyes. Rhusana turned back to her map, fiddling with her claws.

Quick as a flash, Fie saw Tavin fold the blank parchment and slip it up a sleeve. Her heart skipped a beat.

"Are we done here?" he asked, stiff.

Rhusana collected the stack of orders and nodded, sweeping past him and out of the study. "Thank you for your assistance," she called back, a twinkle in her eye. "You ought to go work off that stress with the Sakar girl. You've certainly earned it. And who knows when you'll have another chance?"

Tavin watched her go, glowering. Then he patted his sleeve, which gave a crinkle of parchment, and strode out, shutting the door behind him.

Neither Jasimir nor Fie moved for a long breath, not until they heard the door to Rhusomir's room open and close. Then Fie let the Sparrow witch-tooth go.

"Are you all right?" Jasimir asked immediately.

It was jolting, being asked that by someone who wasn't her own kin. But they'd been through enough, she reckoned they'd grown close enough for him to know the signs. "Not really," she croaked. "We need to tell Khoda."

Jasimir nodded. "Let's finish the map, then we can get out of here."

"It won't be enough," Fie said. "She can find them again."

"Nothing's going to be enough while she's still in power, but we can make her waste her time." He got up and pulled a flag out of the map. "Come on, it'll go faster with the two of us."

If all she could do was vex the queen right now, that was what she'd do. Fie went to help. After a few flags, she said, "I'm glad you're here."

He bumped her shoulder. "I'm glad you're here, too."

The hour-bell began to chime. Fie called a Vulture tooth to see what Viimo had to say and found the skinwitch pacing north-south, pausing in the north. "Khoda wants to meet."

Jasimir stuck a last pin in the flag. "We can bring Patpat with us to the Mother of the Dawn's grave."

Fie blinked at him. "It's a god-grave?"

"Yes?" He said it as if it were the most obvious thing in the world.

"I just . . . didn't feel a grave there." Fie's mouth twisted. "Why's it outside? Doesn't it throw off the . . . the symmetry?"

Jasimir spread his hands like matched wings, thumbs touching to make a head. "Well, the statue's outside, but the grave itself could be right under the thrones. Twelve on each side of the Divine Galleries, then the Mother of the Dawn at the middle."

Fie could have sworn Pa had said there were but two dozen dead Phoenix gods, but Jasimir would know best.

They snuck back to the foyer of the royal quarters, where Jasimir was able to summon Patpat with the crinkle of a wrapped fish treat. The Hawks on guard barely acknowledged them as they left.

Khoda was waiting at the statue for them, scrubbing a marble pedestal that at this point shone like a second sun, so clean it was. He looked to be sore irked with them but tilted his head to the back of the pedestal.

"We have a game changer," he said once they had huddled.

Jasimir made a face. "So do we."

"The queen's mapping our shrines, Crow shrines, with skinghasts," Fie said in a rush. "We fouled up her map, moved the markers around, but she'll find them again. She and Tavin have signed orders to start Hawk raids—"

"It won't get that far," Khoda interrupted. "Until they're crowned, they need the master-general's approval on any Hawk actions. And that's where *my* game changer comes in." He allowed himself a weary grin. "The plague beacons weren't just lit by panicking Hawks. The guards were commanded to ignore the queen and light them. And the one who gave that order . . . was Draga."

CHAPTER TWENTY-THREE

— PATIENCE —

"At this point, I feel like I should just give up on trying to tell you two to stick to any kind of plan." Khoda was doing his best to look severe as the three of them headed to the wing of the palace that housed the Hawks and their generals, but the effect was rather ruined by the fluffy orange tomcat attempting to stand on his shoulder, his magnificent tail waving like a war banner. His leash draped like a garland over Khoda's head. "What else do you want to do while you're here? Steal the crowns?"

"It was a calculated risk, and it paid off," Jasimir said primly. Patpat was walking beside him on a leash fastened to his harness, chirping at the prince every so often as if to hurry him along. They'd stopped by the guest quarters, collected three cats and one of Yula's preapproved requests to send in cat-masters, filled in the relevant information for Draga's office, and set off before the next hour-bell.

Fie had found that Barf liked the leash even less than her harness; she'd flopped on her side and refused to budge, making Fie carry her in her arms. "Granted, if they'd gone near the window seat, they'd have found us. But they didn't, and we're all the better for it."

Khoda cocked an eyebrow. "I've heard stories about the prince and that window seat."

"Please, no." Jasimir covered half his face with a hand.

Fie stared at him, both delighted and wary. "What kind of stories?"

Khoda shook his head, his smirk making the red lines on his face look all the more like whiskers, and gestured to the prince.

Jasimir let out a long sigh. "I . . . may have . . . engaged in certain activities, for the first time, on that window seat last year." Khoda coughed. "And I was not aware Father would be giving a tour of the private gardens to the new ambassadors."

Fie recalled the lovely view the study had had of those very gardens. The windows were crystal, not glassblack; that view definitely went two ways. She let out a gleefully outraged cackle. "You rolled your first lad on those cushions? Why didn't you say anything?"

"What with all the *mass murder plotting*, it didn't seem like the time!" Jasimir's cheeks flushed darker. "Besides, he was my languages tutor and Father had him dismissed by the end of the day, so it was only the once. He's our age and very charming, so I'm sure he had no trouble finding someone new. I'd rather we all forget about it."

"The tutor certainly didn't." Khoda swung the orange tomcat off his shoulders and set him on the ground. "Come on, Jasifur."

"You're not calling him Jasifur," the prince said immediately. "His name is Mango."

"*That's* the objection?" Fie muttered. Khoda and Jasimir didn't seem to hear, embroiled in impassioned debate. She noted with interest that the flush on Jasimir's cheeks still lingered. Khoda might not have been her type, but she could hardly fault the prince for his tastes when she'd just watched her last lover sign death warrants for her kin.

They passed the Hawk training yards, the armory, and finally reached the administrative offices, where they presented the slip calling for cat-masters and were sent up three flights of stairs. A small line of Hawks waited at the far end of the hall before massive twin mahogany doors. One wore the badge of a war-witch.

"I know the witch," Jas said under his breath. "They were one of my mother's closest friends."

"Authorized visitors only," the war-witch called down the hall. "Anyone entering this floor must have their caste verified, by order of the queen."

Jasimir straightened his shoulders. "I have an idea. Let me go first."

"You're the ranking cat-master," Fie returned.

Jasimir strode down the hall, Patpat trotting at his side. "We have a work order for the master-general's suites," he said, holding out a wrist. The Hawks looked taken aback at a Sparrow speaking like a commander, but the war-witch stepped forward and laid their hand on Jasimir's forearm.

A moment later, their eyes widened. They gave Jasimir the slightest smile, then nodded to Khoda and Fie. "Your associates, too?"

"Deputies," Jasimir said. "They're my deputies."

The war-witch only briefly clasped their wrists, looking from Jasimir to them and back. Then they took the work order slip and said, "Let me verify this with the master-general."

They ducked through the mahogany doors. After a minute, they emerged and held the door open. "The master-general says now is an acceptable time."

"Thank you." Jasimir bowed and led them in.

Draga was on her feet, face strained, but she waited until the door shut to ask, low, "Is it really you?"

Fie let the glamours go. Draga dropped into her chair, then motioned for them all to come closer. "I—I thought you'd all be long gone. *How?*"

Barf squirmed in Fie's arms until she set the tabby down. "When all this is over," Fie said, "we're having a long talk about palace security."

"Like I said, the queen underestimates everyone else," Khoda added dryly. "Including a Crow witch with a grudge and a bag of teeth. Do you think Rhusana's lost her hold on you?"

Draga nodded. "Obviously, there's no way to be certain, but it felt like a . . . a hand was on the back of my neck, and an hour or so after the coronation broke down it was suddenly gone. But it was too late by then." She sent a rueful look at Fie. "I should have figured the mess with the ceremony was *your* doing."

"And the plague beacons last night were yours," Fie returned.

Draga winced and leaned back. "Something's wrong here. The crows, the Sinner's Brand, the outbreaks . . . We're in uncharted waters. At least it looks like there's a way out."

"You'll help us against Rhusana and Tavin, then," Khoda said.

"I can fight the queen for the beacons. I can't—" Her breath hitched. She coughed, but it didn't cover the wobble in her voice. "Taverin made his choices. I won't delude myself about whether he can survive them. But it won't be by my hand."

"I could pardon him," Jasimir offered.

Both Khoda and Draga shook their heads. "You'd be leaving an opening for the Oleander Gentry," Khoda said. "They'll take up arms in his name, claiming he's the rightful king."

"I'll support you for monarch, Jasimir," Draga said. "And you'll have my help taking on Rhusana. That's what I can offer."

Jasimir's eyes darted around the room, nervous. He took a deep breath, licked his lips, and asked, "Will I still have your support if Fie is my queen?"

There was a heartbeat of perfect, stunned silence. Then the eruption of noise sent all three cats bolting under Draga's desk.

"*ABSOLUTELY not*," Khoda half bellowed, while Fie, jaw agape, could only manage a "*What?*"

Draga herself was staring at Jasimir as if he'd grown another head. All she asked was "Why?"

"She's Ambra reborn," the prince said in a rush. "It would only be a formality, and——"

"Stop." Draga held up a hand. "Go back. Fie is *what?*"

Fie couldn't make herself answer. If Niemi had heard this, she'd be shrieking with glee at the prospect.

Jasimir wanted to make her a queen. A *true* queen. He'd raise her to a place untouchable, and through that, she'd raise all the Crows into safety.

Jasimir balled up his fists. "She's Ambra. You can ask the Black Swans. That's why they sent Khoda to keep an eye on Fie. And——"

"Can we prove it?" Draga asked. "And I don't mean by interrogation from a Crane witch. What I'm asking is how we convince the rest of Sabor that Ambra, Queen of Day and Night, was reborn as a Crow."

"*She* gets it," Khoda grumbled.

Fie still couldn't find words, but Jasimir was not deterred. "We can figure out something. But if I marry Fie, that elevates the status of *every* Crow. It will be immediate, undeniable protection for the whole caste."

"Until a few monarchs down the line, when both of you are gone and terrorizing Crows is back in vogue," Draga snapped. "Then what? The Crows need protection, but this will only last as long as you do."

"What's the alternative?" Jasimir fired back. "Because Rhusana's getting ready to raid every Crow shrine she can. We can't do *nothing*."

Draga shook her head. "Rhusana's already imploding. She's empty-ing the palace treasury on these parties, she's terrorizing the aristoc-racy, and she's asking all of Sabor to roll shells with the plague. We just need to be patient."

"And how long is patient?" Fie found her voice again, now on familiar ground. "How much of the country's burning plague beacons right now?" From Draga's flinch, she knew the answer was *too much*. "Every day it'll get worse. It'll be more to burn. And the queen's driving the only ones who can stop it into hiding. You tell me how that ends."

Draga scowled and looked away a moment. "I'll keep fighting the queen on the beacons," she said finally, resting her chin on her inter-locked hands. "One more thing to keep her distracted. And . . . she's throwing that ball three days from now, her biggest yet. I can chal-lenge her there, in front of everyone, on how she's handling the plague. Either we force her to back off the Crows, which should cost her the support of the Oleander Gentry, or she doubles down, which costs her the support of every plague-fearing citizen in Sabor. No matter what, she'll be at her weakest."

"I like it," Khoda said. "It could be the right moment to reveal the real Prince Jasimir as well. The nobility will be starving for an alterna-tive to Rhusana."

Draga nodded slowly. "Jasimir can call fire to prove he's a Phoenix, and we'll arrest Rhusana for abducting and assaulting the crown prince, and throw in murder, treason, the standard. It'll be quick, be public, and leave time for the real coronation to happen before the end of Phoenix Moon. I think we have a plan."

There was a knock at the door. Fie snapped the glamours back into place, and Draga jumped. "Gods, that's uncanny," she muttered, then raised her voice. "Yes?"

The same war-witch as before opened the door. "Prince Jasimir is here. He requests a private word."

The four of them exchanged glances. What did Tavin want with Draga?

Draga swallowed. "Very well. Cat-masters, take your leave. We will make another appointment for later."

Jasimir crinkled the fish treats and the cats came running, dragging their leashes behind them. Fie picked Barf up again and glamoured her coat to pure black. No sense in risking Tavin recognizing the tabby.

Tavin was waiting in the hallway as they left, knotting his hands together, and he brushed past them without so much as a sideways squint. His escort of Hawks lingered outside Draga's office, but they paid no mind, either.

The three of them were just passing the archives hall when a handful of people spilled into the courtyard. Some wore Sparrow servant uniforms, but others were in the violet robes of Owl clerks. All of them had one sleeve yanked up, flashing the Sinner's Brand rash on their arms.

The squad of Hawks behind them seemed to be debating something. Fie caught "—*her orders*—" and "—*no room left!*"

"Then take them to the quarantine court for Splendid Castes!" the corporal commanded. "There has to be some room there."

One pointed to the eastern gate. A curl of black smoke was rising; someone had kindled the plague beacon again.

"Thank the Mender," one soldier muttered.

Then the beacon was doused in a puff of steam.

"This is absurd." The soldier planted his spear butt in the ground. "These people aren't sick and we can't—"

"Enough! The last time someone spoke out against the queen, they left without a hand," the corporal snapped, then realized they had an audience. "Move along, Sparrows. This isn't your concern."

The prince, the spy, and the only Crow in the palace traded looks. It was, in fact, very much their concern.

That didn't mean there was aught they could do about it now.

"Of course, sir," Khoda said, and hurried them away.

Behind them, Fie heard the squabble continue as the sinners huddled in the courtyard, wide-eyed and afraid.

CHAPTER TWENTY-FOUR

— CROWS IN THE GARDEN —

*I*N HER DREAM, FIE WALKED THE BURNING STREETS OF KAROSTEI, *fire on every side. At her feet lay a long, long line of bodies: young, old, Sparrows, Owls, Hawks, Peacocks, Lakima, Khoda, Yula, Jasimir.*

The line stretched far as she could see. All their eyes were open. All their eyes were on her.

"Mercy," they whispered as one. The Sinner's Brand climbed up their throats like strangling vines. "Give us mercy, Ambra."

"That's not my name," Fie answered. "That's not who I am!"

The fire roared around her, the sea roared below, they were falling into black, bottomless water and there was no way out—

Fie woke with a start. Barf leapt off her chest.

"Sorry," she heard Khoda whisper. He eased himself back through the door of the guest quarters with a basket on one arm that was giving off a heavenly aroma. "It's just me. No—*scoot*, Jasifur."

"Mango," Jasimir mumbled from the couch. The orange cat left off rubbing on Khoda's ankles and went to go sniff the prince's hand.

"You have terrible taste," Khoda informed the cat. He set the basket on the table and opened the window drapes to let in drastically more sunlight than Fie expected.

Jasimir sat up and cringed. "Why in Ambra's name——er. Why is it so bright out?"

"The sun's been up for about three hours now," Khoda answered. "But I figured you two could use the rest, and *I* could use the opportunity to get my rounds in without having to worry about you running off to assassinate the queen. And I'm afraid I got some . . . disturbing news."

Fie rolled out of the bed and shambled over to the basket, where she found a heap of fresh panbread and stuffed rolls. "All of this mess has been disturbing."

"The quarantine courts are empty," Khoda said. "No sign of the sinners, no blood, not even a blanket. They're all gone. And the queen's only statement is that the situation has been *addressed*."

After a moment, Fie shoved a roll in her face, then went back to bed.

"You're right," she said, spraying crumbs everywhere. "I hate it."

"Can Viimo find them?" Jasimir suggested, helping himself to a roll.

Khoda shook his head. "She needs a possession to track the owner, and the Hawks are burning anything the sinners had with them in the palace. We can try to look if we have time, but . . . there are two days until Rhusana's ball. We'd be better served focusing on what's in our control."

"You say that, but you won't be the one to cut all those throats," Fie said sharply. "How many do you think we're up to now? Two score sinners?" Khoda's nostrils flared, and she knew the count was higher. "Are the beacons even burning?"

"The last anyone saw the sinners, the *only* symptom was the Brand. I don't like it either, but two days from now, Rhusana will be at her weakest, and that may very well be our only real chance to unseat her before it's too late. After that we'll have a new king, and no one will fight Jasimir on lighting beacons then."

"I still think Fie should be queen," Jasimir said abruptly.

Fie's scathing retort died in her throat.

"I know——I *know* what you and Aunt Draga said, I heard it the first time." Jas held up his hands. "But we can all see it, can't we? The crows all over the palace, the, the half plague, the fact that the *real* reincarnation of Ambra is here now. The Covenant wants something."

Khoda started tearing panbread into even strips, slow and methodical. "I didn't want to bring this up in front of your aunt for obvious reasons, but there's another . . . consideration. You'll need an heir."

Jasimir looked to Fie, nervous. "I've considered it. I meant what I said earlier. I could pardon Tavin, and——"

"We've been through this," Khoda started.

Jasimir plowed on. "——and if he and Fie *reconcile* and decide to have children, I'll name one to be my heir, and if not, we'll find another way, but——"

Fie swallowed. Jasimir might be able to pardon Tavin, but even the softest parts of her had tried to forgive him for weeks and failed. It was one thing to near rut Tavin on her own grave; it was another to make him father of her child.

And that wasn't the only issue. "It's not enough for me to be queen," Fie said. "Ambra swore to give up the crown."

Khoda laughed in disbelief. "Hear that? It's not enough to be queen! And pardoning Tavin will only give your enemies an alternative——"

"Rhusana is extorting him," Jasimir insisted. "He said to her face he knew she'd kill him. Tavin only signed those orders because she was threatening to hurt Niemi."

"But he still signed them," Khoda said, cold.

Jasimir looked ready to throw a roll at him. Patpat slunk off the sofa to hide under the low table beside it. "He's my *brother*."

"We need to be consolidating your power, not dividing it," Khoda snarled, "and you'd see that if you weren't too busy trying to save a traitor." He turned to Fie. "You tell me, Fie. How do you feel about raising a child with the man who——"

Something snapped in Fie. "*I KNOW WHO HE IS!*" she bellowed. Even Barf looked taken aback at the outburst.

Fie ran her hands through her hair, then reached for her slippers. "I'm going for a walk."

"Take a cat and a badge," Khoda said immediately.

"I'm just going to use a Sparrow witch-tooth." She stood and headed for the door.

Fie heard the frown in Khoda's voice. "I thought you only had three of those. You should save them for the ball."

Fie sighed and leaned her head on the doorframe. "Well then, here's one more sign the Covenant wants aught from us. I should've burned out the last one days ago. The sparks keep coming back. Can't tell you why."

She called the witch-tooth to life and slipped out.

By now Fie had committed enough of the palace to memory that she felt safe in the gardens, or as safe as she could feel on palace grounds. She saw crows in nigh every tree, but they only tilted their beaks as she passed, blinking curiously, chortling a croak or two in her wake. If they saw through the refuge the witch-tooth gave her, she couldn't say.

Through the leaves she saw the Hall of the Dawn and the upraised hands of the Mother of the Dawn's statue, holding the rising sun. Fie found herself walking toward it. Jasimir had sworn it marked a god-grave, and she could have sworn it marked no such thing. Endless riddles chased themselves through Fie's skull now; she could at least lay one to rest.

It was easy enough to tell once she drew near. To either side swept the curving wings of the Divine Galleries, and from below them she felt the sleepy hum of god-graves. No such hum rumbled from below the statue.

Jasimir had suggested the grave might lie under the thrones. Fie rounded the pedestal and eyed the iridescent panes of glassblack making the back wall of the Hall of the Dawn. They were still streaked with dribbles of gold from when she'd melted their ugly golden sun sculpture, but from what she could tell, most of the wreckage had been cleared away in preparation for Rhusana's ball. The twin thrones sat less than a pace behind the panes.

Fie picked her way over, even creeping into the hedge that bordered the wall, and held her breath.

She could feel not so much as a murmur.

Wherever the Mother of the Dawn was buried, it wasn't here.

Fie's puzzling was interrupted by rising screams from crows. She sank into the hedge on instinct, peering from between the leaves.

The cries grew louder, and a small parade came into view. Sparrows, Owl clerks, a few bewildered Hawks, all were marching toward one of the quarantine courts. Fie's heart sank when she recognized a face: Ebrim was walking with them, shoulders slumped.

Then she recognized an indignant sputter. "This is simply *unfathomable*! When the queen hears of this, you—you'll all be imprisoned for this outrage!"

Lord Dengor was prodded, blustering, into sight at spear-point. The Sinner's Brand had framed his face like an elaborate collar.

The half plague, as Jasimir called it, had reached even the Peacocks.

"Look on the bright side," one of his escorts said sardonically, "there's plenty of room for you in the quarantine court now."

Fie sat down hard and buried her face in her lap. She stayed that way even after the crows had gone quiet.

Khoda might think they could last two days more, but this . . . this was beyond Fie's ken.

All of it was beyond her.

It was a terrible, welcome thing, that thought scurrying across her mind: it was too much. All of it was too much. It had been too much for weeks, maybe moons, maybe centuries.

She'd spent so much of the last few days dashing through sparks and lives and memories in teeth, and she'd seen hardship and pain, but not like this. She'd seen girls like her in Hawks and Gulls and Sparrows and Peacocks and Pigeons, in nigh every other caste. They were weaving crowns of grain and vine for the harvest dances. They were lying on the decks of their mothers' boats, reading the stars. They were sneaking off to share sweets with sweethearts. They were cleaning their armor and trading stories from its stains by the fire.

They got to be young, and not careless, but not care-worn either. They got to measure the distance from girl to woman in years, not scars. It was such a simple thing to want for herself, for every Crow girl.

Yet here Fie was, hiding behind thrones, trying to call a Money Dance with the queen, with the boy who'd broken her heart, with the Covenant itself, simply to keep the Crows alive.

It was too much weight. She didn't know how she was meant to carry it alone.

You think that's how it works? Bawd's voice echoed in her head from what felt like lifetimes ago. *If you fall, we carry you.*

Fie's breath caught.

If you need us, we carry you.

She was a chief. And Pa had told her himself: chiefs couldn't always wait for a call.

A crow alighted on the shoulder of the Mother of the Dawn to watch as Fie found the one tooth on her string that could not be replaced. She pulled it free, rolled it between her palms, called the spark.

And then she opened her hands and brought them close to her lips.

"Pa," Fie said softly. "Can you hear me?"

———◆———

The sun set, rose, set again. Rose again.

As it did, they planned. If any Hawks thought it strange how the master-general's office had had such a terrible outbreak of mice, they kept it to themselves and let the cat-masters in.

As the sky wheeled through day and night, Fie let Niemi Navali szo Sakar stay in hiding, claiming a passing illness, while invitations to tea, breakfast, salons, and more stacked up. Lord Dengor was not the only Peacock taken to the quarantine court. The rest were rabid for distraction.

And Tavin—she would not make herself face Tavin. Not until she had to.

As the sun rose each day, it was on darker and darker spires. Crows gathered thick as rumors, and every effort to scare them off was undone within an hour. The Hawks thrust spears into the trees only for the crows to return minutes later. The Hawks left poisoned meat, but they did not eat it. The Hawks displayed dead crows in the gardens as a warning. Even more crows gathered above, screaming their judgment.

The plague beacons lit, went out. Burned, smoked, went cold. Hawks kindled them on Draga's orders and put them out on Rhusana's, and with each hour, the strain between the two grew more palpable.

The sun set, rose, set, rose. Fie did not think on being Niemi if she could help it. She did not think on Tavin. She did not think on becoming Jasimir's queen.

Instead, she worked on her teeth, knotting them into a collar, a bracelet, an armband, earrings. She worked at her base gown so she could carry her swords, and so her Phoenix teeth could be stashed in a satchel hidden beneath a draping cape. A glamour would turn the teeth into gold, the satchel into sashes, the swords into the ends of a jeweled belt, the base gown's linen into finest silk.

And in the middle of the afternoon, one week before Swan Moon, Fie donned Niemi Navali szo Sakar's face for the final time, and went to a ball.

———◆———

Queen Rhusana had elected to precede the ball with a reception in the Tower of Memories, a broad, graceful tower adjoining the Hall of the Dawn. It would have made sense in a colder time of year; the tower was practically a monument to the Phoenixes, stuffed with sculptures of great conquerors, treasures they had claimed, armor they'd worn into battle, sprawling vivid murals of their triumphs, and on and on.

But at midsummer, even with every window screen thrown open, the late afternoon was sweltering simply from the glut of bodies. Not even chilled wine cut the misery of the gentry crammed into the tower.

Fie took some small glee in it, at least, though she didn't reckon she could claim credit. Crows perched on nigh every branch, every rooftop, every crest of the royal palace now. Even the oleander-walled Midnight Pavilion had surrendered its elegance to the cackling, rowdy birds, leaving nowhere for Rhusana to celebrate herself but the muggy indoors.

"Are you nervous?" Tavin asked.

Fie blinked up at him, arm twined with his. She'd been fanning herself with enthusiasm, part for the swelter and part to hide how her hands were shaking.

Pretend it's about the ball. A tight smile dragged over her face. "A-A little, yes."

It felt strange and sour to mimic Niemi like this. The dead girl's teeth had stayed in the guest quarters; Fie knew the evening would be hard enough without Niemi whining in her skull. It savored even sourer, though, that it was almost too easy to copy the Peacock's manners now.

"Don't be." Tavin reached over and briefly clasped her hand. "It'll be fine." He looked like a prince from a song, all brocade and cloth-of-gold, the circlet cutting a streak of gold through his hair, jewels shining at his ears, his fingers, his throat.

She could almost picture his true face beneath the glamour, and that hurt most of all.

Tonight would not be fine. It would end well for only one of them, and they were about to find out who.

Fie didn't need Niemi's help to keep that to herself as they passed a lovely golden sculpture of Ambra seated on a tiger, holding a banner aloft. She almost sneered at it before remembering a certain degree of reverence was expected.

Particularly under the eye of the queen. Even now, Fie could feel the prickles on the back of her neck. Rhusana was in fine form tonight, her white tiger collared in diamonds that matched her own headdress, more diamonds covering its unfurled glittering wings. A gem-embroidered veil trailed behind her, the full length of a man. Two pale braids secured her headdress, and four more fell at each side of her face, nearly touching the floor. White gold leaf had been pressed into intricate patterns framing her eyes like a mask, and her gown was wrought of thousands of gilded feathers, diamonds fastened at the tips of each. Curiously, she'd had the sleeves and bodice embroidered with fine black thread.

Tavin caught Fie sneaking one more glance at the queen. His mouth quirked. He leaned in and said under his breath, "Apart from the fact that she's wearing enough money to buy Sabor twice over, you know what the worst part of that outfit is?"

"What?" Fie couldn't help asking.

"They didn't really think that headdress through. She has to walk through most doors sideways."

Fie let out the most ungraceful snort she'd produced in the entirety of her near-seventeen years.

"*Shh!*" Tavin said, but he was laughing too.

The other partygoers cast sidelong looks their way, clearly vexed that not everyone was as miserable as they. Lord Urasa's lip curled in particular, and he turned back to his conversation partner with an open sneer.

Then Fie saw who he was speaking with: none other than Rhusana's accomplice in overtaking Draga's camp, Lord Geramir.

Geramir was frowning at her. She saw him mouth "*Who?*" to Urasa.

Fie fanned herself faster. "When does the ball begin again?" she asked Tavin, trying not to squeak. The last time she'd seen Geramir, she'd told him the only Sakar child was dead. If she was lucky, he would have forgotten.

"Quarter hour or so, if we stick to schedule," he said, then followed her gaze to Lord Geramir.

This time, she clearly heard the name "Sakar" from Lord Urasa's lips. Then she heard Geramir repeat it, even louder.

Tavin tensed at her side. "It's awful in here. Would you like to get some fresh air?"

"Y-yes."

Then Tavin was steering them through the crowd, past portraits of dead kings and the swords of dead queens. Out of the corner of her eye, Fie saw Geramir heading straight for Queen Rhusana.

Khoda was going to kill her. Maybe it was still salvageable—she could just tell Tavin she needed the privy, change her glamour, melt into the crowd and hold to her part of the plan anyway.

Maybe that was better. He'd never know the girl he'd been carving kindnesses for in this wretched place had been his downfall all along.

They had just stepped out into a side garden, the sunlight just beginning to steep to gold, when a voice rang out at their backs. "Prince Jasimir."

Tavin stopped, and they both turned. A Sparrow attendant was standing in the doorway, a thin smile on his face. On his uniform was the richly embroidered insignia of the queen.

"Her Majesty wishes to speak with you," the attendant said. "And Lady Sakar."

Tavin took a deep breath. "I'm afraid you'll have to try the guest wing for Lady Sakar. She was feeling poorly, so my friend here, Lady Markahn, has stepped in."

Fie stared at him, then wrenched her expression into a look of mild surprise.

"I see." The attendant bowed and turned to the side, sweeping an arm toward the doorway. "We'll send someone for her, then. In the meantime, Her Majesty awaits."

Tavin unwound his arm from Fie's and turned to her.

"I'll . . . see you in the Hall of the Dawn," Fie blurted out. "In fifteen minutes, right?"

He raised a hand that trembled and briefly, lightly, touched her face, gazing at her as if to memorize every scrap of this moment.

It made Fie want to scream.

Then he leaned in to plant a kiss on her cheek. His lips moved against her skin, breathing barely loud enough to hear:

"Yes, chief."

He pulled back, spun on a heel, and left her standing in the garden as the queen's man pulled the door between them closed.

CHAPTER TWENTY-FIVE

— FAITHLESS —

The first thing that registered for Fie was the pounding of her own heart, a war drum in her ears.

The second were the crows, crying from the rooftop above.

Tavin knew. He'd—known.

How long had he—

Her veins were fire, her bones were ash, and he was gone, gone—

She stumbled over to a bench tucked in the garden's corner, crashed down on it, tried to think, tried to breathe. He'd known. He'd known. But—answers, she needed answers, she needed to scream, she needed to burn this tower down and pull him from the embers.

Crow-song rattled above.

Fie's hands were shaking almost too bad to pry Tavin's tooth from the bit of rag she'd kept it in, but then she had it clutched in a shaking hand, her other scrambling for an Owl tooth. The spark of a long-dead clerk plodded out in her mind, a grandmother cracking her knuckles as Fie woke Tavin's tooth next.

She saw flashes of memory, tried to shut them out; the Owl clerk politely stepped in and whisked them away.

I need—I need—

Fie tried to muster her thoughts into some semblance of a request but couldn't pare it down. *I need help.*

The Owl clerk went to work. After a moment, she said: *It seems the question you have is: How? From what I can tell, these are your answers.*

Fie blinked, and the garden was gone.

———◆◆———

He was nine, and someone was speaking to him: "If you truly love something, you'll do whatever is best for it. You'll give everything you have for it. You understand that, right? Love means sacrifice. It's why your job is so important."

Tavin nodded, though the idea scared him.

"You love your brother. And you love your country. You should be ready to protect them, no matter the cost. Can I trust you to do that?"

"Yes, Your Majesty," he mumbled.

The king smiled down at him. "Good."

———◆◆———

He knelt by the side of the road, by a dead body in the green grass, an empty leather bag at its side.

He could have stopped this. He could have saved her if he'd pushed harder, if he hadn't waited for his mother's permission—he could have saved her—

Fie was dead because he'd failed. He hadn't given enough.

———◆———

"You're hardly a fool." The Black Swan spy regarded him with a piercing stare. "You know the queen has to be preparing a strike, right?"

Tavin knew better than to answer right away. It had been clear Khoda was nowhere near close to being completely honest with them earlier, in his mother's tent. If there were truths he'd squirmed out of stating in front of a small crowd, Tavin had come to pry them out.

But this was a test. Would he accept anything Khoda said because he was an all-knowing spy, or would he reject it because Khoda was clearly untrustworthy?

The way to play these games was neither. He'd survived the palace long enough to know. "She already struck at Fie, who wasn't a threat. It doesn't make sense to just ignore the small army marching behind Jas. But we're all aware."

Khoda nodded, tight-lipped but approving. "Rhusana doesn't do things by halves, so when she hits, we'll know. But that's all I have for you, I swear. Like I said, we can't get anyone embedded close enough to her." His gaze narrowed. "You're not a fool. So I want you to think about this: an army isn't the only way Rhusana can be defeated. If she makes her move, and it doesn't look like there's a way out . . . We *need* someone on the inside."

"I'm not a spy. Besides, Fie and Jas would never let me take that kind of risk."

"They don't have to know," Khoda said.

"No." Tavin felt the ugly fire in him bristle and hiss at that. "I won't do that to either of them."

"Then do it *for* both of them." Khoda looked genuinely unhappy. "This is all still purely hypothetical. But we both know what Fie's capable of. What she and the prince can do together. And we know what lengths they'll go to save what they love." He grimaced. "So if it looks like Rhusana's going to win, if it looks like there's no way out . . . Think about it. You could be what we need to take her down from the inside."

Tavin didn't answer. He didn't want to think about it; he wanted Jas on the throne, and Rhusana in prison, and to stay with Fie as long as she abided him, which was hopefully the rest of their lives. "I'm going," he muttered.

"Just in case," Khoda called after him. "If you think it's a good idea . . . might want to get a haircut."

———◆◆◆———

They were in his mother's tent, Rhusana gloating and sauntering around like she did when she was sure of victory. He hated it, hated her, hated how easily she'd done it.

And now she was gripping his chin, whispering in his ear, and offering him the throne on a white-gold platter.

It was just as Khoda had said. There was no way out.

There had never been a way out. This was what he was supposed to do. This was sacrifice. This was love.

He just hoped that when Fie killed him, it would be quick.

He just hoped this was enough.

———◆◆◆———

The Owl clerk's voice broke through the fog. *Is this enough?* she asked. *Or would you like to see more?*

More, Fie answered.

———◆◆◆———

Whoever had nearly broken into Jas's prison was smart, but they were a terrible spy.

Then again, if Fie hadn't just yelled that the only Sakar child was dead a few days ago, he wouldn't have known. He suspected the person wearing her face now was banking on that.

"Is there an exit over here?" the spy asked, stepping toward the back of the statue. "I'll just leave this way."

"No—!" He seized her arm, reading the caste in her blood to know what he was dealing with—

A Crow.

A witch.

It hadn't even taken her seven days to break into the royal palace and find a prince hidden in a secret prison known only to Phoenix monarchs.

She was absolutely going to murder him by the end of the week.

He'd never been more delighted.

Then he realized: if she had so much as a notion—if she knew the danger he was in, spying on the queen—she would kill herself trying to bring it to an end.

She already had to hate him for the choice she thought he'd made. He had to make sure she kept hating him.

It took everything in him to let her go.

———◆◆◆———

The firebird roared over Tavin's head, smashing into the wrought-gold sun behind the thrones. He liked to think that somewhere, Fie was laughing. He'd made sure she had the best view possible.

It had been a risk, giving Khoda the schedule for the coronation, but the Black Swan had assured him that whatever happened wouldn't be traced back to him. He'd been right.

Fie had made it look like the work of an angry god, of Ambra's ghost. For all he knew, it was.

<hr />

It was night, and he was alone. Not in that hideous bedchamber—when his escort had hurried him up there the night before, after the disastrous coronation, he hadn't precisely been able to sneak away. Tonight was different. He was in his own room, the one he'd spent the last nine years of his life in.

And he was lying on his own bed, face buried in the blanket he'd made sure to take with him from Draga's camp, because it was the only thing in this entire damned palace that still smelled like Fie.

Rhusana had tried to make him kill her today. Not that the queen had known; she'd just tried to make an example of a dissident, with the added bonus of reminding him he was as much on a leash as her ridiculous pet tiger. But he'd seen it, the look in Fie's eyes, when she realized how easily he could end her life at the edge of that terrible well.

She missed him throwing up after.

Now the only thing that gave him even a moment of peace was the salt-smoke-mint smell still lingering in the blanket they'd once shared.

He didn't know how many times he could cry into it before the smell of her would be lost for good.

———————•◆•———————

More? asked the Owl clerk.

More, Fie said.

———————•◆•———————

Khoda's instructions had been simple: Fie would want to go into the catacombs, and Tavin would take her there. They would both be looking and listening for anything strange, and if he found anything, he was supposed to act surprised.

That had been the plan.

It had not involved Fie kissing him.

He should have known better, but she'd looked ill ever since stepping into the catacombs, and it was his own damn fault for fussing over her until she decided to shut him up, and twelve hells, he'd missed this. He'd missed her more with every heartbeat. It could all be nothing, it could just be her playing along, but he wanted to believe she missed him, too, he wanted it like a drowning man wanted air. If he didn't look at the glamour on her face, he could pretend all was as it had been, that there were no lies, no secrets between them.

He could pretend she might forgive him.

And now he was inches away from committing a blasphemy with her on Ambra's casket. Though, admittedly, blasphemy had been something of a hobby of his as of late.

She was supposed to hate him. He was supposed to make her hate him so that when this all came to a bloody end, it would hurt less—at least for her.

It was selfish, this, in the most terrible way. And it was one more sin she would never forgive.

"Do you see the problem?" he asked.

His mother looked at the repulsive decrees spread across her desk, delivered from the queen's footman not an hour ago. "First off, I won't approve a single one of these. She'll have to wait until after the coronation to exercise her right to command the military."

Tavin had taken a gamble, reaching out to his mother after Aunt Jasindra's room had burned. From Rhusana's panic, whatever had been in there was critical to her, and from the shift he'd seen in people around them, he had a hunch what that was.

His mother had all but confirmed it, the loss of Rhusana's influence, as she'd merrily issued orders to light the plague beacons.

"Look closer," Tavin said.

Draga did. Then she covered her mouth.

"It looked close enough. Rhusana didn't check further." It was one of his prouder moments: every single order Rhusana had put in front of him was signed not with *Jasimir* but *Jasindra*. Every one was worthless.

Except for one. He pulled a parchment from his sleeve, one signed by both Jasimir and Rhusana and bearing the royal seal. "I have a proposal," he said. "And I think you'll approve."

"You know this is it," Khoda said.

It was only hours before Rhusana's final ball. He was ready, or at least he thought he was.

He'd done everything he could.

"The master-general won't chase you. But getting out, that's on you. Fie and Jasimir will have their hands full." Khoda shook his head. "If you can make it to the Shattered Bay, give my name to the ferrywoman who works the sundown shift. She can make arrangements to get you across the sea. But there will be no place in Sabor for you after tonight."

Tavin let out a short, harsh laugh, one that made Khoda give him a sidelong look. "Did you think there ever was?" he asked.

He'd done everything he could, given everything he could. He had no more left to sacrifice.

By every dead god, he hoped it would be enough.

———◆◆◆———

The teeth did not offer her more, and Fie did not ask this time.

She sat in the garden, teeth clenched so tight in her palm that a distant part of her thought she might draw blood.

All along, Tavin had been helping her. Undermining Rhusana. Dying by inches. All along.

She'd thought he'd given up. She'd thought he didn't believe they could win against Rhusana, that she was not enough.

But he'd never once stopped believing.

She wanted to sing. She wanted to howl. She wanted to weep and laugh and tear the garden down. She wanted to strangle Tavin and kiss his wretched fool face until her lips fell off.

She needed to—

Stick to the plan. That's what Khoda would tell her. She had every intention of booting him off the nearest suitable cliff for putting her and Tavin and Jasimir through this, but it would have to wait.

Rhusana still needed Tavin. He would play the fool and get away from the queen when he could, and—and he would find her, and—

The hour-bell began to toll.

Fie set the teeth down on the bench and ran her hands over her face, over her hair, until the thunder in her skull retreated enough for her to think. She needed a new face, a new gown, a steady heart. The Peacock glamour shifted, the fabric bleeding from delicate teal to the same crimson as the lantern-lilies, the illusion of Niemi's long braid weaving instead into one that sat over her head like a crown. When Fie stood and caught her reflection in the glassblack window, she realized the face she wore now was none other than Ambra's.

The one upshot of this all, Fie thought grimly to herself, was that, being dead for so long, the artists never got Ambra's face right.

She heard the commotion of Peacocks gratefully fleeing the swamp of the Tower of Memories and slipped back inside, falling in with the crowd. They shuffled out and into the late-afternoon haze, then up the steps to the Hall of the Dawn. Hawk war-witches were at the doors, testing caste.

Fie got in line for the one from Draga's office, who had recognized Jasimir. Draga had said they would be stationed at the door to make certain Fie made it in, and as the war-witch's hand clasped Fie's wrist, she saw their eyes sharpen.

"You may enter," they said, and then added under their breath: "Fortune's favor to you, Lady Crow."

It was a small thing, a scrap of faith, and once it had felt like a burden. Now it felt like another tooth in her arsenal.

Fie gave them the same slight smile they'd given Jasimir, and headed into the Hall of the Dawn.

It was not the same place it had been on the solstice. Layers of whitewash had been slapped over the once-vivid walls, the rich tapestries replaced with filmy gauze of silver, gold, white. The lanterns within the great iron columns had not been rekindled. Instead, fresh white oleander blossoms had been stuffed into the gaps, making each towering Phoenix's portrait look almost as if it had gone rotten and molded over. White petals carpeted the marble floor, the dais, even the thrones, though Fie dearly hoped Rhusana had had the sense to order flowers less poisonous than oleanders for that.

Even the wreckage of the golden sunrise behind the thrones had been twisted and threaded through with garlands of more white blossoms. If Fie squinted, she thought it could be a swan now, but a sickly one for certain.

Servants were picking their way across the flowers with trays of wine and sweets, but there were markedly fewer than at the coronation. All of their sleeves were buttoned above the elbow, displaying arms free of the Sinner's Brand. They all looked worn to near bone—doubtless the work of making over the Hall of the Dawn had fallen on them, too, for no one else could.

It was no secret that Sparrows were fleeing the palace rather than wait to see what would kill them first, Rhusana or the plague. It was a trap Fie knew too well.

Fie wove her way around the knots of uneasy Peacocks, who looked unsteady and garish in their bright garb against the bleak whites and blacks of the hall. Even the music sounded timid, strained, the few musicians clustered on the ground floor.

It felt like when she'd walked the empty halls of the royal quarters at night—too still, too lifeless. It felt like crawling through a glittering corpse.

Fie marked Draga near the head of the hall, looking more than ever like a tiger ready to make a kill. If the master-general had not had a reputation for loathing parties, it would have been perhaps a bit too obvious, but her scowl was perfectly typical.

Jasimir was not out among the servants yet. They couldn't risk him being dispatched on an errand and missing his cue. Khoda, however, was winding through the crowds, his glamoured face the picture of servile serenity.

A swell of simmering fury boiled in Fie's backbone at the sight. Some even-headed part of her knew he'd done what he'd done for her sake, for Jasimir's, for Sabor's.

The rest of her was ready to tear his throat out.

Not yet, her Chief voice ordered. *Not here.*

Fie wandered until she was close enough to the head of the hall to have a clean view. It would be just like the coronation: wait for the right moment, conjure another firebird, throw in a sign that the Covenant favored Jasimir once he was revealed.

She just had to wait for the right moment.

Her heart drummed, drummed, drummed in her ears.

Minutes ticked by. The musicians played on. The sun crept toward the horizon. The queen was late.

Fie saw no sign of Tavin.

He was fine, she told herself, and ran her fingers over his tooth to feel his spark leap for her. Tavin was her clever, brave, wretched fool, and he was not allowed to leave her before she could call him that to his face.

His spark still burned. She didn't know what she would do if it went out.

The Peacocks murmured and whispered as the queen did not show her face. Even Khoda's calm mask was beginning to peel as he held a tray of tarts out to Lord Urasa.

Then a low blast rolled through the hall as two servants blew into the matching hollowed mammoth tusks on either side of the thrones. Mutters of confusion rippled through the crowd: the tusks were to announce the entrance of the monarchs. They were meant to stay silent for another week.

Rhusana glided out onto the dais, alone but for her white tiger still on its leash. On her head sat a familiar golden crown. It took Fie a moment to place—then she realized the last time she'd seen it, it had been fused to Ambra's skull.

"Friends," Rhusana called into the hall, her smile a little too bright, a little too sharp. "A great day is upon us. Prince Jasimir has done me the great honor of entrusting Sabor to my leadership. He has abdicated the throne, and we will make you wait for your monarch no longer. The Phoenix Priesthood has declared me your new—"

"*TRAITOR.*" Draga's voice thundered across the stunned hall.

Rhusana stared at her. One hand twitched toward the black embroidery of her bodice—then fell.

Hair. She'd stitched her fine gown with hair. Fie near spewed.

But Draga's hair had burned with the rest of Queen Jasindra's room, and now the master-general took a spear from a nearby Hawk and strode to the middle of the hall, facing the thrones dead on. "What did you do with him?" she demanded.

Fie felt for Tavin's spark again. It burned yet—but suddenly that felt all the more tenuous.

"It's a crime to raise a blade against your queen," Rhusana said in answer.

Draga deliberately pointed the spear her way. "I'll remember that when I see one. *Where is he?*"

Gasps swept through the hall.

"You are clearly unfit for your rank," Rhusana said swiftly. "I hereby remove you as master-general and—"

Draga took a step forward. "*You* killed Surimir. *You* killed Jasindra. You tried to pass off an imposter for Prince Jasimir to give yourself the barest *whiff* of legitimacy. You let this palace be overrun by the Sinner's Plague because your only master is the Oleander Gentry. You are a coward and a traitor and *you cannot command me.*"

"Arrest her," Rhusana ordered the Hawks at the walls.

No one moved.

"I *order* you!" she repeated, voice climbing, choking at the edges. "I'll have you all hanged for treason, and you can feed the damned crows! *Arrest her!*"

The Hawks traded glances, as uneasy as the Peacocks backing away from the dais.

Fie felt it, the reign of Rhusana balanced on a knife's edge. This was not what they'd planned; this was not how it was supposed to go.

But she could wait no longer. A conjured phoenix was not enough.

She pressed Tavin's tooth to one palm, the Owl clerk's tooth to another. This time she knew square what memory to ask for. Then the Peacock song joined the dance, shifting her glamour once again into something terrible and new.

Fie hoped against hope that Jasimir was not watching. Then she began to push through the crowds.

Peacocks twisted, saw what Fie had woven, stumbled away with ashen faces. Servants dropped their trays, splashing broken crystal and wine into the white petals. Even Draga gaped in open horror.

The crowd split until she could see straight to Rhusana. She knew what Rhusana saw, what they all saw: the specter of Queen Jasindra as Tavin had last seen her, staring down the thrones.

Fie had, of course, taken a few liberties. Jasindra's eyes burned, stark finger-shaped bruises barred her neck, and her hair and robes floated on an unseen phantasmal tide.

Fie drew a breath, pointed at Rhusana, and, in her deepest Chief voice, she called: "*MURDERER.*"

She could see it on Rhusana's face: fear, yes, but wrath, too, and desperation. The Swan Queen knew it was naught but a glamour, because she knew the power of an illusion.

Rhusana knew there were no omens, no ghosts, no Lady Sakar—only a Crow girl with a grudge and a bag of teeth. One who was about to cost her a crown.

Rhusana twitched her hand with a hiss. The white tiger shuddered, then leapt for Fie.

"*NO——!*" Draga threw herself in its path. Fie heard a terrible crack as Draga hit the ground, pinned beneath the great beast. Red splattered across the white petals.

Lord Urasa started toward the dais, bellowing, "*Protect the queen!*"

The room erupted in chaos. Hawks rushed in from the walls, some flocking to Draga, others to guard Rhusana. Most Peacocks rushed to nowhere and nothing but the exits. If any noticed that the specter of Jasindra was bizarrely solid when they crashed into it, they paid no heed.

Fie let the glamour go anyway. It felt oddly exposed, to wear her own face, let her teeth show plain, but there was precious little point in subterfuge now.

A hand locked around Fie's elbow: Khoda. "We need to get out," he shouted.

"But Draga——" Fie twisted to try to see through the pandemonium. She heard the tiger snarling, clashes of blades, shrieks and shouts of guards. Someone had the master-general's arm around their shoulders—the war-witch. Their bloody hand was laid on Draga's head. Fie saw gaps of pink in the crimson and realized the master-general's gashes went to the bone.

"She can manage," Khoda said, shoving them onward. "We need to find Jasimir and get to safety."

"We need to find *Tavin*," Fie spat. "How long did you think it would take me to find out?"

Khoda made a face. "Honestly? I was hoping for one more week. I know you're angry with me, but we need to focus—*hold on.*" He yanked her and they popped through a side exit, stumbling into the south wing of the Divine Galleries.

Jasimir was waiting by one of the statues, wide-eyed. "What happened?"

"It's all rutted," Fie said, "and Tavin has been on our side the entire time, and Khoda's been hiding it from us, and I'm pretty sure Rhusana just figured it out."

"*What?*" Jasimir's jaw dropped.

Khoda looked pointedly over his shoulder at the Peacocks flooding past. "Can we do this somewhere else?"

"No. Not a one of them gives a damn." Fie bent down and started tearing away the bottom half of her gown. "Rhusana's done something to Tavin. I'm going after him."

"Why . . . why would you . . . ?" Jasimir was staring at Khoda like he'd drawn a dagger on them.

Khoda's face almost seemed to break open, furious and guilty all at once. "Because this is exactly what I was afraid of! Hells, you didn't even have to know he was working with us before you started trying to save him! But this is what ruling is about, it's about *sacrifice.* Someone always has to pay the price. Rhusana was going to make it the Crows. I gave Tavin the option to choose himself."

Fie kept tearing the gown. The open air was welcome on her knees. "Funny," she said, frosty, "the ones who always say there's a price never seem to be the ones paying it. You know what my pa says?" She ripped the last of her skirt away. "He says even Phoenixes need ashes to rise. But I reckon you know that, aye. Because it's your job to make sure they're never the ones who burn."

She pulled Tavin's sword free, scabbard and all, and handed it to Jasimir. "The master-general's hurt, and it's a mess in the hall. They need your help. I'll be back with Tavin."

"You can't put yourself at risk." Khoda put a hand on the prince's elbow—

—and the prince threw it off. "I'll decide that."

"Jasimir, *please.*" The note of desperation in Khoda's voice sang so clear, it shook Fie. It wasn't duty, it wasn't agenda, it wasn't born of long-laid schemes.

She wondered when, precisely, the Black Swan had realized his devotion to the crown prince's welfare ran deeper than a throne.

But if Jasimir heard it, too, he had no time for it.

"We can't do *nothing*, so make yourself useful or make yourself scarce." The prince thrust the scabbard through his sash. "Fortune's favor to you, Fie."

"Fortune's favor," she echoed. Then she dove back into the fray, let it carry her out of the Divine Gallery, calling first a Vulture witch-tooth, then a Pigeon witch-tooth. Wishing for fortune was one thing. She needed more than wishes now.

Tavin's own tooth stayed clenched in her fist, an anchor for the Vulture Birthright as it traced his trail. It wove north, dead west, straight down through the gardens—

Dread shot through Fie's gut.

Her Hawk's trail ended in the catacombs.

CHAPTER TWENTY-SIX

—— THE SETTING SUN ——

FIE MADE IT PERHAPS A THIRD OF A WAY INTO THE GARDEN BEFORE she saw the first skin-ghasts.

A Phoenix tooth joined the song in her bones, clearing the ghasts from her path with great sweeps of flame before she realized they were leaving her be. Ghast after slinking ghast slithered by, some loping, some on their bellies like snakes. All of them bore a gash over their throat and the muted pattern of the Sinner's Brand over their arms, and not a one so much as swiveled its eyeless face toward her.

Instead they all rushed past, headed toward the Hall of the Dawn.

Fie reckoned she'd found what Rhusana had done with the plague victims after all.

But there was no sense troubling herself with them if they did

⚜ 341 ⚜

not stand in her way. Whether that was intent or the Pigeon witch's tooth, she could not say. Fie called off the Phoenix fire and kept running.

She passed the Midnight Pavilion, the Sunset Pavilion, found the stone arch with its phoenix perched on skulls. The Well of Grace hummed its dirge somewhere above. The doors of the catacombs were open, ghasts dribbling out of the long tunnel like spittle from a poppy-sniffer. Fie steeled herself, lit her Phoenix tooth again, and plunged into the dark.

She tried not to mind the ghasts slipping past, tried not to start at the dead master-generals watching her stumble down the long stone road, tried not to let the song of so many Phoenix bones rattle her again. Fie heard it more clearly this time: *Welcome, Ambra. Welcome.*

"That's not who I am," she hissed through her teeth, and kept going.

Finally the dissonance grew too great for her to bear. She weighed the Vulture tooth and the Pigeon tooth, then let the Vulture tooth grow cold. There were only so many places to lock up Tavin in the catacombs. Judging from its residents, there was a dire shortage of luck.

Columns loomed out of the dark as she reached the main chamber. She cranked the wheel, lit the brazier, scoured the room for any signs of Tavin. All the blooming fire-lines revealed were more skin-ghasts crawling from every crypt, save for the Tomb of Monarchs dead ahead.

"Tavin?" Fie called. No answer.

The currents of fortune surged. One of the double doors of the Tomb of Monarchs creaked open.

She took the hint.

But when she burst through the doors, the fire-lines only

showed the Tomb of Monarchs, just as she'd last seen it—or almost. Ambra's casket still had its skull, but it was short a crown, an uneven ring of gold rimming her brow where it had been chiseled off. The wheels of caskets still towered above Fie, all those skulls glaring down at her, and four empty caskets waited on the ground level to be fed—

No, three. One had a lid. But it bore no skull.

"Tavin?" His name came out in a half breath. How long could he last in there? If he heard, he wasn't answering—she had to get him out—

Breathe, her Chief voice said. *Panic and you'll foul it up.*

She had good luck, if she knew how to use it. The Pigeon witchtooth was all but begging her to let it help.

Fie closed her eyes, let fortune guide her steps, move her hands. Her fingers found a lever. She pulled it, tried not to think about the scrape of stone. The tooth guided her to a wheel and turned it. The scraping turned to a roar.

There, she could have sworn the Pigeon witch told her. *Was that so hard?*

Fie opened her eyes. The wheel was turning. The lid lifted. She rushed to the casket as a hand gripped the edge.

Tavin dragged himself up, wincing at the firelight, and it was him, not Jasimir's face but *him*, all his scars and scuffs and marks.

"Fie?" he asked in disbelief.

"Aye." She seized his forearms, helped him climb out. His knees wouldn't hold him, and Fie discovered neither could she as his sudden weight sent them both to the floor. "Are you—"

"Fine," he gasped, propping himself against the foot of his casket, "relatively speaking. A little light poisoning."

"Poisoning?"

He cracked a faltering grin. "I didn't exactly climb in there looking for treasure. Don't worry, it'll burn off in a bit. Healing and all. Rhusana just wanted to make sure I stayed put." He reached for her, hesitated. "Fie, I'm—I'm so sorry—I know you have to be furious with me, just let me explain—"

"You absolute ass," she said, choking up. "I already know." Tears rolled hot down her cheeks as she pulled him to her and kissed him, finally without reservation, without glamours, without secrets. His arms wound around her, deliciously tight, and he was kissing her back so fierce and sweet she thought she might drown happy in it. "I'm still mad at you," she told him before kissing him again. "You didn't apologize in advance, so I get to be mad at you as long as I want."

"If this is how you get mad at me, I can live with that," he murmured.

Fie shook her head and made herself sit up straight, scrubbing at her leaking eyes. "I mean it. I don't care what happens to us after this, I never, *ever* want you to die for me, aye? I want you to *live* for me, Tavin, I want you to keep fighting, I want you to be happy with or without me, because that's what love is." She clasped his face in her hands. "Someone told you love means giving up on yourself, and they were lying. I know you never gave up on me. But I never want you to give up on *us* again."

Tavin let his forehead rest on hers, so close she could see the firelight caught in his glistening eyes. "To be fair, one half of this equation just got himself poisoned and locked in a crypt." His voice cracked. "Could . . . could you say that part about being happy again?"

"I don't want you to have to sacrifice for me. I want you to be happy. I want you to live." She kissed him. "Because I love you."

"That," he said raggedly. "That's . . . what I wanted to hear."

"And I'm still mad at you," she added, and kissed him anyway as he laughed, and for a few beautiful moments, all they did was laugh and kiss and dry each other's tears and hold each other close until they had both steadied out.

"We have to stop doing this here," Tavin said as she helped him get to his feet. "I feel like Ambra's watching us, the pervert."

Fie choked. "I, uh. About that."

But before she could figure out how to tell him that, in a round-about way, Ambra *had* been watching them the whole time, a strange, unholy sound lowed through the catacombs.

It sounded like crying. Like a moan.

Like a soul in torment.

Both she and Tavin froze. "That's the noise," she said. "The one the Sparrow man heard. It's something to do with the queen, we have to find it—"

Tavin laced his fingers through hers and headed for the door. "Yes, chief."

The cry faded as they entered the main chamber but swelled up again a moment later, almost *gurgling*. Fie turned toward one of the gaping doorways. "There."

"That's the crypt for cousins," Tavin said, brow furrowing. The fire-lines did not continue beyond the entrance, so he raised one burning hand, his other still tight in hers. Golden firelight caught on dark, wet smears on the ground, and he recoiled. "*Eugh.*"

"Oh. Right." Fie stepped well over one of the smears. "There are skin-ghasts. Reckon that's what Rhusana did with the plague victims."

Tavin shuddered. "A new and horrifying way for her to be creative. Why am I not surprised?"

They made their way into the hall, then into the crypt proper. Coffin-filled hollows lined the walls like larvae in a hive, and more dark slicks polished the floor, spreading from rows upon rows of wet, red heaps of corded muscle and tripe.

A sad kind of wrath coiled in Fie's throat. Whatever the Covenant had meant when it had marked so many with the Sinner's Brand, it couldn't have been this.

Another groan made Fie grip Tavin's hand tighter. It sounded closer, bestial.

He touched his hand to a brazier in the middle of the room. It did not send lines of fire to light the crypt, but as the coals caught, they cast a sullen orange glow over the stone.

At the far end, something stirred.

Fie sucked in a breath. She'd thought it one more body, splayed on a tall stone slab in its final moments. But as she and Tavin watched, its chest racked with coughs like sobs.

"Fie?"

Jasimir's voice made both her and Tavin jump. Footfalls fell across the stone, and a moment later, he appeared in the tunnel behind them. His eyes widened as they took in the gore—then landed on Tavin.

The prince marched across the crypt and pulled him into an embrace. "You absolute ass," he said into Tavin's shoulder. "How *dare* you."

"Funny, that's what Fie said," Tavin wheezed.

"There's still a decent chance I throw both you and Khoda in jail." Jasimir let his brother go. "Assuming there's still a jail. It's a mess up there. People are breaking out with the Sinner's Brand left and right. Rhusana's soldiers have taken the gates, and they won't let anyone in or out. She's holed up in the royal residence with a small army of skin-ghasts. Aunt Draga . . ." He gulped. "She lost an eye. She may lose an arm, too. The prison's rioting, and I only found you because Viimo snuck out. The loyal Hawks are still trying to keep the peace, but they can only do so much."

The figure at the end of the crypt let out a rattling cough.

Jasimir's eyes near bugged out of his head. "Twelve hells, is it still alive?"

"Aye." Fie drew the chief's sword from her belt. "I'll handle it."

Tavin and Jasimir followed her as she walked to the sinner. The closer she got, though, the clearer it became: this was not one of the people Rhusana had crammed into the catacombs, their arms barely mottled with the Sinner's Brand.

This man's skin was so ruined with sores, with the Brand, that everywhere she looked was dried black blood and weeping red along ridges of ribs. His fingernails had withered to half moons of gray, the flesh of his hands gnarled and black; his feet were the same. From the smell, he'd fouled himself, and crusts of long-dry sick streaked down the sides of the stone slab he lay on.

There was something sickeningly familiar about the cut of the man's face, despite his sunken cheeks and bloodstained mouth.

Tavin stiffened at Fie's side, but Jasimir was the one to put a name to the wreckage before them:

"*Father?*"

Rhusana's lie hadn't been that King Surimir had been claimed by the Sinner's Plague.

Her lie had been that it killed him.

Surimir's eyes opened, wandered, closed again, little left but gray cataracts and burst veins. Fie didn't think he knew they were there. If the Covenant had any mercy at all, he would be too lost in delirium to feel the plague's ravages.

Then again, if the Covenant had any mercy for the king, he would have died in Crow Moon.

"How long has it . . ." Fie trailed off, counting the days. "Three weeks since they lit the beacons for his death. He's been down here at least that long." The chief's broken sword shook in her grasp. "This is all wrong. The Covenant doesn't . . ."

It wasn't supposed to be this way.

"Why wouldn't it kill him? Why drag it out like this?" Tavin stared at the king's shivering, fevered form.

"Because," Jasimir said, in awe, in despair, in revelation, "it wanted people to see." He didn't look away. "That's what the plague really is, isn't it? A reminder that no one can . . . can be like him, treat people the way he treated them, and get away with it forever. Not even a king."

Fie found Tavin's hand again, belly-sick. "Rhusana knew that if he died, it would spread. So she tried to hide him where it couldn't reach her, but the Covenant spread it anyway."

She watched Surimir's chest rise and fall in shudders.

Near a whole moon he'd been down here in the dark, slowly burning. Only the Covenant could keep him alive this long.

It was speaking to them now, as clear as the crows flocking to the palace, as clear as the Sinner's Brand creeping through even the highest castes.

It was in the way the Peacocks had watched the queen beat a man bloody without so much as a cross word, then let her savage the one who spoke up. It was in the way the Hawks, sworn to serve the nation first, bowed to a queen who served no one.

It was in the monument to a slow and terrifying death that sat above their heads even now, with centuries of bones at its heart. It was in every inch of the palace, its golden feathers, its cruel-cut iron, the games it played, the ashes from which it rose. It was in the way Khoda and his Black Swans seemed to think they could trade one Phoenix for another like changing sandals, and that alone would be enough to put the country right.

It was a palace built to remind people that only Phoenixes were fireproof. It was built to demand tribute from the rest of Sabor. It was built to make every other caste hunger for scraps of that gold, that power, that fire; to make them swear their lives for just a taste.

Fie was Ambra reborn, by rights the Queen of Day and Night, by rights the heir to the throne, by rights the owner of the crown on Rhusana's head.

But if the Covenant had meant for her to save all this, to set things to rights as a queen, it could have sent her as a Phoenix.

Instead, it sent a Crow.

This is a gift, Little Witness had said, *something to remember. You are not what you were.*

Fie knew what she had to do.

"All those people with the Sinner's Brand now . . ." She shivered into the silence. "Once the king dies, it's going to get bad. I don't know how long they'll have." She squared her shoulders. "I asked Pa to send as many Crows as he could two days ago. If they've made it, we'll have help."

Tavin squeezed her hand. "What a coincidence. Three days ago I got Mother to sign an order for the Hawks to offer rides and escorts to any Crows headed to the palace."

Fie had a number of thoughts then, and most of them involved lowering her standards for where she'd roll a lad.

"So we can stop this." Jasimir ran a hand through his hair. "We can let the Crows in, and isolate the infected, and once the bodies burn . . ."

Fie looked at the chief's blade in her free hand.

Dealing mercy had never gotten easier, in the end.

"Jas," she said. "It's not just the bodies. All of it has to burn."

Jasimir shook his head. "But we can contain the plague. We'll make pyres for the bodies, and then it won't spread."

"It already has. The Covenant's been trying to bring Surimir to light for weeks. We can get the uninfected out, but the plague wouldn't spread the way it has if that rot wasn't clean through the palace grounds by now."

Jasimir's throat worked. "I can't—we can't just burn all of it, can't we try to save *anything*?"

"I think we've *been* trying, Jas." Tavin sounded tired. "Haven't we? You and I have tried our best to survive here without becoming"—he gestured helplessly to Surimir—"this. But if we just burn the dead, clean the palace, and go back to the same damn games . . . Who is that good for? You? Me? Any of us? We told ourselves that if we played by the rules we knew, it'd protect us from people like Rhusana. We told ourselves that people born into castes like ours couldn't be touched by the Sinner's Plague. And it's all been—nothing. None of it did a damn thing to stop it, because the sickness *started* with the king." He put his free hand on Jasimir's shoulder. "What good is *any* of this?"

Jasimir stared at their father, lying bloody and squirming on the stone, an exile from his own tomb. Fie could only imagine what it was like: being raised to believe your father was good as a walking god, one of the Covenant's beloved Phoenixes, chosen to rule the way *you* were chosen.

She could only imagine what it was, to see the rotten heart of it all now.

"It's already gone," she said softly. "The Covenant sent you a Crow, not a queen."

He locked eyes with her.

After a heartbeat, he nodded and whispered, "All of it has to burn."

Tavin and Jasimir were the ones to carry their father from the cata-combs, Fie leading the way, a Phoenix tooth alight in her hand, the lament of the Well of Grace in her bones.

When they reached the surface, the sun had just touched the cliffs behind them, beginning its final descent on the royal palace of Sabor.

— THE FLOODGATES —

Skin-ghasts wreathed the royal quarters above, peering out over the gardens as Rhusana's thousand-eyed sentinel.

Before, they'd not even tilted toward Fie. But now, as she, her lordlings, and the king climbed from the catacombs, one by one, every hollow face turned toward them.

"Don't look now," Tavin said slowly, "but I think we have an audience."

Jasimir shifted his father's arm over his shoulders with a grunt. "They didn't bother me at all on my way here. I think they're protecting Rhusana."

"The queen who hid her damnedest to make sure *this* scummer never saw the light of day again?" Fie jerked her thumb at the king as they passed under the stone arch. "That Rhusana?"

Tavin glanced up. "That Rhusana," he confirmed tightly. "We may want to pick up the pace."

Fie dug in her satchel of Phoenix teeth. "You two go first, and I'll cover our backs. We're going for the main gate."

"Yes, chief," the lordlings said in unison. Fie looped back behind the king's dragging feet—and not a moment too soon, as a skin-ghast leapt toward them from the stairs leading to the Well of Grace above.

It landed in an arc of golden Phoenix fire. "*Go,*" Fie shouted, teeth blazing in her fists.

Through the gardens they half ran, half stumbled, wheels of fire driving off the ghasts, great sweeps of crackling gold from Fie, from Tavin, from Jasimir, leaving trails of lingering flame and scorch marks. They carried the king past the pavilions he'd once ruled, the halls he'd feasted in, the servants' quarters where his name had been little better than a curse.

The sky began to blush bloody. By the time they reached the main gates, it had rusted vivid orange. A mob had gathered in the courtyard where Fie had once bargained viatik from the queen; now the gates were barred shut, penning them in like cattle. She caught shouts of "*Let us out!*" and "*Whatever you want, I'll pay!*" and "*For the gods' sake!*"

Then she heard cries of alarm, of horror. The skin-ghasts on their trail went still as someone gasped, "Is that the *king?*"

"It's over, Rhusana," Fie told the ghasts. "They see him."

The ghasts lingered a moment, then retreated like oil slicks.

Fie returned to the front of their gruesome procession. The crowd drew back as Tavin and Jasimir hauled Surimir onward toward the gates proper. Fie saw Peacocks, Owls, Sparrows, Pigeons, Cranes, a few Swans, all crushed together. She almost let out a bitter laugh. Rhusana had united them after all.

"Is that the king?" someone called more forcefully.

In answer, Tavin let golden fire unfurl from his fingers, then lifted Surimir's limp hand into the air by the wrist. The flames rolled around them both, harmless.

A hush fell over the crowd.

Finally Fie stood before the gates. They were solid lacquered oak, and she saw no bar across the double doors, which meant they'd been sealed from the outside.

"Open the gates," she called to the Hawks standing behind the stone parapets, a score or so in a line, bristling with spears.

They didn't answer.

"Open the gates!" Jasimir's voice soared over her shoulder. In the edges of her sight, she saw him lift a burning hand. "As crown prince, I command you to open them!"

The Hawks only shifted their spears, the sunset flickering along steel.

"There are Crows outside," someone shouted.

A nearby Sparrow nodded. "We heard you shut them out! Let us go!"

"Let the Crows in, you damned fools!" Fie shouted.

"*Fie?*" A voice rose from beyond the gates. "*Fie, is that you?*"

The Hawks did not move.

Fie knew what this was. She'd seen it in more villages than she could number, she'd seen it in the faces of Peacocks and Pigeons alike, she'd seen it in everyone who thought they could yank the Crows about as they pleased because the Crows always, always had to let them. Even on the edge of the plague, they feared the queen more than the Crows beyond the gates.

They should have feared the one within.

Fie lifted her chin, drew the chief's sword, stared them down. "You have a count of one hundred," she said, loud enough to carry out across the courtyard. "Then I cut your sinner king's throat, and you'd best hope you've let in the Crows and gotten far enough from here that the plague won't catch you, because it all goes guts-up from there."

Then she planted her feet on the tiles of the courtyard and let out a piercing, unmistakable scream.

A silent heartbeat passed.

Then the answer roared back like a hurricane, shrieking from beyond the palace walls, carving from hundreds, maybe a thousand throats.

Fie tried not to let her shock show. When she'd asked Pa to send help, she'd expected her band, maybe Ruffian and Jade's.

Khoda had said a conqueror without an army was just a thief. But she had no use for armies, and that Pa had known.

Instead, the Messenger had sent her a flood.

She trilled an order: *Pass it on.* Outside, another chief picked up the commands, wailing sharp as steel. Every stamp shook the ground. Every sweep rolled like thunder.

"One," Fie said.

Finally, one of the Hawks spoke, only to say, "We—we have orders from the queen—"

Tavin and Jasimir let the king fall to the ground.

"Two," Fie said.

One of the Hawks broke, then another. They lunged for something behind them, only for their fellow soldiers to swing spears their way. A scuffle broke out as the rumble and howl of the Money Dance swelled to bursting.

"Three," Fie said. Then she turned to the lordlings and added: "If you've aught to say to the king, say it now."

She did not listen, for the words were not for her. She watched the gates and kept her count.

By thirty, the lacquered oak shuddered like the dying king at Fie's back.

By thirty-three, the gates creaked open.

Beyond them stood more Crows than Fie had seen in her entire life, more than she could dream of. She saw chiefs and masks and teeth waiting for her call. At the front stood Jade, mask in one hand, chief's blade in the other.

Beside her stood Lakima.

Fie's throat closed, but she had no time for sentiment now. She took a deep breath and whistled the marching order.

Crows flooded the courtyard until it was a sea of black crowsilk. They split around her, the lordlings, and the king, pushing the mob back as gently as they could. Then Fie saw Crows stationing themselves about her like a guard, Wretch, Madcap, Bawd, Varlet, all of her kin. Jade, Lakima, Ruffian's band—they ringed her too, giving her shelter.

It felt as if a cord about her heart had cut open, like shedding a too-warm cloak. At some point she'd grown too used to the lonely weight of being the only Crow, bearing the demands of the Covenant on her head. Now her own were here to help carry it for her.

Tavin helped Jasimir stand from where he'd knelt at his father's side, then looked to Fie. "We're ready," he said, low, and stepped back.

Fie crouched by Surimir's ear. For Tavin and Jasimir's sake, she hoped he had heard them, somehow, from the maze of his own delirium. For her own, she hoped he heard her now.

"There's a lot on your head," she whispered. "Maybe you didn't favor the Oleander Gentry like Rhusana. Maybe you told yourself that if you looked the other way, the Covenant wouldn't hold you at fault for all they did. Maybe it just suited you, knowing we Crows would answer your beacons and keep your country whole because it'd kill us not to."

She pulled a Phoenix tooth free, called the spark out, and set it over his heart.

"Pa says the Covenant will bring you to the Crows in your next life, so you can live like us and know what you did awry. I hate that, I do, because it's people like you that make our lives punishment, not the Covenant. You better hope that ends tonight, because here's what I'm supposed to tell you."

Fie laid the chief's blade against King Surimir's throat and leaned in.

"Welcome to our roads, cousin," she hissed. "Remember what sent you."

The tiles of the courtyard ran red with a dead king's blood. Fie stood and let the tooth burn free.

And from every rooftop, every tree, every spire, every dome, crows took to the sky in a jeering, billowing black cloud.

Fie heard a groan, followed by a tremendous crack.

Spirals of gray rot wheeled up the sides of the Tower of Memories, in the same pattern as the Sinner's Brand. More lanced between the tiles of the courtyard, raced over the walls of the Hall of the Dawn, climbed the Hawk barracks, spreading over every surface like dye through water.

Three weeks, Fie realized. Three weeks of plague rot spreading like roots from a dying man's body, waiting for him to draw his last breath and let it bloom. She'd told Jasimir the plague had had to run deep. But now it was growing strong.

She stood and howled, *"ALL CHIEFS TO ME!"*

Jade spun on a heel and strode over. "Twelve hells," she said. "We've an ash harvest on our hands, aye?"

"Aye," Fie said, and only waited for a dozen or so chiefs to push their way forward. "You all pass this to the rest: there have to be hundreds of people in here who are dropping from the plague right now, but these buildings won't hold, either. We *can't* let the palace come down on the victims, dead or alive, or we'll never be able to burn it clean. Jade, split the bands into north, south, and west. Send the healthy out through this gate and bring the sick into the gardens. Clearing them out comes first, then we'll give them mercy, once it's safe."

One of the lordlings cleared his throat behind her but said naught.

"Sabor will never forgive us for it, you know," Jade said. "Burning their beloved palace to the ground. Are you willing to pay the price?"

The question struck a chord in Fie's memory. She couldn't place it.

More coughing behind her. The sky above shivered and fractured with black wings.

"We were always going to pay," Fie answered. "One way or another."

"Fie—" Jasimir's voice rose. "*Fie!*"

There was a quiet thud.

When she whirled about, Tavin had dropped to his knees, coughing.

Dark whorls of the Sinner's Brand were tracing up his arms.

CHAPTER TWENTY-EIGHT

— THE WELL —

B Y THE TIME SHE SEIZED HIS ARMS—*WHY*, PART OF HER THOUGHT, *you can't stop this*—a sweat had already broken out over him. "No," Fie breathed, crashing to the ground before Tavin, "no, no, *no, no, no*," and it became a chant, a scream.

"It'll be all right," Tavin started to say. The words drowned in a choking cough.

No no no no no no—Fie lifted his face, only to find the Sinner's Brand carving lattices beneath his eyes. "Don't," she begged, as if he could do anything about it. "Don't, we can—we can—"

Nothing. There was nothing she could do.

She let out a sob like a howl of rage. Overhead, the crows wheeled and wept with her.

Someone was always going to pay a price.

A hand gripped her shoulder. "I can do it for you," Jade said quietly, broken sword in hand.

The thought of Tavin's blood on the tiles made Fie want to vomit.

Crow-song wailed in her ears. She shook Jade's hand off, pulled Tavin to her. His head rested on her shoulder; his shivers rattled them both, terrible and dissonant in the sweltering midsummer heat. She'd spent nigh seventeen years with the plague. She knew damn well what it did, and she knew now: the Covenant was not tarrying with him.

The sky above warped like glassblack with her tears.

"*I DID EVERYTHING YOU ASKED,*" she screamed to the Covenant. If it could speak to her with its crows and its plague and its teeth that never died, she could speak back, she could demand answers. "*I GAVE HIM MERCY. I CALLED FOR CROWS.*"

If the Covenant had an answer for her, it did not give it.

Little Witness had said she'd failed, life after life. If this was success, she didn't want it. She'd let the plague take all Sabor, she'd head merrily into the twelve hells if it could stop this. But that had been her sin all along. Little Witness had said as much: she'd wanted more than a Crow was meant to have.

Jade set her hand on Fie's shoulder once more. "Don't drag it out."

She twisted, hissing, ready to bite the hand off.

Then a flash of blood-red gold jabbed into her sight. The last gasps of sunset were tracing over the cliffs behind the royal quarters, through the hands of the Mother of the Dawn, through the Hall of the Dawn itself. Just as the monarchs could watch the sun rise from their thrones, she could watch it set from where she knelt in their miserable courtyard.

It was all one straight line, the line of the sun: The Hall of the Dawn. The false grave for the Mother of the Dawn. The royal quarters. The Well of Grace.

The Well of Grace, where she'd felt the hymn in her bones, like standing on Little Witness's grave.

The Well of Grace, where, every time she'd gone near it, teeth she'd burned cold had burst back to life.

You know the price. Will you pay it?

They were the words of the chief of centuries past, holding a hand out to Ambra as she lay dying in her bed.

Ambra, so beloved by the dead gods, it was said, that not even the plague could claim her, no matter how it tried.

You think wanting more makes you less, Little Witness had said, *when you just want what was stolen.*

Fie's hands shook as she cut her satchel of Phoenix teeth loose, then handed it whole to Jade.

"Make sure every chief gets some," she said swiftly, and yanked Tavin's arm around her shoulders. "I've enough to last on my string if need be. Don't call more than one at a time—they'll eat you alive. And try to save them for the skin-ghasts." She braced herself on the tiles. "Bring out the sick, fast as you can, get them to the gardens and deal no mercy."

"No mercy?" Jade gaped at her.

Fie pushed her way to her feet, staggering under Tavin's weight. He let out a startled cough.

"Aye," she gritted, "no mercy, not until I find you. We can't keep feeding Rhusana ghast-fodder. And if I'm wrong, they wait a few minutes to face the Covenant. If I'm right . . ." She shook her head. "It'll be a new day, cousin."

She tried to take a step forward. Her knees wobbled dangerously.

Then the weight eased. Madcap had slipped Tavin's other arm over their shoulders.

"Where to, chief?" they asked.

"The Hall." Fie pointed. They didn't have time to run around it; better to break through the windows behind the thrones and charge right through.

Varlet tapped Fie's elbow. "Let us do the heavy lifting, aye? You just lead on."

Fie let Varlet take Tavin's other side, but couldn't make herself let go of his hand. The Sinner's Brand had near turned his fingers a deep, angry purple, too much like Surimir's for her not to look at them and cry.

Jasimir clasped her free hand, tears welling in his eyes. "I don't know what . . . what ridiculous thing you're about to try, but gods, I hope I see both of you again."

"I hope we do, too," she returned, throat burning. "Can you . . . make sure Barf's not in a bad way?"

He squeezed her hand. "What else is a cat-master for?"

They had spent enough time with each other; they knew when they were out of words. So they let go, and Fie tried not to fear for him as he headed to the guest quarters, not looking back.

It was slower going than she could stomach, the sky fading too swift as Fie and her band crossed the courtyard, even though they walked due west as fast as they could.

When they crossed the threshold of the Hall of the Dawn, the stench of rotting flowers near made her retch. Wilted, gooey oleanders oozed down the cut-iron faces of dead Phoenixes in their cold lantern-columns, and great swaths of the carpet of white petals had soured to gray. Others had turned crimson. Fie saw bodies, their skins not yet claimed by the queen: a few Sparrow servants in their cloth-of-gold sashes, heaps of red-stained brocade or shining armor marking fallen Peacocks and Hawks. Lord Urasa had collapsed against the thrones, a spear in his gut pinning him like an insect.

"Keep clear of the oleanders," Fie warned.

"We know," Wretch said wryly. A tense, broken laugh ruffled through them all.

The sun had nearly fallen by the time they reached the head of the hall. The garlands Rhusana had strung over the warped sun had wilted, the gold tarnished so bad Fie could barely tell it had ever been more than tin. The Mother of the Dawn cast a long shadow nigh all the way to the hall's entrance, dwindling light dancing across the wall of luminous glassblack between the statue and the thrones.

Fie looked about for something to break the panes—then stopped as a horrid wet slap squalled against the windows.

A skin-ghast had flattened itself to the glassblack. Horribly, the sunlight still shone through it, glowing a sick, deep red. Another ghast plastered itself to the window, staring at them, its empty mouth smeared in a silent scream. Then another, and another, fresh enough to still leave trails of blood striping the panes, until the gardens were gone and the last of the dying light sluggishly pushed through wriggling skin.

Fie breathed hard, trying to shake anything out of her thoughts, any last bit of cleverness, any last bit of desperation-soaked grit. If she broke the glass, they'd get in, and she'd have to fight them all off before they could pass. If she went round, through a Divine Gallery to the north or south, they'd lose time, and Tavin—

"Fie," he choked out, and they both knew he didn't have the time.

She looked at him, tears boiling over, and couldn't find the words. He gave a tug to the hand still anchored in hers. "Down . . . please," he gasped.

The Crows lowered him to the ground, where the petals had not yet been touched by rot. Fie sank to her knees beside him.

"I can't," she sobbed. "Tavin, I *can't.*"

"It's enough," he rasped.

"No—"

He unwound his hand from hers, buried his fingers in her hair. A smile tried to chisel its way out only for a trickle of blood to spill from his lips. "It's enough, Fie," he repeated. "You have to let me go."

Fury roared in her heart. It was wrong, it was all wrong, she was so *tired* of it, burning for a Phoenix's mistakes, burning so they could rise.

She kissed his bloody mouth and hissed, *"Never."*

Then she got to her feet. "You lot. I'm about to take a fool's road, and you can't walk it with me. Head out that way, aye?" She pointed toward the southern wing of the Divine Galleries. "I'll find you soon."

Her band traded looks.

"No time to argue," Wretch said swift, and Fie had never loved her more than in that moment. "Don't do aught *too* foolish. Come on, let's move." She hurried the band out as Fie walked over to Lord Urasa and yanked the spear from his belly, lip curling.

Then she stepped down to the glassblack panes, only a thin, clear wall between her and the yawning face of ghast upon ghast. She lifted the spear and swung it as hard as she could.

Fie heard the shatter of glassblack, the creak and squeal as cracks spread over the wall. It buckled in a flood of dead skin. Ghasts plastered over her, wrapped about her, slick and lukewarm. She heard Tavin cry out.

Then the great mass of skin-ghasts yanked them through, swept them through the gardens, swift as a wind from the sea, the horrid whistles peeling from every hole in their hides. Twisting, flaccid arms bound around her wrists, gagged her on dirty skin, shoved her and Tavin up past all the pavilions, up past the Well of Grace, up the stairs of the royal residence itself.

They carried her and Tavin out onto the main veranda overlooking all of Dumosa, the palace spread out below, and spat them onto the beautiful inlaid floor.

A hand seized Fie's hair and yanked.

"You should have died days ago." Rhusana sounded tired, resigned. "You should have died *weeks* ago. It would have been so much better that way. I would have already ended the Phoenixes if you weren't breaking your back to save them."

Fie scrambled to her feet. Tavin was trying to push himself up, but his every breath scraped louder, harsher.

Rhusana slid out onto the veranda. She hadn't changed from the ball, still in her elegant, hair-embroidered gown, still wearing Ambra's crown on her head like a trophy. The chaos had barely ruffled her.

Fie glanced over her own shoulder: the railing was ten paces behind her. That was all that lay between her and a dead drop into the Well of Grace.

"Spare me the 'better' dung," Fie snarled, and darted to Tavin, hooking her arms under his. "You talk about ending Phoenixes like you weren't *calling* yourself the White Phoenix. You only want to change the caste system so you're on top of it."

Rhusana's eyes flashed. She laid a hand on her bangle of wrought oleanders. "You have *no idea* what I want." A low growl curled from the shadows; her white tiger stepped, jerking and twitching, onto the veranda. It tossed its head in a silent hiss, then shook itself.

Rhusana's hand slipped from the bangle, and the tiger let out a low whimper.

Of course. Fie almost laughed. The queen had done what Fie herself had done—conceal the tools of her craft in her jewelry, only with hair instead of teeth. She'd never truly commanded the beast; she'd just commanded it by its hungers and yanked it about by its hide for everything else.

Rhusana held up a finger. Around it she'd wrapped a few strands of black hair.

"I think you want to get away from my pet," she said.

Fie wanted to get away from the tiger. Her own mind filled in the blanks: fear of those bared teeth, the lightning in her veins that came with terror, the way it gave her strength to scuttle across the beautiful floor, dragging Tavin with her.

"I really did want it to be better," Rhusana said, gliding alongside her tiger. "For everyone."

Fie felt her own legs pushing them back, closer to the railing, closer to the edge. She had to, *had to* get away from those jaws—and yet—

"Where's Rhusomir?" she ground out.

Rhusana tilted her head, as if Fie had asked about earrings she'd worn the week before. "What do you care for my son?"

"I don't," Fie said, "and neither do you. But only one of us is pretending they deserve to be queen."

"And only one of us is afraid right now." Rhusana took another step forward, brow furrowing. She clenched Fie's hair so tight it dug into her finger. Fie hoped it drew blood.

A fresh surge of panic sent Fie back again, arms locked around Tavin. The tiger loomed closer as fear clawed at her every thought. She wanted to get back, she wanted to get away—

She felt her spine slam into the marble railing. Even that wasn't far enough. Adrenaline drove her to her feet, Tavin slumped in her arms.

Good. She'd never have carried him all this way without panic pouring strength into her bones.

"You don't know what it's like," Rhusana said. "You have no idea how it feels to never belong anywhere, to have no home, to know that your very existence could get you killed. You have *no idea*—"

The rasp of Tavin's labored breath went quiet.

"I don't have time for this," Fie said, and dragged herself and Tavin over the railing.

The last thing she saw was a sudden blue hush as the sun finally slipped behind the cliffs.

Then all she knew was black water and salt and the weight of Tavin in her arms as the Well of Grace swallowed them whole.

CHAPTER TWENTY-NINE

—— MERCY ——

*T*HEY CALLED HER THE EATER OF BONES, AND SHE WAS THE LAST *of her kind to die.*

One by one, she had seen her siblings to their graves: Gen-Mara in his beloved magnolias, Brightest Eye in her cove, the Mender in their field beneath the open sky. Dena went gnashing into her grave, delighted and furious; Rhensa went dancing, lovely as ever. And when they were laid to rest, she took them to the Covenant, to see the life that came next.

It was a great working, their Covenant: a bargain between the first gods and their thousand children, all for the sake of what were meant to be toys. But toys for gods needed the capacity to think, to breathe, to love. Yet that was what made them more than toys. That was what demanded they choose their own way in the world.

That was what the thousand gods had been willing to die for: choice, true *free will, in a world they would forge themselves. The Eater of Bones had helped build the Covenant that made it so. And they needed her more than any other god, for she was the god of the sunset and sunrise, of the fire and the ash, of the worms that ate the flesh and made the soil that grew new life.*

They called her the Eater of Bones. She was the goddess of rebirth, and she was the last of the gods to die.

———◆———

Fie had not expected saltwater.

It flooded her nose, her mouth, her lungs as she gasped and choked. The hymn of the Well of Grace pounded through her bones, harsh, demanding—she would burst from the roaring in her veins—and then—

Sparks.

The well had eaten scores of thousands of bones over the centuries. Time had worn them down to little but dust in the water . . . but the water had stayed.

So, too, had the bone.

Fie had called for it the moment she sank below the surface.

Now she was drowning in it.

———◆———

Before she laid in her grave, the Eater of Bones made sure her children had their Birthright.

The terrible thing about free will was, of course, that anyone could choose to be terrible. And she and her brethren had debated long and hard about how to spare their children from the worst of themselves.

The answer was imperfect, but the best the thousand gods could manage was this: the Covenant already measured every soul it embraced in death, so it could send them to a fitting new life. If, at any point, it found a soul that would only continue to harm others in the life it led, they gave the Covenant the power to intervene and pluck that soul from the world like a ripe grape. They had built the Covenant and its divine apparatus with all the wisdom, all the knowledge of good and evil, all the love the thousand gods could give, and they knew it would not act lightly.

Still . . . the Eater of Bones was not satisfied.

She wanted better. She wanted more.

And so she gathered her children by her grave, and she gave them the gift of mercy.

Their lot was not an easy one: she had chosen humans who wished a simple life, who valued family born or built, who believed in the dignity of even the lowest creature. Their trade would be the undertakers for wealthy or poor, for lives ended in sickness or violence, for the kind and the cruel.

And the world was bound to be cruel if it could. So she would spare them the cruelty of the Covenant's plague and grant them a gift with which to barter. They alone had the ability to spare others. They needed but two things: a bone for every Birthright, and twelve among them who would welcome the sinner into their own.

———◆———

Fie felt it all: fire, blood, desire, refuge, truth.

Chief among them, though, roared memory. The Birthright of the Owls clung to her, borne on the water, singing to her of the bones at the bottom, kings and beggars and heretics and, before them all: a god.

She saw——she saw——*she saw*——

———◆———

She was reborn just like everyone else, and they called her Huwim, and she walked with her people and carried the dead and spared them from the Covenant's judgment if she could. She taught all the nation to save their milk teeth, to give them freely each year on the moon before the summer solstice, so that her people could seek the Covenant's mercy for them.

She was reborn again, and they had begun to forget what it was to be gods, all of them.

By the third life, they called people like her witches.

By the hundredth, they called people like her Crows, for their black robes and the masks they wore if someone called for mercy. They still offered their teeth once a year, and now they called it Crow Moon.

Too many lives had passed when the ones gifted with fire stole her first bones from her grave, claiming the goddess of rebirth could not possibly belong to Crows who served death. They hid her in a well, so deep she would never be found. They called her the Mother of the Dawn. They called themselves Phoenixes.

They called her Ambra when the Covenant sent her among the fire-bearers to set it right. And that was when she began to fail.

She was invincible. She was vicious. She was a conqueror. She reveled in it: the ability to destroy anything she touched, the security in knowing that destruction could never strike back. She called herself a Phoenix, and the other Phoenixes called her the first queen. And when the Covenant sent its plague to collect her, she conquered it too.

Until it became clear that the Covenant would not forget her oath.

She saw crows in her dreams, every night. She saw them in her shadows. She saw them in looking glasses, in glassblack, in even the waters of her beloved lantern-lily pond.

She stayed in her palace, she banned the Merciful Crows from Dumosa. When Crow Moon came, for the first time, the Phoenixes kept their teeth.

And royal habits caught on.

The Covenant tried twice more, sending her as an heir to the throne so she

could put it right, then sending her as a distant relative to spare her the tempta-
tion of the crown. But it could not be undone; the Phoenixes were fireproof, and
they were forgetting what it meant to burn.

By the time the Covenant sent her back to her own, they called her Hellion,
and she found it a colder world. Teeth were not given freely; they were kept for
payment. Crows were not called to tend to every body, only to those struck with
plague. The memory of their Birthright had trickled away with the last of the
Phoenix teeth. Payment was scarce, and meager when it came, and so they took
to the roads to find work where they could.

Life after life, she failed her oath. She had joined the Crows, but she had no
crown to forsake. Life after life, Sabor grew crueler to her own, because it could.
Without fire teeth, without the full weight of their Birthright, they had little to
offer but a swift death, and little to threaten but mutual destruction.

And then, in a life where she was called Fie, a plague beacon lit over the
royal palace and called her home.

———◆———

Fie saw the nights they gathered teeth in Crow Moon. She saw Ambra
on her tiger, laying waste to her foes. She saw twelve Crows holding
twelve teeth, standing over a figure condemned with the Sinner's Brand.

She saw what had been, she saw what could be, she had the bones of
a dead god on her tongue, she had all her lives in her skull, she had the
weight of Tavin dragging them to the bottom of the Well of Grace—to
the bottom of her own grave—

She was the Eater of Bones. Mercy was her gift.

Covenant be damned, she was going to give it.

She didn't have twelve Crows; she had herself. She didn't have
twelve teeth, but the dust of thousands of bones. And she had a boy
who had told her it was enough.

Fie called the sparks from the water.

It was like calling the Money Dance at the gates, but so much worse: the answer was a cacophony, a primal scream that felt like it would tear her apart. Twelve songs from a thousand throats ripped through her skull. Fie couldn't help but scream back, clutching her head—a metallic tang soured the water in her mouth, she was bleeding—Tavin slipped from her—

She'd promised him she wouldn't let go. She'd come here to keep her oaths.

She let the sparks go, anchored her hand in Tavin's as they sank, and called what she knew by heart: the bones of the Crows. One by one she worked in the Common Castes, the sweet hum of Sparrow refuge, the fluty wind of the Gulls. Then the Hunting Castes, plaintive Owl memory, fierce and steady Hawk blood, piercing Crane truth. One by one the Splendid Castes joined, elegant and full of grace.

Finally, with her lungs burning, with the weight of the well crushing in on all sides, she called for fire.

The song of twelve teeth rang so bright, so pure, she thought for sure it would kill her; she saw her lives all laid out like *The Thousand Conquests*, she heard a voice like an old friend.

What do you want, Fie?

With twelve teeth, one heart, and the boy she loved in her arms, she answered:

"Mercy."

* * *

When they spoke of the night the palace burned, there were many tales.

Some had been pulled from withering buildings, others carried in the throes of the plague and laid out below the amber-pods. Some claimed to have fought by the master-general's side, while others mumbled and looked away when asked where they had stood in the Hall of the Dawn.

One thing alone stayed the same: how the fire started.

Littler fires had broken out in the garden, left by a prince, a bastard, a Crow, and a king making their way across the palace grounds, but they had burned out swift enough.

The true fire began when the Well of Grace exploded. Or it caved. Or it collapsed into the catacombs below. The story wavered there, but one and all, every survivor saw the same thing:

A fire and a flood, burning with all the light and color in the world, sweeping over the palace. The skin-ghasts simply melted away, there and then gone. Everyone caught in the fire tide heard something different: their mother's favorite song, the parting words of a lover, the jest of a friend, the oath of a brother.

When the flood passed, it left the fire in its wake. It let those still inside the palace walls pass without harm and instead feasted on the bones of a kingdom. Every plague-gutted, rot-stained building burned, every bit of gold, every shrine to a dead king, every pavilion, every spire.

And in the gardens, the sinners waiting for their mercy pushed themselves up, marveling at the Sinner's Brand scoured away, the plague banished from their bones. In moments they would learn there was a price to pay.

In the years to come, they would learn it was a kinder world to pay it in.

———◆———

Fie woke in the rubble, arms still wrapped round Tavin. She saw naught of the Sinner's Brand on him; his chest rose and fell without rattling.

She'd done it.

She'd found the Birthright of the Crows. She'd found her own grave. She'd claimed him from the plague.

She didn't want to wake him just yet. She wanted a moment to breathe in the peace, she wanted the beauty of it to last.

Instead, metal claws dug into her scalp and dragged her up. Fie let out a startled shriek.

"You *filthy* little bitch," Rhusana hissed.

Fie could see the burning, crumpled wreck of the royal quarters; the veranda had tilted over, and while Rhusana had survived the fall, it had not been as easy on her as being whisked from the Hall of the Dawn by an escort of ghasts. She'd clawed her way over on hands and knees, her stolen crown gone, her hair straggling from its six braids. Her dress was shedding feathers like a split pillow, mottled red with scratches and scrapes from the collapse.

She kept her grip on Fie's hair but dug the claws of her other hand into Fie's throat, pushing them both up to their knees.

"I think you want to die," Rhusana cooed, teeth bared, dragging so hard on Fie's hair that it brought tears to her eyes. "The world doesn't need another bone thief, does it?"

Fie stared at her. Then she laughed.

She shoved her hand in Rhusana's face. The queen let out a startled, ungainly yelp and tried to push Fie off. Instead, Fie seized a fistful of fat, fraying braid and slammed the Swan Queen's head against the rubble.

A bloody tooth fell from Rhusana's mouth.

Fie seized it. The queen went still, her bones no longer hers to command.

Pa had told her things worked different on his own grave. The well was little more than a slide of shattered stone and glassblack, but it was still hers.

"I'm the Eater of Bones," she told her. "And you're in my home."

She found the spark of Birthright in Rhusana's bones, swatted the memories away like flies; she already knew what had made the queen, and she had no need to roll in it.

She saw unseen strings like hair, and each one conjured a face, a name, a desire: Her attendants, who wanted to feel special among the Sparrows. Her personal guards, who wanted to prove themselves. Her Peacocks, who wanted to believe their fortunes could rise with hers.

Fie snapped each string, one by one.

"No," Rhusana said when the Peacocks were cut free. "Stop," she said when the attendants' tie to her broke.

Fie found one that led to Rhusomir. He wanted her to love him, and she kept it that way.

"Please," Rhusana said.

But through the Swan's own Birthright, Fie could tell: all she wanted was to avoid paying for what she'd done.

She severed the queen's hold on her son.

Then she found what she'd been looking for, as the white tiger picked its way down the rubble toward them. Rhusana's tether held it better than any leash. She could feel the hunger in its belly.

It was a beast; it wanted blood. And the queen no longer commanded its teeth.

Fie yanked out a strand of Rhusana's hair and took a step back, then another, the queen's own tooth still simmering in her fist. "I think you want to stay down," she told her.

And then she cut the tiger free.

A hand brushed her back, unsteady. She turned and found Tavin swaying on his feet.

"Let's go," she said, and slung his arm around her once more.

The queen's screams followed them down the rubble and ended perhaps sooner than they ought. Tavin only looked back once, winced, and shook his head.

"That's over" was all he said.

They half slid, half stumbled out of the wreckage and onto the solid ground of the gardens, and Fie discovered her knees had chosen that moment to give out. She toppled to the ground, taking Tavin with her, and the grass was green and cool beneath her cheek, the palace was burning around them, she could hear shouts of confusion and joy beyond the scorched hedges, and they were alive, and it was enough.

Tavin touched a stinging gash on her face. "Let's take care of that," he mumbled, then frowned when nothing happened. "What . . . why . . . ?"

Fie grinned at him and hoped this would be the last time the night found tears in her eyes.

She found a Hawk tooth and pressed it into his palm, closing her hand over his as the spark stirred—not at her touch, but his.

Then Fie pulled him close and whispered, "Welcome to our roads."

CHAPTER THIRTY

ASH TO RISE

THE SUN ROSE, AND SET, AND ROSE, THIS TIME ON A PALACE'S
ashes.

When it did, it found Fie with the lantern-lilies. It had been a grueling day and a half; after the collapse of the Well of Grace, she and Tavin had been carried to the gardens with the rest of the new-made Crows. When they'd woken in the new day, there was little time to do aught but find the dead, tend to the living, and burn what needed to burn.

In the evening, she and Tavin had made time for themselves, retreating to the waterfall and the pool where the lantern-lilies still spilled, untouched by plague. They told each other what needed to be told, and spoke without words when they could find no more.

But when the sunrise came, they rose with it, for Crows went where they were called.

Jasimir had summoned them to the remains of the Sunrise Pavilion. It had once been a lovely thing, pale blue enamel, lavender tiles, gold trim; now it was a ring of charred, stumpy columns and scorched marble benches. He was waiting for them there, Patpat perched regally on the bench beside him.

So were ten others. Fie saw Viimo cackling as Barf tried to lure her into petting her belly; Khoda was absently petting Mango (or Jasifur— Fie wasn't sure of the outcome of that debate). Draga was not petting cats but instead comparing her eye patch and arm brace to the carved-ebony hand of the new Lady Dengor, who had inherited her brother's title but thankfully not his attitude. Yula was speaking with an elderly Pigeon man in a gray-striped robe, and though Fie did not recognize the Dove in fine-wrought silver, the Gull sea captain, the Crane magistrate, or the Owl scholar, she knew Jasimir would have chosen them with care.

Jasimir's tired face brightened when she and Tavin arrived. A gold circlet shone against his hair, no doubt at Draga's insistence, for without it he could have been another Sparrow, still wearing the simple linen uniform of the servants. Fie couldn't help but notice it was missing the cloth-of-gold sash.

"There you are," Jasimir said, loud enough to muster attention from the rest of the pavilion. "Let's get started. There's a lot to do."

He pointed to the bench beside him. Tavin and Fie traded looks, then took their places next to the last prince of Sabor. Fie reckoned that made them at least as important as the cat on his other side.

Out of the corner of her eye, Fie saw Yula begin passing around a basket of sweet rolls. How she'd managed to procure those in the wreckage of a palace was beyond Fie.

Jasimir cleared his throat. "First we need to talk about the plague. Fie, what happens now?"

She blinked at him, having just stuffed the better part of a roll in her mouth. Viimo brayed a laugh.

"Take your time," Jasimir said, trying to keep a straight face.

Fie swallowed and shoved the basket of rolls his way. "So. Here's how it is. We Crows have had a Birthright all along, but we haven't been able to use it proper. It's mercy, aye? That's our Birthright. The Sinner's Plague can't touch us any more than fire can touch you. And it's not mercy for us alone. Well, not exactly." She frowned. "We can't *cure* it, not like sniffles. But if we think a sinner's worth saving . . . we can make them one of us. To do it, we need a bone from each caste, a Crow to hold each one, and a chief to call the song."

"Then the sinner becomes a Crow and joins their band," Tavin added. "Like me."

Pain and relief flickered in Draga's remaining eye.

"Aye." Fie nodded. "So twelve Crows need to believe that you're worth saving, worth bringing into our own. And then you walk our roads." She twined her fingers with Tavin's. "I'm teaching the way of it to the chiefs here, and they'll pass it along to every chief across Sabor."

Draga sat up. "The order for soldiers to aid Crows is still in effect. Obviously, we're going to see a shift in attitude toward the Crows, since even the worst wretches in Sabor might find their life depends on it. But the Oleander Gentry didn't die with Rhusana, and I'm positive that even now, there are still arbiters refusing to light beacons, so I'll be leaving that order in effect until the roads are safe for Crows." She gave a crooked smile. "We'll see how long that takes."

"What about the supply of Phoenix teeth?" the Crane magistrate asked. "Not to be indelicate, but it seems likely to . . . diminish."

"The Well of Grace was a god-grave," Fie answered. "Technically, mine. It's the resting place of the Eater of Bones, the goddess of rebirth, and every time I went near it, all the teeth I thought I burned out came back good as new. I'm the only chief it happens for. So twice a year, on the solstices, I'll gather chiefs in Dumosa to see to their teeth."

"And I'm not going to let the Phoenixes die out." Jasimir shook his head. "The Phoenix priests were barred from having children in the past so the line of succession wouldn't get murky. We also only allowed marriage and adoption into the caste if someone was joining the immediate royal family. I'm rescinding both of those rules."

"But the line of succession . . ." Lady Dengor started.

"Yes, about that." Jasimir clasped his hands before him. He looked nervous. He looked immovable. "The fact is, we made Rhusana. My father made her, his father made her, and Ambra made her. We made a nation where the only way to be safe and happy was to wrap yourself in money and power and fire, and the only way to reach that was by stepping on everyone you thought beneath you. We made a society where the monarchs could ignore the suffering of their people because it was nothing but an inconvenience, and we punished those who used their position to speak out."

Lady Dengor ran a finger over her carved ebony knuckles.

Jasimir continued, "Now the Covenant has spoken out. The plague in the palace started with my father, and that's where it ends." He drew a piece of parchment from a pocket and unfolded it. It was already signed and sealed. "Today, I am ordering each of you to return to your castes and choose three among you who know your troubles and your strengths. How you choose them, I leave up to you and your people. I will be doing the same."

Tavin inhaled sharp at Fie's side.

Jasimir stood. The parchment shook in his hands. "This decree forfeits my claim to the Saborian throne in favor of a governing council. It takes effect a little under a year from now, on the next summer solstice. My reign will only last long enough to establish the council, the limits of its authority, and the rules by which it governs. I'm sure you all have questions, and some of you may be thinking it's a fool's way out. I'm afraid it's already signed. As for the questions . . ." He smiled. "We have a year. Let's get to work."

The gold circlet in his hair caught the morning light. For a moment, Fie would have sworn it burned like fire.

———◆◆◆———

The Sunrise Pavilion was the eye of a small storm for the next hour, but eventually it dwindled to Tavin, Fie, Jasimir, and Khoda, who had kept his distance and fussed with Mango-Jasifur until the orange tomcat hid under a bench.

When it was just the four of them, Khoda trudged over, distinctly avoiding Jasimir's gaze. "Officially," he said, "you are the only survivor in the royal family. Not counting Tavin, since . . . Crow." He shrugged. "*Unofficially*, you should know Rhusomir survived. I've been ordered to take him to be raised on Yimesei with the rest of the Swans. It doesn't seem like he's a witch, and he's too young to remember much."

"You're going back to the Black Swans, then," Jasimir said, just stiff enough for Fie to hear a cramp in his voice.

"Oh, I'm almost certainly going to be cast out for"—Khoda waved a hand at the swaths of charred rubble—"all this. Probably for the best."

Jasimir straightened, startled. "You want to leave them?"

Khoda didn't answer a moment, throat working. "You were right, you know. Both you and Fie. We helped a monster like Surimir stay in power, and we let everyone else pay the price. And they said it was all to do the best for Sabor, but if that was the best, I don't want any part of it." He finally looked Jasimir in the eye, as if he had more to say, then bowed. "Take care of yourself, Your Majesty."

Jasimir didn't say a word as Khoda strode from the pavilion.

Fie seized Jasimir by the sleeve. "Tell. Me. *Everything.*"

His cheeks darkened. He clapped his hands over them, cringing. "It was just—when you sent me to go find Barf in the guest quarters, I was trying to get her out from under the bed, and then Khoda showed up because *he* thought someone should save the cats, and we were both scared out of our minds, and. *Things.* Happened."

Fie looked at Tavin. Tavin looked at her. Then he looked at Jasimir. "On a scale of one to window seat—"

Jasimir shoved him.

Fie thought of Wretch's parting words to her when she'd left Pa's shrine: *Just because the lad loves you doesn't mean he does right.* It was easier to forgive Tavin than Khoda, and easier never meant easy . . . but it might yet be managed.

"You still have to hold Sabor together for a year, you know," she said. "You could probably use a spymaster."

Jasimir let out a long breath. "I probably could. Especially since . . . neither of you can stay, can you?"

Fie shook her head. "It'll be a hard year. Those outbreaks will have wiped out whole crops, herds . . . I don't know if we can put the land to rights like we did here. It might be just the grave, and even here, it needed to burn."

"And I'm a Crow now," Tavin said. "There's something about that, isn't there? Going where I'm called?"

Jasimir cracked a smile at that. "Then I'll call you both back when I need you."

Fie returned his smile. "And we won't always wait for a call. Though we've a lot of ash to harvest first."

Jasimir pulled the circlet off his head, staring at it a moment, and sighed. "It always should have been the palace. That was supposed to be the price. But I suppose this means we have something to rise from, right?"

"Aye," Fie said.

Jasimir handed her the golden circlet. "Here. Just to make it official. Fie, Ambra Reborn, Oath-Cutter, the Crow Who Feared No Crown . . . I give you mine. Do with it what you will."

The crown sat in her hands a moment, and it felt like fire.

But she had teeth for that. And she'd seen what fire left in its wake.

"Doesn't fit me anyway," Fie said, and handed it back.

Somewhere, the last crow lingering on the ruins of the palace took to the sky.

The chief was taking too long to say her goodbyes.

Her band waited for her anyway, with a company of six Hawks, seven new-made Crows, and enough Phoenix teeth to last her until the next solstice, or so she hoped. Fie had made sure each chief carried enough not just for themselves, but to leave in shrines and pass more to the chiefs they taught to deal true mercy.

She might have organized a discreet raid into the ruins of the catacombs to be sure there were enough Phoenix bones to go around. What Ambra's skull thought of it all, it kept to itself.

The first time Fie had left the palace, it had been with a trophy of Phoenix teeth, two dead lordlings in tow, and a gray tabby in her arms.

This time she left with the boy she loved, the kin who would carry her, and a friend with a crown to lose and an oath to keep. The cat, of course, had only conceded to ride in the cart.

From the top of Dumosa, she could see trails of smoke all the way to the horizon. It would be a hard year, full of ash, but full of hope.

Tavin reached for her. "Ready?"

"Aye." Fie took his hand, took a breath, whistled the marching order.

Together they led her Crows from the ruins of the palace, to the road that would lead them on. Fie did not look back.

She knew her own way home.

Acknowledgments

First and foremost: I would like to acknowledge everyone who read the acknowledgments in *The Merciful Crow,* saw the joke I made to my dear friend Megan, and became immediately and irreversibly consumed with dread re: Tavin's fate. I'd be lying if I said your reactions didn't add about five years to my life. Please don't try to reclaim them; I'm afraid they're non-refundable.

Tiff: Oh my god they were NOT kidding about Book 2! Damn my hubris! Thank you for being the voice of reason and keeping me from going Full Greek Tragedy when I was ready to call it a good run and go seal myself in a cave. I do regret to inform you that I am probably never eating oysters again (and by "never" I mean not without a truly formidable quantity of gin).

I would also like to commission a statue of my agent Victoria for dealing with a screaming, terrified baby, and also her newborn child. If anyone deserves a cat-master badge in this town, it's you (and of course, Deputy Lee). One day I will send you an email that will clock in below 2.7 Tolstoys, I promise.

Thank you so much to the marketing and sales teams at Mac Kids for all your work effectively firing this duology, and me, out of a confetti cannon. You've taken me to places I never thought I'd see, and graciously allowed me to exceed my per diem for terrible puns.

An enormous thank-you to all the booksellers, bloggers, and bookish folks who have championed this duology, too. I started making a list of everyone I could think of and descended into my own immediate and irreversible dread that I would forget someone, so. Everyone who has taken time to set up displays, write up shelf talkers, send me lovely reviews, send me fanart and edits, and made my debut that much better: In the words of *Parks and Rec*, you have done nothing wrong in your entire life, and I know this, and I love you. Your support has meant the world, especially to this ball of anxiety with a weird-ass teeth book.

I'm pretty sure I owe a lot of people drinks, but particularly my fellow authors. From the veterans who have been there with boosts, advice, and blurbs (lookin' at you, Claire, Tessa, Natalie, Shaun, the residents of Deadline City), to my fellow Pitch Wars 2015 classmates (Jen, Mike, Jamie, Sheena, Rebecca), and particularly the long list of people who have patiently let me unhinge my jaw to yarf publishing angst. This includes but is not limited to: Hanna, Elle, Duncan, Ash, Carrie, Linsey, Adib, Laura, Jamie, Julia, Katy, Claribel, Alex, and the kraken-bound: Tara, Kate, Anne-Marie, Emma, Faith, and Chandra. I think I'm forgetting someone. I *know* I'm forgetting someone. If I'm forgetting you, know that it's going to haunt me to my dying day.

To my friends blissfully outside of publishing: Thank you for not being in publishing. (That's only like 50% joking.) You all keep doing things like having beautiful children and buying houses and paying taxes, none of which I understand. Thank you for reminding me of what matters outside of my navel-gazing. (But *I* work in my PJs and talk to my houseplants, so in the grand scheme of things, who's *really* winning here?)

To my family: Look, in the time since I wrote my last acknowledgments, you've survived like five wildfires. Let's keep that energy going.

And finally, I would like to acknowledge my two cats. They still are no help whatsoever, but they've been along for the ride, so here's to my boys—and to everyone else who's gone with me down this road.

Jawbone Gulf

◆ Rhunadei

Teisanar ◆

THE HAVODII FLATS

◆ Nisodei

THE LASH

DOMAREM

THE JARIDEI COAST

◆ Karostei

THE SPROUT

ZARODEI

THE HEM

THE VINE

THE FAN

DUMOSA

Shattered Bay

CHEPAROK

MOREISAR

YIMESEI

Silk Cove

◆ Parilai

◆ Jobelii

Sea of Glass

Map of